The Phoenix

By Denise M. Baran-Unland

Cover art by Christopher Gleason

This book is lovingly dedicated to the reader, whoever you might be.

"You did thirst for blood, and with blood I fill you."
— Dante Alighieri, Inferno

THE PROLOGUE

"oo much fish bait, eh?"

"Totally soshed!"

"Full of the bug juice, ha, ha!"

Across the rustic dining room of Munsonville Inn, twelve-year-old Marie Clare dabbed the corner of her mouth with the bleached linen and resisted the urge to toss her head in disdain, lest she draw attention to herself and cause the dark waves to loosen from its crimson ribbon, which perfectly matched her crimson suit. For more than two hours, she'd suffered the antics of the raggedy domestics from Simons Mansion, Aunt Lula had said; their din rose over the murmurings of the more sedate guests, the ones who understood etiquette and grace.

Some of the rabble had already succumbed to their lack of restraint, with more surely to follow. Marie reached for her water goblet, still monitoring their ruckus with the keen observation her papa had instilled in her. What fool had given his servants such privileges?

Even now, one balanced his gray head between his hands, a head too heavy for his neck to support. Another slumped in his chair and beamed, drooling, into space. Still another, with eyes of slits and a grin like a painted clown, pressed a bottle against the lips of a tiny maid who, with head flopped over the back of her chair, snored like an old grandfather with his afternoon newspaper. The youngest, innocently gazing upon his companions, slid his now empty soup bowl under the table, the rapture of release already overtaking his pained expression. The others, the men *and* the women, clinked their glasses, downed their drinks, and bellowed for refills, which kept Mr. Newton, the innkeeper, a skinny little man with crooked teeth and thick eyebrows, scurrying around the puddles and broken shards to oblige.

"God has surely tested them in order for them to see that they are but beasts." Ecclesiastes 3:18

Mama was right. Overpay the help, even by a cent, and they'll only take to drink.

She turned back to their own dinner guests, all eyes riveted on her papa George Clare, and reached for her French roll, still warm, and split it in half.

Not one lock strayed from George's brunet head or from his immaculately waxed mustache. Not one fleck rested on his brushed herringbone suit. His blue eyes sparkled as he spoke, and his smile was warm and engaging. He held his slight frame erect; he manipulated fork and knife with grace and elegance.

Marie set the butter knife across her plate and took a bite, the sweet butter already melted.

Only a faint pallor on her papa's cheeks and a slight droop to his lids hinted at an internal enemy, more potent than one he fought in the world.

"...to strive for that complete lack of bias does, in fact, makes reporters more like God, not less. Think of it! To attain such pure objectivity, free of ethical attributes, society's prejudices, and..."

Her papa winced as he spoke those words, but slightly, which Marie's mama, Isabella Clare, covered, as she always covered it, by reaching for the decanter with her slim hand, the jewels of her rings and her golden curls glimmering under the glass chandelier.

"More wine, George?" her mama asked, her face flushing with wine and health above her high lace collar.

He held his glass to her. "Please."

She trickled crimson and its smooth aroma of currents and plums into his crystal, while he smiled at his audience, silently engaging them in his patient assent of his wife's interruption. He casually sipped once, twice, and then continued.

"...free of society's prejudices and literary theatrics. Proverbs says, 'The entirety of Your word is truth.' The same should apply to newspapers; make no bones in the canal about it."

Laughter broke out at this last comment, a subtle hint to the reporters who staged scandal in order to write about it, even as her papa, still smiling, winced again.

Marie felt only his wince. She certainly felt no shyness around their dinner companions, as some girls might. These cousins, Leo and Luther Hasset, a dozen years older than she and strangers to her until an hour ago, even this aunt, their mother Lula Hasset, shared The Dream. And The Dream that led them here, to this moment, was more binding than bone, than blood.

Scoop.

That's why they'd come to this little fishing village in Northern Michigan, to scoop the birth of the first child of world-renowned pianist and composer John Simons and his wife Bryony Simons, who was born and raised in this village. The couple lived in a mansion on an estate in the woods, which the musician had constructed as part of his wedding gift. Few people knew the birth was imminent but the Hassets, who published the Munsonville Times, did and leaked the information to George. This time, her papa would grasp such an important story first, today, perhaps. If so, November 2, 1895 would be a day she'd celebrate forever, the fulfillment of The Dream.

Her mama noticed George's wince, too, and nodded; her papa picked up the glass and sipped, a larger and longer sip than he'd taken thus far, almost a gulp, if he'd dared the coarseness of a gulp.

"Which brings me to..." he began.

A thundering of wheels in the distance left his words dangling.

A portly drunk from those uncouth revelers jumped to his feet while another shouted over the commotion, "The fuck is up with Alex Fate?"

"That ain't Fate!" the drunk slurred, tearing to the window as the noise grew louder. "That's one of me carriages!"

Uproarious laughter from the rabble almost drowned the rumble.

Almost.

"Your carriage!"

"Jackson, it'll be a cold day in hell when..."

The cousins exchanged a nervous glance as Lula leaned forward and whispered, "Something must be wrong at Simons Mansion."

George turned white and shuddered; he gripped the table edge.

"Simons Mansion?" he whispered and pulled himself up, the roaring carriage drowning his words.

The drunk stomped his foot; his face boiled with rage. "And that hornswaggler Matthews is driving it!"

George gasped, choked, and convulsed; blood shot from his mouth, spattering the fish loaf, boiled cabbage, apple pudding, and the cheese he had scorned, and staining the white tablecloth with tributaries of scarlet.

ive it back!"

"No!"

Still holding the bottle out of Isabella's reach, Dr. Parks shoved up the window, blasting cold through the heavy air, dispersing the stink of vomit and regurgitated wine.

Isabella lunged at him. "Don't!"

Then he hurled the bottle to its splintering death.

"You bastard!"

Marie raised an eyebrow at her mama's course speech, but Marie remained erect, away from the chair's high back as her mama had taught her, and she clenched hands more tightly, their knuckles whiter than snuff. Her mama never used strong language, and she never raised her voice, not even when Marie was a very little girl and breeched good decorum. Neither did her mama crumple to the floor as she did now inside Room 27 at Munsonville Inn, face in hands and bawling, a mocking harmony to the agonizing groans of her husband.

George lay propped against the headboard over the faded bedclothes at an odd angle – disheveled, white, and bloodied – where the sots, who had lugged him up the stairs, had carefully lain him, a sight as frightening as seeing her mama in a passion.

Isabella Clare was sweetness and gentle smiles, a soft-spoken sentinel of care and perfect carriage, the support structure of The Dream, an angel in pearls and pastel silks. She was unfailingly nurturing, always encouraging, and never tempestuous or hysterical.

Until today, when Dr. Parks smashed the salve of her husband's stomach, their healing balm, a bottle of dry 1846 Madeira.

They shall be one flesh.

Suddenly George arched and screamed, a long scream that rent Marie's heart and ended in a strangled wheeze, but this time no vomit burst forth, only dribbles of bloody slime. He squeezed his eyes and clutched his stomach, writhing and gasping.

Marie dug her nails into the tender flesh of her palms, a signal of her distress only she noticed. Outwardly, she remained poised, observant, and detached, an ornamental observer noting only the facts. Whatever she felt inwardly was her problem.

Dr. Parks lowered the sash and turned to the sobbing bundle on the floor, her skirts prettily and modestly splayed about her.

"Has George ever vomited blood?"

Crying and snuffling, her mama vehemently shook her head, and her studded comb slid to one side, and some of the blonde locks tumbled loose.

"How much does he drink?"

Her mama stiffened and stopped crying. As she slowly raised to her haunches and lowered her hands, her face hardened in an emotion that wasn't exactly hatred, but as close to hatred as the face on an altruistic woman could twist.

Then she flattened those delicate hands on the floor, and Marie nearly gasped at the sight, nearly because Marie was well-schooled in self-control and outbursts weren't her habit. Her mama regularly tinted her pink nails with red oil and whitened their oval tips in lemon juice. She never lifted a fist in anger or to knock on a door, lest she coarsen her spirt or her skin. Now here she was, pushing on the floorboards like a common housemaid to raise herself up, every muscle taut, until she faced the unimpressed Dr. Parks and said in a terse voice, "He does not 'drink.'"

"Mrs. Clare, it's obvious he drinks. The room reeks of alcohol."

'He drinks, yes. But he does not 'drink.'"

They stood there, glowering at each other while the man in the bed groaned and thrashed. Then Dr. Parks removed his double-breasted coat and set it over the back of the desk chair, retrieved his bag, which he'd dropped on the floor in favor of snatching the wine bottle from her mama's hands. He plopped it on the nightstand and rapidly unfastened its thick brass buckles.

12

Isabella flew to the bed and knelt at George's side, stroking his hand and murmuring unintelligible words of comfort. His damp curls plastered his pallid forehead; his lips curled to a sneer. But he responded to her tones. His yells became whimpers; his thrashings to twitchings; and he clutched her hand with the force of a steel bear trap.

She started to dab away the slime with her embroidered lace handkerchief, but Dr. Parks whipped the cloth from her hand and tossed it into the corner, barking, "Diagnosis first. Dignity later." Then, with real respect in his voice, he added, "But do stay. Your presence is soothing."

Somewhat reassured at his confidence, Marie unconsciously relaxed her grip. What might this doctor withdraw from that bag? A stethoscope, most likely, and a sphygmomanometer; that's what Dr. Ritter in Detroit had called it this curious machine that he said measured blood flow in the body. Medicine, too; morphine, perhaps, all items the other doctors typically brought when they called.

But no, Dr. Parks removed a microscope, perhaps an R. G. Mason microscope, like the one in her papa's story about microscope slides, and then set it on the bureau next to one of her mama's porcelain dishes of rose potpourri. Next, he took a glass syringe with a long silver needle, slowly aspirated her papa's slime from his clammy face, and then carefully smeared it on a glass slide to examine it under the lens.

He was a handsome man, tall with curly dark hair and a furry dark mustache on a full face of well-defined features, a real scientist in a white shirt and tweed waistcoat and trousers, and she felt not afraid. Only he and the room's furnishings distinguished this room from the hundreds of rooms, smaller rooms and larger rooms, they and their steamer trunks had inhabited over the years. They never wasted time unpacking, for who could predict when the next scoop might beckon them elsewhere?

This room at Munsonville Inn had whitewashed walls and plank floorboards that creaked at every footstep, not matter how light and nimble, and rag rugs coiled like calico snakes.

This room had a large floor to ceiling window with its white curtains drawn shut.

13

This room had a little round table with three upholstered chairs where they took their morning meal

This room had a large bureau with a hanging mirror, before which George carefully shaved each morning and waxed his mustache, and where Marie and her mama plaited their hair and adjusted their tuckers and jewels.

This room had a roll top desk with a high back chair next to the large bay window, where her mama, eyeglasses in place, recited from the Bible and studied Vogue magazine every morning and every evening, with her hair shining golden in the early light and the fading light; where Marie read, wrote, and worked her sums; and where her papa typed like a man possessed, which he was, when he wasn't feverishly devouring the newspapers, and where Dr. Parks' overcoat now patiently rested.

Being fervent in the spirit, he spoke and taught diligently.

This room had a dark walnut bed, the right size for papa and mama, a deathbed?

Because *this room* held a doctor who dismembered the living. Marie recalled all the news stories on the famous Dr. Parks, ejected from John Hopkins for his experiments on...

"Hmm," Dr. Parks said, rolling the knob back and forth.

Alarmed, her mama turned to look. "What is it?"

"Spirochetes," he said.

Thoughtfully, he returned to the bag and pulled out a glass bottle and a glass beaker. He shook some white chalk from bottle to beaker, measured in water from the bedside pitcher, and stirred the contents with a pewter spoon.

"I'll restrain him," Dr. Parks said, handing the beaker to Isabella. "Help him drink."

Dr. Parks slid next to George and wrapped his arms around him. A little moan escaped George's lips, and his head flopped onto Dr. Parks' chest. Isabella pressed the rim against her husband's parted mouth and tipped. His Adam's apple moved up and down with each grunting swallow.

Someone knocked on the door, and then that someone opened it and poked her head into the room.

14

"Lula!" Isabella breathed with relief as Dr. Parks settled George against the pillows.

At the sound of her voice, George's eyes popped open.

"There, there," Isabella said, patting him back into his mountain of down. "Rest, George. Allow the good medicine to work." And then she answered the question on Dr. Parks' face. "She's my sister."

Lula closed the door. She was as stunning as Isabella but brunette instead of blonde. She also wore eyeglasses and the same lace collars, but her demeanor was less sunny, more sober. Dr. Parks returned with his stethoscope and nodded to Isabella. She stood up and eased away, seeking out Lula's anxious eyes with her own reassuring ones.

Dr. Parks sat and placed the bell on George's chest. George breathed hard, but steady, and pink appeared on his cheeks. Isabella and Lula put their heads close and whispered.

"His lungs are strong," Dr. Parks removed the ear plugs and looked Isabella. "And so his heart."

"My George is a strong man."

He turned slightly to face her, and his eyes held a keen light. "But he's also a man afflicted."

"He has a weak stomach. Nothing more."

"So this is usual for him?"

"Again, Dr. Parks, no. My husband also does not vomit. Ever." She glanced at George, a glance full of love and unwavering devotion. "He seems much better."

As if to prove her point, George struggled to sit straight.

"Lula," he rasped. "Any word from Simons Mansion?"

"Simons Mansion!" Dr. Parks exclaimed. "I rescue you from the brink of hell, and you ask about Simons Mansion?"

A furnace of fire: there shall be wailing and gnashing of teeth...

A lake of fire had churned inside him, until Dr. Parks made milky mud and bade her papa, "Drink." So, Marie thought, who was the blind man now?

Sweat glistened on her papa's face, but his smile spoke of genuine relief.

"It burns," George admitted, his voice still weak. "But the pain has dulled, and I've no inclination to retch."

"He's a reporter," Lula explained to Dr. Parks, adding with a catch in her voice, "and Dick's good friend."

For I will restore health unto thee, and I will heal thee of thy wounds, saith the Lord.

"Lula, please," George pleaded in a weak voice, growing stronger with each syllable. "Have you word?"

Her mama looked hopefully at Lula. Dr. Parks sighed in disgust and packed the stethoscope into his bag. But Lula did not speak. Her eyes darted over each person, who were practically holding their breaths with desire *to know*, until they rested suspiciously on Dr. Parks, who was now setting up the sphygmomanometer on the nightstand.

"Dr. Parks," Lula began as Dr. Parks wrapped the cuff around George's arm. "Should I..."

He held up his hand for silence and then pressed his fingers into George's wrist and inflated the bulb. Lula's eyes narrowed. Marie held her breath with the others.

"Better than I expected," Dr. Parks said when he removed the cuff. "Mrs. Clare, your husband is indeed a strong man."

Her mama smiled encouragingly at Lula, who weakly smiled back.

Sphygmomanometer repacked, Dr. Parks fastened the buckles, took the bag by the handle, and faced the group.

"I'll return in a few hours to check his condition and supply the next dose," he said. "Until then, keep excitement to a minimum and let him rest. Send word if he declines or vomits again." He looked pointedly at Isabella. "And absolutely no alcohol; water only, perhaps gruel later."

The second Dr. Parks left, her mama and papa pummeled Aunt Lula with questions. Any word from Simons Mansion? Was the baby born? And, most importantly, had the news hit the papers?

To each question, Lula had one, very reassuring word: "No."

"Thank God!" Isabella loudly sighed while George actually whooped, and relief flowed through Marie in rolling waves to the extent she momentarily forgot her good breeding and relaxed her back.

"Then we've not lost our chance!" Color fully restored, George eagerly held out his hands, and Isabella even more eagerly pulled him completely up and repositioned the pillows behind him while he gestured to a steamer.

"Isabella, uncork the Bordeaux from Chateau Margaux!" George pointed to the bureau. "Lula, four glasses, no less. Little Marie must celebrate with us."

Crimson splashed into Marie's glass, sweeter and dryer than her papa's blood, which still caked his fine white collar and the front of his shirt, although her mama was already washing his face and hands. Marie held her glass high, so the lamp could illuminate the clarity of the rare liquid from Thomas Jefferson's own collection, one of the last from her Grandpapa's cellar. But they'd saved it for this very reason. The fulfillment of The Dream was near.

"A toast!" her papa cried. "To truth! And ultimate success!"

All except Marie downed their drinks, and her mama poured another round, which they drained as Marie nursed hers, reveling in the dry bouquet that warmed her mouth and throat, because her parents rarely served her wine and because she wanted to linger in their approaching triumph.

An exhilarated smile overtook George, and he looked like her papa again.

But not until her mama served up round three, and their guzzling turned to savoring, did they discuss it.

"Tell me, Lula," George said, eyes half-mast in delight. "If all is well at Simons Mansion, why did Henry Matthews tear up the hill like the very devil?"

Marie's fingers tightened on her glass at the name. Her father hated Henry Matthews, even though they had never formally met him, so she hated him, too. Henry Matthews had once worked for the New York Gazette, one of the most exclusive publications in the country, a newspaper for which George yearned to write. And then just as casually, Henry Matthews had spurned his position, and jilted his fiancée, to manage the affairs of the famous John Simons. But during his reporter days, Henry Matthews had often out-scooped her papa. George had pointed him out to Marie when Marie was just seven. They had traveled to New York to visit Isabella's relatives; Henry Matthews just happened to be dining at the same restaurant. Henry Matthews was short and slim with wavy brown hair and an air of elegance and offhand mockery. But a termite doesn't need tremendous size to wreck tremendous damage.

For the most devastating blizzard in all history slammed into the city during their stay. And Henry Matthews published story after story before George could persuade a single editor anywhere to read his, once again snatching the trophy from her papa's hardworking hands. But this time, her papa had pre-written the story of John and Bryony Simons' baby, a story the whole world eagerly wanted to read. As soon as George had the final details, the Hassets would publish the story. So, of course, Henry Matthews weighed on George's mind. He weighed on all their minds.

"Henry went for Dr. Gothart, who lives at the end of Blue Gill Road," Lula said, but she spoke casually, as if the matter was trivial.

George frowned. "A doctor? For a birth? Is the mother or child in danger? Answer me, quickly."

"I wouldn't think so. Mrs. Simons is fragile and sickly. Dr. Gothart has overseen her care since she was a very little girl. It's natural for him to assist with the baby's safe passage."

"Maybe," George said, but he didn't sound convinced, and his eyes darkened and narrowed.

"If you'd met John Simons, you'd understand, He's uncommonly protective of his wife, far more than most husbands. He's allowed no visitors during her confinement, not even brief calls from Reverend Marseilles, her own father."

George made a face, as if he'd bitten a lemon. "But why did Henry Matthews pick 'that' time to fetch him? And why in such a passion?"

Isabella and Lula exchanged knowing smiles.

"Oh, George, George," Isabella gushed as she sat on the edge of the bed. "It takes time, hours even, before the pains are strong and steady. A considerate woman doesn't waste a busy doctor's time. And remember, Mr. Matthews is unattached. He has no experience with childbirth. We fear what we don't know.

18

He may have misinterpreted Mrs. Simons' distress and became distressed himself."

"All true words," Lula added. "To our knowledge, Dr. Gothart has not returned. Confinements are fickle and unpredictable."

"Well," her papa continued with a tinge of annoyance. "Henry Matthews is connected and sly. He even scooped the story of last year's drownings, a despicable move that falsely showed Dick's life's work in a backwoods light." He held up a finger. "And that despite the asp no longer works for the Gazette."

Marie never met her Uncle Dick, Aunt Lula's husband and Leo and Luther's father, although her papa often spoke highly of his work. Nor would Marie ever meet him. He had died last year.

"George," Isabella began.

"Let's not forget," he interrupted, his voice short and crisp. "He's at Simons Mansion, and I am not."

"But you have us," Aunt Lula reminded him. "Everything is prepared. We only await the update."

"Papa!" Marie finally burst out, each syllable tasting of wine and floating away on eiderdown. "Believe!"

George smiled, but it was a crooked half a smile, and he studied her in wonderment. "Ah, Little Marie, shaming her papa."

But was he pleased? Was he encouraged?

"It's true," Lula interjected. "Dick got his. You'll get yours."

Her mama shaded her eyes and gazed across the room and out the bay window to the approaching dusk.

"The finish line is in sight," she lowered her hand and then smiled into his glassy eyes. "Don't lose heart now."

George swirled the remaining inch and reflected. Marie watched the swirls, hypnotized, and felt a flushing warmth, like glowing embers.

"Yes," he conceded. "The update. No matter the outcome, we need only await the update."

He gulped the remainder and set the glass on the nightstand.

"I'm sleepy," he said with a slight slur as he drew up the covers. "I should rest, as Dr. Parks said. Wake me when there's news."

enry Matthews lifted his sticky face off the cellar floor and studied the mangled body of Chinook.

With a swoop and a few snaps of a jaw that had suddenly become savage and strong, Henry had reduced his Siberian husky to red slush and broken bones, and he didn't care.

And he was still hungry.

He hovered above the dog just away from the knife, the one he'd used to slash John Simons to death earlier this night. John's blood still smeared the floor like red paint on a large palette, fitting considering the obnoxious amount of oils Henry had painted in this room. He wriggled closer to the blade and sniffed that blue gray metal as he once sniffed a fine wine. The scent of heme rushed to his brain, his thirst flared, too. So he lowered himself to lick it, but his tongue felt wadded, as if with batting, and his neck, stiff and raw and swollen, resisted his efforts. The cold stone merged with the chill in his colder hands, but neither cold nor stone made his knees ache, even though he'd mashed them, and his elbows, into the floor during the attack on his dog. The sleeves of his Louis Marche ruffled shirt, and his skin, hung tattered and stained, where the dog had fought back with ferocious desperation. Just moments ago the room had resounded with yowls, snarls, and the faint screams of Bryga, the head housekeeper at Simons Mansion and supplier of John's first unearthly meal. Now, a deathly quiet surrounded him, a silence not broken by the pounding of his heart or the roaring of his breath in his ear as he used to know deafening silences. It was just Henry and the dog, and neither was alive anymore.

Memories flashed in his brain, bright, chaotic memories of all the stories he'd written of murders and suicides and monsters and mummies, and vampires and ghosts who haunt the places of their death. With a quick sardonic chuckle, Henry licked the blood and flesh off his hands at his realization that he'd wound up in one of his stories.

So this was death, he mused, glancing around the cellar of the despicable Simons Mansion. This was hell.

No frozen lake or lakes of fire. No writhing demons or pitchforks. He'd hanged himself to escape the hell of Simons Mansion and woke up, still in Simons Mansion. Like Marley's ghost, he'd forged the noose himself: using Agnes, leaving Agnes, and then worming his way into Simons Mansion as if living near temptation would shield him from temptation, from adultery and more.

"I love you," Agnes said as he kissed her cheek goodnight. "My boy, my hero, my lover forever."

Forgive me, but I must break our engagement, as my heart belongs to another...

He supposed he ought to feel something for Chinook, who had faithfully followed him, even to the gallows he created, but he felt oddly disconnected from the animal, the room, time, and even himself, except for the demand in his desiccated veins for human blood. His canine snack had blunted his need, but instinct told him he needed more and soon. Instinct also warned him of the danger of venturing out to hunt human prey without experience.

But he was his father. He was his uncle. He'd figure it out.

In the meantime, where could he find food in this great empty house? He had a vague recollection, like a dream fragment, of discharging the servants for the day, all except Bryga. He also had a vague memory, as if decades ago, of a certain hunger for lunch, vague because hunger for lunch didn't feel like the craving surging through his frame. In the former, his stomach rumbled, and he'd felt a little faint. In the latter, his soul had snuffed its death rattle, and he never felt more feral than in this moment, not even when fucking, not even when wielding each slashing blow and giving John's body one well-aimed kick before using the noose to take his own leave from life.

No, this need to kill and drink urged him with a force greater than approaching orgasm, and he thrashed and howled, and drove the heels of his hands into his fangs to force it back while he hunted for the memory of his last human meal, the clue where to find the next slaughter.

Henry had trotted down the stairs to the cellar in search of lunch, assembled a tray of cold chicken slices, an entire lobster, a loaf of bread, a jar of pickles, and several apples, items that now had the appeal of dirt. Simple items but Henry had brought them into the main dining room and arranged them on the table with an elegance befitting any spread at his uncle's hidden and mysterious estate – Arcadia.

A shadow shared that meal with him. No, not a shadow. A little girl, about six years old, with a short, blunt haircut framing her large, brown eyes; a little girl in a faded dove-colored dress, with a wide hem at its bottom, and sleeves folded three times at the wrists.

Anna!

He leaped to his feet, sprang up the stairs, and whisked out the back door into the frosty November night, bounding over the expanse of the great estate with enormous speed, the frozen grasses trembling underfoot, until he nearly smacked into the darkened servant's cottage. He zipped around the building, peering into windows for signs of life and tapping on the glass, hoping Anna would see and invite him inside. At every room, the curtains were tied back as if to admit the sun; the coverlets lay at the foot of the empty beds for the morning airings.

Of course! Bryga and Anna had left in the morning for Simons Mansion and never returned.

Henry slapped his forehead, and the crack where skin and bone met skin and bone echoed over the expanse, and all hidden animal life paused in their tracks, quivering; even insects stopped their songs. The pause ripped through Henry, and he writhed and shrieked against it. Life teamed around him, but he was not part of it, and he choked on the perfume of dormant perennials and the exchange of gases between trees and wildlife. Their vitality shimmered through his useless nerves with searing fire, and he yanked his hair and fell to his knees, unable to bear it.

Away, away! He needed to get away! But first...

He plunged his hands into the earth and withdrew moles, which he munched from each hand as he sped back to the mansion. He flew through the back door, stumbling over a knee, an elbow, a forearm, half a face (i.e. pieces of Bryga's scattered corpse) as he soundlessly coursed through each room of the four floors with lightning speed, shouting, "John! John!" with every rapid step, saving the chamber that caused all the trouble for last; the hated tinkling driving him all the way to the meal John mostly likely had claimed for himself.

Henry skidded to a noiseless stop in the doorway. The music box's chimes came from the floor near the bed, where the lumpy covers scarcely blocked the tantalizing smell of the freshly dead mother, the owner of the music box, and her newborn. Henry himself had painted the "bryony" vines all over that box, which played the song that John had composed as his wedding gift to Bryony. Henry himself had crossbred the "bryony" that John had him plant all over the estate and up the mansion John had built for his Bryony. John, of course, had paid Henry handsomely for his time and expertise. But what did any of it matter now?

And yet, Henry stopped himself from pouncing. For Anna and the luscious corpses were not alone.

John Simons, the man who'd become both master and slave, sat on the floor, legs sprawled, giving quite the performance of breathing. His long blond hair hung damp and disheveled; his torn shirt was stained red; and he had the pallor and scent of a cadaver, which, of course, he now was. A hungry cadaver, like Henry.

Anna crouched in the corner, shivering and clutching the now silent music box. Her eyes grew as big as saucers under those choppy bangs as John reached out to wind the box, saying coldly, "You're a big girl now."

The little girl smelled so…alive. Henry clenched his fists.

"Oh, Mr. John, I'm so scared!"

John fumbled for his handkerchief – the one garment touching him that remained unsoiled - and then dried her eyes.

"You must be brave," John said in a dark, flat voice. "You will soon have a new home."

"No!" Anna clasped the music box tighter to her chest.

John pressed her fingers over the lid and his fingers under her chin, raising it and holding her gaze. "It's magic."

"Magic?"

"I am going away."

"No! No! No!" She flailed her legs with each syllable and with far more audacity than even Henry now dared in front of John.

John lifted the lid, and the box obediently cranked out each grating note of Bryony. Anna's eyes glazed, and she slumped against the wall, but she did not drop the box.

"If you need me," John said as he rose to his full height, about half a foot taller than Henry, but Henry hadn't needed height to stab John in the back, repeatedly. "If you need me...play it."

He paused to glance at Anna, mesmerized by the tinkling, Consequently, she never saw the cacodemon towering over her, his cagey sneer, or the darting of his tongue, savoring the delay for the greater satisfaction.

"Gather her things and leave her at the parsonage – alive and in one piece," he murmured to Henry as he passed through the doorway. "I have a plan."

"The parsonage? Is that wise?"

John grabbed Henry's neck, banged Henry's head into the wall, and said in a low, terse voice, "Yes. The reverend should know his daughter, his only child, is dead."

He let go, and Henry instantly sprinted to the cottage, pushed the door off its hinges and ransacked the bureau, randomly tossing clothing into a trunk, forcing it shut and swiping her wraps on the way out, where he leaped to the carriage house, dumped her trunk into a coach, and then rushed back to Simons Mansion and up the stairs – all within minutes.

Anna, still cradling the winding down box, hadn't moved.

In a millisecond Henry was crouching beside her, cranking up the music box, wrapping her, racing to the carriage, hitching Arabian horses, and tearing out of the yard. Anna clung to him every hoofbeat of the way, releasing the stench of excrement, his not hers, which made her choke and gag.

"You smell!" she finally cried, burying her nose in her sleeve.

With a hard wrench on the reins, Henry reversed course and zoomed up the hill. He didn't offend himself, and he certainly didn't care if he offended Anna, whom he would have devoured by now if John hadn't stopped him.

But instinct again told Henry he mustn't offend anyone else.

"Stay," Henry barked as he parked the coach, his words as thick as pea soup, and cranked up the box. He gave her arm a rough shake. "Don't move."

He felt the rumbling of dirt, of John digging a grave for Bryga's pieces. Again, instinct told Henry that leaving human bones exposed meant trouble; instinct sent him flying up the stairs to rip away his clothes, swipe his torn and oozing skin with a dry towel, and then stuff himself into the last pressed suit from his wardrobe. As he slid on the white shirt, the ruffle caught the gold ring on his right hand, nearly yanking it from his finger. Now Henry didn't care about the ring, and he didn't care if he lost it. But Henry knew if his signature ring landed in the bed of a victim, a lynching was sure to follow. With his teeth, Henry stripped the ring from his finger and spat it onto the floor. He slid one leg into his trousers and another faraway memory stirred, of making a careful toilet, of the right tie with the right waistcoat. Tonight he wore his urine and feces just as proudly. Still, he sealed himself in a long overcoat and cloak to mask the stench.

"Look human, don't smell dead," he muttered as he smoothed back his matted hair and grabbed a fresh top hat.

He snorted at the boxes and crates scattered about the room, ready for departure. Well, he wouldn't be going anywhere now. Lucky him.

The music box was winding down by the time Henry retuned to the carriage. He gave it a couple of hard cranks and barreled out of the yard and down the hill with unearthly speed, around the corner and over the path, straight to Munsonville. Anna's limbs slackened, and she gave little jerks, signs of approaching slumber. Good.

He shot out of the woods; moments later, he had ground hitched the horse in front of the parsonage. Henry gathered the sleeping, delectable-smelling child in his arms, who stirred slightly at the movement, and ran up the steps, willing back the need to clamp onto her neck and devour her then and there. He sensed motion and smelled kerosene on the other side of the door; he rapped on the glass, hoping the rap sounded reasonably human.

The door opened, and he came face-to-face, not with Reverend Galien Marseilles but with the reverend's housekeeper. Henry hadn't any idea of the time, but instinct told him dawn was hours away. He nearly laughed aloud. The rumors were true. The village's pastor was a lecher.

"Mrs. Ashmore," Henry said, forcing himself enunciate each syllable, hoping he sounded like the "himself" she knew. "I..."

Henry smelled her apprehension; his eyes strayed to the pink flesh above her collar, as fine as any leg of lamb at Easter and most likely twice as juicy. Reverend Marseilles, tall and thin, with sparsely cropped hair and a long, pointed gray beard, stumbled from the parlor in his clerical suit, reeking of brandy. Neta Ashmore's eyes dropped to the bundle in his arms, which was rousing and mewling.

"Yes?" she quavered, shaking hand groping for the door jamb.

"Bryony...and...her...baby...are..."

Mrs. Ashmore covered her ears and burst into tears. Reverend Marseilles staggered down the hall and slammed the door. Anna opened her mouth to scream, but Henry clapped a gloved hand over it.

"Anna is in shock. Bryga, half-crazed in grief, has fled." He shoved Anna at the weeping housekeeper. "Take her."

To his surprise, Neta did. She sank to the floor with her bundle and cried with the little girl, rocking back and forth.

"I'm scared," Anna whimpered. "I'm so scared."

"Shh," Mrs. Ashmore hugged her rightly. "Shh. I am here. I will keep you safe. All is well." She looked up at Henry. "Thank you, Mr. Matthews. Thank you for entrusting me with this dear child. I shall care for her until her mother is able."

Henry trembled and gripped the door jamb, too, because...

They. Smelled. So. Good.

Not safe, Henry told himself. Not safe. If the humans didn't hurt him, John would. But he had to eat; he had to drink, very soon, or he might...

"I must go," Henry stammered. "I...I'm not feeling well."

"rgghhhhhhhh!"

"There, there, George, shhhhh………….."

From her cot on the other side of Room 27, Marie squeezed her eyes tightly shut against her papa's torment, but terror oozed out and wet her lashes.

Her grandpapa's rare wine soaked her papa's clothes, the bedclothes, the bare floor, and spattered over the bedpan her mama had grabbed too late; the stench of sour vinegar and dirty pennies permeated the airless room and burned Marie's throat.

"Any minute now," Lula's voice soothed with exaggerated reassurance. "Dr. Parks will be here soon."

They'd blissfully drowsed over the wine until George had choked awake when the first paroxysm struck, jarring Marie to consciousness. She roused to see her mama, kneeling at the bedside and dozing with her head against the mattress, struggle to her feet as the deluge poured out, and then teeter across the room in wild disarray, flinging the door open and shrieking repeatedly for help.

Above the faraway frantic voices and pattering footsteps; her papa screamed against the crimson lava that, viciously, and unrelentingly, erupted, erupted, erupted. Marie, floaty, frightened, and full of wine, clung to the only stable item she could, the cot.

But the cot bobbed like a raft on the Ohio River, and the space between Marie's ears rippled in languid waves.

Aunt Lula scurried into the room, babbling that Luther had left for Dr. Parks, and then hurried to the bed, where Isabella was frantically patting George's back.

"There, there," her mama's voice sobbed out in a very non-reassuring away. "Lula, how long?"

"Shh, soon. Dr. Parks will be here soon."

The muddy clay failed because they put their faith in muddy clay.

Thou shalt have no other gods before me... the prayer of faith shall save the sick...

Marie sank into her pillow and descended into its waves of wine, of dreams, of memories...

"Mom," Luther's voice droned. "He's here."

Today signaled the demise of the tannery in Lehigh Gorge, when a forest fire...

...until a loud "Mrs. Clare!" shot her to the surface. Somewhere in her blurry mind, she heard her mother's anguished weeping until Marie submerged once more, fuzzy and weak...

Sliding onto the abandoned bench, George pounded out a rollicking tune: "As swift as time put round the glass, busy curious thirsty fly, jolly mortals fill your glasses, let us drink and be merry."

CRASH!

Marie started and opened her eyes. Splintered glass on the floor, splats on the wall, screams and retching from all sides. She quickly closed them again and drifted into...

George grabbed her hands and twirled her, exclaiming, "Dance, Little Marie, dance!"

His cheeks, rosy; his smile, giddy and wide; his eyes glistening; her giggles bubbling over the fiddle.

"Why did you give him wine???"

Use a little wine for your stomach's sake and your frequent infirmities.

"It's the food. It must be the food in this substandard establishment! He was fine until..."

"Scoop!" George cried, dropping into the chair, spinning a sheet through the roller; clackety, clackety, clackety clack, clack, clacketey, clack, clack, clack...

"Shhh, Isabella. Let's pray. Like little girls."

Six days thou shalt work, but on the seventh day thou shalt rest...all things are possible to him that believeth...thy faith hath made thee whole...

"He's killing George!"
"Isabella..."

"Don't be afraid, little Marie." He tweaked her nose and slipped the paper scrap into her pocket. *"You have good sense. Now go..."*
"But Papa! What if..."
"Shh. 'The Spirit of the Lord is upon me, because he hath anointed me to preach the gospel to the poor; he hath sent me to heal the brokenhearted, to preach deliverance to the captives, and recovering of sight to the blind, to set at liberty them that are bruised.'"

"Stop! You...monster! Lula! Luther! Make him stop!"

"Are you ready to order, Monsieur?"
"Soupe de poisson à la rouille."
"Coq au vin jaune."
"Confit de canard."
"Just the cassoulet, sil vous plait."
"Pissaladière."

"Mrs. Clare, it's just saltwater."

All aboard!
"Your coach is ready, Monsieur."
"Little Marie, here, take my hand. Now up you go!"

"OH, GOOOOOOODDDD...ARRRGGHHHHHHH......."

30

*Her papa sighed and moaned against her mama's breast
while her hand rapidly pumped beneath the quilt.*

"George!!!"

*He held up the bank note: "Fifty dollars! Grab the
glasses!"*

"Get back, damn it!"

*They arrived in Haymarket Square the day after the riot;
they arrived the day after the Oklahoma Land Rush, the day
after the Johnstown Flood.*
*They choked on smoke; they dodged stampedes and
gunfire. They waded through whispering corn; they poured the
wine, slept in brothels, and bought their spring wardrobe, their
summer wardrobe, their fall wardrobe, their...*

"There, there, there, there, there, oh, George! Wake up!!!"

*"Sorry, Mr. Clare. I just ran a story about ...
"Josephine Cochrane's automatic dishwasher,
"George Eastman's Kodak Box Camera,
"John Boyd Dunlop's inflatable tire,
"The opening of the Eiffel tower,
"North Dakota becoming the 39th state,
"South Dakota becoming the 40th state, Montana
becoming the 41st state, Washington becoming the 42nd state."*

"You...MONSTER! You horrid, horrid MONSTER!"

*He held up the bank notes: "Forty dollars! Grab the
glasses!"*

Marie pressed her face into the pillow and soaked it with
silent tears. Was it all for naught? Would The Dream not reach
its happy ending?

*George buried his head in Isabella's skirts, heaving with
sobs and pounding his fists into the seat cushion, while she*

31

rubbed his back and stroked his locks, murmuring, "There, there, George."

He held up the bank notes: "Sixty dollars! Grab the glasses!"

I have heard thy prayer, I have seen thy tears: behold, I will heal thee...

"Nooooooooooooo!!!" Isabella screamed.

Marie rolled to her side and forced her heavy eyelids open.

Her mama was beating Dr. Parks; Luther's arms encircled her waist, tugging and tugging, heedless of his crumpled brown suit and rumpled brown hair. Lula, her face and lace collar streaked with blood, frantically jiggled George's right arm and implored him to wake up. George lay still, white, and drenched in blood.

"Mama?" Marie bolted up, clutching the covers to her neck, her head spinning . "Is Papa..."

Luther yanked her mama off and roughly pushed her into a chair, where she covered her face with bloodied hands and wailed.

"Mama! Papa!"

Dr. Parks, pulled down his cuffs, smoothed his hair back, and faced Marie. Her mama's fists had blotted his waistcoat red like a Monet abstract. He looked composed, but his eyes showed the strain.

"Your papa is fine; your papa is alive." He cleared his throat. "He's alive for now. But he desperately needs a blood transfusion.

CHAPTER FOUR: STRIPE FOR STRIPE

s Henry roared up the hill toward Simons Mansion, a blur leaped onto the bench, grabbed his throat, and hissed, "Turn around!"

Henry did and clattered back down, stealing a glimpse of the figure beside him: The blur solidified into bloody rags, a snarling mass of long straw hair, and glacial eyes in a face of "pallor mortis," a hilarious sight, and Henry chewed his cheeks to restrain his laughter.

The bottom came into sight. Ahead was the lake. Henry instinctively slowed, not because the dead could drown, but because the horses could.

"Drive!" John hissed again.

"To where?"

"Gothart's."

"Why?" He looked at John, openly this time and hiding nothing, not even his mirth. For John's "barely there" mustache and beard was still caked with Bryga's blood, and his face was full of cunning.

John turned aside. "Revenge."

So Henry swerved right, once again in the direction of Munsonville. The horses screamed and thundered down the road, the carriage careened from side to side, and still he thrashed their hides, all the way to the hill and up. Less than twelve hours ago, Henry had made a similar frenetic drive to the same destination: Bryga urging him to fetch Dr. Gothart, because Bryony was in trouble, because the baby was in trouble. The details, the urgency was hazy, as if watching the scene from a distance. His only urgency now was hunger, and that urgency was escalating.

"Just so you know, John, I don't answer to you."

"You will. Once we live again."

He slashed, swung, and slashed again, slashing, swinging, slashing...again he raised the knife and his chest tightened. He flung the knife on the floor and kicked over John's corpse...the noose beckoned...

"John, I hate to break your hopeful little heart, but we won't rise again on the last day."

The musician's dead eyes flickered to Henry, and their hollows smoldered with the same hatred Henry had for John, their forever bond. Then John leaned forward, hands on his knees, eyes narrowed, as if searching for something in the void. "Kellen is a vampire."

"Henry, I'd like you to meet my manager, Mr. Kellen Wechsler. Mr. Wechsler, this is Mr. Henry Matthews. He works for the New York Gazette."

"I know."
"No," John cocked his head at Henry. "A real vampire."
"Like us?"

Henry faced Kellen. "You may join us, if you are available in the afternoon. I suspect you're more of a night creature."

"Yes. And Gothart knew it."
"So what?"
"He knows how to reverse it."
"Maybe he won't." Henry said with more hope than he dared. Reverse it? Fuck that.
"He will."
"You sound so confident of it, John."
"Because you're giving him the reason."
They neared the gated three-story colonial at the top of Blue Gill Road. John sprang out of the coach on all fours and through the tall weeds – gone.

Henry stopped the carriage by the gate and simply sat, chewing through his fingers and grinding his heels into the floor, so desperate, so ravenous, so petrified of John's influence, the smell of blood everywhere. To bolt after John, to tear through every living creature in that house, to drink and drink and drink and drink and drink until the insatiable was satiated – don't do it, the survival part of him begged. Don't do it. Don't do it. The punishment from John would be terrible.

So he didn't. But he reeled with the brutal need for blood; he felt mad with the need, he twisted and thrusted and squealed and snorted to keep himself from lifting the latch and bursting through to carriage to assuage it.

Until he heard a sound.

From the depths of his torment he started, and then paused, listening, sniffing.

A rustle of taffeta. Emerald eyes cutting through the night.

A woman in black, her red-orange hair tumbling over her full bust to her wide hips and her hands in her deep pockets, swished her way to the carriage. Henry stopped chewing and grinding to watch. She was still a beauty, no doubt about it, salacious and wantonly seductive, Lilith clothed in snakes.

Albert Brumfeldt looked away. His uncle looked away.

Two other figures also stood in the foyer, and they were covered in melting snow. The man had auburn mutton chops and thinning auburn hair, gold spectacles, round shoulders, and a slight stoop to his short stature.

The girl...woman...her disheveled red-orange hair tumbling everywhere, gripped him with crystal emerald eyes.

"It's fine," Henry's uncle said quietly. "No one is hurt."

"It was the storm, Henry," Brumfeldt babbled. "The storm frightened the horses and overturned the cart before they turned on their occupants, and then, well... it's unfortunate, but it does happen. At any rate they will spend the night here, as it's impossible to travel tonight, and in the morning, we'll wire for transport and send them on their way."

Brumfeldt had said "here." He had not said. "Arcadia."

Was that for the benefit of the "guests," to preserve a sense of Arcadia's anonymity, all one hundred and twenty-five acres of his uncle's hidden estate? Or was it to assure Henry that these strangers were not previously acquainted with his uncle or his estate? How providential that the horses lost their way off the main road, deep into the woods, and then lost their senses on his uncle's well-concealed property, his estate: Arcadia.

How providential, indeed.

They didn't know Henry had already met Dr. Edwin Gothart at Reverend Marseilles' weekly Munsonville Society for the Humanities, a meeting for men – and Bryony, who was forced to sit on a stool behind the reverend's chair, like Chinook taught to heel, and absorb the conversation.

And they didn't know he was also previously acquainted with his daughter Millicent Gothart, although not by name, when she tried to steal his soul from across room. Instead, she wound up invading his soul and commanding his hand to write words Henry had never spoken aloud.

He kept his soul. She stole every excuse for keeping it.

Revenge... You're going to give him a reason.

Faraway from inside the colonial, a clock struck two with solemn gongs.

The hour of the demon.

Or so he always wrote.

Henry fumbled in his pockets for gloves to cover his ragged fingers and opened the door. He'd hitch the horses to the post after all. He was thus engaged thus when she reached him.

"Good evening, Mr. Matthews," Millicent said in a low voice.

"Good morning, Miss Gothart," he replied. "Do you tarry late or rise early?"

"Does it matter?"

"Not really."

Her eyes, the color of jade, wandered to his lips as she, dreamlike, murmured, "A ghost that loved a lady fair, ever in the starry air, of midnight at her pillow stood; and, with a sweetness skies above, the luring words of human love, her soul the phantom wooed."

He faced her, wondering if she'd sensed his lack of life, wondering if she cared. "Young soul, put off your flesh, and come with me into the quiet tomb." He jerked his head toward the carriage as he looped the rope again. "Our bed is lovely, dark, and sweet."

"'Oh, I couldn't,' Millicent raised her eyes. Their color was solid and offered no clue as to what lay beyond them. "My father would kill me."

You she-devil, Henry thought. You approached me for exactly that.

"I promise you,' Henry said with slight dip of his head. "It will remain our secret."

Millicent shifted her gaze to the house. "How long do you think John and my father..."

"Long enough,' Henry said as he opened the carriage door and gestured.

Millicent lifted her skirts and sprang into inside. But before Henry could follow, instinct whispered in his ear.

Look up, it ordered him. Look up now.

So Henry did. Two figures watched him from the second story window: John, chalky and white; restraining an enraged Dr. Gothart with the strength of death, as the doctor struggled against his captor. For once, Munsonville's Merlin was trapped.

Just the way Henry liked him.

A new emotion flared and seethed through every pore. It was hunger, yes, but more than a relentless need for nourishment. It was also a vengeful fury, more ruthless and bloodthirsty than any anger Henry ever felt when alive. The emotion gripped and enflamed him and, with the all the strength of whatever was left of him, demanded he satisfy it and satisfy it now.

He leaped inside the carriage, locked the door, and then slid across the seat and pulled her close. Millicent's breathing quickened, and each hot breath tore through his flesh like a steam engine, and he groaned aloud to hold it back.

But that only made Millicent smile and edge closer.

"It's my dream come true," she murmured again.

He wound his gloved hands into her hair and held her fast, amazed at the vitality in his butchered fingers, and murmured, "I dreamt you came into my room."

The pulse in her neck quickened. He slipped one hand down to feel it.

Beat. Beat. Beat. Beat. Beat.

"You did? Oh, Henry, when?"

You know when, he thought. Because something of you was there, forcing your way into my mind and toying with the direction of my words. He fixed himself on her eyes, now cold crystalline green, and willed himself to ignore the throbbing in her neck.

"A long time ago," Henry said. "That dream in my room was a long time ago."

"Your room at Simons Mansion?"

Their throat is an open sepulcher; with their tongues they have used deceit; the poison of asps is under their lips.

"No. Another room."

She smiled again, with the slyness of a vixen on the prowl, and her gaze roamed his face before resting on his eyes, the entryway to his nothingness.

Finally she spoke. "Arcadia the night of the blizzard?"

"Yes, Arcadia the night of the blizzard."

The scent of sandalwood, charred, clung to her hair; she exuded copper and algae and rich dark treacle. These were strong smells, stronger than his.

"That was no dream, Henry."

"I know."

She moved the hand on her neck to her breast and squeezed his fingers around it. "I've always wanted you."

"I know."

With her other hand, she reached farther down for him, even as he kneaded her, and he hoped enough blood pooled in his system to fake it.

"You wrote the most remarkable words that night. During the snowstorm." Green crystals glittered with desire. "At Arcadia."

"I did. Twice. In two separate letters." He blew on her lips, and she opened them. "But the recipient of the first letter never received it. And the second, well..."

His uncle slid a folded parchment to him. Henry scanned the lines. Where in the hell was the other draft?

The letter that drove a wedge between Henry and his uncle, penned with Henry's own hand, every word true. No use denying it.

"I did what I had to do, Henry."

"I understand."

He drew her in, and she trembled. He felt the thumping of her heart, the working of her lungs.

"In that dream, you said the most remarkable thing," Henry said. "I never could forget it."

"Tell me, Henry.

He inched his hand back up to her neck and gently squeezed, reveling in its palpating.

"Now, Henry. Tell me now."

He moved his lips to her ear. "Snowstorms don't slash horses to bits!"

Then he tore into her jugular with a ferocity he could no longer control, spilling more blood than he drank.

Ah, but her screams!

So worth the waste.

espite the oily glow of the lamps, night stretched its shadow across Room 27 and blotted any comfort the light strained to give.

Never did the hours between dark and dawn pass so slowly!

Her papa lay flat on the bed in a fresh nightdress, arms limp at his sides. Dr. Parks had stacked all the pillows under his legs, to raise them above his heart and improve blood flow, he had said. But George was still ghostly white, and he breathed with irregular, ragged gasps.

After each of her papa's breaths, Marie, curled up on her cot, covers to her chin, and quaking, held her own breath, straining to catch the next one, and letting her air out again with huge exhales when she heard George's raspy inhale.

Luther had left in search of answers from Simons Mansion, "for Uncle George," he had murmured to his mother before softly shutting the door behind him.

Her mama and Aunt Lula huddled into one of the parlor chairs, weeping softly and clinging to each other as a single entity of bright and dim. Alexander Pope's verses about the conjoined Hungarian twins popped into Marie's mind.

Two sisters wonderful to behold, who have thus grown as one,

That naught their bodies can divide, no power beneath the sun.

Dr. Parks had pulled the desk chair close to her papa. He passed the night still as stone, and absently stroking his chin as he monitored his patient with troubled eyes. From time to time, he checked George's pulse, frowned, and shook his head.

After one such time, he left his post and drew up an armchair beside Isabella.

"Dear woman," he said, reaching for her hand. "Your husband will die without it."

Isabella jerked away, tears gushing down her face. "But it's so...so barbarous."

"All medicine is barbarous."

"It's so...dangerous."

"He's in danger of death."

Isabella looked helplessly at her sister. "Lula, what shall I do?"

Marie heard a soft rap upon the door. Lula eased out of the chair, leaving her sister to cling to its upholstered arm for comfort.

Lula glided across the room like a shadow and quickly undid the locks. Leo, her oldest son and the other cousin from dinner, stepped inside, hat in hand. He was taller and leaner than Luther, although he had the same brown hair neatly combed to one side.

But even through his apprehension, Leo harbored a contented spirit, a contrast to his brother's doleful air. It showed in Leo's comportment, relaxed as opposed to his brother's rigidity.

"What are you doing here?" Lula whispered loudly. "And what about...?"

"Mom, it's fine. I sent Alannah and Eugenia to Mother Kate's last night just in case we..."

Leo recoiled, turned pale, and then swallowed hard and straightened his shoulders. He stared at the still form on the bed for a few moments and then asked, "Dr. Parks, how is my uncle?"

Dr. Parks rose from the armchair. "Dying."

Marie whimpered and clutched the covers more tightly, as if the answers lay in stitched linen and wool.

Leo blanched. "Dying?"

"Yes."

Leo's eyes darted to his mother, his aunt, and then back to Dr. Parks. "You can do nothing for him?"

Lula looked down and away. "He wants to give your uncle a blood transfusion."

"Well, why hasn't he done it?"

Dr. Parks gave a short laugh. "Because they've refused."

Incredulity spread over Leo's face. "Mom, is this true?"

Lula snapped to attention, her eyes sparking behind the spectacles.

"Have you forgotten who this man is?" she spat. "What he's done? The pain and horror he's inflicted on innocent lives?"

"How can you, a longstanding newspaper woman, make these unsubstantiated claims! He's been nothing but kind to his own father since..."

"Dr. Parks!" Lula spat. "Do you deny it?"

Her eyes blazed, and she tightened her fists. Dr. Parks shrugged, a simple movement, like torching grass in a drought.

And flame up Lula did. "Do you deny transfusions kill more than they save? Or that the American Anti-Vivisection Society was formed to stop monsters like you?"

Marie shivered with delight, raised herself up on an elbow, and peered closely at Dr. Parks. She knew about the atrocities of vivisectionists like him, maniacs who cut apart the living to satisfy their vile inquisitiveness, her mama had said. For that reason, Isabella mistrusted scientists and most physicians. But the sober doctor in their midst had treated her papa with deliberation. Even now, with accusations hurled at him, he stood collected unto himself and not the least bit insane, not like the crazed or catatonic patients she had observed at the Buffalo State Asylum for the Insane when her papa wrote about...

George moaned; Leo flinched; Isabella slumped further into the chair and murmured, "Maybe we have not prayed enough..."

Leo dropped to his knees with a thump that shuddered through Marie. He clasped his hands high and bowed his head. Then just as quickly, he jumped to his feet, ripped off his coat, and announced, "We have prayed enough."

Rapidly, he unbuttoned his cuff.

Lula grabbed his arm, but he jerked away.

"What would Dad think if we let his good friend die?" Leo said quietly as he rolled up his sleeve to the shoulder. "Would he rejoice in heaven? Smile down at our good sense?"

"Leo..."

"Dr. Parks, I have blood enough for two. Please take some of mine to restore health to this man whom my father deeply loved."

Isabella squealed and slid to the floor, beating the air and screaming. Lula flew to her side, crouched next to her, and

42

pressed Isabella close to her heart, taking the beating, rocking them both back and forth, muffling the screams.

Dr. Parks slid their empty chair to the bed and bade Leo to sit. Then, as he reached into his medical bag, he caught Marie's eye and paused, hand still in the bag. "What about the child?"

"What about her?" Isabella's muffled voice retorted. "If you are to kill my husband, she should remain."

He whirled to face her. "Mrs. Clare, you can't be seri..."

"He might ask for her before he expires!"

"Mama!"

But her mama did not answer. The Arnold and Dent traveling clock loudly ticked off each minute of delay.

Marie shivered although the room was warm and stuffy.

Dr. Parks drew a deep breath. "Nevertheless, I feel..."

"She's seen men shot to death," Isabella raised her head. "That can't be worse than seeing you slowly bleed out Leo."

Dr. Parks pressed his lips together and closed his eyes. When he opened them, he returned to his bag and removed the items: a copper cup and funnel, tubing, implements with sharp points, a brown bottle. And he removed them with the same methodical coolness he had shown earlier this night.

A lifetime of objective observation had attuned Marie to subtleties others missed. Although concerned, Dr. Parks was more than confident in his treatments; he was practiced. He removed each item with the precision of a doctor who had set up each item in the same way for similar reasons many times. He knew the steps to take; he understood the results.

Marie's mama took her cues from Marie's papa, who took his cues from the world. George Clare noticed, analyzed, and reported, and he did all three with thoroughness and zeal. To Isabella, if George thought it true, she thought it true. But George could not assure Isabella now, so she was afraid.

All night, as she watched the macabre show, Marie had trembled with her mama's fear. But now, in this moment, her papa's training surfaced, like cream in milk, an action so automatic it happened before Marie realized it.

As her papa always said, "One can't refute truth." Something unwound inside Marie as she watched Dr. Parks; her limbs slackened; her fists released.

Dr. Parks twisted off the cap and poured a little of its contents on a piece of cloth. He rubbed the cloth across the under portion of Leo's upper arm. He did the same to George's left forearm and all the sharp points of his instruments.

An oily sweetness, like syrup on wood tar, lingered in the air.

Dr. Parks turned to Isabella, who was still on the floor, clasped to Lula's breast and weeping. "Please stay at his side. Your presence calms him."

Isabella shook her head.

"Very well."

As Dr. Parks picked up a needle and moved it close to Leo's arm, Marie called out, "I'll do it."

Slowly, Dr. Parks turned, the needle pointing directly at her. "You?"

Lula gasped, and Isabella yelped, but Marie slid off the cot and presented herself to Dr. Parks, feet bare, hands clasped behind her nightgown. "Yes. Papa trusts me, too. I am not afraid of blood or death."

Dr. Parks raised an eyebrow and looked her up and down, a slight bewilderment to his face. But Marie held firm. She had spoken the truth. She did not wish her papa to suffer, and she did not want her papa to die with The Dream unrealized. As Isabella had said, Marie had witnessed plenty of blood and death in the last decade, and neither typically frightened her. Her papa in such a state: that frightened her. But she would not say it or show it.

He shrugged. "Then, well, sit on the other side and take his hand."

Marie dragged the other parlor chair close to her papa's bed, digging a set of fine grooves across the wooden floor. After settling herself on the cushion as primly as she could, she learned forward, took her papa's clammy hand into her little round one, and murmured, "There, there Papa. The good doctor will soon restore health and vigor."

Dr. Parks knit his brows together but did not speak. He lined up the needle to Leo's arm and pricked the skin, much as one would pierce the crisp skin of a good roast chicken. Leo bleated like a lamb, but then he clamped his lips and made no other sound, not even when Dr. Parks threaded a tube into his arm.

Leo's blood seeped into the tube and toward the funnel. Dr. Parks repeated the same on George, who did not cry out, not so much as a moan. But sweat dampened on his forehead and one eye twitched. The blood continued leaking through the tubing toward its destination, her father. The process was not a quick one, and Marie kept one eye on her papa during the procedure and one eye at the sky outside the window.

Not once did Leo open his eyes, but he need not open his eyes to complete the task. The needle and cannula did it all for him. He only need sit still and let the apparatus do its job under the watchfulness of Dr. Parks, who sat, chin in hand and monitored the transfer of vitality from one man to the other with a rapt expression.

Although George did not respond, Marie intuited quickening in his lethargic form. This intuition crystalized into a vague certainty as night grew old and tired and her mama's traveling clock announced each passing hour.

Just as mauve streaked the raven sky and lifted the gloom, so did pink splotch her papa's white complexion, more beautiful to observe than Easter dawn.

At the appointed time, which only Dr. Parks seemed to know, he pronounced the transfusion complete, removed the tubing from each man's arm, and bandaged it. George remained still as stone but instead of appearing near death, something resembling sleep returned to him, for his breathing became slow and easy, and his eyes moved back and forth beneath his lids.

Leo started to straighten, and his head flopped back.

"Easy, son," Dr. Parks said as he steadied him. "Rest a few minutes." He turned to the sisters, who lay on the floor in a jumble of arms, legs, and disheveled clothing. They'd spent the intermittently dozing and whimpering. "Mrs. Clare, have you any more wine?"

"Yes," she mumbled without opening her eyes. "In the trunks."

But neither woman made a move to retrieve it, so Marie said politely, "I will bring you a bottle of very fine wine, Dr. Parks," and then she walked, head high, to one of the steamers. She returned shortly with a favorite from her grandpapa's – an

1869 Chateau Lafite – two clean glasses, and silver corkscrew with the head of a wolf.

'This is very fine wine," Dr. Parks said, holding up the bottle and examining its label.

"Why serve cheap alcohol to my father's savior?"

Dr. Parks smothered a smile, but the lines of his face relaxed. He uncorked the wine, poured half a glass, and handed it to Leo. Then he poured a full one for himself.

The door banged opened and slammed shut.

Marie swerved to the sound. Lula's eyes popped up. Luther slumped to the floor, his face puffy, red, and streaked.

"Luther?" Aunt Lula began as she peeled her sister's grasp away.

He buried his head in his arms and blubbered, "Mom, they're dead!"

CHAPTER SIX: RED MEAT

 enry felt a tug, and then he crashed to the floor.

Once again, John Simons had cut the rope. Once again, Henry had returned from nothing to darkness and a hunger so strong, he immediately scrambled to his feet and then sprang up the stairs and out the back door to appease it.

As he silently vroomed through the Simons estate and through the frozen woods, Henry easily grabbed and sucked out the blood of ground squirrels, wood-chucks, skunks, cottontail rabbits, foxes, and snowshoe hares.

But these were merely the hors-d oeuvre, the potage, the oeuf, the farineaux, the poisson, the entrée. Henry snapped the head of a mole and drank its contents, the sorbet. They tamed his starving beast and allowed his stealth to emerge, even as he emerged from woods and slunk into the cemetery, a cunning predator ready to dine. He mentally tied a bib around his swollen neck in preparation for the releves and roti. With the desperate part of his appetite tamed, he was in no hurry to attain the rest.

Munsonville held nearly four hundred souls, far more dining opportunities than the actual number of restaurants in New York and Chicago combined, for his uncle had homes there, too. Each human held trillions of tantalizing red blood cells, and their aromas wafted around him, more tempting than a savory joint and gravy.

Whom must he taste tonight?

Henry pondered the menu selections as he strolled his shrunken frame up and down the streets of this wretched fishing village as he once strolled Fifth Avenue with his uncle, except this time he kept to the shadows, much like his uncle kept their blood relationship in the closet.

"Welcome to New York, Nephew," a voice beside him said.

The moon, not quite full anymore but waxing with a soft glow, revived him as gently as an April morning at Arcadia way too many years ago, and invigorated him more than sleep and a tonic.

They followed the wide path of smooth stone to the chateau. The sun warmed Henry with brilliant rays as it climbed higher in the sky. Incredible the clarity of sunshine when it didn't have to fight smoky grime.

Feigned light for feigned life, and he cared about neither. He wondered, briefly, at the fate of Arcadia after his uncle's death and realized he didn't care about that either.

"Simplicity, peace, and happiness. Such is the definition of the word, the name for my estate, all one hundred and twenty-five acres." His uncle fixed his gaze on Henry. "And you shall be happy here."
"Yes, sir."

Blood.
He cared about blood.
Not family blood, but the blood of families laid out in their beds like quail on a serving platter. He flinched and shuddered at the thought of that delicate bird roasted in its juice with black pepper and allspice. The only quail that quickened his palate was raw, bloody, and ebbing from life.

Tonight should he dine on blood ripe with maturity? Or blood tinged with youthful freshness? Thick, rich, and raw? Or light and slightly sweet?

He raised his nose and sniffed the aromas, teasing out the one that appealed to him tonight over the rest. Ah, there it was! So fresh, so delicate; he burned; his whole body burned until it dissipated into mist and wafted its way to the house of his next meal, a balloon frame on Pike Street. He floated at the window and watched the final preparations of his lovely feast; he actually twitched with anticipation. Her flaxen hair spread across the pillow like golden gossamer. Her lashes fanned above rosy cheeks like well-placed herbs. One rounded arm had slipped out of the blanket and hung by the side of the bed. The thin coverlet slowly rose and fell with each gentle breath.

Now.

Henry slipped through a window crack, slithered down the wall and across the floor, fastening his gaze on the repast; not once did he blink. He slid up the bed until he sat next to her; he smoothed back the strands to expose the white neck, hypnotized by each beat of her pulse.

She stirred; he leaned down.

"Shh," he whispered in her ear.

She unconsciously raised a hand as if to swat a fly; the hand dropped to her side, she drifted off again; he moved in, mouth parted, aim precise. She bolted up; he clamped a fierce hand over her mouth, pushing her into the pillow and tasting his victory. The warm, sticky fluid freely flowed from her into him. His veins ballooned as she deflated, and Henry drank and drank until she shrunk to the size of peeling stick doll, and he approached the roundness of a trout with the bloat. He never removed his hand until long after she passed, frozen-eyed, into eternity. He licked the red smears off her neck, a throwback to his childhood and its scarcity; one never wasted food, no matter now meager or spoiled. He felt satiated but not completely, just enough to carry him over to the legumes course, opossum, perhaps, maybe raccoon.

But before Henry departed, he bent and kissed her cold forehead, his compliments to the heavenly chef that fashioned her. Then he slipped through the window in search of the next course.

By dawn, Henry had worked his way through the blood of grouse, ermine, wood frogs, turtles, and bats; in other words: the salade, buffet froid, entremets, savoureux, fromage, dessert, and the final boisson of the night: the blood of a sparrow, whose early morning song Henry silenced by snapping its tiny neck.

Finally Henry, as plump as a Thanksgiving turkey, wobbled his sleepy way through the lightening cemetery and the long stretch of woods back to Simons Mansion. He stumbled through the back door and all the way to the basement where he tottered to the secret room, which John had prepared for them once again.

The door was wide open; of what need had they for locks now? John already lay crumpled and dormant on the floor, in the exact position where Henry had killed him.

He kicked over the corpse. Blood oozed from the corners of John's swollen face, ruddy now, but that wouldn't last. He studied John's sightless eyes, jealous that John had arrived at nothing first. The noose beckoned him, but his eyes first swept over rows of easels and the flames of many strategically positioned candles, glad John had once again seen them, and even more glad John had also lit them once again. Henry hoped the view haunted John before he hibernated. He hoped the view would always haunt and harry him.

Then Henry stepped onto the stool, sipped his head into the noose, a noose once again made from bryony of all the fucking things, and kicked the chair away.

Henry felt a tug, and then he crashed to the floor.

Once again, John had cut the rope. Once again, Henry returned from nothing to darkness and a hunger so strong, he immediately scrambled to his feet and then sprang up the stairs and out the back door to appease it.

As Henry grew more experienced, he needed less time to make the rounds of all the courses. Soon, he was arriving at Simons Mansion long before dawn or what Henry called "the dormant hour." On this particular night, brisk piano music greeted him as he teetered on distended feet through the back door. Henry seethed with rage at the sound.

How dare John keep the one piece of life that mattered to him when he, Henry, had lost everything?

But Henry had already taken John's wife and John's life. Henry had nothing more to take.

So Henry merely stood in the middle of the floor as if one of his orange trees from the greenhouse his uncle had built for him at Arcadia had taken root on the spot. He clenched his hands and jaw and waited for the fury to stop.

Which it finally did. Abruptly.

In the middle of a movement, Henry heard a discordant bang of the keys, a slam of the lid, and a scuffle as John shuffled from music room to the basement door. John's own vibrancy from the night's kill was quickly fading.

Their dead eyes met.

"You bastard," John said quietly as he kicked Henry square in his distended stomach. Blood shot out as Henry buckled to the floor.

"You bastard," John said, punctuating his low words with repeated kicks, which caused more blood to erupt. "You bastard. You bastard."

Henry groaned with each blow. His dinner exploded across the floor and spattered the walls. Finally, he slipped flat and lay gasping in a pool of assorted blood.

John bent down and pulled Henry up by his hair.

"Do you hear it?" John tilted his head, leering. "The Fisher Farm cock crows. It's time."

Abruptly, John let go, and Henry's head dropped with a loud clunk. Then the musician spun on his heel and headed for the stairs. Henry crawled after him like a whipped husky, the instinct of survival spurring his movements since moving hurt so badly. He tumbled down the last few steps and then couldn't muster the strength to pull himself up. So, grunting with each inch, Henry dragged himself along the cold stone floor, inch by painful inch, until he finally reached the hidden room.

John already lay crumpled and unseeing on the floor, knife a few paces away from him where Henry had tossed it. The noose of bryony beckoned to him, a hypnotic summons he must accede. So Henry obediently climbed onto the stool, placed his head in the noose, and kicked the chair away.

One night, Henry felt a tug, but he did not fall. He opened his eyes, and a vision swam before him.

The vision had auburn mutton chops, thinning auburn hair, wire spectacles, round shoulders, and it was smoking a pipe and holding a lantern high. His pipe was polished dark wood with a large bowl and gold lid, trim, and mouthpiece. The gold glinted in the flame's light and made Henry's eyes hurt.

John cut the bonds, and Henry crashed to the floor amongst an assortment of the dead and dying. Dr. Gothart kicked one over to him.

"Hurry up and eat," Dr. Gothart said. "You have work to do."

John had already split open the neck of his first course and was greedily devouring it, much like Chinook had once devoured a rib-eye. So Henry quickly did the same, while the barely alive moaned in terror. He and John roamed the basement floor on hands and knees, each picking and drinking to his liking.

When they'd reduced their meal to hair, skin and bones, Dr. Gothart reached down, snapped off someone's femur, and hovered it over Henry's head.

"Upstairs," Dr. Gothart said quietly. "Now."

"Fuck you," Henry said.

The bone cracked onto Henry's skull, and Henry shrieked. Dr. Gothart thwacked him again and followed that up with a splintering kick to Henry's ribs. Delivering one wallop after another, Dr. Gothart drove Henry up the basement stairs and then up the rear staircase to the second floor and through the door of Henry's study, where he yanked Henry up by his grimy collar and towed him to his desk chair. As Henry struggled to catch his non-breath, Dr. Gothart set the leg on the desk next to a stack of telegrams and the gold heirloom ring Henry had spat onto his bedroom floor that first night of his turning.

Dr. Gothart relit his pipe, took a drag, and then perched at the edge of Henry's desk, smoking.

"Read them," Dr. Gothart said.

Trembling, Henry picked up a telegram and skimmed it. Then he picked up another and another until he read them all.

"Start typing," Dr. Gothart said.

Henry vehemently shook his head.

Dr. Gothart grabbed the leg and smashed it into Henry's face.

Henry yelped like a prairie dog, at least, how Henry always imagined a prairie dog might yelp. Then he bent over the keys, clacking so fast his fingers blurred before him.

CHAPTER SEVEN: WEEPING COMETH BY DAY

ith excruciatingly slowness, George crawled back to life in Room 27.

He interspersed sleeping with periods of cranky wakefulness where he complained of headaches, which Isabella soothed with strips of cloth dipped in cool chamomile tea.

He spoke curtly when he spoke at all, for the mental effort to compose even five words exhausted him, necessitating a nap.

He craved juicy meats of all kinds only to spurn them when the kitchen help finally delivered them. Besides, struggling to sit unsettled his stomach. So Isabella took to feeding George one patient bite at a time, which, more often than not, he spewed into the chamber pot minutes after he swallowed it.

Dr. Parks still called three times a day. Each time, he mixed more clay, and George drank it with two hands around the beaker and eyes fixed on Dr. Parks. He drank as docilely as any obedient child. And George's stomach always accepted it.

But the hands on her papa's Vacheron Constantin took many circular trips (He insisted on checking that beloved timepiece whenever he awakened) before George could remain upright for an hour without dizziness and panting for breath, and before Dr. Parks pronounced George's pulse as "nearly normal."

Yet the head spasms and general lassitude persisted, enough to confine George to bed, albeit propped against the pillows, even when he wasn't dozing on Isabella's shoulder.

While George recovered, and Isabella oversaw his recovery, Marie managed the routine.

Each morning after Marie left her cot, she ducked behind the solid walnut screen to use the chamber pot and otherwise prepare for the day. The screen was older than Marie and traveled with them from place to place. Isabella insisted upon it and pressed on Marie the necessity of carrying out any personal business behind it so as to never offend George with the coarseness of femininity.

53

So Marie did.

Elimination, bathing, grooming, dressing: Marie accomplished each one, if not in total secrecy, which was impossible when three shared a room most days of the year, then at least hidden from view. Marie always emerged "fresh as a rose," as Isabella liked to say, ready to stand before the bureau's mirror to plait her hair and fasten her jewelry.

Today she chose an eighteen-karat gold drapery necklace with blue sapphire teardrops and a blue sapphire ring and matching comb for her hair, adornments from her Grandmama Sage's collection. She also chose her newest charm bracelet. Marie owned many. Her papa began the tradition when she was just four. Every time they visited a place, George bought her a charm. They'd visited so many places that Marie's bracelets ran out of space. This new one had just three charms: a cat (Cat Spring, Texas), a ladies boot (Natchitoches, Louisiana), and scissors (Cut Bank, Montana).

Finally, Marie reached for her ivory hairbrush, almost like hard lace with its deep rose carvings. She watched her reflection pull the bristles through each tangle, starting at her scalp and down to its ends. She hadn't the hint of a smile, not even in her blue eyes, the color of her papa's eyes except hers lacked his vivaciousness that only illness could snuff out But why she should smile? Her papa was driven; her mother was beautiful; and she was Marie.

Once Marie was fit for society, she undid the bolts, opened the door, and brought in the covered dishes that the kitchen help had left at their door. This part of the routine Isabella generally managed, so Marie knew it well. But George's need for care did not end at sunset, and neither did Isabella ever deny him that care. She was ready to serve him any time day or night, the reason why Isabella, for now, often slept through the early part of the day. And that is why Marie often ate the countrified breakfast alone. Such a simple meal did not bother her. She'd eaten many kinds of breakfasts over the years: fried cornbread and boiled eggs, goat's milk with cold bread and butter, fluffy omelets with griddle cakes or toast, mutton chops and rice, sausages with fried potatoes, chunky soups and stews, stewed fruits and sweet custards, and thick puddings and toast. Some breakfasts were served on fine China, others on tin, still others in chipped pottery.

This morning it was mashed fish and potato cakes with bread and translucent dewberry jelly, for jelly was a must for her mama, and every kitchen always managed to deliver it. This morning's repast was presented on white ironstone. Marie silently ate hers and left the rest covered. When Isabella finally stirred, Maria was sitting at the desk, silently reading the day's selection from her mama's Bible, which Isabella always marked. After first tucking the covers around George, Isabella disappeared behind the screen. By the time she emerged, Marie had transitioned to schoolwork.

Unlike many children her age, Marie needed no prompting, and why would she? For routine balanced the adventure, and Marie found security in both, even though she perceived her family as a scalene triangle, with herself at the farthest point of the Yin and Yang of her parents.

But Marie never minded her place at the apex. For it allowed her to see what others did not see.

She turned a page and began copying the next algebra problem into her notebook with her gold-filled mechanical pencil, reveling in the sunshine from the nearby window that the cold glass could not contain.

This was the most daylight the displaced Clares could currently enjoy: spreading apart the curtains and basking in the glass-blocked sun. They must not, must not, open the window, not the slightest crack, Dr. Parks had warned earlier in the week, even more severely than he warned against wine for her papa.

For a mysterious illness had settled in the village they'd yet to explore. It shut down industry; it bottled people up in their homes, where no one heard the wails of families mourning their dead.

So even as George gradually improved physically, they all declined emotionally and drowned in mutual dejection. But for Marie, routine kept dejection at the perimeter of her life and offered escape from the despair that would surely follow.

For once again, they'd missed their chance; once again they'd missed the scoop, a scoop in place, ready to fire. And now they were living in the midst of a scoop-in-progress, and her papa was too weak to nab it.

As George had predicted, the disreputable Henry Matthews had squashed The Dream once again. It started with Henry Matthews scooping their story on John and Bryony Simons, a story on which her papa had labored for weeks, but Henry's sabotaging didn't end there.

Henry himself had quickly written and telegraphed his entire feature to the New York Gazette before even the village, much less The Munsonville Times, heard the news that Bryony Simons and her baby were dead, and that the anguished John Simons had fled the village.

The wire officially informed the cousins of the missed opportunity, shortly after Luther had unofficially blurted out the news to her papa's sentinels at the conclusion of the blood transfusion.

George had wept the next morning as he read the copy aloud, despite Isabella's objections and attempts to shield her husband from the newspaper that Dr. Parks brandished over her head.

"He's a man, not a child," Dr. Parks said as he placed the folded Times in George's eager, outstretched hands. "Truth won't hurt him, only wine."

Isabella had glowered at him, if only to show Dr. Parks how greatly he had displeased her and to remind him of his extremely limited role in their lives. But when he paid no need to her umbrage, she settled on the bed and cooed sympathetically to George as he read each heartbreaking word aloud.

Deadly tragedy leaves music world, Michigan fishing village bereft
By Henry Matthews for the New York Gazette

At half past seven o'clock on Nov. 1, in her private chambers at Simons Mansion in Munsonville, Michigan, Mrs. Bryony Simons and her unnamed son died shortly after the child's birth.

Dr. Edwin Gothart, the attending physician, blamed abruptio placentae during the confinement. Dr. Gothart had treated Mrs. Simons for chlorosis since she was a very little girl. He said her chlorosis mostly likely contributed to the placenta's detachment.

Mr. John Simons, renowned pianist, composer, and husband to Mrs. Simons, left Munsonville shortly after the deaths of his wife and son, vowing never to return.

Dr. Gothart said Mr. Simons departed in a distraught state, even though Dr. Gothart pleaded for Mr. Simons not to travel in such a passion. Mr. Simons' whereabouts are unknown at the present time, leaving the music world stunned and in an uproar.

Mrs. Simons' fragile health often left her unable to travel with Mr. Simons on his engagements, which grieved him greatly. He had canceled all engagements this year in order to remain at Simons Mansion and oversee his wife's care.

At this point, no one knows when the great piano master will perform again.

Reverend Galien Marseilles, Mrs. Simons father and pastor of Munsonville Congregational Church, refused to comment. Burial services were private; Marseilles and no one else.

For a village still reeling under last year's tragic drownings, not to mention the loss of its leader and founder Owen Munson a few years prior, this current tragedy is nearly too much to bear.

Mr. Munson's birthday is celebrated with great festivity in Munsonville every June 28.

With contorted face and savage hands, the most energy her papa had exhibited since he fell ill, George wadded The Times, threw it to the foot of bed, and burst into racking sobs.

No one moved or spoke, even Isabella.

"Another defeat," George finally gasped as he wiped his streaming eyes and dripping nose on the bed sheet.

"There, there," George," Isabella said as she reached for his arm.

But George pushed her hand aside and covered his face.

"I am a worm and no man," he muttered, "a reproach of men and despised of the people."

Because they had lost access to servants during the quarantine, Isabella hand-washed George's soiled laundry herself, repeatedly soaking his bloodstained clothes in milk until she had rubbed out every stain from his fine garments. But no amount of carefully placed potpourri could blot the stench of their confinement, and Marie often paused in her schoolwork to gaze out the window, longing to take deep breaths of the cold, fresh air.

Aunt Lula and the cousins, of course, stayed away, because of the quarantine and because they kept the village informed about the strange malady that stole souls away in the night. But Isabella did write daily notes of George's progress, which Dr. Parks hand-delivered to The Times.

Even the servants, Dr. Parks told them, could not return to Simons Mansion, and Henry Matthews, the last person remaining at the great estate, was not allowed to step out. But Henry had direct access to a telegraph and newspaper publishers in Chicago and New York, which George, even if he had the strength to cover stories, did not.

And so they were stuck inside Room 27 at Munsonville Inn.

To Isabella's chagrin, whenever Dr. Parks stopped with George's medicine, he always brought the latest edition of The Times.

Mysterious Illness Claims More Souls
By Luther Hasset, Editor-In-Chief, The Munsonville Times

The quarantine continues in Munsonville.
Each day, at least one family rises to find a loved one has perished by night.
Dr. Gothart said has no explanation for the mysterious illness.
Only a few moved freely about the village: Dr. Parks; Dr. Gothart; Leo Hasset and Luther Hasset, to deliver the news doorstep to doorstep; and the grave diggers.

But at least, Marie often told herself, at least they weren't digging a grave for her papa. Twice the Grim Reaper had called on George Clare in Munsonville, and twice George had not only repelled him, but limped away in the opposite direction.

"Any notion of the cause?" George asked one morning, sitting against the headboard with such a look of profound curiosity and professional concern that Marie almost felt as if she had her papa back.

"It's baffling," Dr. Parks agreed as he buckled his bag. "They go to their beds healthy and never wake up."

"No sign of illness?"

"All rosy before repose, pale as linen by morning, even their gums, and sapped of life."

Servant Girl Still in Care of Village Woman, Mother's Whereabouts Unknown

By Leo Hasset, Publisher of The Munsonville Times

Anna Czarnecki, the eight-year-old daughter of Mrs. Bryga Czarnecki, Simons Mansion housekeeper, is still under the care of Mrs. Neta Ashmore.

Henry Matthews had brought Anna to the church parsonage after the death of Mrs. Bryony Simons and her newborn son when Bryga, an attendant at Mrs. Simons' confinement, could not be located.

Many fear Bryga herself fell victim to the mysterious illness plaguing Munsonville, especially since Henry Matthews, the only resident remaining at Simons Mansion, may be ill himself and unable to conduct a thorough inspection of the premises.

A search party cannot be dispensed at this time, also due to the quarantine.

Mrs. Ashmore, widow of entrepreneur Blair Ashmore, is the current housekeeper of Reverend Galien Marseilles, pastor of Munsonville Congregational Church and father to Mrs. Simons.

Mrs. Ashmore stepped up to serve the parsonage after longtime housekeeper Mrs. Bertha Parks, the previous housekeeper, had to assume full-time care of her husband Mr. Orville Parks.

Mrs. Parks was also the foster mother to Mrs. Simons. The reverend was widowed when Mrs. Simons was just three years old.

"It figures Henry Matthews would escape the scourge," George said disgustedly the next morning as he folded The Times and handed it back to Dr. Parks. "Vermin have an innate talent for survival."

"Mr. Matthews is a recluse, I've heard," Dr. Parks said as he set the publication on the little table. "His self-imposed isolation may have protected him. Or he may have contracted a weaker strain. But Dr. Gothart is his attending physician and knows more than I."

"Sick or not, he keeps out-scooping Munsonville's own publication. He's disgusting."

"That may be. But perhaps his 'timeliness' is protecting your nephews. The more he reports, the less they mingle with others, reducing their chance of illness and...and death."

Marie started at the catch in Dr. Parks' voice. But her papa, enmeshed in his own distress, missed the distress of his Savior.

"And he's destroying their father's Dream, the migrating cockroach."

Daughter, Fiancée of Village Physician, Succumbs to Mysterious Illness
    By Luther Hasset, Editor-in Chief, The Munsonville Times

Miss Millicent Gothart, daughter of Dr. Edwin Gothart and fiancée of Dr. Martin Parks, son of Mr. Orville and Mrs. Parks, is the latest victim of the mysterious illness to befall Munsonville, bringing the total number of deaths to fifty-six.

Like the other souls who met a similar fate, Miss Gothart had bid her father good night before retiring and never appeared in the morning to prepare his breakfast. Dr. Gothart discovered the tragedy soon afterward.

Burial services were private, just Doctors Gothart and Parks.

We at The Munsonville Times find it peculiar that the attending physicians seem to be immune to this mysterious illness when the other villagers are in danger.

Soberly, George folded The Times and set it aside. A tear ran down his cheek. Isabella whisked a lace edged handkerchief from her reticule and blotted it. But more tears followed, faster than Isabella could dry them.

"What grace of God that I'm to be treated by such a courageous man!" George exclaimed.

Isabella's face hardened. But she kept dabbing.

"What dedication to his patients that he does not falter, even when his own heart must be broken beyond repair!"

"Why, George, your tea has grown cold. Surely this will chill you." Isabella placed the back of his hand against the pot. "You see? I'll send for more directly."

"Forget the tea," George said shortly. "My head hurts. Little Marie, close the curtains."

George folded a pillow over his face, rolled onto his side, and sank into a heavy sleep. Marie turned back to her book, but her mind kept returning to the last line of Luther's story. Why *were* the doctors immune to the illness?

Dr. Parks arrived shortly before the noon meal, no less self-composed and with his same careful solicitude of George. Marie studied him as he checked her papa's pulse, blood pressure, breathing, and then mixed and dispensed her papa's clay; she tried to analyze her observations and the knowledge she had of him. Was this kind doctor a callous monster as her Aunt Lula had intimated? Or did extreme heroism cover inward suffering at the death of his true love?

Marie rose respectfully as he prepared to leave. Her movement caught his attention, so she said, "I'm very sorry for your loss."

She noted a flicker in his eyes. Was it sorrow?

Dr. Parks bowed slightly to her.

"Thank you, Miss Clare," he said.

His gaze met her mama's; mutual dislike passed between them.

Then Dr. Parks retrieved his bag and left.

As George gradually recovered, they gradually altered the rhythm to their day. Isabella once more took command of their routine, and Marie returned to her supporting role.

After rising before day to carefully groom herself behind the screen, for she still would not appear less than angelic before her husband, Isabella, fragrant with rose oil, carefully washed and shaved him; she even waxed his mustache before pulling off his soiled dressing gown and slipping on a fresh one.

She read from the Bible while they awaited the arrival of their breakfast trays, for two of the village women remained quarantined at Munsonville Inn in order to serve the inn's few guests. The trays usually contained hashed codfish, fried potatoes, poached apples and dewberry jelly for Isabella and Marie, and gruel and a soft egg for George.

With the morning meal cleared from the table and the dishes and chamber pots left outside their door for the help, Isabella worked on needlepoint and listened as George read aloud in a weak voice from the morning edition of The Times.

At the conclusion of these activities, George settled into his pillows for a nap. That's when Isabella turned to life's crudest chores, laundry, dusting, and sweeping, chores that would beset George if he saw Isabella's debasement on his behalf, and both Isabella and Marie shrank at the thought of causing the gentle man more torment.

Indeed, George always awakened shortly before lunch to serenity, to his wife rereading the latest issues of Vogue or daintily running a needle of colored thread through linen, the sunshine trespassing through the dirty glass and streaking her golden hair with golden rays; and to his Little Marie sitting at the desk reading her lessons, diagramming complex sentences, or working her sums.

At noon, the trays contained roasted meats, potatoes in their jackets, boiled root vegetables and fresh warm rolls for Isabella and Marie, and gruel and a soft egg for George.

The afternoon repeated the morning.

In the evening, the trays often contained soup, fresh baked bread and dewberry jelly for Isabella and Marie, and bone broth for George.

Dr. Parks still came three times a day, to examine his patient, to dispense clay, to which George submitted with slackened limbs, trust in his tired eyes, and a countenance full of respect, a clear annoyance to her mama, who sat rigidly by George and tried to smile cheerfully to him through tight lips.

Then came the wonderful day when Dr. Parks tested her papa's stomach with boiled chicken and potatoes. And her papa's stomach did not rebel, a relief to all, especially Isabella, who longed for the day Dr. Parks need not cross their threshold again, and they could resume their pursuit of The Dream.

But not a day passed without another death. And so, the quarantine remained.

Outbreak in Simons sphere: Has the New England vampire panic moved to Northern Michigan?
By Henry Matthews for the New York Gazette

Who can forget the Rhode Island hysteria of just four yours ago, where rural folk mistook victims of tuberculosis for victims of demons and mutilated the corpses of their loved ones in futile attempts to protect themselves?

Well, it seems as if the plague has moved to Munsonville, Michigan, home, until very recently, of world-renowned pianist and composer John Simons.

Ever since Mrs. Simons and her son died in childbirth, an inexplicable illness has ravaged the tiny fishing village that looks, indeed, as if actual vampires might be preying on them.

Healthy residents retire at night; a random few expire before dawn. Could a mutated tuberculosis be the cause? A new plague from distant lands that migrated to these soils?

It seems unlikely the cause is demons, not with a rumored vivisectionist practicing in their midst, who could easily stake and dismember any prowling vampires.

For the safety of all, a quarantine remains in place, which all are heeding.

Except the vampires.

"Vampires!" George exclaimed as Isabella hastily removed the newspaper from his shaking hands. "Innocent souls dying in their beds, and he mocks the tragedy! How can any editor take this man seriously? He's a disgrace to the very nobility of the profession!"

"Shh, George," Isabella said as she fluffed up the pillows behind him. "Forget about Henry Matthews and rest. You'll put him to shame soon enough."

"Soon enough" couldn't come fast enough for Marie. She couldn't wait until her papa's hard work silenced scoundrels like Henry Matthews. She opened her grammar book and began copying sentences.

One night, as Marie drifted into sleep, she heard her mama softly murmur, "George."

"Shhh. What about Little Marie?"

Her eyes popped open; she stared in the dark, her back to their whisperings.

"She is asleep."

"Then speak."

"Read this."

A rustle. And a heavy male sigh.

"Oh, George…"

"The thief has come in the night, as we…"

"I'll talk to Lula. Maybe she can loan…"

"Please don't."

"George, you're not thinking clearly. We can…"

"No, we cannot. It's time this grasshopper stops fiddling."

CHAPTER EIGHT: FROM CELLAR TO CEILING

enry felt the familiar tug and plunged to the floor, face-to-face with a bruised and splotchy human lump. Blood conveniently flowed from lad's nose, which was twisted and molded to his cheek, and smelled positively scrumptious.

One hand inched toward Henry. The other arm lay broken and useless by his side.

"Help...me," he pleaded.

"Hurry up and eat breakfast," John said coldly. "We're meeting in the music room."

Meeting? Music room?

We?

Henry gave the youth's shoulder a pat and smiled reassuringly.

"I'll help you," Henry promised.

He speedily sent his victim to heaven, less for reasons of mercy and more for gratifying his hunger, his curiosity about the rendezvous upstairs, and his gratitude that, once again, food came to him instead of the other way around. Thirst slaked, hunger cooled, Henry hastened up the steps and through though the open double doors to the music room, where a fire danced in the fireplace and a peculiar party had gathered.

An enormous grand piano ruled the center of the room, which merged with an outer room, a library full of books, a few well-placed chairs, a second fireplace, and a desk in the far corner. Both spaces were richly decorated in crimson and brown, a film of dust, and a light draping of cobwebs. Alive or dead, John always preferred this space above the others. True to form, the acclaimed pianist, composer, widower, and, for now, decomposing corpse with stringy long hair, occupied the piano bench, unmoving, not smiling.

Kellen Wechsler, John's manager, was lounging in a wingback far away from the fire, sulking and smoking a cigar. He wore only black, the same shade as his hair, eyes, goatee, nails, everything except his waxy skin, which was pale as death. Unlike John, Kellen sported a certain "freshness," like when a butcher presses blood into spoiled meat for reselling.

Near the fire, Dr. Edwin Gothart smoked in a haze of aromatic tobacco and an unhurried air. The gold on his pipe glinted in the firelight and stung Henry's vision.

The biggest surprise, although reflecting back, Henry realized the man's presence really shouldn't have surprised him, was Dr. Martin Parks, the famous vivisectionist and former fiancé of the now deceased Millicent Gothart, may she never rest in peace. Dr. Parks sat tall, although not as tall as John, and nursed a decanter of Bordeaux. Also unlike John, Dr. Parks had a full head of dark hair, a furry dark mustache, and absolutely no signs of decay. In fact, Henry detected a strong and rhythmic heartbeat and a robust capillary system, along with deep and regular respirations.

Interesting, Henry thought. Maybe tasty.

Dr. Gothart gestured to Henry with the pipe. "Take a seat."

The tone, pleasant; the words, nonchalant; the intent, malignant and with no leeway for trifles. Wary, Henry selected a chair in the farthest corner and eased his bones into the velvet cushion, nicely crimson, so staining needn't trouble anyone.

"First of all," Dr. Gothart said quietly, glowering first at John and then to Henry. "Stop killing in Munsonville."

Henry blinked. "What?"

"In fact, stop plucking humans anywhere in this century. You're risking exposure and staking."

"Correct," John said. "Because no one ever staked a thirteenth century Bulgarian vampire."

Kellen chuckled and waved the cigar. "Oh, John, John, you darling neophyte. You don't stay in Bulgaria long enough to get staked. You…"

"I don't intend to stay dead long enough to get staked anywhere," John said, replying to Kellen but looking at Dr. Gothart. "My current vampire state is merely temporary."

"Temporary, yes," Dr. Gothart shifted slightly. "But perhaps more temporary than you like."

John's features hardened; his irises crystallized to blue ice. "You don't have a remedy?"

"I'm working on a remedy. I have a partial remedy. In the meantime, we can restore a façade of humanity."

"Like Kellen's facade?" Henry piped up.

With a hint of a smirk and the flames crackling behind him, Dr. Gothart tipped his head and contemplated Henry. In that instant, Henry knew Dr. Gothart not only knew Henry knew, Henry realized Dr. Gothart had known Henry's suspicions about Kellen for a very long time.

But Dr. Gothart only removed his pipe. "Somewhat. Kellen is a hybrid and prefers to remain so. The extent we restore you and John depends on your goals."

"Our goals?" John asked.

Henry snickered loudly and stretched pleasantly. "You know, John. Goals. The end toward which you direct your efforts."

John glared at him, and Henry thumbed his nose in response, but John had already redirected his attention to Dr. Gothart. "And what do you mean by 'hybrid?'"

"Fully human is not an option – yet," Dr. Parks interjected. "In the meantime, Kellen enjoys moving about time with a foot – or should I say 'fang' – on both sides of the grave. Dr. Gothart has worked quite extensively with him to achieve it."

"Why the hell are you here?" Henry demanded.

"To kill you – and him," Dr. Parks said casually, jerking his head at John. "Or I ought to feel that way if I'd tied more of a bond with Millicent. And if Millicent had been a normal woman."

Dr. Gothart opened his mouth to remonstrate him, but Dr. Parks held up his hand for silence.

"But as the matter stands," Dr. Parks continued, "I'm conflicted. I miss her even though she frightened me. Her depravity was part of the thrill, perhaps. However, my marriage to Millicent would have made my working with Dr. Gothart natural and expected and would have repaired some significant relationships in my own life. But you," he turned fiercely to Henry. "You destroyed all of that when you assassinated…"

Henry broke out laughing, and Dr. Parks rose halfway out of his seat, fists clenched.

"Simmer down, Martin," Dr. Gothart pointed the pipe at the chair. "This solves nothing. I mean it. Sit."

Dr. Parks hesitated, and then he complied and resumed his little discourse as if no breech occurred.

"...yes, assassinated, for that is my estimation of your attack on a defenseless sorceress. You hoped to destroy her, and instead you empowered her even more."

"Fortunately for you," Dr. Gothart said as he leaned into the chair's cushioned backrest, still monitoring Dr. Parks for signs of a second outburst. "She's left the area in search of greater pursuits. I doubt we'll see her again."

But Henry was watching Dr. Parks. He appeared relaxed, but his pupils were dilated.

"You're really still frightened of her?" Henry asked.

"Hell, yes!" Dr. Parks actually shuddered. "And if you were still alive, you'd be frightened, too. She..."

A brief string of sharp, brisk chords cut off the rest.

Silence.

Except the spit and snap of the flames.

John coolly shut the lid and faced Dr. Gothart. "So how do you accomplish our...transformation?"

But Dr. Gothart proceeded to smoke while observing John with amusement. John merely gazed back, self-assured and at ease, for Henry knew time meant nothing to John, and it meant everything to Dr. Gothart.

"An ancient legend," Dr. Gothart finally said, reflectively, as if calling the words to mind, "says minute amounts of blood consumed from one human source neutralizes vampirism and restores life."

"Ha!" Henry exclaimed, plopping his feet on the ottoman and clasping his hands over his chest, as if he were settling in for a drowsy evening of refreshment and not a fantastical discussion of the implausible life beyond the afterlife. "So you don't even know it's true!"

"Oh, it's true," Dr. Parks insisted. "It worked for Kellen."

John stiffened; a shadow crossed his countenance; and he lowered his head, as if Dr. Parks' words weighed him down. Kellen noticed and jumped on it.

"Oh, come on, John, don't act so betrayed," Kellen said smoothly, but Henry detected a slight rise of panic . "The terms of the contract were quite simple, and you agreed to them. Fame and fortune for you, and blood for me without demise to you. Just..."

"...sips from time to time," John muttered. He raised dark eyes to Dr. Gothart. "So one host accomplishes it?"

"Yes," Dr. Gothart said. "And the closest the host is to the vampire's continuum, the more effectively treatment appears to work."

Henry snorted. "What the hell does that mean?"

"Family blood is ideal," Dr. Parks explained. "Second choice is blood to which the undead forms a particular attachment."

"Such as Kellen's for John's," Henry said triumphantly.

"Exactly," Dr. Gothart took a long, thoughtful puff. "Back to goals. John, what do you wish?"

John straightened his shoulders. "My goal remains unchanged. Worldwide acclaim above other musicians. As a human. Soon. We invent a story about my grief to explain my brief, very brief, absence. Dr. Gothart does the rest."

Dr. Gothart took another puff. "And you, Henry?"

"I have no goals," Henry said simply. "This is fine."

"What is fine?"

"This," Henry slapped his chest. "It's simple, and it suits me."

Dr. Parks swerved to him. "I don't understand. You wish to remain undead?"

"Yes," Henry insisted.

"But...I thought..."

"Martin," Dr. Gothart said with a hint of mirth, as if he found the exchange especially entertaining. "I don't believe you've been properly introduced. This is Henry Matthews."

"I know, the reporter for the Gazette and Albert Brumfeldt's nephew." Dr. Parks was still studying Henry. "You really don't want to rehumanize?"

"No."

"Martin, he's not Brumfeldt's nephew."

"Huh? Then why does everyone..."

"He's Lord Girard's nephew."

John's jaw dropped.

"WHAT?" Dr. Parks jumped up and then dropped into his chair and rubbed his face, as if the act made the story more believable. "But Lord Girard didn't have any family, only his sister, who ran off with ..."

He lowered his hands and stared in horror at Henry. "Oh...God."

"You really are loathsome," John said to Henry with genuine hatred in his voice.

"You can see why Lord Girard didn't formally claim him," Dr. Gothart said, unruffled.

"But what about his lordship's fortune?" Dr. Parks insisted. "His vast fortune?"

Dr. Gothart closed his hand around tinder box. "All left to Albert Brumfeldt, Lord Girard's..."

"Friend," Henry said evenly. "Friend and colleague."

"Cut out of his will, and still you defend him," Dr. Gothart sneered and struck the match with a loud scritch.

Henry flipped him off with a grin. Dr. Parks cleared his throat and topped off his wine with a slow trickle.

"Well," Dr. Parks picked up his goblet. "While you're developing and refining your vampire skills, you'll need to relearn the art of moving from 'beast' to best.'"

"Why?" Henry stretched again and yawned. "I'm not reverting."

"Why?" Dr. Parks mocked. "Why? Because a vampire with the appearance of a human is more likely to go undetected, that's why."

"Oh, and get plenty of moonlight," Dr. Gothart instructed.

"Why?" Henry asked again, enjoying the game.

"A moon that reflects light helps rejuvenate beings that also reflect life," Dr. Gothart said. "Benefits include wound healing and gradual adaptation to small amounts of sunlight."

Dr. Parks set down his glass. "Before I forget..."

He strolled to the desk in the library, retrieved a stack of papers, and then strolled to the far part of the room, where he dumped the telegrams into Henry's lap. Henry rapidly shuffled through them, scanning the lines. Yup. All from Brumfeldt. Again.

With a dramatic flourish, Henry pitched them over his shoulder. "I'm not writing anymore. Not for Brumfeldt. And certainly, not for you." He nodded in the direction of Dr. Gothart.

"I replied to them for you," Dr. Parks said, ignoring Henry's objection. "At the request of your attending physician, I informed him you were afflicted and under quarantine. That will buy you some time."

"I don't care," Henry spat. "I'm not doing it."

"You better care," Dr. Gothart warned. "And you better do it. Your survival as a vampire depends on it. As we've already said, the more you behave like a human, the better you protect..."

"So what about me?" Kellen shrieked. "What about my humanness? Every day I lose a little more, and it's all because of HIM!" Kellen threw his cigar at Henry, who simply snuffed into the chair fabric.

"Your goal is easy," Dr. Gothart said, still calm. "We simply find you a new host."

"I had a perfectly good host! That shrimp of a dandy stole my host!"

"Let me do my work," Dr. Gothart soothed, but his green eyes sharpened. "Perhaps you may drink from John again one day."

"Over my dead body," John retorted.

All eyes turned to John.

"Joke," John said with a shrug, not smiling.

Kellen flew out of the chair and lunged at Henry, grasping his neck with two hands and then yanking him up and violently shaking him.

"He's already dead," Dr. Parks said.

Dr. Gothart picked up the poker. "Use this."

Kellen leaped to Dr. Gothart, but Dr. Gothart swept the poker out of Kellen's reach.

"You sure?" Dr. Gothart's voice was low and silky. "You can't destroy Henry without destroying John, at least, not until John is human enough to survive on his own without him."

"Who cares? John's blood is gone! The little coward spilled it! And now I'm going to plunge this poker through his bitty canary heart!"

Kellen swiped for the rod again, but Dr. Gothart, again, held it at bay.

"Think carefully," Dr. Gothart advised. "To the world, John is still alive. To the world, John is grieving his wife and..."

"Fuck her," John said.

Dr. Parks started and began to speak but John added, "And fuck that bastard child."

"'Bastard' child?" Dr. Parks said in alarm. "Do you mean...?"

"Moi!" Henry beamed and slid further in his chair, reveling in the shock on Dr. Parks' face, as white as a vampire after a twenty-four-hour fast.

"...and also to the world, YOU, Mr. Kellen Wechsler, is still his manager, who receives a handsome portion of the..."

"And fuck Kellen," John said.

Henry sighed in mock despair. "John, I'm hurt. No 'fuck you' to me?"

Dr. Gothart charged at John and jabbed the poker over his heart. Henry leaned forward, clasping his hands again, still enjoying the fun.

"You killed an innocent woman and somebody's child." Dr. Gothart's speech was taut, and his face was full of menace. "Tempt me again."

"Better for an adulterous woman to die in her bed than in the county jail," John countered. "Do you think I'd let such a crime against my name pass? Besides, you let her die."

Dr. Gothart pressed harder. "You poisoned her, and I can prove it."

"No, you can't..."

"No? Then why do you keep sweet clover powder in your chambers?"

John glared at Kellen, and Kellen chuckled as he groped inside his shirt pocket for another cigar.

"Bryony bled to death," Dr. Gothart said with a push of the poker for emphasis. "You filled her with your blood after I forbade it. Whether she bled out due to vampire venom or sweet clover powder is a matter of semantics. Cross me, John, and I'll end your miserable legacy once and for all."

Dr. Gothart eased off and sauntered to the fire, where he replaced the poker and settled into his place.

"So I'm tied to Henry because of...her?"

"You and Henry are tied in death due to the manner of your deaths."

"Explain."

"I can't. That's just how the laws of unnature work. Until you and Henry are free to roam the earth as live men, both of you must always return to the basement by dawn, first you and then Henry."

"What if I don't? What if I find an empty coffin and stretch out there for the day?"

Dr. Gothart shrugged and resumed smoking. Kellen, chin in hand, pouting, and grousing under his breath, forgot about the cigar, smoking itself in a saucer on the little table next to him. Dr. Parks had closed his eyes and was massaging one temple.

"One last thing," John said. "Where is Anna?"

Dr. Gothart lifted an eyebrow. Henry flinched as if someone had doused him with water.

"I left Anna with Neta Ashmore at the parsonage," Henry said cautiously. "Just as you told me."

"She's not there." John insisted. "Find her."

"She's been adopted," Dr. Gothart quickly replied.

"By whom?"

"I can't imagine why this is important," Dr. Parks said impatiently as he rose. "But I can inquire."

"Isabella, listen to this."

George sat at the little table for the first time in weeks, perusing The Times and sipping a fragrant eighteenth-century Madeira, another leftover from the cellar of the late Daniel Sage, Marie's Grandpapa.

Villagers Successfully Test Own Theory of Illness
By Leo Hasset, Publisher, The Munsonville Times

For the time being, the mysterious illness has come to a halt.

The credit belongs, not to Dr. Edwin Gothart and Dr. Martin Parks, but to Munsonville Times Editor-In Chief Luther Hasset.

Frustrated by the doctors' inability to quell the mysterious sickness, Luther proposed a theory that a beast of some kind was ravaging the blood of the victims.

Last week Luther wrote a column suggesting villagers sleep in shifts. If a beast were the cause, the person on duty could prevent the next attach.

Both Gothart and Parks disputed the beast theory, citing no evidence of forced entrance or disarray.

But whether illness or beast, Munsonville has lost no souls this week.

George smiled at Isabella, but the smile was weak and lacking his characteristic enthusiasm. With a heart and fingers of lead, Marie diagrammed compound-complex sentences. Her papa was still a man afflicted, even if his physical affliction was waning. But children were seen and not heard.

Isabella glanced up from her needlework and returned the smile with a warm and genial one of her own.

George took another sip. "Dick would be proud."

A festive mood hung in the air, but Marie's heart still felt heavy. They'd celebrated Thanksgiving yesterday, just the three of them due to the quarantine, and they celebrated with creamed white soup, roast turkey and gravy, stuffing with giblets, mashed potatoes, roasted vegetables and stewed squash, cornbread and freshly baked French rolls, and apple pie and pumpkin pie. A hint of sage, mace, and warm buttery yeast lingered in the room long after they'd savored the meal. But the rich, comforting aromas were not enough to blunt the sour odor of a room in desperate want of a good airing.

The rich food caused only a slight indigestion in George, which Isabella chased away with a glass of the Madeira. George slept undisturbed that night, and he now partook of fried codfish and potato balls, griddle cakes, cottage cheese – the biggest surprise to Maire, for George was particular about his cheese – and baked apples, along with the rest of the Madeira, which he now relished, slowly, as not to overload his delicate stomach.

"Isabella, here's another. Listen!"

John Simons: Dead or Alive?
By Luther Hasset, Editor-in-Chief, The Munsonville Times

It's been several weeks since the death of Mrs. Bryony Simons and her unnamed son during Mrs. Simons' difficult confinement.

Dr. Edwin Gothart had previously reported that world-renowned pianist and composer John Simons had fled from Munsonville that very night in a distraught state.

But just as a malady of unknown cause is spreading through Munsonville, John Simons has mysteriously disappeared.

None of his friends in Chicago or New York have seen him, other reports have said, and people who know him locally have expressed concern.

His housekeeper, Bryga Czarnecki, disappeared the same night, leaving some to speculate the two may have disappeared together, on purpose, although this is doubtful due to Mr. Simons' exceptional devotion to Mrs. Simons.

Perhaps Mr. Simons and Mrs. Czarnecki were the first victims to this as yet unnamed malady and perished out of sight.

"Ah, this is fine reporting, indeed!" George closed the paper, grinning and turning to Isabella, who looked quizzically back at him. "My love, you do realize The Times is the first publication to even raise these speculations."

The jubilance on her papa's face cut Marie to her soul. Speculation was not reporting; her papa had said so many times and severely criticized anyone who resorted to it. What was happening to him?

Nevertheless, she smiled, a false smile that hid her bleeding wound.

"Can you believe Luther out-scooped Henry Matthews! The wire is certain to pick this up! Isabella, grab another bottle. Yes, and for Little Marie, too! Such a moment cannot pass without celebration!"

So she "celebrated." That night, while her papa and mama slumbered sweetly, Marie lay still on her cot, paralyzed with fear. She sensed a malevolent presence in Room 27. She knew it by name.

Death.

"Isabella, listen to this," George said excitedly as she arranged breakfast on the little table.

The Beast Strikes Again, Doctors Strike Back
By Leo Hasset, Publisher, The Munsonville Times

The reprieve was short-lived.
Sleeping in shifts soon wore out even the hardiest of men, as the tragedies of the last few months has chiseled away their stamina.
That night, one of them succumbed to slumber and then caught death in the act. Here's what happened.
Mr. Paul Drake said he had dreamed of indigestion, with his stomach gurgling so loudly in the dream he jolted awake as a shadow slipped through the wall.

76

*His little four-year-old daughter Amanda Drake lay still
in the bed. The gurgling came from a wound in her throat, but
she was alive. He awakened his wife Mrs. Phyllis Drake and
then ran up the hill for Dr. Gothart.*

*Dr. Gothart came immediately and transfused blood from
the frenzied father into the little girl.*

*At the time of this writing she is alive and enjoying a
nourishing soup.*

George set the paper aside and picked up his fork and
knife. "Amazing. The quarantine will soon end, and it will be
Dick's sons who helped accomplish it. I couldn't be prouder than
if Little Marie had solved the puzzle herself."

"George," Isabella admonished as she poured his tea.
"One doesn't fight the devil with the devil's tools."

Marie mulled over this statement for some time. Was her
mama correct?

Because stories over three days reported three more
cases caught at the point of death and those all died shortly after
the blood transfusion, The Times reported.

"But flesh with the life thereof, which is the blood thereof,
shall ye not eat," Isabella calmly said as she uncovered her
breakfast tray. "No good will come out of these...transfusions."

"Perhaps," George said as he buttered his toast. "But it's
technically not eating. And see how the blood of the son of my
'closer than a brother' friend restored me to life? These poor souls
were already close to heaven's gates. They may have succumbed
even without the transfusions. Let's not judge until we have all
the facts."

However the facts favored the transfusions. Several
weeks passed and several more people were transfused. Yet not
one person died or even approached death, The Times reported.
The quarantine was lifted in time for Aunt Lula and the cousins
to gather with the Clares at Munsonville Inn's dining room for
Christmas dinner, the first time the little family had left Room
27 since the night George first became ill. Paper chains looped
around the room and around the crooked pine in the corner, from
which walnuts and pinecones hung from the branches. They ate
fish and potato balls, roast turkey and dressing, peas and onions,
rice croquettes, fresh rolls, and minced meat pie. The wine freely

flowed (except in the case of Leo's wife Alannah, who did not drink wine) as did highly animated conversation about the Clares remaining permanently in Munsonville. This way, George could join the small staff at The Munsonville Times and share his editorial talents and years of expertise.

Death.

The presence had pursued Marie into the dining room. She glanced around the table. All smiled and chattered with great animation, all except Marie and Luther; he mostly kept his gaze to his plate. Unlike Marie, who remained silent throughout the tortuous meal, Luther occasionally added a pleasantry, even though he never smiled and every line in his face remained taut.

"Occasional" was key – until the conversation turned to speculation of the source of the strange illness that vigilance and blood transfusions had vanquished. Then he looked as sullen as Marie felt, a sullenness she could not shake.

Leo said both Dr. Gothart and Dr. Parks blamed a parasite, one that caused rapid internal bleeding.

"By retaliating with blood transfusions and driving it away with watchfulness, science successfully eradicated the parasite." Leo glanced at Alannah's empty cup. "More tea, dear?"

"Please, Leo."

George stroked his waxed mustache with thoughtful strokes. "How would such a parasite find its way to Munsonville?"

"The parasite most likely lives in the woods, Uncle George," Leo said as he poured more of the clear amber fluid into Alannah's cup. These woods extend for many, many miles on three sides, almost to Thornton on the West and beyond Evansville on the east. No one, not even our founder Owen Munson, has ever explored the length and depth and breadth of them."

Lula nodded. "A parasite or wild beast was our theory when Mr. Blair Ashmore died a few years ago. Do you remember, George?"

"I do." George wiped his lips and reached for the decanter. "Very intriguing, a story still worth exploring."

"I look forward to exploring it with you, Uncle George."

Lula and Isabella exchanged glances, their eyes brightly shining.

"We've found the perfect place," Leo said, noting their happiness as he set down the pepper mill. "It's two doors down from us on Pike Street."

"Ah, Little Marie will have a family at last. Now, you say no one is still not allowed inside Simons Mansion?"

"Correct," Leo swallowed a forkful of mashed potatoes before he spoke again. "Apparently Henry Matthews is quite ill, but the symptoms are different. Dr. Gothart and Dr. Parks are not certain if the 'parasite' caused the illness, or if his ailment is new. Until they grasp it, Mr. Matthews doesn't leave, and the servants don't return."

"They won't be returning anyway," Lula interjected. "The outsiders left town before the quarantine took effect. The villagers have found other positions."

"It won't matter," Leo said with a quick shrug as he speared a piece of turkey," if John Simons isn't planning to come back."

George leaned forward, eyes flashing. "Don't you find it peculiar that Henry Matthews is the catalyst to the entire Simons story?"

Leo paused, his fork in mid-air. "Catalyst? Uncle George, what are you saying?"

George sat back and folded his arms. "Let's review the order of events. Seven years ago, Reverend Marseilles hired Henry Matthews to paint his daughter's portrait. That's how the family became acquainted with him, true or false?"

"True," Leo said. "At the time, Mr. Matthews was a reporter for the Evansville Courier. He also wrote rather scandalous fiction in serial format, which the wire, and we, picked up."

"Those stories were quite popular among our readers, too," Lula interjected. "So, of course, Dick continued running them."

George grimaced, and Isabella quickly refilled his glass, her jewels sparkling under the chandelier's lights.

"So from there, he randomly attends some sort of literary society at the parsonage a couple of times before moving to New York to work for the family-owned New York Gazette."

"Also correct," Leo said. "Remember his uncle, Mr. Albert Brumfeldt, owns the Gazette, among other newspapers across the country. One clarification: Henry Matthews didn't just 'appear' at the literary society. An acquaintance was a longtime member of that society, which even my father occasionally attended. It was that mutual acquaintance who arranged a meeting between Reverend and Henry Matthews regarding the painting of a portrait. So his attendance wasn't necessarily random. Reverend himself might have invited him, as an expression of gratitude. And, Uncle George, as much as it irks you to hear it, Henry Matthews is artistically gifted. The portrait was lovely."

"And then," George continued, as if Leo hadn't spoken at all. "And then just as randomly he shows back up in Munsonville, after a crime lord's daughter jilts him, and brings John Simons with him. Now here's my theory: I believe Henry Matthews intended to marry Agnes King for her money. I also believe Agnes King learned the true nature of his ardor and escaped his hellish clutches by seeking asylum in a House of God. But where shall the asp find its next prey? Ah, in his 'friend,' the very rich and renowned John Simons. But how to get his money? Could it be he schemed with Miss Marseilles to seduce Mr. Simons and then slither his way into their home?"

Leo dropped his fork.

"Uncle George, I don't trust Henry Matthews any more than you do." Leo groped for the fork with a trembling hand. "The sight of him turns my stomach. But I've known the late Mrs. Simons since childhood. She was simple, quiet, and God-fearing. Such a rouse would not be in her."

"And yet," Lula added bitterly. "Look how quickly she spurned Luther once she snagged a better prospect."

"Mom! Luther never formally courted her."

Baby Eugenia woke up and began crying. Like her mother, Eugenia had a rose tint to her flaxen hair, rounded limbs, and a cherubic face. Alannah fumbled with her bodice and arranged a soft blanket over the baby to retain her modesty and not offend the men. Still, Marie caught a glimpse of Alannah's conical breast and her brown areolae before the baby clamped its lips onto it.

80

"He might have," Lula insisted. "If Henry Matthews had not brought John Simons to town."

Luther pushed his plate away and reached for the decanter. Marie noted disgust, not unease. Was the malignant sensation merely fancy, a ruse of her overwrought imagination?

Marie's cocktail of strong emotions, consternation mixed with despondency and surliness, persisted through breakfast the next morning and when she later attacked her studies. She answered in blunt monosyllables to any question her parents posed her, the only time she spoke.

Finally her papa addressed her bad temper. He actually picked up one of the padded chairs and carried it across the room without huffing, a good sign of a renewed constitution. He placed the chair next to Marie without making a sound, and then he sat and leaned close. She felt him scrutinizing her, but she kept her gaze on her notebook and scribbled away.

"Little Marie, why must you pout? You should rejoice; The Dream is to be realized at last."

"Yes, Papa, I'm very happy for you."

"Happy girls don't invert the corners of their mouths. Do not lie to your papa."

"Then don't insult The Dream by belittling it."

"What a queer little speech. Well, you are growing up."

"Yes, Papa."

George sighed loudly, and she set aside the pencil and looked accusingly at him. He took one of her hands, clasped it between his cool slender ones, and kissed it, lingering over the kiss and stroking her hand against his bristly cheek before he spoke again, this time in a low voice.

"You dream by night; you know the nature of dreams. When dawn arrives, you eagerly allow dreams to fragment and disperse in favor of daylight and sunshine. Well, Little Marie, I am like a man wakened from a long sleep. It is time that I, too, walk in the light. Have you no comment?"

"Yes. Remember Satan himself is transformed into an Angel of Light. Be my Papa who holds fast to The Dream. Do not become a Father of Lies and transform this room of healing into a place of perdition."

With that, Marie picked up her pencil and began to jot x 4 − 2x 3 + 2x 2 + x + 4, if only to grasp an absolute truth.

 afely concealed in the farthest dark corner of Cosmos Café, Kellen took a tiny sip of his cheap coffee and watched the hulking man clump through the door, cradling a stack of binders.

The other customers paused in their activities to observe his entrance, too; well, who would not? Just his manner of dress invited gawking as the man hailed the wait- ress (Becky Cosmos, the owner's daughter) and scanned the room. He wore bleached and faded jeans nearly bursting at the seams, a T- shirt stretched over his barreled chest, and a blazer patched in colorful squares of polyester. He had mop of thick, curly black hair and a small-squared off mustache. Thomas Carnacki, he was not. But he'd do.

Kellen gestured for the man to join him. The man saw; his face brightened. He swung his hips to and fro as he squeezed between the tightly packed tables, very much like an upright hippo mimicking a go-go dance, until he finally arrived at the booth.

"Mr. Kellen Weschler," the man panted.

"Cornell Dyer."

"*Professor* Cornell Dyer."

"Of course. Please have a seat, Professor."

Cornell eased onto the seat cushion, which set off a series of protesting squeaks at his bulk. As he set the stack near the wall, Kellen slid the menu across the table "Order what you like, Professor."

Kellen snapped his fingers, and Becky appeared. She was young, maybe twenty-one, plump and juicy and with an auburn ponytail, just the way Kellen liked his women, when he had a taste for women. He cared less about the other diners, especially now. They'd all taste like charbroil and onions for the next few hours anyway.

Cornell rattled off a long list of sandwiches and a couple large fizzy orange drinks while Kellen nursed his coffee, and

Becky scrawled his requests. After she moved away, Cornell dropped his voice, and said, "So I'm here to kill a vampire?"

"No. "Kellen leaned close and murmured, "Tell me how to kill a vampire."

"I can kill it. That's what I do."

"No."

"Why not?"

"This particular vampire is not easily...accessible. As I told you, I will pay handsomely for your knowledge. Ah, here is your food."

Becky delivered a full tray: a large platter of assorted sandwiches cut into triangles and two tall glasses of bubbly orange drink, which she placed in front of Cornell.

"More coffee, Mr. Wechsler?" she asked.

Kellen covered the cup and shook his head. "No, danke."

She turned to Cornell. "Anything else for you, sir?"

"Ketchup. A big bottle."

Becky scurried away to retrieve it. Cornell quickly stuffed half a tuna sandwich in his mouth and reached for the first binder. Kellen removed a ballpoint pen and a little memorandum book from his pocket, riffled to a clean page and clicked the pen, his fingers trembling with excitement. "Please begin, Professor."

"Well, as you probably know, the most traditional and long-lasting method of killing a vampire is a stake to the heart."

"Of course, yes." Kellen nodded and wrote. "Does the type of wood matter?"

"Ash, hawthorn, maple, and oak are preferred, but even iron can work."

"Good, good," Kellen said, scratching away. "This is foolproof, you say?"

"Nope. Removing the stake revives the vampire, unless..."

"Unless, what?"

Becky set the ketchup bottle at the edge of the table. Cornell choked down rest of the sandwich, while Kellen tapped the pen.

"Well," Cornell turned a page. "For added protection, you can burn the body with a match or by dragging it into the sunlight."

"Any particular time of day?"

"Noon is ideal. Early morning works, too, but it takes longer to reduce the vampire to cinders."

Kellen nodded again and noted it. Cornell picked up a grilled cheese sandwich, peeled back the top slice, and squirted ketchup swirls over the melted cheese.

"Now for good measure," Cornell said as he replaced the bread. "You can scatter the ashes to the four corners of the earth or bury them in four different locations." He bit through half the triangle, talking as he chewed. "Or you can place the ashes under running water, say a park fountain. As long as the water runs on the ashes, the vampire can't reanimate."

Kellen recorded that and looked up in time to see Cornell work through another half sandwich, egg salad this time. "Anything else?"

Cornell flipped to another page. "Well, you can cut out the heart and intestines and then chop the rest of the body into four parts, one limb per quarter. But you have to use a knife with a silver blade, or the vampire will simply regenerate." He grabbed another sandwich.

"So chopping is not as effective as staking?"

Munching, Cornell shook his head.

"Why not?"

"You still gotta stake him first." Cornell said. "You start chopping limbs off an unstaked vampire, and he's gonna get pissed."

"I see." Kellen found a clean page, added that detail, and then waited while Cornell drizzled ketchup between all the layers of a bacon, lettuce, and tomato triple decker.

"Now," Cornell took a large bite. "You can also decapitate the vampire, again with a silver blade. Then you stuff his head and neck with plants that are toxic to vampires."

"But what about...?"

"The staking? Yes. Always stake first."

Kellen, out of pages, scratched **always stake** first in the margins and then underlined each word. "What are the toxic plants?"

Cornell pulled out folder at the back of the binder, removed a sheet of paper, and pushed it to Kellen. Kellen scanned Cornell's messy penmanship (*holly, juniper, lemon, linden, mayflower, millet, rowan, wild roses, and wolfsbane*) while Cornell polished off the club and started gulping the first orange drink. Kellen carefully folded the paper, tucked it into his shirt pocket, and glanced up. "Next?"

"Drowning," Cornell said.

"You can't drown a...!" Kellen started to exclaim and then caught himself. "a...a dead man."

"But you can waterlog him so he can't move. He'll sink to the bottom and stay there."

"What if someone rescues him?"

"If someone pulls him from the water and dries him out, he'll be as good as new, definitely. But if you dump him in, say, the Atlantic, there's a good chance no one will pluck him off the ocean floor."

Cornell slurped around the ice and then removed the straw and slid the empty glass next to his empty plate. Kellen gently pounded his forehead as he reviewed the details. If he could still get headaches, he'd have one now.

"Anything else, Professor?"

"Garlic," Cornell said as he plopped the straw into the full glass.

A convulsion ran through Kellen, and he hissed, "Garlic doesn't kill vampires."

"Sure it does."

"It merely repels them."

"Really? Why do you think vampires back off?"

"Because it stinks."

"Because it kills. Stuff a vampire full of garlic, and the toxins will fry him from the inside out."

"You're sure?"

Cornell leaned towards Kellen, elbows on the table. "Mr. Wechsler, I am Professor Cornell Dyer, the world's greatest supernatural super sleuth. I specialize in amulets, fortune-telling (with and without cards), ghost-hunting, horoscopes, numerology, palm-reading, potions, séances, spells, vampire-slaying, zambies, and disabling pink Moravian goblins. I am insulted that you would doubt, or even question, my supreme capabilities when I am internationally renowned and sought out for my knowledge and skills. So maybe we should just terminate our..."

"No, no, no!" Kellen flapped his hands at Cornell. "I'm not questioning your authority or methods. I'm simply surprised, and I bow..." Kellen dipped his head. "I bow to your superior intellect and judgment. Please go on, Professor."

Cornell narrowed his eyes, moved closer, and studied him. Did he know, Kellen worried. But...but...but Kellen had taken many precautions. He had liberally sprinkled himself with scented powder before the meeting and freshened up by guzzling gallons of John's blood, which "Dr. Gothart" had stored in a freezer circa 1980.

But Cornell leaned against the seat, took a couple of noisy sips from his second drink, wiped his mouth on the paper napkin, and scanned the next page.

"Garlic works in other ways, too," Cornell continued, as if no breech had occurred. "For instance, garlic thins out any blood vampires consumes, so their veins can't bulk up. The vampire will literally starve to death."

The gnawing in his belly, the dizzies in his head: these remained, as constant as his mother's whoopings, his duties toward his blind grandmother, and shaping manure bricks.

"So no matter how much he eats, he won't get full."
Kellen slowly nodded. "Makes sense."
"Finally, he withers to nothing."
In tiny, wiry script, Kellen crammed this new information between the lines of the old information. "How do you stuff a vampire with garlic?"
"Wait until its dormant. Then pack every orifice with the stuff, like it's a Thanksgiving turkey."

Donna, a clean apron neatly tied over her red-checked house dress, was cutting up leftover roast. Hash again, but it was good hash, the kind that made coming home so worth it.

"So, Professor," Kellen said, pen poised. "The garlic must be packed into the vampire? What if the vampire simply touches it?"
"Like I said, garlic is to a vampire like acid is to a human. So touching garlic is bad, for vampires. If you get enough garlic

and swathe him in it, I guarantee the plant will burn him to a crisp. Crosses, holy water, and consecrated wine have the same effect."

"So even if I can't get garlic, I can substitute any of these items?"

"Yep. But to prevent reawakening, you gotta do one more thing with the ashes."

"What's that?"

"Feed 'em to a wolf."

Nothing left except the back cover. So Kellen jotted it there.

"So, yeah, it's not my most popular option, unless you know some hungry wolves. But that's problematic in itself."

"How?"

"Some vampires befriend wolves. Some vampires ARE wolves in disguise. And nothing sabotages a vampire execution quicker than a vampire summoning his friends to rally against you."

"Anything else, Professor?"

Cornell slapped the binder shut and reached for another.

"Well, I do have one more," Cornell skimmed pages while sucking out the last drops of the last drink through the straw. "But I've never tested it, so I can't guarantee it works."

"Which is?"

"Arithmomania?"

"What?"

"Arithmoman..." Cornell started to repeat but Kellen snapped his fingers.

"I know what 'arithmomania' is, Professor. How does it kill a vampire?"

Cornell raised the glass to see if any more orange drink remained. Crestfallen, he set the glass back down.

"Well, legend says vampires are compelled to count tiny objects. They literally can't stop until they've counted them all. So if you put seeds or grains of rice or millet in its path for, say, hundreds of miles, the vampire will keep counting until he either starves to death or the sun comes up and disintegrates him."

"Hey, who's owns the motor home?" an angry voice rang out. "It's blocking the road!"

Kellen hastily added arithmomania to his napkin and said without looking up, "Professor, you'd better go."

But instead of moving, Cornell extended his hand. Kellen peered at the other patrons as he clicked off his pen. Satisfied no one was spying on him, Kellen opened his coat, withdrew a small cloth sack, and gave it a little shake; the contents lightly clinked. Cornell snatched the bag, fumbled for a gold coin, and then bit it.

"If someone doesn't move this damn motor home, I swear, I'll call..."

Cornell, clutching binders and sack, struggled his way out of the tight space and dashed out of the café.

When Becky returned with the bill, she found the booth empty, except for a plate full of scraps, two tall glasses streaked with orange, a crumpled paper napkin, and a nearly full cup of black coffee.

Becky sighed, ripped off the sheet, and headed to the kitchen where her father was grilling hot dogs. They seemed to attract more and more deadbeats by the minute. He kept talking about selling the café. She wished he'd do it soon.

For the rest of the day, Kellen lay in a stupor six feet beneath the ground deep inside Simons Woods while visions of staking danced in his head. Once the sun set, Kellen crawled to the surface and reappeared at an auction in the 1970s, where he easily outbid all attendees on an "authenticated" vampire killing kit.

"Authentic my ass," Kellen chortled as he sorted through his prize: several bottles of fairly new holy water, along with a cheap plastic crucifix from the 1950s, oaken stakes, a mallet, a dusty rosary of wooden beads from 1890, a prayer book from the 1930s, an 1859 pistol, and three silver bullets.

Then he stopped at a greenhouse for gardening gloves and a sack of garlic, freshly harvested from the dark, rich, fragrant, luscious soil.

"Can you double bag that?" Kellen asked the clerk, holding his nose at that stench of that repugnant plant.

The clerk made a face at the odd request. But he obliged the customer.

The problem with vampire-on-vampire murders, Kellen mused as he left with his purchase, is that both creatures are active at night and dormant by day. In order for Kellen to successfully stake John, his timing must be perfect. Kellen needed to be alert enough, and John needed to be narcosis enough, for Kellen to successfully drive a stake into the dead heart without risking his own leathery hide.

So Kellen stopped at a drugstore and bought a windup travel alarm clock in a plastic case. Before digging his hole for the night, Kellen devoured a substantial daytime snack and then used the mallet to quickly kill, and bury with him, an early evening breakfast.

Kellen set the alarm for late afternoon and then tossed and turned in the dirt, struggling to lose consciousness with the incessant ticking, which reminded him of toddler heartbeats and made him hungry. Frustrated and exhausted beyond all patience, Kellen finally rolled over in his grave and faced a set of staring eyes from a blotchy face with its blackened tongue hanging out.

"You've got it easy," Kellen told his future breakfast. "An eternity of rest, and you don't even have the decency to thank me."

Kellen flung himself onto his back, pillowed his head with the metal box holding his vampire slaying implements, closed his eyes, and mentally counted jumping spiders.

BRRRRINGGG!
BRRRRINGGG!
BRRRRINGGG!
BRRRRINGGG!
BRRRRINGGG!
BRRRRINGGG!

Kellen fumbled in the dark for the alarm, gorged his silent partner until only a set of false teeth remained, and then lay there in the silence, a jumble of non-nerves, trying to stir up the motivation to emerge and stake John. He was so tired, he almost gave up the notion, but losing John as a host AND a future slave really nettled his lost soul.

So Kellen clawed his way out of his crypt with his phony vampire kit in his hand and reemerged behind Simons Mansion, ready to do his evil deed, which Kellen assured himself was really a good deed, like culling deer.

He misted through a crack in the foundation and solidified in the basement's hidden room. Henry still hung from the noose, eyes bulging and tongue lolling, while John was a scrunched wad on the floor. Henry's knife, John's first murder weapon, lay inches from his head.

Dusk was approaching. Kellen had to hurry. He scratched his head, trying to recall Cornell's instructions. Was he supposed to stake first and then stuff John with garlic or vice versa?

He couldn't remember, so Kellen dove into his pocket and brought up only lint. No notebook. No napkin.

WHAT???

How in the hell did he lose them?
Kellen mentally retraced his centuries....

Ponder. Ponder. Ponder. Ponder. Ponder...

Kellen looked down at John's still form that wouldn't stay still for long if Kellen didn't hurry.

Garlic.

He'd stuff John with the garlic first. That ought to immobilize him and make the staking easier. But what hole should he stuff first?

Something easy and exposed, Kellen mused. Like...the ears.

Kellen slid on the gloves to keep his own hands from burning, tied a scarf around his face to blunt the gagging smell and keep his nostrils from blistering, and then he gingerly picked up the loathsome perennial by its hairs.

90

But no matter how hard Kellen pushed, the limp stalk wouldn't penetrate John's ear drum, and the bulb didn't fit at all.

Hurry, damn it!

Kellen pulled John's collar away from his neck and stuffed the plants beneath John's shirt. Then he unsnapped the box, unscrewed the bottles of holy water, and poured them onto John's head, causing a rapid rising of thick smoke. He took up the mallet and stake and placed the point on John's back, which Kellen hoped was directly over John's heart. He raised his hand to swing, and John twitched.

WHAP!

Kellen hit the stake hard and then he hit it again. With a groan, John groped behind him, fumbling for the stick as Kellen raised the mallet again, and pulled the stake out. He struggled to his feet, a little dazed, until he saw Kellen.

John threw the stake on the ground and stalked up the stairs.

With a scream of rage, Kellen snatched the pistol, loaded it, and scampered after him, catching up just as John slinked out the back door.

BANG!

John caught the bullet, spun around, and hurled it at Kellen's forehead, knocking him down like a tenpin.

OW!!!

Kellen scrambled to his feet and bounded across the grounds and into the woods, rubbing the dent in his forehead, sniffing this way and that, trying to catch John's scent. Over the expanse Kellen ran, nose in the air. But the smell of other people's blood assaulted him and masked the scant amount of John's own remaining natural pheromones.

Wait! Was that John? Up head, by that cove, stalking a lone fisherman?

Kellen sped up and vroomed through the woods, marveling at John's audacity at killing in present time and in present place, after Dr. Gothart clearly warned not...

He hoped the water on the back side of Lake Munson was really, really, really deep.

With a roar, Kellen leaped into the air and landed feet first on the dock, which trembled at the force.

"Saving your life," Kellen gasped to the gaping fisherman as Kellen shoved John into the lake.

NOOOOOOO!

The water was only waist high, and John was already sloshing his way out, glaring at Kellen.

Kellen jumped up and down, tearing his hair and beard.

No! No! No! No!

Kellen crouched, poised for another shove. But John gave himself a brisk shake, spraying droplets on Kellen, and then stalked into the woods. Enraged, Kellen swiftly killed and ate the fisherman, called it a day, and dug himself a new hole, shaking with fury.

He arose at nightfall, starving. So he headed for a remote mountainous village in the sixteenth century, gobbled up its inhabitants, and then headed to an early nineteenth century general store in Virginia and bought a hundred-pound bag of rice.

Thus fortified and with eyes closed (lest he be compelled to count), Kellen took his time sprinkling the rice all over the woods, with plenty of "tee-hee-hees" escaping his lips as he envisioned John struggling to collect them all the while growing weaker by the second.

Kellen arrived at Simons Mansion around midnight and followed the piano sounds straight to the music room.

"John, did you see what's outside?" Kellen asked, nudging John's arm.

The nudge caused John to plunk wrong note, and the clunk rang throughout the room. He whirled around and seized Kellen by the throat. As he did, John's eyes strayed past Kellen and to the window.

"You bungled my piece for snow?" John asked.

Snow? SNOW?

WHAT???

Kellen bolted to the window. Sure enough, a good measure of Northern Michigan November snow was falling thickly from the sky. It had already covered the ground with a heavy coat and showed no signs of slowing.

He flew to the fireplace, plunged his hand into the flames for a log, and then rushed at John, waving the burning torch and screaming, "I'll kill you!"

But a hand of steel stopped him from striking a single blow.

"Put it back," Dr. Gothart ordered. "Now."

"No!"

John sniffed he air, puzzled. "What's that smell?"

Dr. Gothart kicked Kellen in the testicles so hard he skidded across the room. None of that hurt, of course, but Kellen did jam a hand inside his trousers and fumble. One, two. Good.

By now, Dr. Gothart had ripped off John's coat and shirt and was throwing the offensive plants in the fire. Yesterday's garlic and holy water had melted into John's neck and back, leaving blackened craters and a colony of maggots happily glutting themselves on the dead flesh.

Dr. Gothart plucked Kellen's ear and hauled him up.

"Bathe those wounds in the moonlight," Dr. Gothart told John, giving Kellen's ear a viscous tug. "Hurry!"

He dragged Kellen by that ear all the way to his colonial and all the way down into the dungeon, where he hung Kellen off one of the hooks in the wall and flogged him until Kellen's skin split like an overripe plum, and Dr. Gothart's frenzy was spent.

"Get down," Dr. Gothart commanded him with one final lash before yanking Kellen to the ground.

Kellen clambered for the corner, where he huddled and repeatedly whimpered a single phrase: "You promised. You promised. You promised. You promised."

"And I kept that promise. You had him. For a while. No one said forever."

"You promised!"

Dr. Gothart threw down the crop. Then he strolled across the room and crouched before him. Kellen whined like an injured puppy and shrank back. Dr. Gothart stroked Kellen's hair in a reassuring way.

"But nothing's changed It's a temporary hiatus. The goal is a return to humanity. 'John Simons the Product' still needs managing. John makes music. He needs you to book his venues and handle the contracts. Those take time. John wants to produce, practice, perform. He's not a businessman. That's your specialty. Also, since you wanted to vampirize him to make him your slave, we'll just gloss over the first part and just make him your slave. Part of my rehumanization contract with him includes the stipulation he retains you as manager. You earn twenty-five percent of his profits forever. And he lets you drink from him again when he's one hundred percent human."

Kellen snuffled. "Promise?"

Dr. Gothart rose. "Of course, I promise. Not quit snuffling and get up." He held out his hands and pulled Kellen to his feet. "Go bathe your wounds. There's work to be done. You've lived in both worlds for several centuries. They need you to teach them how to act human."

"Fine."

He might as well, Kellen thought as he headed out to the woods. He only had one trick left, and he'd probably fail at that one, too. Sawing into neck bones is no easy task, even with a silver blade.

*nd he shewed me a pure river of water of life,
clear as crystal, proceeding out of the throne of
God and of the Lamb.*

With a weary sigh, Dr. Parks removed
the clear tube from her papa's arm and
bandaged the wound with carbolated gauze.

During the entire water infusion,
Isabella sat on the bed at George's left and
Marie did the same on his right, inducing Dr.
Parks to mutter, "the two thieves" when he set
up the procedure, a remark Isabella appeared
not to hear.

But Marie heard it. She studied each of Dr. Parks'
movements and ruminated on the man who executed them. Did
this man have discernment? And to what depth did he cultivate
it?

The outside of George remained washed in, not the Blood
of the Lamb, but his own blood and that of Leo's, which had shot
from his body with alarming force shortly after lunch on New
Year's Day, so shortly that the dishes were not yet cleared from
the table, and the bottle of 1860 Bordeaux was not completely
drunk.

It was the sight of that bottle that caused Dr. Parks to
stop short in the doorway, hat and medical bag still in his hands,
and stare at that bottle as if he'd never seen a bottle in his life
and the very sight frightened him. All the while his patient, with
Isabella cradling his head, continued to heave nothing into the
bedpan, as he had nothing left to heave.

"Don't just stand there!" Isabella had screamed. "Help
him!"

"It's too soon for Leo to donate again. I'll need to find..."

"No! No! No! You will not give him any more blood!"

That's when Dr. Parks sprang into rapid action, not even
stopping to remove his overcoat. Within minutes, he was
infusing George with saline solution.

"It's to replenish the lost fluids," Dr. Parks had said to Marie although she had not asked the question aloud.

But even after Dr. Parks completed the transfer he looked very, very, very worried.

"'For every one that thirsts, come you to the waters," Isabella murmured as she rubbed George's hand with both of hers. "I will cleanse their blood that I have not cleansed: for the Lord dwelleth in Zion."

Water was pure, Marie thought as she clung to her papa's cold blue hand. Water was lifegiving. Surely water would restore health and vigor to her papa.

For I will pour water upon him that is thirsty, and floods upon the dry ground... you shall be like a watered garden, like a spring of water, whose waters do not fail.

Dr. Parks mixed the clay with water as clear as the water that had infused life back into his patient. He offered the beaker to Isabella and raised an eyebrow. She accepted it, her answer, and nudged the rim to her husband's lips. But George refused it.

"Bring wine," George mumbled.

Dr. Parks drew a sharp breath and narrowed his gaze, not at George, but at Isabella. "No. Wine."

"Doctor," George gasped. "Please."

"Good God, man! Do you want to die?"

George turned blanched, clutched his stomach, and retched loudly onto the covers, producing only noise. Panting, he raised his eyes. "Wine for you, good doctor."

"I'll bring the wine, Papa."

Marie slid off the bed and headed for the trunk, where she brought forth a clean goblet. She then carefully filled half of it with some of the Bordeaux from lunch. Any less would make them ingrates; more might be wasted if Dr. Parks practiced temperance, a possibility as he didn't finish the last glass she'd offered him, the night he'd transfused Leo's blood into her papa.

She returned with the goblet as Dr. Parks removed the stethoscope from his ears. The empty beaker, insides coated with chalk, sat on the nightstand. Isabella lay against the headboard, cradling George against her breast.

"For you," Marie said, hand outstretched.

But Dr. Parks only looked inside the goblet, as if hypnotized by its ripples, and she wondered what he saw: the wine's deep color, almost black with a plum blush near the top, or something beyond the wine.

For if one peered closely, one might perceive nuances of its bouquet: elegant, smooth, and mature, a wine to be savored in all its complexities. A more reflective person might detect the high regard the family had for its head – and the head's physician – since only the best was served up to them. One who pondered spiritual truths might understand the medicinal depths this wine represented, both to the drinker and the one who poured.

But most people didn't look that far. She extended her arm to full length.

"Dr. Parks," she said clearly and without emotion. "For you. For healing my papa."

He jerked his head toward the nightstand. "Over there." Then he nodded curtly at Isabella. "Please move."

She settled George against the pillows with a loving little pat and eased off the bed, glaring at Dr. Parks.

Marie placed the goblet next to the beaker. An empty glass of clay, a half one of wine. One for the patient who needed healing, one for the healer. Sure God would approve works wrought in such faith.

But we have this treasure in earthen vessels, that the excellency of the power may be of God, and not of us.

Dr. Parks wrapped the cuff around George's arm. Isabella was pouring water into a basin, and George, white as bismuth, followed her movements with anxious eyes.

"My dear, take some wine for you, too. You're disquieted and tense. Little Marie, pour a glass for..."

"George, don't vex yourself. I'm fine."

"My devoted Isabella, so concerned for my care. Please - a drink."

"Soon, George. When you're refreshed."

Satisfied, George plunged into heavy slumber. Dr. Parks packed up his supplies and then picked up the wine and drained it in three gulps.

Isabella, gathering fresh towels, did not look up from her task as she said flatly, "Dr. Parks, thank you."

"You're welcome."

He set down the empty goblet and reached for his coat.

"Doctor Parks, please wait."

He froze.

Uncertain, Isabella faced him and stammered, "He...he seems so weak. Are you certain the water will help him?"

"Maybe." He turned around. "But a blood transfusion..."

"Humph! You and your blood transfusions. I'm so sick of hearing about blood transfusions. Look at him! Much worse since the 'transfusion.'"

"Because of the wine you gave him. Not the transfusion."

She clenched her fists. "Wine nourishes the stomach."

"Wine also eats it away."

"Dr. Parks, how does your 'fountain' gush forth fresh water and bitter water?" She took a step toward him. "How can you bring both blessing and cursing?"

He opened his mouth to reply, but Isabella held up her hand. "Your vile reputation is well-known, even if my husband won't admit it. Yet it's also clear the spirit of the Lord is upon you, that he has anointed you to bring healing. Why do you persist in opposing the God who's gifted you?"

"Mrs. Clare, it's you who's blocking your husband's healing. Why do you persist in giving this man alcohol when it's clearly detrimental for him?"

"Not 'alcohol,' Doctor. Wine. And not just any wine. Not even the highly touted tonic wine, but pure wine of the highest quality, wine my own father..."

"Wine is still alcohol. Your husband's stomach is wounded. Giving him wine will..."

"...bind his wounds, as the Samaritan did for the poor beaten man at the side of the road. And calm his stomach, as it did for young Timothy, disciple of Paul."

Dr. Parks' features hardened, and deep lines appeared near his mouth. He took a deep breath and then quoted, "He shall separate himself from wine and strong drink, and shall drink no vinegar of wine, or vinegar of strong drink.'"

Isabella tossed her head. "Dr. Parks, I'm not interested in hearing you twist scripture to support your intemperance theories. Drink lightly, if you must, but don't force your beliefs on us. You are here to treat my husband, not moralize."

"I'm speaking as a medical doctor, as one who's observed the detriment of alcohol abuse in his patients. I implore you…"

She cut him off with a wave of her hand, her eyes flashing.

"Any good medicine that's abused, Dr. Parks, will cause detriment. My own cousin developed a craving for laudanum after her physician prescribed it for her insomnia. However, the wine my George drinks is not 'abuse.' He drinks to calm his afflicted stomach. God's very word recommended it, and …"

Dr. Parks sighed and rolled his eyes. Isabella flushed with rage, took another step, and raised her voice.

"…and the Messiah himself has visited and instructed us. We cannot disobey!"

Dr. Parks picked up his hat and bag. "Mrs. Clare. Please. Do not give this man any more wine. I'm not even certain the infusion and bismuth will be sufficient. Not this time. He really needs more blood."

She lifted her skirts and ran across the room, grabbing his arm as he reached the door. "The only blood my George needs is the blood of his Savior! Which comes from wine! Which God Himself hath given to us!"

Dr. Parks set down his bag and hat on the table and tried again. "Mrs. Clare, alcohol increases acid secretion. It…"

"Wine protects the stomach!"

"This acid has eaten a hole in his stomach." He leaned into her, his nose hovering just above hers, his face taut. "Do you understand? The continual consumption has left this hole bleeding and raw and full of tiny spiral-shaped creatures that are having a 'continual feast' at the peril of your husband."

"You…you vivisectionist! Of course, you'd know that. You dice people into bits to satisfy your morbid curiosity! The only holes in people's stomachs are the ones you brutally chop into them!"

"I learned about the detrimental effects of alcohol by treating its aftereffects in fools like you and your husband."

Isabella pointed to the door. "Get out now!" She stamped her foot. "Now!"

Marie held her breath, her heart racing. Her mama was nearly purple with rage. Her eyes bulged. The cords on her neck looked ready to snap.

Miraculously, George did not stir. He lay still and white as smooth stone, mouth slightly parted, breaths faint.

Dr. Parks reached for her hand, but she yanked it away. He took a breath, and then he took a longer one before speaking.

"Mrs. Clare."

"Shut up!"

"Mrs. Clare," he said again, punctuating each syllable with his hands. "He's bled so much he's in danger of death, and you won't even allow me to replace the blood. The most we can do is hope, and that is hope only, no guarantees, that the fluid I've replaced, along with rest and time, will allow your husband's body to heal and recreate his own blood."

Isabella's shoulders sagged. She lowered her head, thinking – or praying. Then she looked back up at Dr. Parks, her face brightening.

"Yes," Isabella whispered. "That is the best way. For we are fearfully and wonderfully made." This time, she took Dr. Parks' hand, and he did not withdraw. "I do thank you, Doctor, for being the channel of healing for my George. Don't you see? He now only needs a little wine for stomach. Remember God always says, 'Give strong drink unto him that is ready to perish, and wine unto those that be of heavy hearts.'"

"No. More. Wine."

"But God Himself has advised us!"

"Look, all scripture is based on personal interpretation. It's not as if God himself returned to earth..."

"But he did! The Messiah himself sat next to us on a train and spoke to us, face to face, one person to another."

His jaw dropped.; incredulity spread across his face. "Mrs. Clare, do you actually expect me to believe that the Lord Himself came down from heaven to join your family on a train?"

"Well, of course not."

"Good. Because I was beginning to think..."

"We were on our way to Denver when George became afflicted. As George writhed in pan, the conductor approached us and said the Messiah was on the train and, if we so desired, he would send for him at once."

Dr. Parks dropped into a chair and rubbed his face, all words gone. Isabella, keyed up with the story, hardly noticed his retreat as she babbled away.

"George asked his name and he responded with 'I am.' Then he asked where we stored the wine. The Messiah blessed all of it, selected one bottle and called out for a loaf, which a customer fished out of a bag. Then he blessed the wine, gave thanks to the Father, and told George to drink. After a time, he blessed the bread, gave a portion of it to George to eat. This bread, blessed by God, did not cause him distress."

Dr. Parks raised his eyes to her. They looked stunned, mystified, as if they disbelieved what his ears were hearing.

"He told us George's affliction was his 'thorn in the flesh,' but he exhorted him to 'take a little wine for his stomach' that he may bear it. So how dare you, Doctor, to contradict the will of the Almighty God?"

Slowly he stood, thinking hard on the way up.

"Mrs. Clare, you've spent your lives chasing down the scoop that will make the world notice your husband's ingenuity and talents. Now why, in God's great name in heaven, did your husband not interview 'the Messiah' when he had the opportunity? And please don't tell me the Messiah refused!"

"The delicate nature of George's health often interferes with timely reporting. This has been his great frustration. Why do you think we're here, if not to report on the birth of John Simons' child? And even that opportunity was stolen from us by the repugnant Henry Matthews! As for interviewing the Messiah, do you think we are gullible? Naive?"

The look on Dr. Parks' faced showed exactly that.

"Impertinence!" Isabella dug her fingers into her hips. "How dare you disrespect me! Do you know who I am? Do you know who my father was? Do you realize how much money he donated to John Hopkins? Dr. Parks: we knew this man was the Messiah because other newspapers had already reported it. I'm assuming you read newspapers? A story from George about the Messiah would not be fresh news! A story about the Messiah would not advance The Dream!" She sighed. "Besides, it's too late. He's returned to the Father."

Dr. Parks shook his head, dazed. "Mrs. Clare, I'm so confused."

"The Messiah. He went to Mexico this year and vanished, just as he did forty days after His resurrection."

Dr. Parks rubbed his face with both hands. Then he rose and picked up his hat and bag. After glancing at his patient with a mixture of grave concern and pity, he trudged to the door and opened it.

Then he paused and turned around. His face looked kind. But the anger in his eyes, terrible.

"Mrs. Clare, his stomach needs rest," Dr. Parks said quietly, "If you pour him another drop, I'll send for the constable."

CHAPTER TWELVE: A LITTLE WINE FOR YOUR STOMACH, PART TWO

"Here, ye! Here, ye!" Kellen called from the back of the library, which he had commandeered for the occasion. "The Kellen Wechsler Finishing School for Young Vampires is called to order!"

He'd tied his sleek black hair into a short queue to underscore his authority over his larvae. In one hand, he held an old golden cowbell, which he now rattled with annoying vigor, and in the other he clutched an antique, leather-bound "Straf Mich Gott" Bible. A mouthwatering smell hung in the air, reminding Henry, who lay across the rug propped up with his thin hand, he hadn't eaten nearly enough. This smell was an interesting mixture of blood, sweat, charred oak, cadaverine, putrescine, beeswax, and tobacco. Thick candlesticks, a few candelabra, a lone oil lamp, and the swaying, snapping flames in the stone fireplace provided the room's only illumination, and even that was for the benefit of the humans only, a compromise of enabling their sight while preventing instant disintegration of the quickened corpses.

The school, Henry noted was small, just two pupils: John Simons and himself, both looking war-starved in suits too spacious for their gaunt frames, and, consequently, unfit for serious study, not that Henry was taking any of it seriously. John's hollow eyes sank into his skull, and his wrinkled skin sagged on his pallid face. His bony hands draped over the chair arms, for he sat behind his desk, a silent reminder to Kellen, whom he regarded coldly, yet calmly, of the real authority in the room. Henry was even more withered than John and cared even less. Yet unlike John, Henry was smirking, ready to heckle, and hoping Kellen's address to the class was brief. Henry was starving, and he already had his family picked out.

"Before we begin, I'd like to introduce the school's headmaster, Dr. Edwin Gothart, and his assistant, Dr. Martin Parks."

Dr. Gothart lounged near the fire, sucking on his pipe. Dr. Parks occupied the chair opposite his senior, pen and notebook in hand, ready for the lesson to commence.

"Charmed," Henry said, not bothering to hide the sarcasm in his tone.

"As lead researcher of the 'blood is life' project, Dr. Gothart will ensure your training is..."

"...thorough and correct," Dr. Gothart said with quiet emphasis on "thorough" and "correct," which put Henry on alert. Whatever the scheme, this wouldn't be fun.

John jerked his head toward Dr. Parks. "And him?"

Dr. Parks smiled. "I'm here to learn, too, and take notes. To restore a semblance of life to the dead is an idea that, well, intoxicates me."

Henry raised his hand. Kellen recognized him with a curt nod. "You, there, lounging on the rug: state your name."

"Henry Matthews, O Wise One, and when is recess?"

"Insolence! I shall make you crouch in the corner with a dunce cap and..."

"Just get on with it," Dr. Parks said with a frustrated sigh.

Kellen dropped the bell with a loud clank. "Due to the small class size, we can dispense with the usual attendance-taking and move straight into..."

John's gaze flickered to Dr. Gothart. "Is this necessary?"

Dr. Gothart removed his pipe, smiled slightly, and his eyes gleamed. Kellen noticed and cleared his throat loudly.

"I am, AHEM, here at the behest Dr. Edwin Gothart, who is overseeing your return to humanity. My purpose is two-fold: to help you understand your current state and to prepare you for the restoration yet to come. Any questions so far?"

Henry yawned loudly and rolled onto his other side. Kellen snapped his fingers and a little square, richly carved, rosewood card table appeared.

"Hey!" Henry scrambled to sit. Now he was interested. "How'd you do that?"

The table held five goblets and two cut glass decanters of blackish red liquid: one with a taut, supple clarity and the nauseating aroma of currents and smoke; the other heavy, viscous, and mouthwatering.

Bordeaux, Henry thought, sniffing hard and choking on the obnoxious scent. And, of course, blood.

"First, we'll discuss your enhanced senses," Kellen said. "Later, I'll introduce a few techniques to refine your new vampire abilities. We'll also discuss habits that give the illusion of being alive. Any questions?"

Henry raised his hand again. Kellen ignored him.

"But I have to pee!" Henry cried, squirming and clutching himself.

All eyes turned to Henry, which didn't bother Henry in the least. But he did drop his hands and say, Fine," in resignation. Kellen turned back to the group.

"By now," Kellen boomed out, "you've realized the increased acuity of four of your senses. Darkness and distance are no barriers to seeing, and the faintest of noises are as loud as shouting. Your nose teases out the most subtle of aromas for hundreds of miles, which is exquisitely attuned to blood. In fact, the taste of anything other than blood will repulse you. Any questions?"

Henry raised his hand, which Kellen still pretended not to see, and then Henry glanced at John. No expression. He glanced at Dr. Gothart. Puffing contentedly. He glanced at Dr. Parks. Pen poised, waiting for more. He lay back down and tried to ignore the smell of live human blood and his internal clamoring for it. He knew he should eaten that grandfather, too.

"The only sense that suffers is touch," Kellen continued. "But your skin will resensitize as you enliven. The same is true with any pleasure except your nightly feasting. You can enjoy worldly revels, yes. Nevertheless, full satisfaction will elude your grasp, however desperately you swipe at it. You've been warned."

Skeptical, Henry's fingers reached for the chair leg closest to him and closed over it. He sensed its smooth rigidity, but the full perception of the wood was lacking, as if his hands, numb with their death chill despite his recent meal, were bundled into thick gardening gloves. He'd never paid attention to this blunting of touch until Kellen pointed it out. But did it matter, especially now that his grip had superhuman strength? He used hands to snap the necks of his victims. He wasn't taking up cabinetry.

"...now, you already know the basics: hunting down the victims and optimal methods for bloodletting, but we should talk about a few other skills you may not have considered. Behold!"

Kellen snapped his fingers and a large blackboard on an easel appeared. He selected a nub of white chalk in his left hand and scrawled:

Teleportation
Sunlight
Hypnosis
Mind reading
Shapeshifting
Real food

Henry groaned. And he used to think his tutors at Arcadia were tedious. Dr. Parks just scribbled away, as if he sat in a lecture hall instead of among hungry vampires. Five minutes, no three, was all Henry needed to rip into Dr. Parks' neck and suck him dry. But he daren't, not with Dr. Gothart on his left and John, who apparently had shrugged off starvation, erect at his right.

"First, teleportation. You dwell outside the corporeal world. Thus, it cannot constrain you. Later, tonight, when you perform your pre-dawn hunt, note how fast you sprint through the void and push yourself to greater speeds. Time is for the living. Place is for the living. Not for vampires. We are..."

"...creatures who don't venture out by day," Henry said, indicating item number two on Kellen's syllabus. "Which makes us obvious to a suspecting general public."

"Not necessarily. As you become older and more experienced, you'll be able to withstand some sunlight. But until he evolves, John will perform at night and 'sleep' by day. You as a reporter will be trickier to manage, but these two brilliant doctors are working on a plan."

He pointed Dr. Parks, as serene as if he were enjoying a night at the opera, and then to Dr. Gothart, leering at Henry and puffing steadily. Terrific, Henry thought. Gothart and Parks.

The replacements for Girard and Brumfeldt. The new architects of his future. Even in death, Henry wasn't free.

"Note that it's perfectly fine to simply attack and take. A vampire's superior strength and speed is suited to it, and it's ideal for a quick meal."

Well, that's what Henry wanted. A quick meal. He wished Kellen talked as fast as he feasted. At this rate, dawn would snuff out any opportunity for further dining, and they'd starve to dust. Thankfully, Henry saw only darkness through the windows. He couldn't wait to eat and go dark.

"But when you begin regenerating, it's best if the hosting victim is willing and cooperative, and even better if you let the victim believe the hosting is his or her idea."

"That's impossible," John said, his face twisting in disgust.

Kellen snapped his fingers, and a pointer appeared in his hand. He tapped the tip to "hypnosis" and then to "mind reading" and then said, "Yes, I do."

"Huh?" Henry asked, momentarily distracted from his woes by the ridiculous statement.

Kellen smiled, a bit too smugly for Henry's liking, and said, "John was wondering to himself if I read minds. So I replied."

You forgot hypnosis, Henry thought as he monitored Kellen for changes in demeanor.

"No I didn't," Kellen stuck out his blackened tongue. "Can you prove the chalkboard is really there?"

Dr. Gothart snickered. So did Dr. Parks, but he smothered it behind a hand. Wise asses.

"Also, if you've tagged a good fit for you, host-wise, but the victim resists, just wheedle through the doorway of dreams. You're dead. They're vulnerable. It's an easy 'yes.'"

"What's the point?" Henry asked.

"Because once the victim welcomes your attack, he or she stays under your power and you can come and go as you please."

"It's just dinner." Henry snorted to underscore his point. "And speaking of dinner, are we almost...?"

"Or it's a reentry to life," Dr. Parks said evenly. "For vampires with more ambition, for vampires who advance the cause of science."

Dr. Gothart removed his pipe. "Not for contented slugs."

Henry started, and his eyes widened. Slug? Did Merlin just call him a...?

"Also, remember that, because you are dead and have ceased existing, you may shift into any shape you desire," Kellen said. "Popular choices for vampires include wolves, bats, rats, other humans, and mist."

Henry raised his hand.

"Yes?"

"So let's say I want to shapeshift into a fish. Do I change into a live fish or a dead fish?"

"You will shift into the appearance of a live fish," Dr. Gothart said. "But you technically aren't a fish at all. You are nothing. That's why you can present as anything."

"So I never actually become a fish?"

"No."

"Will I look like a fish?"

"Yes."

"Will I perform fish functions: exchanging gases through gills, swim by moving my fin joints, digest food with..."

"Yes."

"Will live fish recognize me as a fish?"

"Pay attention," Dr. Gothart said with quiet menace. "Your outward appearance resembles a man, or a fish, or whatever you choose, but all similarities end there. Your life force, some people call it a soul, is gone, and, with it, your humanity – or fishity. Blood does indeed sustain you, but it won't return life..."

"...without consistent feeding from one single host source," John said, his voice cold and flat, his face expressionless. "So until Dr. Gothart perfects..."

Kellen cut him off with a swoop of his hand. "But we'll teach you how to mimic a life force."

"Goody," Henry said.

"To that end, Dr. Parks suggested we use the Bible's 'fruit of the spirit' as a guideline for practicing human behavior." Kellen raised the "Straf Mich Gott" high. "Otherwise, the deadly traits that allow you to survive might tip off the living that you do not belong to their club. Obviously, you need to keep your vampire skills sharp to remain undead but not so obviously sharp as to appear inhuman. I shall demonstrate."

He walked to the table. "Note these two decanters. One is filled with Bordeaux, and the other is brimming with a luscious sanguine fluid, our beverage of choice. Now, many of us here tonight, when we lived, also enjoyed a nice glass of Bordeaux. As some of your pneuma returns, you will tolerate small amounts of both food and drink, which keeps the illusion in place. The trick..."

Kellen poured a goblet half full of blood and raised it to his lips.

"...the trick is to prepare your shrunken stomach to accept what it no longer needs. So first, the blood."

Kellen drained the glass and finished with a loud smack. Then he refilled the goblet with wine.

"Now that my stomach has a nice coating of hemoglobin, I can drink this..." Kellen tipped his head and downed the wine.

Henry gagged and swallowed it back. He was growing hungrier by the second, and he wasn't about to waste any of his last meal – just in case he didn't get any more until tomorrow night. His veins gnawed with hunger and a raging appetite for the humans in the room.

Kellen turned over the empty goblet, beamed, and patted his stomach. Not a drop spilled, from the glass or from Kellen. "See? I can drink this and not get sick." He grabbed a clean glass and trickled another serving.

"I'm not doing it," Henry said.

"Me neither," John agreed.

"Not yet you aren't," Dr. Parks warned as Kellen handed him the glass.

"Dr. Parks is right," Kellen said. "Eating and drinking are for advanced students only. But you'll get there. Now," Kellen opened the "Straf Mich Gott" and thumbed through the pages. "Here are qualities you can start imitating now. Implementing them into your studies will allow you to move about the world believably human. Ready?"

"No," Henry said, averting his gaze from Dr. Parks, who was glowering at him even as Henry was mentally tying a napkin around his neck.

"So the fruit of the spirit is love, joy, peace, longsuffering, gentleness, goodness, faith, meekness and temperance. These will be difficult to learn, I know. Vampires are naturally indifferent, restless, impatient, selfish, impulsive, self-centered, immodest, and prideful. So let's start with something easy. Let's start with love, romantic love, because that will..."

"...lead to courtship," John said darkly. "Again. No."

"Don't be so prideful, my former darling little pet. After all, you ate rabbits as a human, Don't deny it!"

Henry blinked. What did rabbits have to do with...?

"Yes, but I didn't need to chase one to eat it."

"So instead of chasing food, food will chase you. Courtship is only for hosting. The rest of the time, be charming, mysterious, seductive, and then..."

Henry yawned again. "Or wait until they're asleep, kill 'em, eat 'em, and move on."

Kellen turned to him and narrowed his eyes. "For cowardly vampires who cower in hiding. Not for strong, independent, virile, and masterful vampires who wish to mingle in society. Not for John, who has women offering themselves to him."

"I don't care," John said.

"John, don't argue with Uncle Kellen. You're the grieving husband. It's very attractive."

"Luring women to my room to kill them will end my career. Are we done?"

"No," Dr. Gothart said and then nodded at Kellen to continue.

"Well, maybe it's too early to practice something as complex as love. Let's try something simpler, like joy. Think of something that delights you."

"Nothing," John said.

"Not music?"

"No," John said.

"Aha! Not true. You yourself have said music makes you happy. Close your eyes. Visualize. You're playing the piano. How do you feel?"

"This is stupid," John slumped and rubbed his forehead.

"Answer the question." Dr. Gothart's voice was low but full of malicious warning.

110

John glared back, obviously not intimidated. "I don't have an answer."

"I'll make it easier." Kellen picked up the chalk and then drew a large circle on the blackboard. Inside, he drew two half-moon eyes, a snub nose, and a long curvy line that turned up at each end. "This," he traced lightly over the line, "is a smile. People who are alive move their mouths this way when they feel joy. See?"

Kellen smiled as broadly as he could move his alabaster facial muscles, which made him look like a grinning death mask, hardly useful for opening the doors to high society. "Now you try it. On the count of three, everyone will smile. One, two…"

John bolted up and stalked out the room. Dr. Parks started to follow, but Dr. Gothart pointed his pipe at Dr. Parks, saying, "Sit, Martin."

"But he…"

"He'll be back," Dr. Gothart insisted. "When he realizes he can't get what he wants any other way, he'll be back."

Kellen faced Henry. "Now you try it."

"No."

"Why not?"

"Seriously?"

"You've attended masquerades, right? Well, a smile is just a mask. It hides your vampire nature and keep you safe."

"Smile," Dr. Gothart said, and the menacingly way he said it warned Henry he wasn't playing.

"Fine."

So Henry simpered and batted his eyes in Merlin's direction, feeling more like a Parisian moll than a fiend in disguise.

"Good start!" Kellen exclaimed. "Now back to love. When you wanted to seduce a woman, what did you do?"

Henry shrugged. "Nothing. They came to me."

"What about the one you lured from the convent?"

"We recited poetry, and I twiddled her."

"You snake." John had returned and was wandering near the piano. "No wonder Jacob King hates you."

"Come on, John, don't be coy," Henry retorted." Music boxes, flowering estates, custom mansions, wedding songs. It's a lot of effort just to get your dick wet."

"I don't answer to you."

"Actually, yes, you do, John."

"Boys! Boys!" Kellen wagged a claw at them. "Ironically, this brings us to peace. That's a challenging one because vampires are restless by nature. So we must practice serenity."

"The only time I'm serene is when I'm comatose," Henry said.

"Ditto," John said.

"Fine," Kellen said irritably. "And then there's longsuffering, because sometimes you must be patient in waiting for the right move with a certain victim."

"Only if you pursue money and power," Henry said. "I pursue nothing. I don't need to wait for it."

"I'm actually rather impatient at Dr. Gothart's lack of progress." John lifted the lid. "It's been two months, and I'm still not restored to life. I canceled concerts only through April."

"John, as I told you, these things take time."

"Now onto gentleness," Kellen said hurriedly. "Vampire reflexes are brisk and fast, so brisk and fast that you might appear clumsy in front of a human. Think in terms of making very slow, highly exaggerated movements."

"Like pianissimo?" John played a brief example.

"Yes, John, well done. Henry, effective seduction is like that."

"Similar to the time you kept Agnes waiting for her marriage," John said.

"Fuck off, John," Henry said.

"Next is goodness. You should practice this well."

"Why?" John asked.

"Because many people who are alive are attracted to it. If you appear 'good,' they will come to you."

"They came to me anyway when I was alive, and I didn't need to fake it," John said.

"And that leads us to meekness, which is the opposite of aggression."

"So a pushover?"

"No, humble and kind."

"I can't stomach this." John dropped the lid with bang and strolled away.

Henry said in a gruff voice, "Please may I rip into your neck and drink you dry?" Then he quickly switched to high falsetto: "Yes, please, I've waited all night."

Kellen put his hands on his hips. "Look, if you're not going to take this seriously, I won't be responsible for..."

"Serve the refreshments!"

Kellen whirled around and bowed. "Yes, Dr. Gothart." He retrieved the cattle bell and clanged it with all his might. "Hear ye! Hear ye! Recess will now commence!"

"The first decanter is for Dr. Parks only," Dr. Gothart continued. "The rest will drink from the second."

Kellen hustled the rest of the Bordeaux to a grateful Dr. Parks and quickly splashed blood into the remaining goblets and sent them 'round the room.

"The blood of an Austrian maiden," Dr. Gothart raised his glass to John. "A little wine for your stomach that thy may bear thine present infirmities."

John held up his glass and peered at its crimson innards. "It's not coagulated." He fixed his gaze on Dr. Gothart. "Is this a trick?"

"Tincture of white clover," Dr. Gothart countered. "From your room."

Dr. Parks held out his glass. "Bottoms up!"

In a single gulp, Henry drained his glass.

"Please sir," Henry stretched out his hand holding the goblet. "I want some more."

"More?" Kellen roared.

"Yes, more," John said through his teeth. "Or I'll leave now and kill my own."

Kellen snapped his fingers and two tin buckets brimming with blood appeared. Henry scrambled on hands and knees to the first bucket and thrust his entire face into it, lapping and gulping until he reached the bottom. When he came back up, face sticky and dripping, he noticed John had done the same. Kellen rapped on the board for their attention, and Henry dried his face with his sleeve.

"Recess is ended! We shall now discuss faith. Because you will encounter a church from time to time. Or you will, at least, must act like you attend one."

"How?" Henry asked, lying back on the rug, satiated and drowsy. "We'll spontaneously combust the moment we step inside. Won't that give us away?"

"Eastern European legends do such injustice."

"So this won't hurt you?" Henry made a cross with his arms. "Hey, you're right."

"You might have trouble with sacred objects," Kellen said. "But we can work on building up your resistance. Finally, temperance. Not more eating or drinking like a pig."

"Pigs don't drink blood from buckets," Henry retorted.

"Look, you can cultivate elegance and civility like a decent human being."

"I'm neither decent nor human."

"That's true," Dr. Gothart said. "But John must pretend both if he wants to return to the world – and onto the stage."

John darted up from the bucket, heedless of his smeared face. "Mustn't I be fully human to perform?"

"No," Dr. Gothart said with a wink and evil shining in his green eyes. "Just close enough."

ou...rascal! I'll...I'll...!"

George heaved between each breath, and his skin shone with sweat. He pointed across the room with a shaking finger; his lips curled in rage.

"Hush, George, lie back," Isabella said as she guided him toward the pillows that Marie hastily fluffed and restacked. "See how cool and light."

George twisted free. His eyes, glassy and suspicious, darted around the room, dark save for the dim illumination from the kerosene lamps. Marie had lit two: one on the wall near the door, the other on the desk, lamps George did not perceive. But then, George seemed unaware of Isabella's and Marie's presence, too.

"Try and stop me! Come on! Now!"

George swung and collapsed, sinking almost immediately into fretful, restless slumber. Within minutes, his entire body jerked with the forceful contractions Marie herself had experienced when overtired and dropping quickly into sound sleep, only to be momentarily jolted awake with the sensation of falling. From time to time during that weary, dismal night, where the hands of the Arnold and Dent traveling clock inched around the face so painfully slow, George broke his stupor with muttering, shouting, and even growling and barking.

They dozed in hardback chairs at George's bedside. While Isabella cared for George, Marie cared for Isabella.

"More wine, Mama?" Marie held out the bottle more than once, a bottle that grew lighter with each offer.

"Please," Isabella gasped in a strangled voice as she tucked the covers around George and blotted his face with a soft cotton cloth.

Each time Marie splashed more of the ruby tonic into the goblet, releasing its heady tart scent. Gradually her tired little hand grew less steady, and Marie often wound up bringing her mother a liquid as dark as her papa's old blood but inside a vessel sticky with Marie's carelessness. She then sank back onto

115

her chair. At one point her gaze fell on the clock. Three o'clock in the morning. And another half bottle of wine drunk, by her mama and not her papa. Dr. Parks' threat about "sending for the constable" had scared Isabella, so now Isabella languished in a prison of indecision, too frightened not to help her husband with the old reliable remedy and too petrified of the consequences if she did.

For several hours now Marie and Isabella had kept watch, chasing away delirium each time it flared with comforting words, gentle pats, and repositioning of bed covers, while Dr. Parks' words, "He really needs more blood," replayed like a mantra in Marie's overtired and so very fear-stricken brain.

At one point, Marie asked in a timid voice, "Should we send for Dr. Parks?"

But Isabella slowly shook her head, her exhaustion obvious with the effort it took for her to execute that simple movement. "No. He'll be here in a few hours to give the bismuth. What more can he do?"

Not even twelve hours had passed since Dr. Parks had infused her papa with water and then argued with her mama. And yet, how long the hours since Dr. Parks had left, when Marie and her mama had cleared the little table as soundlessly as they could and set the dinner dishes outside for the help to take away. They dared not tidy up the room; any sound might disturb George's sleep.

"Dr. Parks said his stomach needs rest," Isabella had murmured, more to her wine goblet than Marie as she reached for the decanter.

So they'd spent the evening in quiet pursuits: Isabella with needlework and Marie with her studies. Isabella patiently worked golden stitches around an amber stem in a colorful garden of stitched sunflowers, bluebells, roses, and leaves. But although Marie dutifully bent her head over her grammar, sparks of panic disrupted the pathway between her mind and the written characters, and she spent most of the time stomping them out.

She had never felt so terrified.

Not six years ago when she witnessed the massacre of Wounded Knee because George gleefully rushed to cover it, taking her and Isabella with him.

Not five years ago when they were among injured, although not mortally injured, of the 1891 East Thompson train wreck that killed two passengers.

Not three years ago when two men fell dead at her feet during a tavern brawl.

Not even in early November when George ruined their first dinner with family of long ago by vomiting blood over the food.

For Marie had never doubted a doctor could not alleviate his agony. Wherever The Dream had taken them, they could always locate a doctor who understood George's affliction. Her papa never languished for long. And certainly no infirmity, of the stomach or otherwise, ever extinguished the fiery passion that pressed George Clare to the culmination of The Dream. George's stomach, no matter how weak, never snuffed the gleam of ambition lighting his eyes.

Until now.

If suffering was the price for attaining The Dream, hadn't her papa paid it a million-fold? How many times could his feet not carry him to a juicy story because his stomach rebelled like an unruly child? Or, if he'd already snagged the story, how often had his fingers pecked out letters too slowly, or pecked out the wrong letters, because he was typing while groaning and doubled up at the typewriter? He never surrendered to the relentless colic, but like the sleeping hare, he almost always crossed the finish line last. News published too late spoils, like old milk, her papa always said. News tastes best when fresh.

With trembling hands all through that awful evening, Isabella slowly moved her needle up and through the cloth, again and again, ripping more stitches than she placed. More than once, Marie caught her wiping tears away with the muslin or staring blankly at her work, letting the tears fall and blot the fabric.

At ten o'clock, Isabella had insisted Marie take her own rest, while Isabella herself ignored the sensible words and refused Marie's offer of the cot. For Isabella would not disturb

George's repose and refused to go anywhere near the bed while George slept.

"Let me sleep in the chair, Mama," Marie had insisted. "I can curl up and be quite comfortable."

"No," Isabella had mumbled as she, again, refilled her goblet and settled in the chair near the window. "No, I shall doze here and keep watch."

"I shall keep watch with you."

Isabella hiccupped and then glowered at Marie as if Marie, and not she, had breached good etiquette.

"Miracle Child," she reprimanded with a slight slur. "What will your papa say when he wakes up, refreshed and rejuvenated, ready to follow The Dream, and you dawdle because you're exhausted? Why, once the infusion takes effect, we'll be moving into our new home on the hill, tomorrow, perhaps. So we need to be revitalized and prepared."

Isabella took a swig and stared at George with drooping eyes.

Marie glanced anxiously at the wan figure. He had not stirred since Dr. Parks' departure. Did it matter? He had already deserted The Dream. Although she rarely back talked, a surge of dread caused the words to spill out before she could stop them: "Mama, you're wrong."

But Isabella didn't fly out of her chair to give Marie's mouth the smacking it deserved. Instead, she rolled her head toward Marie and studied her with a glazed expression.

"Of course, he may need an extra day to recover," she reflected. "This, of course, is due to Dr. Parks' savagery, filling your papa with the blood of another man, even though God commands against it, and then taking away his wine, the catalyst for Jesus' first miracle and the balm for your papa's affliction. But," Isabella continued, now speaking to the blackish red liquid inside her glass. "I have faith in the lifegiving properties of water. Hadn't God affirmed it? I've no doubt it will flush out all the blood that does not belong to him and cleanse him from this iniquity. Then, when we are safely away from this horrid little inn, your papa can reestablish the healing regime the Messiah laid out for him. So, Marie," Isabella waved to her daughter's cot, "do rest."

"Yes, Mama."

118

Marie ducked behind the screen, the first step in obeying her mama's directive. She poured water from the basin to wash her face with smooth olive oil soap and clean her teeth with gritty tooth powder. One by one, she shed each of her daytime garments and exchanged them for an ivory cotton nightgown. She carefully refolded each day garment and then placed them in the trunk that held their dirty laundry, for Aunt Lula had found a village woman to launder, starch, and press their wardrobe during their confinement. Marie then emerged, bareheaded, for the steam heat in Room 27 kept the room comfortably warm, no need for a night cap.

Averting her eyes from her papa's immobile form, she strode across the room where Isabella was sitting at the window and gazing into the darkness. She had just refilled the goblet, and the bottle next to it was nearly empty.

"I am ready for bed." Marie lightly kissed Isabella's cheek. "Good night, Mama."

"Good night," Isabella whispered.

Marie walked to the cot, keeping only the cot in sight. She pulled back the covers and slid between them. Outwardly, she had fulfilled her mother's wishes. Inwardly, her brain burned with a strange fever, even though her forehead felt cool to the back of her hand. She lay rigid and alert, clenching her toes and fingers while her stomach folded over itself like bread dough, and fear sizzled through her nerves like a match to a fuse.

At some point, she drifted off, only to be startled awake by her father shouting at an invisible Henry Matthews. So Marie and her mama passed the night with him, waiting at the edge of his twisted abyss, each moving their lips in prayer that George's torment might soon end.

The next morning Dr. Parks came early with bismuth and saline. By then, George's terror had passed, and George had fallen into a deep sleep, so deep he did not hear Dr. Parks set his bag on the table or set up his medical equipment; he did not stir when the help brought the breakfast trays and The Times. But he did surface briefly when Dr. Parks spoke his name. He dozed during the infusion and drank the bismuth in semi-alertness with Isabella stroking his hand; he turned to her with the dazed expression of a boxer who'd suffered one too many blows on the head and didn't notice as Dr. Parks retrieved the beaker.

"My love," George sighed. "The Times."

Isabella slowly blinked and her mouth parted slightly, as if to summon her frazzled mind into understanding. She looked rumpled and disheveled in yesterday's clothes, her frizzy hair and the smudges on her cheeks added to her lack of decorum, all clues, Marie surmised, to the state of her mama's psyche.

"George, The Times?"

He nodded. "Read to me."

So Isabella did. With the halting voice of an overtired brain, Isabella read the entire newspaper to George and re-read the stories that kindled frenzy in his eyes or made his nose flare with renewed verve. She read the stories from the wire and the stories composed by his archenemy Henry Matthews. Marie kept the daily routine to the drone of her mama's voice.

For the next few days, Isabella read to him day and night, stopping when consciousness forsook him, during which time she slumped in her chair and fell soundly asleep, the paper dropping from her fingertips and scattering across the floor. But she just as abruptly shot to vigilance the moment he awakened and bid her to "read."

Isabella's voice grew hoarse under the strain. She no longer asked for wine and not for the sake of wine; she shunned all manner of food and drink. So again Marie kept the routine, with the additional role of nursemaid added to her duties. She fed her mama tidbits of her meat and bread and dewberry jelly between pauses at paragraphs and offered sips of water whenever her mother's voice turned from clear to croak.

But George consumed nothing except sips of bone broth and even this required protracted coaxing from Dr. Parks while Isabella read aloud to George to keep him awake for the meal.

Then after Dr. Parks left, if George was still alert, she read.

Isabella read how the Mormon Church finally renounced its evil practice of polygamy, which allowed Utah to be admitted as the forty-fifth state in the Union on January fourth.

She read how the first women's six-day bicycle race would commence on January six at Madison Garden and speculations if weak feminine constitution would withstand it, when even men broke their collarbones, fractured their skulls, and went queer in the head on such rides.

She read how Fannie Merritt Farmer released her first cookbook on January seventh: The 1896 Boston Cooking-School Cook Book, the first cookbook to standardize measurements so that all cooks, regardless of skill, might be able to replicate each recipe every time.

She read about how three students at Davidson College in North Carolina experimented with X-rays on January twelfth and commentaries about how applications of this "Roentgen's Ray" might successfully aid difficult surgeries. She read how a demonstration of these new rays would take place on January eighteen in New York City.

Whenever Marie awakened in the night, Isabella was at his side, cradling his head, or wiping his bottom as one might wipe the bottom of a tiny babe, or helping him with the urinal Dr. Parks had brought for him. Whenever Marie awakened in the morning, Dr. Parks was often already there, infusing another saline solution into a man who roused less each day. She read low numbers on the sphygmometer. She counted each movement of the mouth when Dr. Parks held her papa's wrist.

"It hurts," George moaned one day, raising a shaky hand to his forehead, pale as a corpse.

Dr. Parks finished counting and then lay George's other hand back on the bed. "What hurts?"

"My head. It...it pounds so."

Isabella immediately lay a cool cloth on George's forehead. At its touch, he began to shiver and shake.

Marie immediately dragged her own covers to George's bed. Dr. Parks carefully arranged them over George, which reduced the chattering in his teeth.

"Marie," Isabella said in a voice thick with fatigue and unremitting worry. "Bring The Times."

"Yes, Mama."

Dr. Parks held up his hand. "Wait."

Something of the mother lion kindled inside Isabella at the sound of that single word. A warning appeared in her eyes. In a sharp tone, as stark and cold as window frost, she said, "He's not a child, remember? He's a man."

Dr. Parks winced in memory of his little speech. "But his brain is now feverish. We need to cool the flames, not fan them."

"You've taken away his medicine. Must you take his mind, too?"

"I'm trying to preserve his mind."

Isabella breathed hard and fast, as if catching her breath from a six-day bicycle race, and then spoke through tight lips.

"You...doctors. We've spent all our resources on men of science and chasing The Dream. Well, physicians happily pocketed our money and yet failed to cure him. All that's left is The Dream."

"Mrs. Clare, your husband might never recover. Doesn't that worry you?"

"Dr. Parks: when all a dying man has left is a dream, why would you squash it?"

To Marie's great surprise, Dr. Parks hung his head. When he raised it again, he looked as if he might cry.

Without another word, he picked up his coat and hat and bag. Silently, he closed the door behind him.

CHAPTER FOURTEEN: NONE GREATER CAN BE CONCEIVED

ohn opened his eyes and stared at the steel knife, bloody with his blood. The cold stone floor pressed into his colder face; his head boomed as if someone had smashed it with a hammer; and muscles blazed with unquenchable fire, the agony of a dead nervous system that's forced to function. But none of these compared to his back. Filleted by a savage cuisinier, it smarted with a searing smartness, as if someone had rubbed a pound of salt into his raw, slashed flesh.

This jolting from oblivion was his most formidable hurdle of the night. Once John grasped the knife and wrestled himself to his feet, he could manage the rest. Getting there: that was the struggle between his battered casing and a tenacious will that refused to die.

Tonight the will triumphed, as it must always triumph.

He staggered through the easels of oils he'd commissioned of Henry to the bryony noose where Henry swayed: body limp, swollen tongue out. Swiftly, John sawed through the bonds and watched Henry smack into the ground. Once Henry started to stir, John staggered up the stairs and out the back door, the part John loathed more than anything he had ever loathed in life or death, except Henry and Savannah. But a vehement thirst for blood would not yield until it spent itself, and it would not spend itself until John had killed, and killed violently, until he not only filled his veins with the vitality of his victims, but until he was sodden with it, when every single decaying cell was overflowing with blood that was never his. Only then could John lope back to Simons Mansion and settle at the piano for a night of relentless and fruitless pursuit of replicating the music that won for him the adulation that belonged to his talent and his alone.

He paused, relishing the silence of three thousand barely breathing men and women. Then his hands struck the keys, a joyful waltz broke forth, and the applause exploded.

Except duplication dodged him.

The pieces were exquisitely executed, each note perfect in precision. But its essence was lacking. Whatever elusive, nondefinable quality that had made audiences sigh and nod their heads, knowing they were swooning to a John Simons composition, was lacking, and John couldn't reproduce it, no matter now long or hard or persistently he tried.

That was frustration number one. The second was Savannah.

He'd mentally killed her hundreds of times and ways since his summer at the Holloway Farm, each time he allowed his mind the slightest wavering in the direction of her memory, which was rarely. He hated her nearly as much as he hated Henry. Only one reason ever prevented the living John from seeking her out and finishing her off: her demise at his hands would have severed his acclaim with the world. In the end, that's what kept her alive. He loved his image of himself more than he despised her.

"Your pay," Savannah smiled, a cool unperturbed smile. "For your services this summer."

Since death, he'd let his vague notion of slaying her ripen into a dark, disturbing need. He must act quickly, before he regenerated, for murder would sully his golden reputation among the masses. So he faithfully practiced the teleportation lessons Kellen, whom he also loathed, laid out for him. But although John made progress, all the way to Jenson one night, that progress came too slowly for him, not when he craved to torture, maim, and then destroy her by his hands – finally.

"I changed my mind." Savannah squeezed his fingers. "I want you to stay the night."

He launched into another piece.

Steinway Hall. The Metropolitan Opera House. Castle Carden. The White House. Carnegie Hall. Canada. Exposition Universelle de 1889. Royal Albert Hall. St. James Hall, Drury Lane: he'd conquered them all. His murder cut short the next frontier: a full-scale European tour – with an undead promoter more formidable than Kellen.

John blinked. "You worked for P.T. Barnum's circus?"
"I was a bareback lady."
"A bareback lady."
"Yes, on an elephant." Savannah laughed, a full deep melodious laugh.

He trilled the high notes, blithely skipping up and not too far down, a melodic enthusiasm climbing higher and still higher, magical tinkling chords that rose and rise until the waves crashed in a thunderous refrain and merged into dissonant chords and a macabre melody of music that the music swelled, dark and distended, thundering notes and then drowsy waves and plundering shades and downward spirals with hard abrupt chords; a pause and then sad, single notes. Some went up the scale, and some went down; some stayed the same, a monotonous half-melody he repeated again and again.

"Phenomenal performance, Mr. Simons."
"Well done, John!"
"What a phenomenal success, I tell you!"
" Your music is truly beautiful."
" Extraordinary!"
"So bewitching was the music."
"Just a natural feel for the instrument,"
"John, you were wonderful!"
"A musical genius. A master of melodies."
"Uncanny. It's like hearing the great master himself."
"The celestial springs from human fingers: my Jenny Lind of piano."

His crescendos plunged the walls; the keys tinkled like gentle rain. John played and played and played and played. He played a prelude, and then an etude and then a waltz, and then a mazurka, and then a nocturne, and then a polonaise, and then a serenade, and then a scherzo, and then a ballade, and then parts of a new sonata and an older concerto.

Wild clapping filled the air... he exited to a standing ovation... the clapping following him offstage, unabashed admiration from New York's finest, for him, for his music...their enthusiasm as he strutted off the stage sounded louder and longer than any of the previous concerts, and he basked in the applause... the ensuing applause: longer and harder than any at...

And then all too soon it was time.

All too soon John lowered the lid and shuffled up the stairs to the second floor, completely drained, much like his victims by the time he discarded them. Several times he paused, gripping the railing and panting hard. Then he resumed his ascent. Almost to the landing he stumbled, and he braced his hands at the top of his thighs, willing up the energy to complete the climb, for climb he must or perish in place. He took a step, the memory of the last time he mounted this staircase as a man more vivid, more acute than the actual event. When he finally reached the top, he turned left for the opportunity to turn right was gone; he must only turn left; he was incapable of turning any other way. Then he crawled across the hall, passing Henry's study on the way to the rear, creeping down the staircase like a whipped animal instead of the lord and master of his home, and then slithering like a worm along the hard cold stone, for all strength had vanished from his limbs. He pulled himself inch by inch by the might of his famous, musical hands until he reached his place in the hidden room and could finally stop, a broken heap fixated on the flickering lights.

These candles were positioned around the oils, hundreds of them, commissioned from John to Henry, but they blazed in the room as if it was noon.

"Portraits?"
"A surprise. For Bryony. For our anniversary."
"Two portraits? Three?"
"I made a list. And prepared a room."

Each canvas quickened something in the painted image of Bryony, making her appear as John had known her in life, the kudzu that choked off his soul. Each image invoked a memory more excruciating than any thrust of Henry's knife.

Bryony sat at her dressing table brushing her long tan hair, her blueish green eyes dreamily half-closed.

"I won't raise the child of a whore."

Bryony gazed out her bedroom window and over Simons Mansion's spacious grounds, bryony vines framing her face.

"The night is ours," he murmured. "Let's go home."

Bryony held the music box, rapture on her face.

"Oh, John! I do believe in us."

Bryony played dolls with Anna.

"Bryony, you indulge that child too much."

Bryony sipped tea in the morning room.

She calmly took another sip. "I'm not going."

Bryony sipped wine in the small dining room.

"Anything you want, darling."

Bryony stretched high to pick a ripe, red apple from one of John's prized trees.

"Well?" She searched his eyes for his approval. "Doesn't it make you hungry?"

Bryony sat in full concert dress, her face shining, her eyes on a performance she could not see.

"Mrs. Simons, would you like to see the White House?"

Bryony paused in a half-twist before a full-length mirror, admiring her Parisian wedding gown.

"And with all my worldly Goods I thee endow."

Bryony stroked the nose of one of John's Arabian horses.

"Do you like horses, Mrs. Simons?"

Bryony stood poised with a croquet mallet, about to take her winning stroke.

"Your wife is rather good with a mallet. Perhaps, someday, I shall triumph."

In an aquamarine ball dress and diamonds, Bryony checked her dance card.

"You're so beautiful," he whispered. "I want you. Now..."

He heard a thud and then a scuffle: the trudge of the dead.

It wouldn't be long. He was forever ready and always unprepared.

The first blow came before he braced himself, it always came before he braced himself, but he took it. And then he took another and then another until all went black.

"I sabella, please stop."

"I can't," Isabella whispered in a voice strained with many days or reading aloud as she turned the page. "Lula, I just can't. George isn't allowed wine, and water isn't helping. Only this," she stroked that day's copy of The Times. "Only this can save him now."

Lula wore a stunning gray gown trimmed in violet satin and high color with a black satin hat with a violet satin bow, and an expression of concern bordering on alarm.

Marie was also dressed for the company in amber and gold, and she was fastening a gold locket that contained actual hair from her Grandpapa and Grandmama Sage while her aunt and mama argued. But Isabella had not washed or changed her clothes for many days, and she smelled as grubby as she looked, nothing like rose water. But her appearance, although contrary to Isabella's habit, didn't worry Marie. George's did.

He lay so still, so ashen, so cold. A ghastly blue tinged his lips and fingertips, the color of periwinkle, the color of poison. He breathed shallowly, sometimes very slowly, as if he might not breathe again, and sometimes quite rapidly, in little gasps. But his eyelids no longer flickered when Isabella read to him, a strange omission from a man who consumed words as a glutton consumed food and drink. But Marie understood now, even if the others did not.

Somehow, an ominous presence had slipped into Room 27 and concealed itself until Marie finally perceived it, yesterday right after lunch, during Dr. Parks' second of his regular thrice-day visits.

Dr. Parks' look had gone from worried to puzzled as his fingertips darted about George's wrist, until they finally found the rhythmic little thump and rested there. He counted it, and then he counted it again, and his expression grew more somber with each count. Twice, Dr. Parks counted to one hundred and thirty-five when, on previous visits, he always stopped counting before he reached one hundred and twenty. When he finished, he laid George's wrist gently on the bed and gave his hand an even gentler little pat. Soberly, he infused George with more saline, but he could not rouse George enough to safely give the bismuth, not even with Isabella squeezing his hand, stroking his cheek, or murmuring encouragements into his ear; not even when she read the latest scourge to The Dream: a brief, exclusive interview with the still grieving John Simons by the despicable Henry Matthews.

"I'll try later," Dr. Parks said as he buckled his bag. "If we force it, he may aspirate."

Tears streaked Isabella's cheeks at this setback. But she nodded, her full attention on George.

Dr. Parks put on his overcoat and then picked up his hat and bag with effort, as if he'd aged considerably overnight and the lifting of these common items taxed his muscles to their limit.

"I'll return at nightfall," he said with a quaver, which he immediately covered by clearing his throat. "Please send word if...if I'm needed."

No one answered. He shut the door behind him with a light click.

That was at noon. Now twilight was approaching, and Aunt Lula had arrived to ensure they were ready for dinner. Last night, Aunt Lula had called to announce that Lillian and her husband were coming to Munsonville in the morrow, and they wanted to see George. Marie knew all about Lillian and her family from their letters. Lillian Betts, the last the cousin Marie had yet to meet, was Leo and Luther's sister, slightly older than they. Lillian was married to Milton Betts, whose family predated the Hassets' arrival to Munsonville by a few years. Both lived and worked in Jenson, a college town the Clares had passed on their way to Munsonville. Lillian was a copyeditor for the Jenson Reporter; Milton assisted the chair of the philosophy department at the Jenson College of Liberal Ats. Although Lillian and Milton were married a few years ago, God had not yet blessed them with a baby – or if He had, they'd already shipped the blessing back to Him.

But Isabella looked confused at her sister's words, almost as if she were hearing the names for the first time. She smiled at George, but her gaze was wistful as she smoothed the limp curls off his brow.

"They want to see George?" Isabella had repeated, as if Lula had spoken those words in a foreign language, and Isabella needed to repeat them to comprehend the meaning. "But why?" Bewildered, she looked up at her sister. "George has not recovered. George needs rest. Ask them to call next week, after we move into our new home."

Lula had started to speak, hesitated, and then hurried to Isabella, crouching near the chair and wrapping her arms around her. She lingered over the embrace, which Isabella acknowledged with an absent pat on her sister's arm. After a long while Lula straightened and as she did, she noticed Marie, and Lula's eyes misted. She rushed across the room to hug Marie, but the touch felt odd, and Marie did not return the act. She'd never received affection from anyone except her parents, so the sensation of pressing against another woman's bosom, even one of her own blood, sent prickles up her back. But Lula was her mama's sister, and her mama had taught Marie to be kind and useful. So if the hug consoled Aunt Lula in her distress, Marie knew better than to refuse it.

Finally Aunt Lula pulled away. She placed her hands onto Marie's shoulders and drew her back, trying to smile with confidence.

She failed.

"You are such a brave, dear girl and a great asset to your parents."

"Yes'm."

Lula blinked at Marie's clipped remark and then peered into Marie's eyes, and Marie noted waves of tender emotion passing over her face. Finally, Lula pressed a light, little kiss on Marie's forehead and stroked the side of Marie's head. Then she left.

Now here she was again, pulling her mama out of the chair, which caused The Times to fall and Isabella to sob aloud. Isabella dropped to the floor, frantically collecting the scrambled sheets and arranging them in order as if her salvation depended up on it.

Lula knelt beside her to help, tears running down her cheeks, too.

"I can't stop reading," Isabella cried in a hoarse voice. "I have to keep reading. George needs me to read." She clutched The Times to her breast. "Oh, Lula, what shall I do?"

"Mama, I am ready for the company," Marie said with feigned assurance as she turned away from the mirror. "I can read to Papa while you bathe and dress."

The slight deception in her attitude did not trouble Marie any more than saying, "We will eat sweet peaches in four years" after one plants a tree. The feigned assurance was the seed of the honest fortitude Marie intended to grow. For she no longer merely sensed the shade, she saw it, a congealed shadow lurking near her papa's bed. Of what use now was fear? Dismay, despair, dread: none had brought benefit to her papa, her mama, her. Fear only served itself. It didn't encourage judicious decisions; it didn't prevent troubles and predicaments; and it couldn't delay the inevitable. Fear devoured soundness of mind and stoutness of heart faster than starving interlopers at a private banquet, so Marie resolved, in that moment, to deny fear the least crumb, no matter how much fear wheedled and cajoled. If fear could vanquish the specter, a specter that even now stretched out its arms and wiggled its fingers to snatch the person most dear to her heart, Marie would gladly quiver and quake the rest of her days.

But fear had failed her. Fear always failed her. She had given fear one last chance to speak prudent advice instead of vague whispers of doom, and fear once again had failed to deliver on its promises. In all his torment, her papa had never given fear a foothold. From this day forward, neither would Marie. So Marie chained and bolted her fear and banished it to a remote part of her spirit, where it could harm her no more. And then she stationed guards at all entrances to ensure fear stayed far away.

She was the "Miracle Child" of George and Isabella Clare. She was Aunt Lula's "dear, brave girl." Starting now, Marie would live the role.

Isabella rolled her head up at Marie, her eyes looked glazed and unfocused.

"Yes, yes that is a wonderful idea," Lula said, nodding encouragingly at Marie. "Come, Isabella, I will help wash and dress you like we're little girls toileting for a party."

Isabella swerved back to the bed. "But..."

"George will be fine. Marie will read to him. And we won't be in the dining room long, just a quick dinner."

Aunt Lula helped Isabella up and then helped her taking mincing steps across the room to get ready behind the screen. Marie retrieved the abandoned newspaper, settled into her mama's chair, and then calmly flipped through the pages, seeking a story that might interest him.

"Now, Papa, would you like to hear Henry Matthews' latest piece?"

But the only movement from George was the weak and irregular movement of his chest.

No matter. Marie read Henry's update on the missing John Simons with precise inflection so her papa would not miss a single syllable.

George slept on and did not react. As soon as Marie concluded one story, she began another. If George heard any of the words, he gave no sign. But Marie continued reading. Even if it the words didn't stir her papa, the recitation of them comforted and reassured her mama.

Finally Isabella and Lula stepped out from the screen. Isabella wore a ruby and black suit, which ordinarily complimented her rosy skin and golden curls. But with her pale complexion and dark circles under her eyes, she looked more like Brunhilda in Johann Ludwig Tieck's *Wake Not The Dead* than an ornamental heiress. But Marie did not reflect on her mama's vampiric appearance for long; a knock on the door cut those thoughts short.

"I'll answer it." Marie set the paper down and then patted George's hand. "Papa, I'll be right back."

She opened the door and faced Briana Miller, one of Alannah's sisters, come to stay with George. Like Alannah and Eugenia, Briana had a rose tint to her flaxen hair, and she had the same rounded limbs and cherubic face. But whereas Alannah emanated serenity with her relaxed features and the unhurried way she executed each action, whether she was putting a fussy baby to her breast or responding to a question,

Briana oozed energy and vitality. Marie saw it in the flashing of her eyes, the flush on her cheeks, and her bright smile.

Perhaps, Marie thought, if Briana sat close enough, some of the girl's vigor might transfer to Papa.

Briana gave a quick, little curtsey. "Ma'am."

"Come in," Marie said, motioning the girl through the doorway with as if leading a child, even though Briana looked about eighteen, and Marie was only twelve. But Marie was yards above this girl's station, and they both knew it.

Marie led Briana to the bedside and then gestured to The Times on the nightstand. "Please read the news to him. He likes it very much. Even if he does not appear to comprehend, keep reading to him."

"Yes'm."

"Please, if he's...come get me," Isabella begged.

Briana gave another of her brisk curtsies, which reminded Marie of a jumping, mechanical toy. "Of course, Mrs. Clare."

"Come, Isabella. It's time."

Lula led Isabella from the room, and Marie followed them, catching a glimpse of Briana settling near George with The Times as Marie closed the door behind them. Isabella leaned on Lula during the walk through the hall, down each step of the staircase, the clicking of their heels on the boards announcing their descent, and all the way into the dining room. Lula, in turn, kept hold of Isabella's waist and Isabella's arm during the entire short trip. Marie trailed behind them and leaned on no one.

The guests were gathered in the back of the dining room, where the help had pushed two tables together. They were the last to appear; even the food had arrived – platters lined up in single file, ready to serve the hungry. In addition to her, Isabella, and Lula, the party included Luther, Leo, Alannah (with baby Eugenia nursing under a small blanket), and the reason for the party: Lillian and Milton Betts. Lillian reminded Marie of a Gibson girl, with her slender, symmetrical figure, stylish clothes, and soft brunette pompadour. Milton looked awkward by contrast, despite his fine clothing. He was tall and skinny, with sandy hair and freckles. Everyone except Alannah rose when they entered the room; next came a jumble of introductions, handshakes, and hugs. Milton concluded his hug

134

with an affectionate pat on her back; Lillian's embrace felt warm and assured, and Marie detected nuances of orange and cloves. Still, she did not return one hug, and no one appeared to notice.

"How was your trip?" Lula asked as they settled back in their seats, with Marie nestled her mama and Lillian.

"Very pleasant," Lillian smiled wryly. "For January."

Milton held up the pot. "Tea, anyone?"

Tea, everyone, Marie noted. And then the dishes made their rounds: place to the left, take a small amount, pass to the right, and the repeat. They ate fish and potato balls, boiled fish with gravy, peas and onions, rice croquettes, fresh rolls, and dried apple pudding, and Marie tuned out the chatter of polite and trite.

"...for Boswell Pike," Lula said.

Isabella looked quizzically at her.

"He was Munsonville's first mayor," Milton said as he poured cream over his pudding. "He served a long time."

"How long?" Alannah asked.

Milton screwed up his face. "From 1875 to 1887, if I'm remembering rightly." He picked up his spoon. "Even back then, he was teaching philosophy at Jenson College, so he traveled back and forth from Munsonville every day. We lost our leader about the same time Professor Pike was asked to serve as department chair. So he resigned as mayor."

"That's when the college hired Milton," Lillian sipped her tea. "Milton was already working unofficially for him, you see. But the Pikes were kind that way."

"How so?" Alannah asked and then she blushed a little, a sweet blush. "Forgive my questions, but I've only met Professor Pike once, at my father's funeral."

"They gave poor kids like me a chance, and I'm grateful they did," Milton took another bite of pudding and swallowed. "At first, he paid me out of his own wallet to assist him with his mayoring and teaching duties. When the college offered him the position, he made it part of the deal that it hire me, too."

"The Pikes invited Milton to live with them," Lillian continued. "Then when Milton and I became engaged, they talked to the Jenson Reporter on my behalf and invited me to live with them, too."

"We've been there ever since," Milton said with a broad smile.

The conversation turned to the cultural aspects of living in Jenson, and this interested Marie, especially when Lillian talked about her enjoyment of bicycling, sketching and violin lessons at the college, and theatrical as well as choral performances, also at the college. Lillian was active, poised, and living her Dream. Marie stifled a sigh. Why was it so easy for her and so difficult for her papa?

"I've enjoyed Aunt Isabella's letters through the years — so full of adventure," Lillian said to Marie.

"Yes,m."

Lillian placed her hand over Marie's, briefly squeezed, and then picked up her spoon; but Marie had felt an electric jolt at the touch of the woman fingers, and she felt it still and wished to feel it forever. She had a sudden impulse to know Lillian through and through, down to her skin and straight to her soul, which Marie imagined as a crystal gem. A little fantasy sprang up in her mind and took shape. Might Lillian, out of concern for George, decide to spend the night? Of course, she'd slip behind the screen with Marie to ready for bed. Because of her great beauty and confidence in her essence, Lillian would feel no shyness at disrobing in front of Marie or letting Marie see her perfect, teardrop-shaped breasts and pink areolae. She would share Marie cot and take her hand as they drifted off to...

"...but you're staying with us tonight?" Lula asked.

"Yes," Milton said with an even, slightly strained tone. "We shan't be long at my parents' home. Too...too many bad memories."

Leo, Alannah, and Eugenia left first. Eugenia was fussy and required rest in a proper bed, Alannah explained half-apologetically. Luther must put the paper to its own bed; Leo promised to join him as soon as he took Alannah and the baby home. But Lillian and Milton went upstairs with Isabella, Lula, and Marie, with the sisters, hands clasped, leading the way up the staircase. Milton and Lillian followed, also holding hands, and murmuring and smiling to each other, their faces radiant with love. Marie held her head high, arms rigid at her side, fingers slightly curled to her palms. Each footstep landed in the middle of the stair and brought her closer to – what? Hope? Despair?

Briana had not budged from George's bedside and was dutifully reading from The Times in her sweet, uplifting voice. Marie's heart sank at the sight, and Isabella turned even more pale and might have fainted if Lula had not eased her onto Marie's cot. George had absorbed none of Briana's vitality, nay, he had transferred some of his listlessness to her. The lilt that had caught Marie's ear had dropped to subdued and slightly troubled.

She knows, Marie thought. She knows.

Marie did not greet Briana, nor did Marie did say, "Welcome to Room 27," to Lillian and Milton because they had not paid a social call; they had paid a first and final call. In fact, Marie had said nothing to Lillian and Milton since they'd the dining room Neither did her mama, but she lay limp and dazed on Marie's cot, too broken for courtesies. Neither did Lula speak to her daughter and son-in-law, for she was tending to Isabella, sitting beside her, stroking her hair, and whispering reassurances.

Briana rose, curtsied, and said she'd wait downstairs for her mother to walk her home. So Lillian took the chair Briana had forsaken; Milton brought one from the table and set it on the other side of the bed. Then the two of them, Lillian and Milton, made light conversation with George for the next hour while Isabella slept on Marie's cot, moaning from time to time, and Lula held her hand. Marie sat stiffly at the desk and watched the company watch her papa as they talked to George and around George. Not one of their words registered in her mind; their mouths moved, and sounds came out, but each intonation meant nothing, just like all this visiting meant nothing to George. Not one syllable stirred him; not one topic affected him. He did not respond to their words, not a single one, nor did he start when unfamiliar hands reached for his limp ones.

Dr. Parks arrived at twilight. Lillian and Milton took that as their cue to rise and retrieve their outerwear, for they still had to pay an actual social call to Milton's parents. Lula wavered, torn between departing with her daughter, whom she seldom saw, and staying with her emotionally fragile sister. A looked passed between Lula and Dr. Parks, a silent communication that they seemed to understand. Lula gave Marie a hug and then she gave Marie an extra hug, and then she gave Marie an exceptionally long hug, and Marie did not resist. Then Lula smoothed Marie's hair. And then Lula, crying, dashed from the room.

When Milton and Lillian approached Marie to say their goodbyes, Marie rose, extended her hand as was proper, and said in carefully crafted words, "On behalf of my papa, thank you for support, care, and concern."

Marie did not say, "Thank you for coming to Munsonville."

Because Munsonville killed The Dream.

Munsonville was death.

CHAPTER SIXTEEN: SMALL BITES

"ere, ye! Here, ye!" Kellen stood at the head of the table in the formal dining at Simons Mansion, shouting over the frantic squeaking of mice. "The Kellen Wechsler Finishing School for Young Vampires is called to order! Please," Kellen bowed low and swept his hand. "Take your seats."

Someone, Henry surmised, and most likely Kellen, had set five places around the table, complete with name cards. These "cards" were actually used envelopes with their names scratched on the backs and folded so they stood up behind the plates like little tattered tents. Henry found his name and slid into the chair at Kellen's right, the same chair he had occupied during his lunch with Anna. John sat across from Henry; Dr. Parks and Dr. Gothart settled into two seats at the opposite end of the table. The table was set for a formal dinner, although the silverware was unwashed, unpolished, and haphazardly scattered in the general vicinity of the plates. Each vampire, plus Dr. Gothart, had his own decanter of blood, while Dr. Parks had one of Bordeaux. He immediately poured himself a glass, much to Kellen's consternation at jumping ahead of the rest.

"Fortification for this class," Dr. Parks said with a smile and a sip.

In the corner, Henry glimpsed a cloth bundle; its smell: unmistakable. The bundle was actually a tablecloth, hastily tied up by its corners. Spilling out were remnants of that last lunch: dirty dishes, slimy chicken slices, a lobster shell, half a moldy loaf, an empty jar of pickles, and several mushy brown apples cores. Ah, yes. The lunch Human Henry had shared with Anna. Before Bryony and her baby died. Before Henry murdered John and hanged himself. The last meal. Still hanging around. The way Henry was not still hanging. Fitting.

A fine dust coated the gold-flecked wallpaper, chair arms, wooden floor, and Oriental rug. Not the dining room Henry recalled, but so what? A long candelabra, lit and swathed in lacey cobwebs, stretched across the part of the table where the two doctors sat. This would enable the humans to follow the lessons for vampires, of course, had superior eyesight and didn't require any light to see, a real asset when light in any form dehydrated the undead. Two covered dishes were also on the vampire side of the table. One was a long silver tray with a lid that rattled as if bewitched (the source of the squeakings), of which Henry detected musk and ammonia; even though the rich coppery bouquet from the rest of the decanters partially masked it. Beside the tray was a porcelain bowl topped with a plate; this emanated a faint vinegar scent.

"Now, you may think this is a generous school where we serve refreshments in class," Kellen purred. "But, actually, the 'wine' is preparation for your stomach, to help train it to accept the type of food you ate as a human."

Alarm flashed in John's eyes and vanished as quickly as it came.

"We're eating actual food?" Henry asked, suspicious.

"Well, it depends on how you define 'real food.' But, yes, you are eating some..."

"Absolutely not!"

Henry sprang to his feet; Kellen's hand clamped onto his shoulder and pushed him back.

"We aren't starting with Châteaubriand with a Béarnaise sauce," Kellen said with a roll of his eyes. "We're practicing with simple creatures you already catch and whose blood you already consume. And we're only doing two courses."

"Courses?" John asked warily.

"Yes, You will suck the blood out of your course as I serve it, and then you will eat a minimum of one bite. Or, at the very least, you'll sink all your teeth into it."

John turned every shade of white, and Henry swallowed very, very hard.

"And more good news! You can ignore the utensils. They're here for 'show,' to reacquaint you with a more civil form of dining. Goblets, however, are not optional and neither are napkins. Please slip them out of the ring and spread them across your laps. Now, do you remember the first step?"

No one moved. Henry was still stuck on the words "more good news." His eyes drifted across the table: Claude Bernard,

Victor Frankenstein, the animated "banquet" desperate for escape, the Phantom of the Opera, and Lord Ruthven. Nope. Not one speck of good news anywhere.

John slowly reached for the decanter, and, even more slowly, poured himself a glass of someone's blood.

"Yes," John said, haltingly. "The first step is to prepare your shrunken stomach to accept what it no longer needs. So first, the blood."

Kellen chucked John under the chin and cooed, "Somebody was paying attention in class!"

John swatted him away and took a sip, glaring at beaming schoolmaster.

Abruptly, Henry grabbed his decanter, poured a glass and gulped it, more from nervousness than from hunger, since he'd eaten a huge party shortly before class. Kellen wrenched Henry's goblet out of his hands.

"Not like that!" Kellen screeched. "Where are your manners?"

"Give it back!"

"Say please – politely."

"Please," Henry mocked. "Politely."

Kellen slammed the glass onto Henry's "tent," flattening it. Henry repoured the glass, raised it high, and glanced around the room. Dr. Gothart sipped his blood with the elegance of a visiting lord at a dinner party. Dr. Parks, pen poised, looked as if he might burst into laughter.

"To your health!" Henry sniffed it, took a sip, and gently swished it. "Volatile acidity, full-bodied, rich. I'd call this an 1822...male...emphysemiac..." he swished again, "from London."

Dr. Gothart snickered and exchanged smirking glances with Dr. Parks. With a trembling hand, John topped off his glass, thoughtfully sipped with quivering lips, and eyed the now gyrating, squealing lid with trepidation. Henry took another sip and said, "Lovely evening, isn't? I do believe we're due for..."

"First course!" Kellen picked up the bowl.

He removed the plate and picked out a wolf spider, about an inch and a half long, wiggling its mottled legs in a desperate attempt to free itself, terror in all eight of its dark eyes. But

Kellen plopped the creature onto John's plate where it froze in fear and didn't even try to escape. John gagged and looked away.

"One for you," Kellen crooned and then reached into the bowl for its "amour," which he placed on Henry's plate. "And for you..."

Henry scooted his chair back. "I'm not eating that."

"And one for me. It's tasty. Look!" Kellen quickly sucked the spider to jerky, dropped it into his throat, and washed it away with a mouthful of blood. "Ah! Delicious! And...go!"

John shuddered, eyes on the spider, which had dredged up enough courage to creep to the edge of his plate.

"Fuck that," Henry said, again starting to rise. Again, Kellen pushed Henry onto the chair and shoved it close to the table.

"You'll be fine," Kellen patted him hard on the head like a loving benefactor to an orphan. "That's why you drink the blood first, so your stomach will accept the flesh. Remember? A little wine for your..."

John snatched up his spider, sucked it flat, and swallowed it whole. He reached into the bowl for another. Slightly emboldened, Henry slowly siphoned the blood, and bit off a leg, choking and spraying blood and leg onto the floor.

Nonplussed, John reached for another spider.

"Don't overdo it on the first day," Kellen admonished him. "Your stomach isn't used to a heavy load of..."

John quickly desiccated the spider and swallowed the hide. "The sooner I'm human, the sooner I can end this loathsome existence."

"Fucking showoff," Henry grumbled, as his spider bravely tried to wriggle away on one less leg, and Henry willed down the rising nausea.

"Why, Henry, your dinner is escaping," Kellen clicked his tongue again and wagged his finger. "Are you going to let an itsy witsy spider outsmart you?"

"Yep."

"Well, while you work on that first course, John can move onto the entrée."

Kellen raised the silver lid, and three frightened deer mice rushed out, streaming urine behind them. John snatched one, bit the brown furry head off, noisily slurped its blood as one might finish off a fountain drink through a paper straw, and took another huge bite. He convulsed like rabid dog and then blood, spiders, and a mouse torso shot across the tablecloth. Sputtering, choking, and groaning, John rose halfway out of his seat, grabbed the decanter, and downed its contents; he collapsed onto the chair, panting.

"See? If you'd listened to Uncle Kellen, you'd..."

Henry laughed. "Ha, John can't hold his vermin."

"Shut the hell up!"

"Really, John, what disgusting manners. Look at this: tiny legs, the blood of God knows how many people, and ...is that a mouse whisker?"

"Shut up!" John leaped over the table, yanked Henry out of his seat, smashed Henry's face into the mess, and then tottered off.

Henry darted up, wiping his face onto his sleeve and yelling, "Go ahead and run, John! You've got to return to the basement sometime! And when you do..."

"Well, Henry, if you won't eat your spider, you can go tease out your own meal." Kellen lay his hand on his forehead and slumped a little, as if he might faint. "Oh, the hours I spent chasing arachnids and rodents, and you don't even appreciate it." He swept the dishes off the table with a loud clatter. "Class dismissed!"

Now Henry hoped this meant Kellen was ready to abandon his mentorship. But as soon as Henry smacked the floor the following night, John kicked him and told him to hurry up with his hunt, that they were gathering by the grand staircase in thirty minutes. None of that hinted of "food" to Henry, but just in case, he drank a few extra courses. Consequently, he was late to class, and Kellen's was already clanging that fucking cowbell with all his might.

"Here, ye! Here, ye!" Kellen called at the bottom of the stairs. "The Kellen Wechsler Finishing School for Young Vampires is called to order! I trust you've all had a good bloodfast, and you're ready for another night of learn..."

"Just get on with it," Dr. Parks said shortly.

"Tonight's lessons will be held in the penthouse," Kellen announced. "Pay attention, for Dr. Parks will perform a short examination of your skills. Now follow me. Oh, and Dr. Parks?"

"Yes?"

"A warm fire and bottle of brandy are waiting for you in the library." Kellen gave a stiff little bow. "Enjoy your refreshment." Then he turned to the vampires. "This way, larvae." Kellen headed up the stairs reciting, "Follow me to school today, school today, school today. Follow me to school today..." He peered over his shoulder with a leer. "You know, if you were more advanced in teleportation, we'd have arrived by now. Did you ever see a vampy, a vampy, a vampy? Did you ever see a vampy go..."

They'd reached the landing. Kellen turned right, singing "this way and that" and headed down the hall. The papered walls of outdoor scenes, of lakes, woods, and people strolling, riding, or boating, the gilded mirrors, and the chandeliers: these felt familiar and foreign. When he was alive, Henry had strolled along this hallway multiple times each day on his way to the gleaming wooden staircase, now coated with dust, and back again to his study, never imagining that the place he'd once called home would become his place of eternal unrest, one he'd haunt until...until when?

Forever, Henry thought with a jolt as he trailed the Singing Sanguisuge, the permanence of his situation finally "dawning" on him as Henry fully realized for the first time that he was now exactly the same as Kellen.

"go this way and that way, go this way and that way. Did you ever see a vampire go this way and...here we are," Kellen finished abruptly, giving Henry a hard shove past the threshold.

Henry started to exclaim, "What the fuck is this?" but caught himself, stunned and aghast at the sight. Maroon foil lined the walls, and black carpet with trails of blood covered the floor. A heavy bedstead ruled the center of the room, although its black curtains were torn from golden rings and lay scattered across the bed's rumpled black and red quilts. The sole light was a swaying flame atop a black candle on the nightstand. Dr. Gothart was standing in front of the toilet table, arranging items: two basins of water, soap, shaving knife, nail clippers, toothbrush, toothpowder, a bottle of bay rum, a stack of Turkish towels, an ivory comb and brush, and clear glass jars filled with water and...were those worms?

144

"What do you mean, 'What the fuck is this?'" Kellen mocked. "This room is…"

"I don't believe it," John said.

"Run, John, it's a trick!" Henry exclaimed, giving John a playful push. "They're staking us and preparing our bodies for burial! Finishing school? More like finishing us off!"

Kellen sighed. "You're half right, little larva. It's a 'refresher' course in basic body care."

"I don't need refreshing," Henry said, eyeing the items even more suspiciously as John rolled up his sleeves and gingerly flicked water across his face. "I bathe in moonlight, per our eminent doctor's orders, and consume plenty of hemoglobin for 'improving, beautifying, and preserving my complexion.'" He pinched and patted his cheeks. "See?"

"True, the blood keeps you fresh," Dr. Gothart said. "But by evening, decomposition has once again begun. So you also need to keep yourself clean or bacteria and flies will break down your tissues to the extent moonlight can't regenerate. Tonight you'll also wash away the remains of past slaughters and your own body waste from the time of death."

"Why?"

"We've established that," John said irritably as he gingerly slid the shaving knife down his cheek, paring away a layer of skin with the whiskers. "To look human and smell, somewhat, human."

"Why do I need to look and smell human?"

Kellen gave him a frustrated kick in the shin and raised a fist. Henry ducked; Kellen grabbed his hair and give it a vicious tug. "You're really not courting a host?"

"Highly unlikely."

"Your 'uncle' will eventually wish to see you," Dr. Gothart settled into the toilet chair and brought forth his pipe. "So you have no choice. You smell like the clothes you died in."

"Those are in the study. I changed into these before I took Anna to the parsonage."

"Why the leeches?" John asked, reaching for the comb, heedless of his oozing cheeks.

"Leeches?" Henry, curious, stepped closer. Sure enough, the glass jars held leeches, not worms. "I don't recall leeches as part of New York and Chicago's polite society, but perhaps the rules are different here at Simons Mansion."

"Leeches eat any dead skin that doesn't regenerate by moonlight," Dr. Gothart said.

"Let's go," Kellen prodded Henry to the toilet table. "Don't keep Dr. Parks waiting."

"What does Dr. Parks have to do with it?"

"He will inspect you," Dr. Gothart said. "Now hurry. You don't have all night."

"And change your clothes," Kellen ordered.

"Death's turning into a lot of trouble."

Kellen snorted. "You don't remember how to get dressed?"

"I can manage it."

Two hours later, the pallid debutantes, toilet complete and wardrobe refreshed, moved to the parlor, where Dr. Parks was drowsing in his chair, since the hour was nearly midnight, but he sprang up, fully alert, by the time the vampires presented themselves in front him, and Dr. Gothart had settled by the fire and lit his pipe.

"Martin, do you have your checklist?"

"I do."

John had chosen trousers striped in several shades of brown with a matching cutaway, single-breasted coat, along with white shirt and black vest, but they hung from his frame as if tailored for a man of greater breadth. His eyes were sunken, his cheeks had collapsed, his wizened skin was gouged red where John had misjudged the force of his shaving blade, and his once gleaming fair hair dangled sparse, stringy, and greasy. But it wasn't John's ghoulish appearance that delighted Henry, even though Henry knew he hardly looked better and most likely far worse since he scarcely applied himself to the grooming and even less to the dressing. It was the fact that the great, so full of himself John Simons, who once elevated himself onstage before thousands, now planted himself before a has-been vivisectionist, desperate for his approval.

Henry raised an eyebrow. "Checklist?"

"Yes," Dr. Parks said, turning a page in his notebook "I'll be inspecting you for body odor, flesh fragments, blood stains, sweat, and signs of decomposition."

146

John fared far better than Henry for he quickly dabbed smeared camphor under Dr. Park's nose ("That's cheating, John!" Henry had exclaimed), which masked any lingering death stench. John had also dutifully removed all signs of blood streaks and assorted grime, even ordering Kellen to cleanse any place John couldn't see or reach.

"Oh, hell no!" Kellen had exclaimed when they were upstairs, shaking his head and backing off. "No! No! No!"

But Dr. Gothart had underscored John's request with the threat of a whip to Kellen. So John happily stripped, spread his legs, and bent over the toilet table, to make the task easier for Kellen.

"I don't get paid enough for this," Kellen grumbled as he dutifully scrubbed a very tight space.

"That's your problem," John countered. "You negotiate the contracts."

Dr. Parks also docked John for some slight decomposition on his back, but that was from Kellen's garlic attack and not completely John's fault, Dr. Gothart decided.

"But spend less time at the piano and more under moonlight," Dr. Gothart admonished. "Or you'll be severely chastised next time."

Henry, in addition to stinking to low hell, was found to have three species of skin behind his ears, blood on his molars, and signs of decomposition in the perineum, which Henry said didn't trouble him because he "didn't give a fuck anyway."

"Get it?" Henry said, grinning as he hiked up his trousers.

No one else was laughing.

"So, full moon during a full moon?" Henry tried again as he tucked his shirt into his waistband. "That's the remedy, right?"

Dr. Parks snatched Henry's collar, pulled Henry close, and gave Henry a little shake, as one might shake a rambunctious puppy.

"You think you're so smart," Dr. Parks said quietly as he smacked Henry, first on one side of his face with the front of his hand and then on the other side with the back, while Henry tried to twist himself free. "Well, I'm fed up with it." He smacked Henry again. "Really fed up with it." He let go and boxed Henry's ears before Henry could jerk away. With a howl, Henry dropped to the ground and covered his ears, whimpering. Dr. Parks squatted in front of him. "Anytime you'd like a different existence, let me know. I'll have you quartered and disemboweled before you can say, 'Albert's my uncle.' He slapped Henry across the head. "Got it?"

"Kellen," Dr. Gothart said. "Set up the game, so we can dismiss them."

They played "Going to Jerusalem" to practice teleporttation, which Kellen won every time, both to his triumph and chagrin, while Dr. Gothart puffed, and Dr. Parks snored.

"This is terrible," Kellen said, dropping into a chair and pulling a cigar out of his pocket. "You'll never attain mastery this way."

"So you're giving up?" Henry asked, hopefully.

"Not at all," Kellen said smoothly. "But I must ponder the problem to devise a solution."

A few nights later, as John cut Henry's bonds, a shrill voice rang, "Here, ye! Here, ye! The Kellen Wechsler Finishing School for Young Vampires is called to order!"

Henry hit the ground with a thump and a crack. Dazed, he opened his eyes, wondering if he'd broken his neck and if that mattered. Before him was a giant carriage, yes, a carriage was in the basement, with Kellen sitting on the bench and holding a black snake of a whip. Instead of horses, John was already hitched to the right.

"Our first lesson in teleportation is about to begin." Kellen snapped his fingers, and Henry found himself on all fours, hitched next to John.

"I know you're weak, famished, and dried up for lack of blood," Kellen said. "But a hungry vampire makes a motivated student." He snapped his fingers again. A stick appeared in front of Henry. A rosy, but dead, baby dangled from it, rope tied firmly around its neck.

"The fuck!" Henry exclaimed as he glanced at John, but John also had a swinging baby inches from his face.

"They look scrumptious, don't they?" Kellen smacked his lips. "Unbaptized kiddies from 1967 Oklahoma. You'll have to run fast to catch them. Oh, and we're leaving by way of a tiny crack in the foundation, so quickly dissipate into mist so you don't shatter any bones. Giddyap!"

Kellen cracked the whips over their necks. Henry screamed, writhed, and charged through the wall, bruising his shoulders but otherwise with vaporous transformation complete. Although Henry often ran on all fours when pursing his prey, he'd never tasked his arms and legs beyond their superhuman abilities. But Kellen lashed at them as one possessed and spurred them to speeds that Henry, at least, couldn't execute without sustenance. The landscape, and even the baby, blurred to gray before Henry's keen eyes, and blood streamed into his eyes, and still Kellen thrashed them over and over and over and over again, until Henry's legs finally gave out, and he collapsed on the cold stone of the basement's hidden room. A drove of hares dropped in front of them, which he and John savagely devoured.

"Tsk, tsk," Kellen said. "You'll have to do much better than that. Class dismissed!" He snapped his fingers and was gone, along with the carriage and babies.

Henry dragged himself up the stairs after John, too exhausted to stand. He crept gingerly out the door onto the grounds, drinking what he could grab and hoping the blood of small mammals might sustain him through the day. Thus fortified, he crawled back down to the basement and up to the noose just as dawn was breaking.

Kellen gave them a night to rest up and kill before returning to play "carrot and stick" with them on the third night. This time, Henry and John did slightly better, having caught their prey, just as the Fisher Farm rooster crowed its morning bedtime call.

It continued that way for a couple of days. But Kellen's trick worked like a snake's charm. Their hunger drove Henry and John to impossible tempos until they could span miles and millenniums in mere moments.

"Here, ye! Here, ye! The Kellen Wechsler Finishing School for Young Vampires is called to order!" Kellen called from the back of the library. Tonight we will work on mind reading and hypnosis."

By now, their routine was set. Dr. Parks summarized the details of the class while Dr. Gothart smoked. John still displayed his authority by sitting behind the desk but Henry, still not taking the classes seriously but, at least, finding them amusing now, had moved from floor to wingback and cooperated with the current agenda.

On this particular night, the rosewood table held a square-shaped covered object. Its appearance was not due to Kellen's conjuring it with a snap of its fingers; no, it was set in place before Henry entered the room.

"Mindreading is nothing more than perceiving vibrations in the networks of neurons in the brains of the living and dying," Dr. Parks explained. "Learning to read minds is like learning to read text on a page. You mastered each individual letter and then their phonetic sounds, which led you to decode the words. When you read a book or newspaper, you no longer think about the process; it's become automatic to you. In due time, so will this reading of minds. So in order read minds, you need lessons in deciphering electrical impulses in order to 'read' what another is thinking."

"Unfortunately," Dr. Gothart interjected, "this is one skill you will learn mostly on your own."

"Why?" Henry asked.

"Because Dr. Parks and I are the only humans that know you're now vampires," Dr. Gothart said. "And we can hide our thoughts behind mental doors."

"But we can still play parlor games with them," Dr. Parks said. "Think of a color, a number; button, button; hide the thimble: things like that."

"But first..." Dt. Gothart said, rising.

Pipe in hand, Dr. Gothart walked to the little table and removed the cover, revealing a tall wooden box with several glass dials on its front in various sizes, four coils in the center, and a metal stylus hanging off a hook to one side.

"John, come here," Dr. Gothart said. "Kellen bring a chair."

A look of distrust passed over John's face. "Why?"

"To help you hear the vibrations."

For a long moment, John didn't move. Then he sprang up, briskly crossed the room, and settled into the chair. Dr. Gothart picked up the rod and pushed it through John's temple. John's face immediately lit up, and Henry sat up and leaned forward.

"That's incredible," John murmured.

"What do you hear, John?" Henry asked.

"Clicking."

"More specifically, electrical subvocals," Dr. Gothart said. "Each click and combinations of clicks correspond to pre-thoughts."

The expression of John's face approached one of near rapture. Dr. Gothart leaned in.

"It's like music, eh?" he asked. "Notes become chords become symphony. Clicks become thoughts become..."

"Control," John said with most assurance Henry'd heard from him since their turning. "Absolute control."

Dr. Gothart turned slightly to Henry. "Try it?"

Curiosity overcoming snarky, Henry submitted to the rod. It pierced his skin, which caused no pain, just pressure, but Dr. Gothart was persistent, and the probe easily slid into his brain. The sounds it produced were indeed clicks, much like a telegraph machine might make if it was part tropical bird.

After a few moments, the pressure released, and Dr. Gothart was hanging up the pen.

"You will need 'reading' lessons," he said. "But the machine will assist you until you sense the sounds on your own."

Before too long, Henry, as well as John, could interpret enough rudimentary sounds as to practice their newly acquired skills through games originally played by chance, such as "hunt the thimble" and "twenty questions." They also learned that "dream penetration" was merely a more sophisticated form of the same expertise.

"Instead of 'reading' the thoughts, you're simply reading the impressions of very fast electrical activity in the brain while the dreamer is asleep," Dr. Gothart explained. "Practice before you eat. Watch the victim sleep. Sense the vibrations. This will also help you with shapeshifting."

"How?" Henry asked.

"Because shapeshifting uses the power of illusion and hypnosis. You are dead. You have a corpse form. But you can leave the corpse form and travel by spirit, assuming another form that you let others see. It's a type of hypnosis."

"Dr. Gothart is right," Kellen said. "You've done well with mist, such as passing through walls to feed. Let's try some other shapes."

Soon Henry the vampire bat was creeping down the wall toward Kellen the wolf, who loped around the room, pausing to sniff the air, pretending he didn't see Henry, who trod easily and stealthily on his toes, hopping behind a chair whenever Kellen turned around or growled. The moment Henry landed on Kellen's ear, Kellen gave a brisk shake and knocked Henry to the ground, which caused everyone to laugh, even John.

"Ow!" Henry cried, sitting up in his real self and rubbing his head.

Dr. Parks jotted a few more words, yawned behind his hand, and then looked up. "John, your turn."

John didn't move.

"Go on, John," Henry said, now standing and pouring himself a goblet of blood, of which he took a sip with a loud smack. "It's fun. You can even change into your father and let Kellen slaughter him for pretend."

Kellen scowled. "Shapeshifting into a person take extreme skill and experience. Even I haven't mastered that one yet."

"Nor shall we tonight," Dr. Parks said, rising and swallowing the last of his Bordeaux. "It's after midnight. I'm going to bed."

Over the next several classes, Henry and John practiced other skills, such as the safe lighting and carrying a single candle. They then graduated to oil lamps, candelabras, and finally, the most sophisticated "fire" task of them all: starting and maintaining a fire in the fireplace. They also made progress with food, eventually consuming entire mice and spiders with no ill-effects, and then moving onward to a little beef, a little potato, a little wine, a little bacon, a little bread.

Sunlight, they learned, was for later or so Dr. Gothart explained one night when Dr. Parks was absent, due to an "emergency," Dr. Gothart said. To tolerate sunlight, vampires needed to "age" or "ripen," he said.

"It's because you, as deceased, are bereft of bodily fluids," Dr. Gothart explained. "You are dried out and dusty. Exposure to sunlight quickens the decaying process. An older and more experienced vampire retains a bit of "plumpness" from decades of bloodsucking, which provides the ability to withstand the ravages of bright light in small doses, A vampire that is

152

currently being "hosted" has that ability, too, so I encourage you to tag that host as soon as possible. Even if a vampire like you," Dr. Gothart pointed his pipe at Henry, "that just wants to loaf all day and feast by night, the ability to withstand a bit of sunlight is to your advantage, in the event your final resting place is discovered, or you must do a 'day challenge' to 'prove' your humanity."

"Then why do holy items burn the skin?" John asked.

"Because they are infused with the 'energy' of eternal life, as opposed to the energy of eternal unrest. Life always trumps death. Even demons understand this. Again, the closer you grow to life, the greater your ability to handle these items will become."

Kellen lit a cigar and leaned back. "John, be patient."

"I'm scheduled to play Mass at Notre Dame when we go to Paris in September, remember?"

"John," Dr. Gothart said. "You'll play. Complain that you're cold and wear gloves except when you're actually at the piano. You can practice dipping those gloved fingers into holy water or touching sacred relics in the weeks leading up to it. Experiment with attending Mass."

"What about taking Communion?"

"I don't advise it under any circumstances until you are fully human," Dr. Gothart said. "Eucharist will burn right through your tongue, mouth, throat, and stomach."

"I understand," John said.

CHAPTER SEVENTEEN: IN WHICH A DISCOURSE ARISES BETWEEN DR. PARKS AND LITTLE MARIE

ll nights are dark, but some nights are darker than others.

Like Room 27 after Lillian and Milton left and Dr. Parks came and never went.

George had slept through Dr. Parks' evening exam, and he did not wake for medicine or nourishment. After Isabella roused enough to shut the door behind the guests, she took two weaving steps toward the bed, wavered, and then staggered back to Marie's cot, where she immediately passed out.

Dr. Parks made no move to leave; he offered to send for another cot. Marie declined his offer; she offered him wine.

And he declined her offer of comfort, too.

So they sat and silently passed the night, Marie on George's right, and Dr. Parks on the right side of Marie.

As the Arnold and Dent traveling clock ticked off the minutes, Isabella never so much as twitched, worn-out from many, many days of worry and care for George. So Marie stayed by her papa and held his hand while Death's shadow lengthened and deepened in blackness, and George's spirit grew fainter. She now understood the necessity of belief in God: to bar Death's ultimate victory.

For the Grim Reaper stood ready with his scythe, and he cast a wide veil over their hope, even though they'd put their whole strength at keeping George Clare on the green side of life. Death came for souls, that's the nature and purpose of Death, and once Death entered a room, it would not leave without its harvest. All the world's stores of bismuth and water could not vanquish Death when Death was determined to take.

As Isabella had intimated, Marie had witnessed plenty of deaths: shootings, stabbings, explosions, and fires. The Death Marie knew was the Death that suddenly appeared and just as suddenly left with its spoils.

But she had never witnessed the gradual taking of a soul, of Death at its leisure, plucking away a person strand by strand. Looking back, she recognized Death's hand where she had previously missed it: every scoop narrowly missed by someone faster, healthier, and more connected; every story filed too late, same reasons. Even if Dr. Parks and his bismuth cured her papa's stomach affliction, neither could revive the flame of his ambition. The man who reported unvarnished truth now called compromise The Dream. Who now could trust his judgment?

"Dr. Parks, the hour is late," Marie murmured, still contemplating the wan, unmoving figure on the bed, her little warm hand curled loosely around her papa's cooler one, wondering when the reaper might complete its harvest. An hour? Two days? "Why not go home?"

"He's a sick man."

"He's a brilliant man."

"Who's chained his family to an illusion he cannot satisfy."

"You do not understand my papa." Marie met his judgmental stare with an almost defiant one of her own. "He is the paralyzed man lying by the pool." Her vision blurred, and she averted her gaze. "He sees when the angel stirs the water, but he has no one to carry him in."

She sensed Dr. Parks' incredulity; she heard marvel in his voice as he said, "Insightful speech from a child."

Marie shrugged, and the wave passed. "When one lives in a such a situation, one observes much. But of what use is insight? Grandpapa's inheritance ran out, and we have no more resources to chase The Dream."

"You've lived off an inheritance all these years?"

"Mama is…was…a very wealthy woman. And occasionally Papa was paid for his efforts."

"Your father is indeed fortunate to have a family who supports his dreams."

Marie faced him, puzzled. "Don't all families support the dreams of their own?

"No." His face hardened. This time, Dr. Parks turned aside. "No, Marie, they do not."

She studied the pallid face of the man who meant the world to her, the man slipping away from her, like sand through her fingers at Ocean Grove.

"What pitiful families," Marie finally said, only half-aware of her remark.

For a long while, neither spoke. Marie watched the irregular rising and falling of her papa's chest and listened to the sound of her mama's barely audible snore and the ticking of the Arnold and Dent travelling clock.

Abruptly, Dr. Parks broke their silence.

"I knew a man once, Marie, who said to his parents, 'Give me your resources, so I can study hard, make you proud, and care for you in old age.' Because they loved their son, they gladly sold all their possessions to further his dream. But because they did not understand their son, they did not understand his arduous labors. And so they disowned this beloved son and moved far away, requesting he not contact them ever again."

Marie glanced up at him, but he was leaning forward, eyes narrowed and fixed on nothing, as he softly cracked his knuckles.

"Did he squander their assets?" she asked.

Dr. Parks leaned back in the chair and sighed, a rather irritable sigh, it seemed to her. "No, Marie. He toiled relentlessly in his work, work that would astound the world if they comprehended it. And now, the son is well able to care for his parents, to repay all the kindness they bestowed on him, especially since the father is ill and requires advanced care. But they've spurned his advances, content to live apart. And so, the son found a companion, but the companion also left him. So now the son lives alone, miserably and in rejection."

Marie sat quietly a moment, pondering his words.

"Dr. Parks, it seems to me the son should go to his parents and say, 'Father, Mother, I have sinned against heaven, and before thee and am no more worthy to be called thy son.'"

He stopped cracking. "But the son has not sinned! Why should he debase himself when he's done no wrong?"

"But Dr. Parks, he has done wrong. He has disrespected his parents' wishes for him. He should acknowledge that he is not worthy to be called their son, for he is not."

"So he should abandon his calling, a lifetime of astounding works?"

Marie shook her head. "No, the son must be true to himself. But he should also beg his father and mother's forgiveness for not being the son they wanted. If they are true Christian folk, they will be moved to pity, bestow forgiveness, and once again open their hearts to him."

The word "hearts" drew Marie's gaze to George's chest, where breaths came slowly, weakly, and too far apart. "He will die without more blood, won't he, Doctor?"

Dr. Parks said nothing.

Marie traced her thumb over George's cool, pale one. "But even with blood, his Dream has died. Is it fair that he should live when his Dream cannot? What then, would life be to him? Should a man dead to himself struggle to stay dead?" She looked pointedly at Dr. Parks. "Would it be kinder to allow him rest?

"Marie, try not to be negative..."

Suddenly a light flashed in eyes, and he jumped up. His face was flushed, and he beamed, as if he'd drunk too much wine.

"Marie, despite your youth, you are wise indeed. We shall restore your father's physical health. And then we'll work on that dream."

CHAPTER EIGHTEEN: BAD FRUIT

he second John cut the bonds, Henry heard, "Here ye! Here ye! The Kellen Wechsler Finishing School for Young Vampires is called to order!"

Henry hit the floor flat on his back and blinked. Kellen stood over him, dressed in a cleaned and pressed black suit with a fresh rose at the lapel. A pair of round dark spectacles perched on his nose, and he carried a leather crop and a brass megaphone.

"Tonight is very special night, the night of our first 'practicum scholarum.' So quickly attack your people. Raise their blood vessels and fill yours well! Drain your appetites, for tonight; oh, tonight! Uncle Kellen is treating you to a feast you won't soon forget!"

Kellen slid his shiny boot top under Henry's ribs and flipped him onto his belly as a disagreeable boy might flip a cockroach before crushing it. Scattered victims with twisted, broken limbs covered the floor and moaned in terror as Kellen kicked them closer to Henry, singing:

> *Little Tom TU-cker*
> *Sings for his SUP-per.*
> *What shall we give him?*
> *A vein full of blood, mmmmmmmmmmmmmmmm...*

Henry ravenously tore into one body after another. Kellen squatted on Henry's death chair, like a frog preparing to catch flies, and urged Henry and John to hurry with rude, sarcastic remarks: "Come on, eat up!" "Don't let anyone go to waste!" "This will help you grow big and strong!" and "Tastes just like chicken!"

After they finished off the last person, Kellen announced, "Party time!" Then he struck them with his crop and struck again and again, driving them up the basement stairs and through the hall to the main staircase, where John coolly picked up stride and put distance between him and the crop master.

Henry trotted behind him, taking the steps two at a time.

"He's annoying as fuck," Henry puffed. "Why do you listen to him?"

"Because he always delivers," John tossed back as he reached the landing and turned right. "Death suits slimy slugs like you, so stay dead. Dealing with Kellen is part of the path to re-life."

"Right you are, my money-making musical man!" Kellen called out as they hurried down the hall.

"You gave a poor imitation of it, John. I saw the way you tore into those jugulars. What a bloody mess you made. Here, look."

Henry grabbed John's arm as he whipped out a grimy handkerchief and swiped John's cheek. "Dear, dear, so untidy."

John flung Henry off. Henry off. Henry fell backwards into Kellen, who roughly pushed him forward.

"Boys! Boy! Stop this roughhousing or Uncle Kellen will whip you, and I mean whip! Now hurry! The moon is high, and our feast is nigh!"

"We just ate," Henry complained, feeling as if he'd puke blood and guts if he ingested another corpuscle.

"Well, you're going to eat again," Kellen leaped onto the wide windowsill and gestured to the toilet table, still in disarray from the previous lesson, with bloodied towels and soiled clothing strewn across the carpet. "That's why you ate first. We're taking a school outing to practice your 'life' skills. The basins are refilled with fresh water and, John, Henry is right. You're a bloody mess. Clean up!"

Reluctantly, Henry stripped off his grimy, slimy finery, the same clothes from his first exercise in performing his ablutions, when he and John processed before Dr. Parks to await judgment. Then he plodded to the toilet table and started splashing cool water onto his colder face with slow, hesitant splashes. He didn't want to go anywhere with Kellen, and he certainly didn't want to practice "life skills." He'd made it plain and clear that he wasn't returning to life, that he liked being not just a "slimy slug" but a grimy one, too, and that he wasn't interested in vampire finishing schools. Yet however assiduously he tried to avoid it, Henry couldn't resist the compulsion to attend; he wondered from whence that compulsion came; and he shuddered at the punishment awaiting him should he refuse.

As Henry grabbed the bar of castile soap, Kellen began to sing.

> *This is the way we wash our face,*
> *Wash our face,*
> *Wash our face.*
> *This is the way we wash blood from our face*
> *This cold and frosty evening*

Remembering how he failed to pass Dr. Parks' inspection, Henry carefully rubbed the washrag behind his ears and between his legs, scowling at his spineless acquiescence to this useless exercise as the rag turned from white to red. John was already untangling the knots from his hair. Henry had just picked up his own comb when Kellen launched into verse number two:

> *This is the way we comb our hair,*
> *Comb our hair,*
> *Comb our hair.*
> *It's impolite to save bugs that do bite.*
> *So comb them right out of your hair.*

"I'm going to stake him," John said as he unscrewed the jar of tooth powder.

Henry pitched the comb over his shoulder and reached for his toothbrush. "Hard to stake something that teleports faster than you."

John narrowed his eyes, dipped his brush, and Kellen sang out as John opened his mouth.

> *This is the way we scrub our fangs,*
> *Scrub our fangs,*
> *Scrub our fangs*
> *We don't want our breath to smell of fresh death*
> *And cause any mortal...*

"Shut up!"

160

Kellen stuck his tongue out at John, who opened the wardrobe door with a bang. Henry, toilet complete, headed for the door.

This is the way we put on clean clothes,
Put on clean clothes.
Put on clean clothes
We shan't smell like shit not one little bit...OW!

Henry whirled around. Kellen was lying on the ground struggling against John's foot on his chest as he futilely swung his crop.

"Behave!" John growled.

"Fine!" Kellen retorted. "Now let me up!"

Henry trudged all the way to his room. Except for shedding his garments twice in the last few months, he had not "se promener tout nu" since he'd died, so he gave himself a quick look, more out of curiosity than any concern for his appearance. Naturally, he looked gaunt, but "gaunt" didn't quite summarize the appearance of his frame. Every bone – hand bones, rib bones, leg bones, toe bones – pressed through his wrinkled white skin like bas-relief. His penis had shriveled, and his scrotum had deflated, but his belly, due to his recent feast in the basement, was hard and distended. Yet with the wasting of his body came a restless, unearthly energy and a keenness of senses. Although not one light shone in Simons Mansion tonight, Henry perceived each object more clearly than if someone had fully turned up the gas; he heard the scuffling of carpet beetles and the tapping of spiders behind the walls. He smelled the excrement on his "hanging" clothes that still lay on his study floor, and the field mice in the scullery. His "frail" hands might fumble with buttons, but he could snap a collar bone as if it were a twig.

He paused in the doorway, annoyed with himself for not telling Kellen to fuck off and irked at the weird post-death umbilical cord attaching him to John, shackling their fates, and obliging him to cooperate when he'd rather vegetate. He surveyed the scores of crates and trunks, peering through the wood to quickly discern what items lay folded where, and then mentally composing a checklist for tonight's eveningwear. Let's see: starched white linen shirt with ruffled cuffs and white collar; sapphire blue silk necktie; gray paisley waistcoat; black wool trousers with white pinstripes; black frock coat; gold cuff links, shirt studs, and ring, although not the gold heirloom ring he'd discarded that first night; wearing *that* in public would be plain stupid. As he layered garments over his corpse, buttoning, snapping, tying, clasping, Henry decided the whole business of grooming and dressing wasn't worth the effort and wondered why he'd ever spent so much time engaged in it.

When he completed the task, because, yes, it was most definitely as task, Henry checked his appearance in the full-length looking glass, swerving from side to side, impressed at how handsomely human he looked, especially with his face scrubbed and shaved, and his hair washed and combed into place. The earlier glut of blood had swelled his tissues quite nicely. It gave a live-ish tinge to his face and allowed a reasonable pre-mortum fit of his clothes, an unexpected surprise after noting his skeletal nudity.

He nodded and smiled at his reflection.

"I'd eat me," Henry said aloud.

"We can do better than that!" Kellen purred in his ear.

Kellen snapped his fingers, and they were standing beside a carriage at the rear of John's estate, beyond the servant's cottage, near the woods, with Kellen already crooning:

When, what to my wondering eyes should appear,
But a hellbent old coach and eight racketeers
With a centuries' old driver, so lively and quick,
You *knew in a moment I might be Old Nick.*

Someone had hitched a team of eight twitching, gurgling, gargoyles to the coach, and they writhed and strained against the reins, their eyes rolling white into their sockets, and their blackened, forked tongues lolling from their mouths. The carriage itself gleamed crimson and black; and its golden embellishments – pentagrams along with the numerals 666 – glinted in the darkness.

The hell?

Kellen opened the carriage door and chanted:

More rapid than demons my workhorses came,

And I whistled, and shouted, and call'd them by name:
"Now, Mammon! Now, Moloch! Now, Lilith, and Legion!
"On, Belial! On, Baal! On, Azazel and Abaddon-gion!

"Messiers Simons and Matthews, step right up, step right in," Kellen bowed low with a swooping gesture. "Our celebration awaits!"

Henry glanced uneasily at John, who shrugged and readily climbed inside. A strong hand grabbed Henry at his collar, raised him off the ground, and dumped him next to John; Kellen slammed the door, rocking the coach. Henry bolted up, retrieved his hat, which had tumbled near John's crotch, and scooted to the edge of the cushioned bench. John shifted his weight, and Henry noted a slight apprehension in John's eyes. Good. So much for John's confident proclamation of "Kellen is the Way, the Truth, and the Life," blah, blah, blah.

Kellen hopped onto the driver seat and punctuated each syllable with wild lashings of the "horses."

"Pay heed to my crop! Don't ignore my shrill call!
"Now flash away! Flash away! Flash away all!"

They shrieked; oh, how those "horses" shrieked! Even John started at the sound, although John didn't start as hard Henry did. Henry's start was a violent sort of starting, as if he were having an epileptic fit. Even dead, Henry had never heard such high-pitched, reverberating shrieks, shrieks that ended in a prolonged and deafening screech and a sudden upward lurch of the coach as it soared into the black, misty air.

Kellen, the provoking bastard, continued to sing:

Over the river, and through the wood,
To an old brauhaus we go;
Our guide knows the way to keep us at bay
From the ones we used to know-oh!

Henry tugged on the curtain, but it wouldn't budge, as if held into place by an invisible hand, one with the strength of a thousand dead men. Or so the alive Henry had once written in "Carter Jones and the Sunset Ghost."

Over the river, and through the wood —
Oh, how the whip strikes blows!
It stings ours toes and bites ours nose
As over the ground we go.

And then suddenly, Henry remembered another meeting, another dinner, back when Henry still esteemed life and honor.

"A toast," John had whispered that night as he held his glass high. "To prosperity." With an unearthly gleam in his pale eyes, John had tapped his glass against Henry's. "For the blood, my friend, is the life."
"John, thank you for the offer, but I must refuse."

I refused, Henry thought bitterly. I refused to play Faust and I still wound up here.

Over the river, and through the wood—
And straight through the barnyard gate,
Get us untied; we'll hurry inside
For food piled high on a plate!

On and on and on they rode, and on and on and on and on and on, through mutterings and screamings first described by Dante:

Various tongues,
Horrible languages, outcries of woe,
Accents of anger, voices deep and hoarse,
With hands together smote that swell'd the sounds,
Made up a tumult, that forever whirls
Round through that air with solid darkness stain'd,

Where had his end begun? With the white kitten that had stumped him and his first editor, Horace Fuller, for weeks? Or had his end originated with the storm?

"It was the storm, Henry," Brumfeldt had babbled. "The storm frightened the horses and overturned the cart before they

turned on their occupants, and then, well… it's unfortunate, but it does happen. At any rate they will spend the night here, as it's impossible to travel tonight, and in the morning, we'll wire for transport and send them on their way."

Maybe his end had begun in eyes as green-blue of Munsonville's shore and as eternal as its depths, eyes replete with magic and mystery, the foam of an agitated sea, the beacon of vivid imagination during stormy seasons, the ebbing and flowing of wistful dreams…

Had his end begun in Bryony's eyes?

Over the river, and through the wood—
Now the innkeeper's cap I spy!
We want meat on a bun! Is the pudding done?
Hurrah for the possum pie!

"I don't give a fuck for possum pie!" Henry shouted, more irritated with himself now than with Kellen.

The coach jolted to a stop. The door flew open, and Kellen was standing beside it, pointing ahead to a stone roundhouse with a thatched roof, alone in the middle of a field of thistles. The windows glowed tangerine, the only illumination, thankfully, in the dark moonless night, for the dead travel best under the cover of blackness. Still, how brightly did those lamps burn? Enough to accentuate their pallid complexions and melt their flesh?

"Step this way, gentlemen – yes, you are gentlemen tonight," Kellen said, and his tone was low and as smooth as butter. "Our feast awaits!"

Head high, Kellen sauntered across the grass to the ghostly pumpkin of a building with John tagging behind him. Henry lagged, partly from consternation, partly from indifference, and mostly because he loathed Kellen, loathed Kellen's classes, loathed this push toward rehumanity, and, quite frankly, had reached the end of his patience with the lot of it. If he couldn't stay dead, then Henry just wanted to kill and go belly down. But, no, he was out in the middle of a wasteland with creatures he hated, and he would soon enter an abode full of humans under the expectation he would eat their food and not them.

All too soon, Henry passed through the arched door and into the jack-o-lantern. The entire room emanated an apricot radiance. A cottony fungus covered the walls; simple wooden blocks served as tables and benches. Kellen led them to a table in the back and bade them to sit: Henry first, Kellen next, and John across from them both.

Kellen snapped his fingers, and a waiter appeared with a bottle of Blaufränkisch wine and three pewter goblets. He had a pointed face with a dog's nose, a rounded body with a humped back, and long hands like flippers. He pulled a rusted corkscrew from his pocket, which Kellen snatched from his hand.

"Thank you, Hertwig," Kellen said. "Tonight is my treat. Allow me to pour."

Hertwig bowed. "Very good, sir. Shall I bring the usual?"

"Yes, the usual."

"Usual?" Henry asked after Hertwig departed, as in left their table, not dearly departed.

Kellen dropped his voice. "Yes, that's why I chose this...place. They know me here, and the dishes are very, shall I say, friendly to your current state."

He stabbed the silver worm into the cork and turned the handle, a goat with slanted eyes. Then Kellen trickled a half-inch of Blaufränkisch into each glass as he monitored the room. As soon as he set the bottle down, Kellen swiftly dove into his overcoat for a flask and just as swiftly topped off the wine with blood.

John stared at his glass with a thoughtful expression.

"That is why we ate first," he murmured.

"Right you are, my magnetically mysterious musician," Kellen whispered with exuberance. "I've not only prepared your stomachs, I've considered your diets in your menu selections tonight, all while keeping other diners safe from your 'charms' and you safe from hunger usurping your control. So drink slowly – but drink up!"

John took a cautious sip, slowly swallowed it, and then took an assured sip. Henry, not as easily swayed, raised his glass and sniffed. The blackberries, currants, and alcohol, especially, stung his nostrils and flooded his brain in an unsettling, drowsy way, but the glass contained no more wine than he'd drunk in class. He touched the rim to his lips and allowed a small taste.

"What happens when your stash runs dry?" Henry asked, eyeing the bottle of Blaufränkisch, which was still fairly full.

With a sly look, Kellen opened his coat an inch. The inside was lined with pockets, and each pocket held a flask. Henry started to exclaim, but Kellen raised a claw.

"Shhh," he cautioned, his coal eyes glimmering. "Uncle Kellen thinks of everything."

Henry relaxed, a little. As they nursed the "wine," the small party practiced idle banter by discussing the weather, but even a thorough deliberation didn't take long. The view was dark; the air was cool; and no one could think of more to add. So John turned the topic to John's upcoming European tour, and Kellen happily latched onto it, as he snapped his fingers to produce a thickly folded itinerary. Henry yawned behind his hand (another lesson in etiquette learned) and experimented with small sips.

Hertwig arrived with a tureen of congealed blood. Kellen immediately grabbed the ladle and plopped the glop into their bowls. Even the stink of cloves, onions, and peppers didn't mask the mouth-watering aroma of pig blood.

"What is it?" John asked, suspiciously.

"Schwarzsauer," Kellen said, reaching for his spoon. "Blood soup. With pig's feet and snouts."

Scattered victims with twisted, broken limbs moaned in terror around him as Kellen kicked them closer to Henry, singing...Henry tore into body after body after body...

The memory from earlier this evening felt distant, and Henry's thinking felt sluggish. How far had they passed through time? His hunger flared at the sight and smell of that soup, so — a great deal of time?

Henry picked up his spoon and skimmed it across the surface, which quivered at his touch. John did likewise; astonishment spread across his face at the first taste.

"This is quite good," John said, dipping his spoon again and then again.

"I knew you'd like it." Kellen smirked as he refilled his bowl and then Henry's.

Hertwig brought more courses. Henry detected flour, bacon, butter, and onions, and more pig blood, which was lighter, sweeter, and not as satisfying as human blood but not completely disagreeable to the palate.

"Blutwurst," Kellen set a sausage link onto each of their plates. "And Hofer Schwaaß or Gebackenes Blut."

This "Hofer" bit was a square of gelatinous blood, crispy on top. Lastly, Kellen set a reddish brown "blood roll" on their plate.

Henry, using his knife and fork, an act that didn't win him any "brownie points" since Kellen and John had returned to their, tête-à-tête, cut into a blutwurst, and brought a morsel to his nose. Savory and coppery. He nibbled the edge. Sweet and metallic. He popped the bit into his mouth and chewed. A texture not unlike human intestines. Somewhat delicious. He eyed the Hofer square. Was this a good dish or a bad dish? Emboldened, Henry slid his fork through the square and eased the tiny chunk past his lips. Hemoglobin with a crunch. He pinched a bit of the roll. Chewy with a piquant bloodiness that compensated for the disgusting wheat and yeast.

Kellen and John continued reviewing John's concert schedule, starting with John's return to Carnegie Hall in mid-May. Bored, Henry studied the other patrons as he dined and not one of them tempted him. Neither did they shoot uneasy glances at the trio against the back wall, despite their formal dress. For these other customers wore baggy, loose-fitting layers, with caps for the men and wimples for the women. This crowed ate and drank and chattered and sang, with glasses raised high and with loudness and gusto. For the first time since he'd died, Henry mingled with the living, and the living accepted him as one of their own. He found the concept interesting, and one he digested with the meal, enjoying the mellow haze. As the portions dwindled, and Henry filled to bursting, he debated if he really wanted that last sausage and decided he did.

But as he stretched out his fork, Henry noticed how languidly he performed that motion, and it felt vaguely familiar, a sensation he'd experienced in life, when he'd drunk one too many glasses of wine.

Wine.

Henry scanned the table. Empty bottles of Blaufränkisch lay on their sides next to empty food platters, stacked at least a foot high. He saw the crumbs and greasy smears on his plate and on John's, but not Kellen's – no, Kellen's plate was still filled with food. A hard shudder tore through Henry, and he gagged as the first wave of nausea passed over John. Kellen grabbed their hands with his left, snapped with his right, and instantly they were crouched on the Simons estate, hurling blood and bacon over the verdure. Blood shot from Henry's mouth with projectile force, over and over and still over again, but blood and bits also erupted from his nose, ears, eyeballs – out every orifice and pore of his skin – and still he vomited, with chattering teeth and racking spasms.

In the midst of his fog, Henry glimpsed an agitated Dr. Gothart sprinting over the grounds. The doctor skidded to a stop, punching Kellen to the lumpy ground, where Kellen happily lay, rubbing his jaw and chortling.

"How dare you!" Dr. Gothart roared.

But Kellen was laughing hard now, laughing and pointing at Henry and John, who were still retching and spluttering.

"You said to train them," Kellen gasped out between guffaws. "They'll experience it at some point; they should know how to handle it. You yourself know blood doesn't always 'take.'"

"There's a difference between 'taking' and trickery! You set them up!"

"So what if I did? They deserved it, especially him," he jerked his head at Henry, "for stealing my pet." He sneered at John. "Take this as a warning. If you ever turn against me, I'll..."

Dr. Gothart cut him off with a kick to the jaw. "I'll punish you later. Dr. Parks needs my help with a medical emergency. Get them to the cellar now! Dawn's approaching! He kicked Kellen again. "Now!"

"All right, all right."

Henry's face fell into blood-slicked grass. Finally, the end was near.

But as soon as Dr. Gothart disappeared, Kellen grabbed their hair and dragged them over their mess and across the yard to the house, through the door, and over to the cellar steps, bumpity, bumpity, bumpity all the way down.

"Aw, it's hard to leave the party when you're not sleepy," Kellen cooed. "But Dr. Gothart said you must, so we must."

The stone floor scraped Henry's knees and elbows as Kellen hauled them around the passageways to the secret room, where dropped them, side by side. He snapped his fingers, and a herd of frightened, frozen-in-fear deer appeared, standing in formation, like soldiers headed to Hades.

"So you don't starve to death during the day. Come on! Drink up!"

But Henry could not raise his head. He could not open his mouth or even wiggle a finger. He was done.

"Here. Uncle Kellen will help you."

Kellen pierced the neck of the first victim and held John's face over the wound, massaging it so the blood flowed into his mouth, as tenderly as any nursing mother feeding her beloved babe, flinging each dehydrated deer hide past its comrades and into the corner the moment he emptied it. Then Kellen did the same for Henry. Kellen even set the knife in Henry's hand and closed Henry's fingers around its handle.

"There. And there!" Kellen moved Henry's fist up and down on John's leg a few times, stabbing him here and stabbing him there. "That should do it. Tonight's murder is complete. Now go up to your noose. It's way past your dead time. Look at John. See? Your much bigger ex-friend is already tucked under himself on the floor, dead to the world. If you want to be biting heads off tomorrow, you need your eternal rest."

Kellen hoisted Henry by his armpits and lugged him onto the chair. "That's it, there you go. You mustn't keep the nice noose waiting." He slipped the vines around Henry's neck. "See how soft the pink flowers are tonight – and the vines, how they long to wrap their tendrils around your neck and hold it close. That's it. Lay your head down; kick the chair and cares away."

Then Kellen snapped his fingers and a glittering jeweled throne appeared. He settled himself against the high back, crop in hand, and sang in a tranquilizing voice:

Rock-a-sick body
Flog it to stop.

When wild wind blows
Salvation will rock.
Then your neck breaks,
Your soul starts to fall.
And down,
down,
down,
down,
down,
down
          will
                    come
                         body...

SNAP!

Kellen was gone.

he sixty minutes between the second Dr. Parks shut the door behind him and the moment he reopened it was the longest, most tortuous in Marie's short life.

For despite the struggle to master her nameless fear, nameless because Marie held firm on not handing Death any additional power by giving fear an identity, a vague unease crept up her spine, and she alternated her gaze between her papa, her mama, and the apparition's scythe.

Alone.

She struggled against that fear alone. Although three occupied the room, only she knew it. Her mama and papa, while not actually dead, were dead to her, themselves, and each other; perhaps they were even dead to dreams. George breathed so faintly, he appeared not to breathe at all, and Isabella's light snoring had long since faded to hush.

Only the Arnold and Dent traveling clock made any sound, the clock and the deafening noises inside Marie's head. Her heart banged like a bass drum with an overly enthusiastic drummer at its command; her breath roared like the ocean in her ears; and her head buzzed with a thousand whispers; she sensed dark wisps slip into the walls. She sat alone in an eternal solitude, as if Dr. Parks had never occupied the room. She held the cold hand of her father and watched the easy movements of her mother's bodice. Nothing else existed; nothing else had ever existed.

But when Dr. Parks returned in the hour before dawn, he did not return alone. Just one glance at Dr. Parks' companion, and Marie immediately knew Death had an enemy, a force more robust, more sinister than Death had yet encountered, a force that smelled, not of brimstone, but of aromatic pipe tobacco.

"Miss Clare," Dr. Parks whispered with a sidelong glance at Isabella as he set his hat on the table. "Meet Dr. Edwin Gothart."

Marie knew the name. Dr. Gothart. The stories in The Times said he was the attending physician for Bryony Simons, the doctor present at Bryony's death and the death of her baby. but this was the first time she connected a being to the name. Dr. Parks, never Dr. Gothart, had always attended her papa.

Dr. Gothart had auburn mutton chops, thinning auburn hair, wire spectacles, round shoulders, and brown eyes flecked with green and ageless knowledge. A pipe of dark polished wood trimmed in gold peeked from the pocket of his wool overcoat like a familiar from the warlock's ceremonial robe. He set his hat next to Dr. Parks' and then unbuttoned his overcoat. Dr. Parks had his halfway off.

Then, without bothering to look at George, Dr. Gothart snapped open his case, selected a glass vial, and inserted a metal rod. He strode across the room, flipped up Isabella's skirt, and plunged the needle through her drawers and into her thigh; Marie screamed and bolted for the door.

But Dr. Parks barred it, with hands outstretched, like Christ on the cross. His gaze was not full of humility; it was fiercely determined.

"Stop," he said quietly but firmly. "If your mother interferes, your papa will die. It's just morphine. Sit."

She spun around. Dr. Gothart was arranging a copper cup and funnel, tubing, implements with sharp points, and a brown bottle on the nightstand. She looked back up at Dr. Parks, confused.

"A blood transfusion for my papa? But we have no donor."

Dr. Parks was already walking across the room, rolling up his sleeve.

Marie blinked. "You?"

He settled into one of the chairs near the bed and smiled genially at her. "And there are three that bear witness in earth, the spirit, and the water, and the blood: and these three agree in one. 1 John 5:8."

Dr. Gothart twisted the cap off the brown bottle and poured a little of the bottle's contents on a piece of cloth. He rubbed the cloth across the under portion of Dr. Parks' upper arm. He did the same to George's left forearm and all the sharp points of his instruments.

An oily sweetness, like syrup on wood tar, lingered in the air. Now Dr. Gothart was holding the needle that would pierce Dr. Parks' skin, so Dr. Parks could shed his blood for her papa so that her papa may live.

Soon Dr. Gothart was threading a tube into Dr. Parks' arm. Marie watched as Dr. Parks' blood seeped into the tube and toward the funnel. Dr. Gothart repeated the same on George, who did not cry out, not so much as a moan. The blood continued leaking through the tubing toward its destination, Dr. Gothart monitored the transfer of vitality from one man to the other with a stern expression.

Marie glanced at Isabella, sleeping soundly but snoring only lightly, which nearly made Marie laugh aloud. Even drugged, her mama's good breeding repelled her baser nature like oil to water.

Be ye therefore wise as serpents, and harmless as doves.

But the urge to even smile faded as quickly as it appeared. Her papa was dying, and the man her mama presently hated more than anyone in the world, yes, even more than Henry Matthews, was infusing the one substance in the world her mama didn't want inside her husband.

I have set before you life and death, blessing and cursing: therefore choose life.

Moses spoke thus to the Israelites who, after wandering in the wilderness for forty years, were preparing to finally enter The Promised Land. For years, she, her papa, and her mama had wandered from scoop to scoop in search of The Dream. Here, now, in Room 27, God was setting before them the way to life and death, the way to blessing and cursing. God was exhorting them to choose life. Marie peeped uncertainly at Isabella. She peeped even more uncertainly at Dr. Parks. One way led to George's death; one way led to George's life. But which was the right way? Which was the right life?

Honor thy father and thy mother: that thy days may be long upon the land which the Lord thy God giveth thee.

174

Honor thy mother? Or honor thy father?

Slowly, in fits and starts, Marie sidled across the room on trembling legs until she, somehow, reached Dr. Parks. She lay a timid hand on his other arm and stammered, "Will...will this help him?"

He was still smiling and looking at her with an earnestness that melted her heart. Was God giving her a sign? Or had the serpent smiled the same way to Eve as he whispered, "Ye shall surely not die."

"Marie," Dr. Parks said kindly but firmly. "Your papa has the most spirit I've ever seen in a man. That's one. I've infused him with water. That's two. All that's needed is more blood."

Her eyes burned with sudden tears; they darted to the man in the bed wavering between death and life and then back to the man in the chair, willing to his share own vital fluid with him. "You would give up your blood for my papa?"

Dr. Parks gave a little sigh, and his entire demeanor softened even more.

"You and your mama have bolstered his spirit. I've replenished the water, and ... and 'almost all things are by the law purged with blood; and without shedding of blood is no remission.'"

She gaped in wonder at his queer response and Biblical acumen; she had no other reply.

He smiled again. "For the life of the flesh is in the blood: and I have given it to you upon the altar to make an atonement for your souls: for it is the blood that maketh an atonement for the soul."

Atonement for the soul.

Now Marie understood.

The battle in this room extended beyond her papa's physicality. They had fought, they all had fought, for a reward their imagination could scarcely conjure. Faulty perception had caused all the trouble.

How right, Marie thought, that this man, who understood healing on all its messy levels, should become her papa's blood brother.

"Because the blood..." Marie murmured aloud, lost in her musings.

"...is the life," Dr. Gothart finished.

Marie jerked up and met his stare.

And Dr. Gothart's eyes glowed like a cat's at night.

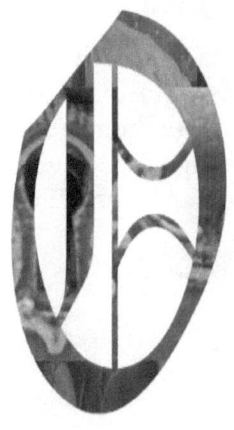ne plink.

That's all John heard.

One plink of one note.

But it was enough to make him pause, cold, blue hands hovering over the keys.

A second plink, lighter, followed the first followed it – and then a few more, each a successive stair-step higher than the last.

Pause.

Another two notes, a rest, and then a third, then a pause. More tinkles, a pause.

John smiled, hands still hovering. Anna, his Fountain of Life, had finally summoned him through Bryony's music box.

The notes trilled up and away, a melody as viney as the woman for whom he'd composed it. With a harsh, almost happy chuckle, the first twinge of pleasure since his death, John resumed his practice with renewed vibrancy; the room rang with his delight. He never doubted Anna would revere Bryony's music box, the box that enchanted Anna when Bryony was alive, but finally hearing those chimes solidified his resolve that Anna and no other was the one, the special daughter from his own Father of Lies, conceived before he'd invited Henry to sow his seed all over his estate.

"Astonishing. From New Haven, you say?"
"Yes. Can you transplant it?"
"Probably."
"And cross-breed it?"
"Definitely."

Bryony.

Not Bryony his bride but bryony a gift for his bride, the bryony vines from Granny Spencer, which once wound through his mother Lucetta, one of many plants Lucetta transplanted from his Granny's garden to her bedroom hothouse. John's father had destroyed Lucetta's plants, but John knew where to find the originals, in Granny's long forsaken, overgrown garden.

So when he asked Henry to crossbreed bryony, he meant the plant. Apparently, Henry had other ideas.

That thought birthed more thoughts, each one more heated than the last, simmering thoughts that grew hotter until they boiled out of him and into the keys; he banged them with the brutality of a sadistic overseer. But only his fingers received the punishment, an ache in those delicate bones that intensified each time his clawed hands struck.

Twice, Granny warned John. Twice, he missed it.

"Bryony!" Granny screeched, her nose touching his; her talons clawed into his neck as she spat, "Poison!"

Granny peered at the viney pattern and then knocked the clay cup to the ground, smashing it in a two-footed single stomp. "Out! Out! Out! Out!"

His fingers stomped in staccato bursts like demons cavorting around a bonfire, except the fire blazed within him, and WOULD NOT GO OUT!

The bryony weeds smothered Granny's garden after her death, yet did he heed it?

Did he?

DID HE?

Nooo, he wove them through his estate and set it to music. He carried it into his home and into his heart, where the venom, unhampered, reveled in its freedom and diffused, like a drop of blood in a glass of water.

"How lovely!" Bryony breathed as his metallic notes gushed from the box, each one crafted especially for her during those months of separation.

He plunged his hands over and again, up, down, dark notes hinting of shades and vipers, of brimstone and foaming blood and NOT the lyrical strains of pink blossoms and green vines that he'd composed for her and housed in a music box Henry constructed from cherrywood. He envisioned Henry

178

assembling it, polishing it, and painting it to resemble the bryony he'd crossbred for the Simons estate alone: green with tiny pink flowers, and then he envisioned Henry "sowing his seed."

Goddamn him!

She wrinkled her forehead. "I'm not certain I know that piece."

Third warning. Rule of threes.
Omne trium perfectum.

"You don't. I composed it just for you, as my wedding gift. We shall dance it together for the first time on Christmas Eve."

He yanked the gold pocket watch from his shirt pocket with a satisfying rip of the expensive linen. Huffing and panting, which he found strangely hilarious since he didn't breathe anymore, he studied its ivory face, black Roman numerals, and silver hands. He pushed a tiny button and released the same hypnotizing melody: *Bryony.*

Kellen had arranged the watchmaker in Switzerland who imprisoned the tune in a pocket watch for John.

Bryony didn't understand, not then, not ever.

Hypnotizing. *Same.*

With roar that reverberated throughout his hollow spirit, he pounded his fists across the keyboard and then slammed the lid and leaped to his feet, sweeping sheets of notations to the floor and tearing his garments and his long, stringy hair, the hair of a puppet, a marionette, who'd foolishly danced to the wrong tune.

He paced through the library, the music room, and back again, up and down the dusty carpet but nowhere else, desperate for solace and relief. He'd wait for the Fisher Farm cock to crow three times before he'd crawl out of his sanctuary. Not a second sooner. He kicked a chair leg as he passed it and then rammed the chair through the wall; he threw his head back and howled as he dropped to the floor, beating nothing, relentlessly swinging as someone should have flogged him when he announced his intentions to marry a weed.

Equally unyoked yielded...

"Our trunks are nearly packed. We leave in the morning."
Bryony calmly took another sip. "I'm not going."

...a marriage of missteps.

"Do me another favor, please, John."
"Which is?"
"Don't mention our 'trip' to Henry."

He jumped up and paced some more. He listened to her. Then he listened to Dr. Gothart. When he should have listened to...

"John why not give her a baby? That's what everyone woman wants."
"No baby."
"Well, she'll go mad with despondency if you don't address it. The isolation is affecting her mind."

So he took Dr. Gothart's advice.
And then so did Henry.
He paused at the Schwechten, tracing a gaunt finger through its burr walnut swirls as if noticing them for the first time. He and his piano: both well-played.
He paced some more, back and forth between the adjoining doors of the music room and library.
Yes, they played him well: his wife (two words that seared through him like a branding iron, and he paused, one hand on the wall, doubled in pain), and the snake who wormed into his house and into his wife.
Bryony would bind them for all eternity if John didn't cut the ties with a set of human scissors.
Plink.
Tonight, he was so grateful for the plink.

"I've missed you, Mr. Simons."
"Do we have an understanding, Miss Bryga Bednarczyk?"
"Indeed, sir."

180

"Then let's go."

The lapse with Bryga cost him thousands, although she did repay him by making a tasty first post-death meal. Tonight his money and her scheme stopped mattering, and it was all because the sounds of Bryony hadn't come from his piano.

A second plink, lighter, followed the first and then a few more, each a successive stair-step higher than the last.

Anna was "bone of his bones and flesh of his flesh," the one living creature on the planet comprised of his family dirt. He couldn't wait to reward her. He could wait to soil her more.

Another two notes, a rest, and then a third, then a pause. More tinkles, a pause. Then the music trilled up and away,

How swiftly teleportation works when one concentrates! There Anna was, on the other side of the glass in her Detroit home, smiling softly in sleep, still clutching the music box that still tinkled *Bryony*. Her blunt haircut spread across the pillow like strands of hay at the Holloway farm, where he'd worked during that summer of 1881, the summer he turned eighteen and received a post-graduate education that didn't hurt him enough – oh, how he still wanted to hurt Savannah!

straw-colored hair piled under a wide-brimmed straw hat...hazel eyes twinkled with amusement...held out her gloved hand...put her hands on his shoulders...raised her eyebrows...smiled, a half-smile of surprise and intrigue...grasped his face and eased it from side to side, as she bit her lower lip...dazzling in white linen, trimmed in tiny buttons and ruffles at the high collar and wrists...face framed by a few rebel tendrils from her regal pompadour...caressing a glass of burgundy wine...dreamy eyes...face softened...eyes brightened...grinned with girlish delight...leaned forward and motioned with her finger...moved aside his hair and brought her lips to his ear...hair tumbled down...with a rapturous smile...turned her face to the ceiling and closed her eyes...opened her eyes and looked at...placed a hand on his...brushing one of the thoroughbreds...shrugged and held out an apple...wrapped in charcoal blue and barely pink...beige ruffles at the collar, shoulders, wrists, hem, and down the middle...brushed away cascading hair...accepted the cup with one hand while yawning into the back of another...two hands around as she blissfully sipped....tracing gold lines with a finger...lost in reminiscing... cupped her hands and drank...stretched out in the grass, flung her arms above her head...a full deep melodious laugh...reached out and tweaked his cheek...crawled away on hands and knees... pressed the fruit between his lips...briefly parted her lips...quickly dismounted...rapidly unbuttoned her shirt... kicked off her boots...stepped out of her pants...twisting water from her hair...face in his hands...forcefully kissing...held her fast...entwined her fingers in his hair...threw a strong leg over his waist, and scooted closer...pointed out each item...tilted her head and smiled teasingly...mouth was full of mirth...leaned over the piano, wine glass in hand...mist in her eyes...pulled her tight and tasted salt...stirred, stretched, and smiled at him...playful smile...climbed to her knees and threw her arms around his neck...tossed her head...kissed her again, easing her back onto the bed...curled against him...a shadow crossed her face, and she said no more..

No more Savannah. He needed no more Savannah.

He would not drink from Anna tonight, he thought as he watched her sleep. But he would drink very soon.

Although the entire process of vampirism disgusted him, and would always disgust him, a wisp of intrigue stirred within him as he contemplated the blood coursing through Anna's body, so similar to the blood Henry spilled from him. He imagined the first lick, the first sips, its taste. Might he feel contentment, wholeness, the emotions his piano teased from him during life? He ran his tongue over his lips and pondered, wondered.

John couldn't control the compulsion to seek out and feast on the living when the sun went down. But he could control his choice of victims. He could control when and if and how and where and, even more importantly, who might "host" his reentry into life.

In the meantime, he had someone to kill, someone he'd waited and yearned to kill for an exceedingly long time...

He stared at the outline of the barns and the farmhouse, bound by ancient sycamores, against the midnight horizon of New Haven. Despite their age, they appeared sturdy and maintained, almost as if recently built.

"Well, well, what a surprise."
John turned at the woman's voice. Her straw-colored hair was piled under a wide-brimmed straw hat, which perfectly matched her blouse and neatly fitting trousers.
"I'm seeking the Widow Holloway."
The woman's hazel eyes twinkled with amusement.
"That would be I." She held out her gloved hand. "Savannah Holloway. And you are?"

He wafted around the empty barns, where he once dutifully scrubbed compartments and replaced hay and fed and bathed the thoroughbreds and made love to her for the first time, and nothing pricked up its ears at his wisp of cold.

As John was brushing Bella, Savannah appeared out of nowhere. "Would you like to ride her?"

He seeped past the farmhouse's walls, through the kitchen where he'd prepared scrambled eggs, flannel cakes with maple syrup, toast and butter, and newly-made applesauce; and into the dining room, where she presided over dinners like Helen of Troy with her hair tumbling about her shoulders; into the drawing room where he'd filled her mind with his music, and she'd slashed his heart with cool words and a banknote; and up the planed staircase, to her bedroom, where she...

"For God's sake, John!" Savannah kicked off her boots. "Why are you staring? I'm neither a mawkish schoolgirl nor a country maiden. I thought you could handle that fact."

Where was she hiding?
Why couldn't he find her?

A few nights later, John reappeared at Anna's window. Bryony's music box stayed near her as she slept and emanated the melody that outlived the woman that inspired it, which kept memories of Bryony replaying in his mind, too.

"John who was that woman?"
"Savannah Holloway."
"Why did you invite her?"
"Meaning is she essential to my career and was I ever intimate with her?"
"Are you still in love with her?
"I loathe her."
"Do you ever think of her?"
"When I think of Savannah, I think of ripping her limbs from their sockets, stripping her muscles fiber by fiber, and crushing her bones to powder."

He would find her. And her death would be no accident.

After a week, he came to Anna again and kept watch at her window through the smallest hours, gloating at her fretful sleep as he vanished.

He repeated the elusive act with greater frequency, not because the gong of the dinner bell or Anna's savory aromas tempted him, no matter how often she summoned him with his music. No, these visits were merely preparations for the banquet, the chopping of vegetables and whisking of roux, but each step inched him closer to the main course.

True, Anna frequently played the music box, especially at bedtime. But Anna must be more than willing, more than ready.

Anna must be welcoming and initiating.

Until then, he'd keep her on ice.

CHAPTER TWENTY-ONE: SABBATH DAY

atching someone ease back from the brink of death felt nearly as torturous as watching the approach.

Despite Marie's resolve to leash fear, anxiety whipped her all through January, although she tried to keep it cloaked for her mama's sake. The many weeks of constant agitation showed on Isabella, too. She never wavered in each of her caretaking duties; to Marie, Isabella had appeared to redouble her dedication. But Isabella's nerves were shattered to the point of collapse, and it showed in the languor of her movements and dullness of her eyes – except, that is, when Dr. Parks stepped through their threshold three times a day. Although Isabella never spoke to him anymore than necessary, and even then in flat speech, the wrath she harbored for him twisted her features into something so weird and hideous, Marie could scarcely recognize her. But a simmering pot filled to the brim will eventually boil into the flames; the question was not "if" but "when." Like the Greek goddess Adrestia, Isabella had become "she who cannot be escaped."

For even with the help of Dr. Parks' blood, George's recovery was painfully slow, and his body showed the ravages it had withstood as it now tried to repair them. He'd lost weight, quite a bit of weight, and his muscles had shrunk. Assisting with dressing or attempts to bathe himself in bed necessitated a nap and so did his pathetic efforts to stand on legs of shaking twigs. Once he tried shaving, but his hand trembled so violently that Isabella had persuaded him to give up the blade, a relief to Marie, who feared her papa would slice his jugular.

In the meantime, Dr. Parks prescribed leg and arm movements George could perform in bed to build up his strength. But even these proved taxing. With teeth tightly clenched, fingers clawed, and grunting and bearing down as if he had a stoppage, George struggled to lift his shriveled arm above his head, much less to hold it in place as Dr. Parks had instructed. More often than not, he arm dropped limply to the bed clothes before it completed its journey, with George breathing hard and sweating harder. He fared no better in raising his legs, one leg at time, to the level of his hips. Most exercises ending prematurely with George falling fast asleep.

Dr. Parks also sent a tall glass of egg-enriched milk on George's food tray at each meal and at bedtime to help George regain the lost weight. That proved particularly thorny for a man with no appetite; not even the choicest roast chicken or succulent side of beef tempted him, and he frequently nodded off in mid-chew, so he needed close monitoring lest he choke.

George also slept fitfully, had frequent nightmares, and complained about his eyes feeling "gritty" when he was awake. During periods of alertness, when George wasn't attempting to carry out his exercises or, at the very least, stay awake while Isabella fed him, George's moods vacillated between soaring with elation and thankfulness to the great God in heaven for this second chance at life and descending into a very dark despair that neither Isabella nor Marie could reach. On Valentine's Day, Dr. Parks provided another round of his blood while Isabella curled herself into a fetal position in the chair by the window and wept. And yet, just one week later, George could finally sit in bed without a nap and a week after that he briefly bore his own weight, with Dr. Parks and Dr. Gothart holding him on either side.

One Saturday night in early March as he slid the stethoscope off his neck, Dr. Parks made a pronouncement.

"If you don't leave this sick room and breathe fresh air," he said looking directly at Isabella, who had cuddled into George during the entire exam, "I'll have two new patients. I've arranged respite care for George. Tomorrow you'll spend the day away from the inn."

Isabella gasped, and her eyes widened in alarm. "Leave George?" She violently shook her head. "Unthinkable! Why…"

But George gazed up at her with a mixture of tenderness and quiet authority. "Listen to Dr. Parks. He knows best."

Marie's heart was already pounding. Leave George alone at the inn?

"No, George!" Isabella hugged him closer, a vise of an embrace, not even bristling at the "Dr. Parks knows best" message. "I won't do it!"

Dr. Parks held firm. "You and Marie are to, at the very least, attend church and join your sister for lunch. After that, if you're still consumed with anxiety, you may return. But I'd prefer you hold out until after dinner."

The next morning Dr. Parks arrived to check on George, who was sitting up in bed and feeding himself a hearty breakfast of bread and milk with Isabella encouraging each bite, and he didn't tremble with the effort. His face was finally losing its peaked look and a faint pink was returning. But Dr. Parks was not alone.

With him was Briana and her widowed mother, Kate Miller, a tall broad-shouldered woman with thick russet hair and a sad, but warm and kind, smile.

"Please don't worry about your husband, ma'am," Kate said with a little curtsey. "I have plenty of experience tendin' the sick."

"Thank you," Isabella said crisply, scarcely able to contain he contempt that this woman, so below her station in life, would replace Isabella in her caretaking duties. Marie also sensed a tinge of jealousy that another woman, regardless of the reason, would touch her husband.

Kate, for her part, gazed admiringly at Isabella as if she'd just seen a goddess and gave another curtsey.

Only Isabella's eyes betrayed her exhaustion; only the rigid lines of her face proclaimed her hatred of the doctor who saved her husband's life. And only for George did Isabella even attempt to hide these defects in her demeanor. Although good breeding dictated Isabella's deportment, only her fervor for George drove her to appear nothing less than angelic in his sight, now that he was awake to notice and appreciate it. And the light in his eyes, and the yearning on his face whenever he looked at her, showed he indeed noticed it.

He certainly noticed it this morning. Isabella was dressed in royal blue and impeccably groomed. The matching hat atop her golden curls, the fringe of her lashes, her carriage; these George studied with eagerness shining in his eyes. Marie, also dressed in blue, knew her papa approved of her beauty, too, but differently. He approved of her filial duty to appear presentable in public as proper to church services.

"Luther is downstairs waiting for you," Dr. Parks said.

"Thank you, Dr. Parks," Isabella said in carefully formed words. She squeezed George's hand. "I'll return shortly."

George's eyes were already drooping, but he smiled and nodded. Briana removed the tray. Dr. Parks opened his bag. Isabella held out her hand to Marie and said shortly, "Let's go."

They clasped each in other a relaxed way, but Marie's fingers felt tight, and she sensed the tension in her mama's too, as they walked out of Room 27, across the quiet carpeted hall, empty except for them, and down the stairs to the lobby, the space between them and around them empty with George's absence. Never in Marie's young life had she attended church services without her jovial papa leading the way. Although they had studied the Bible twice each day before George's illness, they did not always attend church, and always for reasons relating to the news: they were traveling, lodging in the outskirts, or on deadline. These weren't excuses as others who shrank from proper observance of the Sabbath Day as some might shrink from a corpse. George reveled in Sunday services no matter the denomination and ensured he and his family attended them as many Sundays as they could. No matter how afflicted his stomach, the spring in his steps always grew brisker, and the animation in his eyes always shone brighter, the closer they moved in the direction of a church building.

Luther waited for them near the front desk, top hat in hand, wearing a brown overcoat and a blank expression. But then, Luther rarely smiled or showed any emotion except an overall antipathy for life.

"Good morning, Aunt Isabella. Good morning, Marie," Luther said. The words were flat, matter-of-fact, polite. Luther was executing his duty and nothing more.

"Good morning, Luther," Marie and Isabella said nearly in unison, with Isabella's voice trailing off.

Luther offered his arm, and Isabella accepted it.

"Thank you for allowing me to escort you to church," he said simply.

"You're welcome."

After these awkward pleasantries, they walked the way to the Congregational church in silence, even though they'd joined a foot train of others from Munsonville Inn headed in the same direction. Despite the sunny sky, the cold air bit through

Marie's cloak and made it hard for her to believe Easter was just a few short weeks away. They hadn't gone far, when Luther veered right onto an unnamed street, which was less packed than Main Street but dustier, so Marie and Isabella held their skirts high during this stretch of the walk. To their right, villagers surged down the hill from all three streets, a three-pronged parade with the church as their destination.

"Good morning, Luther," a stocky woman pushing a carriage said in a large voice.

"Good morning, Mrs. Bass," Luther returned. "This is my Aunt Isabella and my cousin Marie."

"Pleased to meet you," Mrs. Bass said to Isabella. "How is your husband? I understand he's been ill."

"He's recovering, thank you."

Marie found the baby much more interesting and wished Mrs. Bass would slow down so Marie could study the child. It was if God couldn't decide if this baby should be pretty or ugly, so He settled on a look that fell between the two, with a collection of features so exquisite Marie had no idea how to categorize them. She had the wan appearance of a sickly child combined with the energy of a well-nourished one, and she brimmed with curious attention at her surroundings. She had a snub nose and thick eyebrows and short, thick lashes. Yet her brown eyes held a faraway, dreamy look that made Marie think of saints, angels, and sirens.

They'd reached the church. It was small and the color of new cream, and they fell into line with the rest, passing through the narthex to the nave and then halfway down to the left, where Lula was already sitting with Leo, Alannah, and the sleeping Eugenia. Isabella slid into the pew first, so as to sit by Lula. Marie sat next to her mother, and Luther took the end beside Marie, his duty as the man. The whitewashed nave was plain, just a raised platform near the front, a podium and unadorned wooden cross. A pretty woman with a round face, pink cheeks, and frizzy blonde hair, was sitting at the piano and turning pages of a large hymnal. She launched into *A Mighty Fortress is our God*, and everyone rose and began to sing, Marie included, for she had memorized the lyrics to this hymn and many others years ago.

A mighty fortress is our God,
A bulwark never failing:
Our helper He, amid the flood
Of mortal ills prevailing.
For still our ancient foe
Doth seek to work his woe;
His craft and power are great,
And armed with cruel hate,
On earth is not his equal.

The pastor, a regal-looking man with blue-black hair streaked with gray, walked to the podium as they sang. When the hymn concluded, he motioned people to sit. The service was pleasant, the message heartfelt, the rest of the music upbeat, but the church was oddly sparse on male attendance. Perhaps, Marie surmised, the men fished on Sundays. That thought slapped truth back into her face, and she looked away from Luther, lest he perceive her wicked thoughts. No, the men weren't fishing on Sundays, or any day, anymore. Not since the tragedy that killed her uncle, her cousins' father, her father's best friend.

At the service's conclusion, Marie, under Luther's protection, followed her family outside. Lula excitedly introduced them to a steady stream of people, underscoring her introductions with the news that the Clares were staying in Munsonville and that veteran reporter George Clare would be joining the staff of The Munsonville Times. Marie noted each name and face, and the avalanche of information did not overwhelm her; she'd plenty of practice through the years. In addition to officially meeting Pastor and Mrs. Demars (the pianist), she met Milton's parents Sebastian Betts (short, square head with grayish auburn curls, who insisted on making sure everyone knew he was Munsonville's former mayor) and his vulgar wife Clarice Betts (hair curled with an iron, deep red rouge, and reeking of scent); and the real mayor, James Fisher and his wife Maybelle Fisher (both short, fat, and graying). Mrs. Fisher was as sunny and chatty as Mr. Fisher was morose and silent. At this moment, Mrs. Fisher was chatting to Mrs. Bass.

"...a part of this village," a woman with missing teeth said to Marie. "Welcome to Munsonville, Miss Clare."

"Thank you."

Eventually, the crowds thinned out, and Marie and her mama joined the parade on its return ascent on the hardpacked hill. The Hassets lived about halfway up Pike Street in a four-bedroom Cape Cod, near the Clares' new home, and Marie looked away when she passed it, lest she catch a glimpse. She would see it soon enough. The villagers had constructed their houses in a stair-step fashion, with the smaller ones at the bottom of the hill and the larger ones at the top. Odd was the only word Marie had for it, but she was of good breeding and would not say it. Despite the plainness of the house's clapboard siding, the inside of her cousin's home was charming. The limewashed walls and the open shutters made the parlor airy and light; the carefully framed photographs of New York, Detroit, and her cousins in childhood added character; and the vases of columbines, forget-me-knots, and everlasting peas added color and sweetened the air. The wide plank floors gleamed as did the legs and arms of beautifully crafted furniture, with cushions featuring Isabella's precise needlework.

"Bass and Betts," Leo explained.

Marie blinked and looked at him. Leo grinned like the Cheshire cat.

"I saw you admiring it," he said, taking the drooling baby so Alannah could remove her cloak. "Milton's dad runs the woodworking shop. He crafts beautiful furniture."

"Mr. Bass?" Marie glanced at Luther. "As in Mrs. Bass, the woman we..."

"Yes," Luther said shortly.

Leo's smile faded. "He drowned, too. When our dad did."

Marie's face burned, and she started to stammer an apology, but Leo stopped her. "Don't be sorry. How could you have known?"

"Lula, your house is beautiful," Isabella said, following her sister to the kitchen.

"Wait until you see yours."

Leo handed the baby back to Alannah and motioned Marie to the kitchen. "Lunch is ready."

"So soon?" Marie asked, surprised.

"We prepare cold sandwiches on Saturday night," Luther explained.

Leo nodded. "We work so hard with The Times. Sunday is our only day of rest."

Lula had set out several platters of various kinds of sandwiches on the table — all cut into triangles — and Isabella was laying out Flow Blue plates and flatware. The kitchen was as open and pleasant as the parlor; it also had shuttered windows that were folded back to admit the late morning sunlight. The wooden table and chairs matched the cabinets and shelves, the copper-lined wooden sink and even the ice box. No heat emanated from the iron stove on its day of rest.

Soon they were sitting around the table, hands folded, while Leo said grace. They partook of cold fish sandwiches, onion and tomato preserve sandwiches, potato and creamed spinach sandwiches, and even jelly sandwiches for dessert. They passed hot tea and even hotter coffee, and Marie accepted both, one at a time. She had not tasted coffee for weeks and wondered how her papa was faring with Mrs. Miller and Briana.

Despite Lula's and Leo's attempts at generic pleasantries, Isabella answered shortly, and then sharply, growing more agitated with each response until Lula and Alannah finally offered to accompany her back to Munsonville Inn.

"I don't wish to trouble you," Isabella began.

"It's no trouble at all," Alannah assured her. "The baby needs her afternoon airing."

"Would you like to see the rest of the village?" Luther abruptly asked Marie, looking directly at her. He did not smile.

"No, thank you."

Isabella squeezed Marie's shoulder, but she spoke to Luther. "I think that's a splendid idea. Marie should enjoy some young society and explore the place she can finally call home. Marie?"

"Yes, Mama. I'll stay."

"Don't worry about the mess, Mom," Leo said as he noticed Lula's eyes roaming around the kitchen. "I'll tidy it up."

Luther remained silent all the way down the hill, and Marie wondered why he offered the tour of the village when he could be enjoying solitude in the quiet house.

He marched her past the church and then back toward the inn and onto Main Street. That's when Marie stopped to examine this village from all sides. The hill lay to the north, Lake Munson and the fishing cabins to the south, comprising one half of the activity on Main Street. The other half contained a timbered sidewalk and brick buildings, although where residents of a fishing village obtained bricks, Marie had no idea. Village Hall started the lineup at the west. This was followed by a general store, the woodshop, The Munsonville Times office, a storehouse for fishing and lumbering supplies, the inn, and finally a whitewashed building about the size of the general store, which Luther said was the school. Of course, all the shutters on all the buildings were closed, as was proper for the Sabbath Day.

"This is it," Luther finally said, breaking the silence. "This is Munsonville."

Marie strolled along the wooden walk, pretending the sights interested her and that Luther's attitude didn't annoy her. Suddenly, Marie spun around and faced him.

"I see sadness in your eyes whenever someone mentions Mrs. Simons," she said with the same flat tone he used to address her. "Did you love her?"

"No," Luther said, much to Marie's surprise that he bothered to reply. She expected an upbraid for her rudeness. "I thought I did. But I didn't really know her at all."

"Often love is based on an illusion of our minds," Marie said. "We think we're beholding our beloved, but we're really infatuated with our own reflection."

"Maybe," Luther said. "Either way, I can't wait to forget her."

He crossed the empty street toward the lake, so Marie trailed him, between a pair of weathered cabins and then onto a dock, proceeding to its edge. For a long while, they shaded their eyes against the sun's glare on and the icy blue waters while the cold breeze stung Marie's nose and cheeks. Then, abruptly, as if joining a discussion in progress, Luther said, "We're honored a newspaperman of your father's caliber will be joining us. I'm eager to learn from him."

"Whatever."

This time Luther looked surprised. "Aren't you excited to have a real home?"

Marie lifted her chin and quoted:

Tis home where e'er the heart is,
Where e'er its loved ones dwell,
In cities, or in cottages,
Throng'd haunts or mossy dell.
The heart's a rover ever.

"Your dad's a rover, that's for sure," Luther said, easing himself onto the dock, heedless of his Sunday finery, and crossing his legs, so Marie sat, too, and arranged her skirts to protect her modesty, as Isabella had taught her.

Then Marie tossed her head and retorted, "He's from France."

"I know. The Lozere region."

"Also known as Gevaudan."

"Famous for cattle farming and tourism."

"And cheese."

"If you say so."

"Famous now."

"Makes for good lore, at least."

"Right. Because cheese is how my papa and mama met."

"I don't tell folks we're related to the Sages," Luther turned to her. "No one would believe it."

"Benjamin Sage, the great banker, saving America from financial ruin," Marie said proudly. "And his son Daniel Sage, my grandpapa and your grandpapa, a Wall Street financier."

"Our grandmother died young."

"Giving birth to my mother."

"I know. I'm sorry."

Marie shrugged. "It happens."

"Yep."

Marie's cheeks burned. Bryony Simons. The woman who'd spurned Luther had also died in childbirth. She opened her mouth to retract her callous remark, but Luther had already moved on.

194

"Of course, Uncle George has his own interesting back story, starting with poor parents: French mother and an English father.

"Who ran a cheese shop."

"Cheese that Grandpapa found delectable."

Luther turned to Marie and smiled. Marie relaxed and smiled back.

"Papa is very particular about the cheese he will eat." Marie sighed. "Except Papa didn't want to make cheese. He wanted to report the news. He even wrote for a small weekly in Lozere."

Luther nodded. "So he traded his skills: he would teach the Sage family chefs how to make the Clare brand of cheese. As payment, Uncle George could write for Sage's underground newspaper, a newspaper he started in 1876 to favor James Blaine, which is also how Uncle George met Dad."

"Because your papa also wrote for that underground newspaper."

"Funny how neither cared for that paper or its political leanings."

"They cared about The Dream."

"Right. Dad's dream was to run his own newspaper, which Grandpapa's money could provide. Uncle George's dream was to scoop the biggest story and get into one of the country's major publications, which Grandpapa's money could also provide."

"But Grandpapa died on the ship during the return voyage."

"Leaving our mothers heiresses. And giving Uncle George his scoop."

"Papa wrote the story for the New York Gazette and was paid well for it," Marie's face darkened. "But he did not receive an offer of employment."

This time, Luther shrugged. "Those are hard to come by. Especially for rookies."

That stung. So Marie shot back, "And your parents were lovers, but Grandpapa had forbidden the marriage. But with his death, they could marry – and quickly since Aunt Lula was already pregnant with Lillian."

Luther's jaw dropped, and he narrowed his eyes at Marie. "Who told you this?"

"Didn't you know?"

Luther scowled, picked up a pebble, and threw it into the water. "Of course I knew. They invested the money until they had enough to hide here, start The Munsonville Times, and live out their lives."

"In the meantime," Marie said a bit smugly. "Mama fell in love with Papa and his charm."

"And Uncle George fell in love with her infatuation and an easier way of life."

Marie nodded. No sense in denying it. "It's true. And when Mama proposed marriage, he, naturally, accepted."

"And they've lived as nomads ever since." Luther threw a stick. "In search of that elusive scoop."

"Some people," Marie said reflectively, more to herself than to Luther. "Some people think Papa is the yang because of his passion for chasing scandals, fires, robberies, murders, inventions, and train crashes, and for our vagabond lifestyle. But he is actually the yin, for receives all their actions and depends upon my mother to be the yang, to be the light to his life, to bring him constant and stability. So even though it appears she is the passive female, she is really the active male force in their marriage. And she was quite active in preventing me because she had no room in her heart for anyone but my papa."

Luther stared at her with incredulity. "They told you this?"

"Yes. My parents would not lie to me. Mama calls me "Miracle Child" for God placed me in their lives despite her best attempts to thwart it."

"Well," Luther said with a wry half-smile. "I guess, it's not everyone who can claim she's someone's miracle."

Marie tossed her head. "I symbolize hope, the realization of all things impossible. But now the money has run out and Papa, while burying The Dream, is worried Mama will now live a life of tribulation. That would break his heart."

"Your dad has covered so many stories," Luther said with real admiration in his voice. "You must have seen it all."

Marie took a deep breath.

"I have seen much," she reluctantly agreed. "But the only thing I've wished to glimpse has remained out of view.

"The realization of The Dream?"

"Yes. And now I am not to see it at all."

Luther picked up a rock, stood, and stretched. Marie took that as her cue to stand, too, which she did, smoothing her skirts down and brushing away debris.

"I used to dream," Luther said. Then he cocked his wrist and flicked the rock across the lake. It skipped, skipped, skipped, skipped, leaving widening circles in its wake. "But I don't anymore." He looked pointedly at Marie. "And If you wish to live at ease with yourself, I advise you to do the same."

CHAPTER TWENTY-TWO: THORNS WITH POISON

February 13, 1896

Dear Sophia,

Just dropping a quick line to see how you and Jozsef are faring in your new role as parents. I imagine you are quite busy, for this is the longest lapse in our correspondence since Blair and I first moved to Munsonville, when we had no regular address to give you.

My arrangement at the parsonage is still going well; I am thankful for the work, the provision, and the com-panionship. I hope you don't regret taking Anna into your home. I prayed long and hard before asking this great favor of you. As you know, I almost kept her myself, but a child needs two parents, and this I was unable to provide.

I remain as always,

Your devoted Neta

February 23

    Dear Neta,

    I'm so glad you wrote because I desperately need your guidance. I've put the question to the ladies at church, but their advice was so conflicting, I felt at a loss which piece to take. I'm sure my inability to decide arises from my inexperience at this sort of thing. If I'd become a mother at the proper time instead of at the advanced age of thirty-two, I'd have the experience to manage this type of situation.

    You can't imagine how much Jozsef and I love Anna, as much as, perhaps more, than if she'd been born of our union. The joy she's brought into our lives these past few months is immeasurable. As you know, the child was shy and withdrawn at first, a very natural reaction, I'm sure, to being abandoned by her very own mother.

    But as you know, "the shell must break before the bird can fly." It seemed as if the child were pecking through her barrier – we'd had a lovely Christmas, as you recall, full of nuts and sweetmeats, and little paper dolls we cut out from wrapping paper. But then she retreated once more. In fact, Anna is not only reserved, she's secretive as well, and I'll tell you why I think that. Something has bitten her, I'm certain of it, but Joszef said the marks are not those of the bed bug or the cockroach. He's wondering if the culprit's at the park, for we've been liberal with our walks lately now that mild weather is returning. So although I'm uneasy, I'm inclined to agree with him. Indeed, I've not seen so much as a fly in this apartment, yet we still applied boric acid and smoked the house with peat. But why would a child lie about an insect bite?

Lately, Anna shuns us except for meals and church. She prefers to remain in her room with only the music box for company. She plays it nonstop, even at night. I'm at my wit's end, Neta. I don't know what to do.

Any insight will be much appreciated. You are as dear to me as my own sister was. Be assured, I will take your words to heart and apply them.

Other than that, we are all well. Anna's color is fairly good and so is her appetite. As for Joszef and I, we are never ill; you yourself know that.

He's diligent at his work and keeps the hardware store's accounts in perfect order. I've never seen such a man for facts and figures!

Be assured of my prayers and love. Pray for us and reply soon.

Love,
Sophia

March 7,

Dear Sophia,

Thank you for your prompt reply! I'm relieved to know you, Joszef, and Anna are overall well, but I was grieved to hear you are having some trouble with Anna.

Having lost my little Joel at birth, I'm scarcely a paradigm of mothering wisdom. Still, I do know some of the details of the child's short life, which may help put Anna's perplexing behavior in the right light.

Anna's parents worked for Mr. John Simons, the musician who just lost his wife and child during his wife's confinement. Their employment began when Mr. Simons lived in New York, long before he met Mrs. Simons.

If my memory is correct, Anna's father served as Mr. Simons' personal valet, and Anna's mother worked as his housekeeper. At some point between Mr. Simons' travels and his relocation to Munsonville, the valet grew sick. Despite the calling for the best physicians, the poor man succumbed. This might have left Anna and her mother penniless and without a friend in the world, if not for the kindness of Mr. Simons. He sent them to Munsonville to help the other servants prepare the home he had built for himself and his bride. Here's the high regard Mr. Simons felt for their faithful service: he even had private quarters built for Anna and her mother on his very estate.

Mr. Simons treated Anna as if she were his actual daughter, to the extent she had quite the run of the main house, and he showered her with presents. Mrs. Simons became like a second mother to the little girl and kept her quite entertained by playing games with her or spinning amusing little stories.

So you can see, Sophia dearest, this child has lost more than a mother. She has lost her mother, her father, a set of surrogate parents, and two homes. I have no idea why a mother would run off and abandon her child — I visit Joel and Blair every day and weep over their graves — but God has not called us to judge our fellowman but to be compassionate in all circumstances. Perhaps Anna's mother, in her extreme grief, ran into the woods to cool her despair and met with a cruel or wicked end.

Have you spoken to Dr. Mroviak about her? Perhaps an examination to allay your fears and a tonic to perk up her spirits might do wonders.

Write soon. Your letters are such a comfort.

I remain as always,

Your devoted Neta

March 15

    Dear Neta,

    Thank you so much for your timely letter! Your insight into Anna's past was invaluable and so was your suggestion that we contact Dr. Mroviak. He, of course, had thoroughly examined her shortly after the adoption, but since she hadn't any overt signs of illness, it never occurred to Joszef nor me to bother the dear man again and incur an added expense, too.

    As the matter stands, we did right in summoning him, for she has lost weight and grown rather pale since his initial visit, which is dreadfully upsetting, especially since her appetite is quite good, like that of a young man working on a railroad. She especially craves meat – I never did see such a child – and we have done right by giving it to her; Dr. Mroviak said she should eat all she wants. Fortunately, we have the means to provide for her. If we hadn't, I don't know what I should have done!

    So that is the plan for now. I shall keep you posted on Anna's progress. Now I'd like to turn my attention to you, dearest Neta, and your current situation. I don't know how to broach the topic, so I'll be quite blunt: news has reached even our old friends here in Detroit, and the remarks they are making in your direction are quite unwholesome. And if news of your indiscretion has reached us, what must people be saying out of earshot in Munsonville?

    I know you are quite alone in the world, and that you are independent and freethinking, but even modern women need to consider their reputations, and you are no exception, especially since "he" appears to have no regard for it at all.

Now Neta, please don't think I'm scolding you; I'm not quite as moralistic as that. I'm just advising you, as a closer-than-a-sister sister, to perhaps not be so overt. It distresses me that others see you as fast and loose, especially when I know you to be upstanding and virtuous in the other areas of your life.

Please write back soon and reassure me you are not angry with me for speaking thus.

Be assured of my prayers and love. Pray for us. I always pray for you.

Love,
Sophia

March 23

Dearest Sophia,

My precious sister, I never could be angry with you. How could I when you've loved and cared for me all these years? In fact, I love you all the more for bringing this matter to my attention. Although I suspected the gossip was true, I didn't know it to be fact; and yet, this does not, and will not, change my mind, at least for the present time. Since you've spoken so frankly to me, I pray you won't mind if I speak thus to you about Galien, for that is the given name of the Reverend Marseilles, and he is more than the church pastor to me.

Sophia, no one except God and you knows how bitterly I grieved the loss of my Blair after he was attacked and killed in the woods. And then to lose our child — how could God be so cruel?

Although the Demars are like family to me, and Algernon is Galien's former pupil, friends now, so they've been close for many years — sometimes a woman needs more than family to comfort her. Now, don't interrupt, dear; I can already hear you objecting and assuring me of your undying love, of which I am most grateful.

But you have not lost the love of your heart. Although you can imagine how the loss of Joszef might tear your heart apart, you have not experienced it. Galien lost his wife when his own daughter, Mrs. Simons, was just a little girl, so young she had no memory of her own mother. And now his daughter is gone, too.

It's hardly a secret that I like men who are intellectually strong. With Blair gone, I also lost our stimulating conversations. Like Blair, Galien is learned on many levels and is able to hold deep conversations on a wide variety of topics. His own wife was also a new woman and that, I believe, was the basis of their attraction.

Now I am not Adele, and Galien is not Blair. No one can take Blair's place in my heart. But keeping company with Galien passes time in a way that's pleasing to both of us. As far as keeping house for him, his former housekeeper is now needed at home as her husband is an invalid.

So although I appreciate your concern, Sophia, truly I do, I think that, I'm going to please myself and not try to stop the wagging tongues of busybodies. At least if they are wagging about me, they are leaving others who may be feeble in heart alone.

I pray you and Joszef are well and that Anna is doing much better.

I remain as always,
Your devoted Neta

April 6

    Dear Neta,

    I cried heaps of tears as I read your last letter! Your words rent my heart; please don't be angry with me! For it hurts me deeply to hear disparaging words about people who don't know you as well as I do. But you always did know your mind, and I trust you will make the best decisions for your life.

    Now about Anna. She has not improved; in fact, she is much worse. She's lost more weight, and her complexion is devoid of color, save for dark smudges under her eyes. Dr. Mroviak feels certain her condition is a combination of melancholy and the city air, which isn't suiting her constitution. He inquired as to our next visit to Munsonville as a change of air and return to familiar surroundings might improve her health.

    However, Joszef can't get away from the shop until early June, end of May at the soonest. I shall have to wait for him, because it's too dangerous for a mother and child to travel so far without male protection, and the thought of staying in a fishing cabin alone with an ill child is absolutely ludicrous. In the meantime, Dr. Mroviak did prescribe a tonic, even though she eats like a whale at every meal.

    I hope by the time we arrive, you will have finished with spring cleaning at the parsonage and can make time for some stimulating conversations with me, too - although I understand if you're unable to leave the minister's side. What would he do, I wonder, without your solicitude? May God reward you for you constant and dedicated efforts in his regard.

Have you read _The Woman Who Didn't_ by Victoria Crosse? It's all the rage right now, and I want to hear your thoughts.

Be assured of my prayers and love. Pray for us. I always pray for you.

Love,

Sophia

CHAPTER TWENTY-THREE: THE DEAD MAN RISES

n Easter Sunday just before noon, George shocked and surprised the inhabitants of Room 27 by walking from the bed to the dinner table, where the feast sat under the silver lids and filled the room with savory aromas.

Now a beaming Dr. Parks did hold his arm, and George did take unsteady, halting steps. Through blurry eyes, Marie watched Isabella watch him. And Isabella watched with bright open eyes and tears streaking her cheeks, her dewberry jelly forgotten, as he lifted one foot after the other and slowly traversed those few feet, breathing hard and never once moving his gaze away from her face.

"Oh George," she wept as he bent and placed a tender kiss onto her forehead.

Dr. Parks, grinning and looking extremely pleased with himself, eased George into the seat next to her.

"I suspected he had the strength a week ago," Dr. Park said as he drew up a chair for himself "But he wanted to save it for today, his Easter gift to you both."

He glanced at Marie, and she nodded solemnly. She could not speak, not with the lump stuck in her throat, but neither could she smile. Her eyes held a brimful; any movement might cause leakage, unacceptable.

"Dine with us, Doctor," George said with a weary, happy smile. "Little Marie, ring for another tray."

Dr. Parks held up his hand. "Not today. But I will take tea."

"Little Marie, please bring another cup and saucer."

"Yes, Papa."

George insisted on pouring, and, after Dr. Parks enjoyed a couple of mouthfuls, George got to the point.

"Doctor," he said, his voice trembling with eagerness. "When is it safe for me to leave the inn?"

Now Marie had expected a number of reactions from Dr. Parks at this question: concern, worry, happiness, hope. But she hadn't expected a glint of cunning in his eyes or the slight grin he tried to smooth away with his hand.

"Have you acquired a home?" Dr. Parks spoke steadily, but Marie detected hints of mirth in those few syllables.

George glanced at Isabella, who looked away and coolly replied, "Yes. But it's not quite ready."

Dr. Parks took another sip to hide his smile, which kept breaking out despite his efforts to squelch it, and his eyes were merry. "I believe it will come together at the proper time."

"Ah!" George exclaimed. "Then I am satisfied." He, too, smiled, but fondly and openly at Isabella. "We shall need some adjustments, my love." He moved another glass of dewberry jelly close to her and tapped its spoon at the edge. "But we shan't skimp of the jellies. I shall starve before you are deprived."

Isabella returned the smile, a forced, terse smile.

"Speaking of adjustments," Dr. Parks cautioned with a sidelong look at Isabella. "You'll need a special diet. No wine again, ever. Even one drink could be fatal. Bland food. Nothing spicy. No irritants."

George's face lit up, as if he'd heard the most delightful news. "Dr. Parks, I'm content to sup on pap and gruel all my remaining days."

Dr. Parks chuckled, and his demeanor relaxed. "Extremes aren't necessary. More like boiled vegetables and rice, stewed meat and fruit. Weak tea with sugar. Farina."

Grinning, George held up a finger. "And no alcohol."

"Especially no alcohol."

"Then I propose a toast. Isabella, more tea? Little Marie?"

The teapot and the sugar bowl went around the table. Marie accepted only tea and covered her cup when George tried to add a spoonful.

"No sugar, Little Marie?"

"Not today, Papa."

Unsweetened.

The way Marie would approach life now, in stark, unvarnished reality.

George held up his teacup. "To our new future! And to Dr. Parks, my blood brother who returned the future to me – and returned me to my wife and child."

Marie raised her cup and slowly took a small sip. Isabella, her expression stony, moved the cup to her lips, pretending to taste and then quickly blotting her lips with her napkin after the act. Dr. Parks downed his tea and stood.

"I must go," he said, hastily laying his hand on George's shoulder as George was already halfway out of his chair. "No, stay. I'll return this evening to check your progress. Although," he beamed with genuine happiness, "I anticipate a brief visit." He bowed to Isabella and then to Marie. "Enjoy your Easter dinner."

They passed the fish soup, boiled ham, roast beef with horseradish, boiled potatoes in their jackets, stewed squash and stewed tomatoes, apple fritters, dewberry jelly, and fresh rolls for Isabella and Marie, although, to Marie, all of it tasted like cardboard. George had his own tray of boiled chicken, blanc mange, and milk toast, but he savored each bite as if he were dining on salmi of wild duck. Isabella absently pushed her food around her plate, occasionally taking a bite, but her face was taut, and her narrow eyes flashed.

"My love," George finally said with the utmost tenderness in his voice. "Tell us about our new home."

So Isabella told him about the little Cape Cod on Pike Street with three rooms downstairs – a kitchen, a parlor, and cubicle for George's office – and two bedrooms in the dormer, but her tone was flat, as if giving a weather report. Finally George gave up and reached for The Times, which was still folded at the edge of their table.

He read silently, each turning of the page rustling loudly in the silent room. Slowly Marie forced her food, one small bite at a time, down her very tight throat.

"Well," George finally said, subdued at the impassive way Isabella picked at her celebratory meal. "The village is also inching back to life. The sadness at Mrs. Simons' untimely passing is ebbing, and people are making new plans to enhance the economy as it's obvious John Simons will no longer make Munsonville his primary home."

He spoke with a slight catch in his voice, the only hint of lingering sorrow that his last swipe at The Dream had eluded him for good.

Isabella jumped to her feet. With loud clinks, she began haphazardly stacking their dishes onto the trays. Bewildered, George set his hand on hers. "Dearest, what troubles you?"

"Blood brother!" she spat. "You have the blood of a monster flowing through you!"

George peered into her cup. "Why, Isabella, you've scarcely touched your tea. Do try it. The flavor is nice, chamomile, with grassy undertones."

Isabella picked up the cup and threw it across the room. It crashed to the floor, splashing tea everywhere. "Don't ignore me!"

"I..." George stared at his own tea, suddenly finding the amber liquid fascinating. The man who effortlessly poured forth the most eloquent of prose now faltered. "I...I wish to abstain from words that...bite."

"'If only ye had abstained from meats offered to idols, and from blood, and from things strangled!'" She leaned over the table, jabbing her finger dangerously close to his nose. "How can you, a man of God and a man of truth and man for life, sit there and be fine with the blood of a 'doctor,' who's tortured animals and humans to satisfy his own barbaric pleasure, flowing through your heart and pumping over every inch of your body? 'Be ye not unequally yoked together with unbelievers: for what fellowship hath righteousness with unrighteousness and what communion hath light with darkness?' And now you're yoked forever with...Oh, George!"

Isabella rushed to the bed she'd forsaken all these months and flung herself across it, face down and crying out in a muffled voice, "George, how can you bear it?"

She wept as if her heart were breaking; she poured out all the hours of worry and terror she'd endured these many months. Marie sat as still as a statue, taking the passion in, letting none of it out, scarcely breathing, heart pounding in her ears. George still gazed upon his tea, but he looked distressed, as if he needed a little wine for his stomach.

He looked "afflicted," as Dr. Parks might say.

The bed covers muzzled Isabella's cries, but no one could mistake them.

George took a deep breath and turned around. "Isabella."

She shook her head and buried it deeper, wailing, screaming, and kicking her legs.

George's shoulders sagged, and he ran a trembling hand through his hair. "Can you not look at me? Because you see a monster?"

She cried harder.

hat is up with you?" Henry asked one night as he tottered through the back door of Simons Mansion after his nightly kill.

For Kellen was dancing a lively hornpipe through the halls and singing:

*When Johnny comes marching home
again, Hurrah! Hurrah!*
*When Johnny comes marching home
again, Hurrah! Hurrah!*
*We'll give him a hearty welcome then
Hurrah! Hurrah!*
The men will cheer, the boys will shout
The ladies they will all turn out,
And we'll all feel gay when
Johnny comes marching home.

As Kellen hopped and skipped over to Henry, he grabbed Henry's hands and swung him around, trilling, "I'm so happy, happy, happy. I'm so happy, happy, happy. I'm so…"

Annoyed, Henry broke away. "Happy about what?"

Kellen stopped. "Haven't you noticed the change in John?"

"Yes. He's dead. Nothing new."

"Ah, but not quite so dead anymore!"

"You're saying he's alive?"

Kellen's shoulders sagged. "I didn't say that either. But he's more than dead, and that's a good sign. And soon…soon…" Kellen ran a tongue over his lips. "Soon the blood of…"

At that moment, John walked through the back door with a spring in his step and a small plate in his hand. The plate held a bit of cooked beef, a roasted potato chunk, and a stalk of boiled asparagus. Humming under some actual breaths, John passed Henry without a word, strolled directly into the music room, and shut and locked the door. Soon, lively music filled the air. Kellen skipped out the back door, chortling, which left Henry alone, glowering. Yes, Henry had noticed the change in John, not that he'd admit the fact to Kellen. And he didn't like it.

John, of course, was fully aware of these changes in himself. He monitored them each night in the looking glass that he'd dragged into the music room. Tonight he contemplated those changes are he slowly nibbled and exuberantly played.

First of all, he didn't appear so dehydrated. His face looked fuller, younger, and his skin was approaching taut and plump, with a rosy tinge that reminded him of life. His hair regained some of its previous thickness, and it gleamed in the room's candlelight.

Yes, candlelight.

Quite often John lit several of the candles or turned up the gas when he played as some of his penetrating night vision had slightly declined. John also noticed a similar decrease in his sharp hearing, and his brisk reflexes, the latter an asset when lighting the fire. In fact, he liked running a comb through his hair and noting the shine of the strong strands. His muscles had grown hard from weeks of bolting through the woods on all fours in search of prey. Better muscle mass plus a good blood feast helped him fill out his clothes, almost to their original fit. The more he looked human, the less he needed to hypnotize Anna, which also pleased him. Better to save his energy for more important pursuits - such as his triumphant return to the stage. He'd delayed the European tour out of respect for Bryony and "their" new baby, quite possible the worst decision of his life, but Kellen had since scheduled a summer tour of the east coast and hadn't cancelled it.

John's foul breath was the hardest to mask, but he found chewing wild mint, which grew abundantly in Simons Woods, effectively covered it, at least from a socially polite distance. Up close, well, he certainly wasn't planning on kissing anyone, except the kiss of death, and he'd abandon even that once he returned to life. Until then, anyone who received his kiss of death had more problems than his malodorous breath.

His new routine now looked like this. After tapping into Anna, John would sweep through an inn and whisk a small serving of food, which his stomach never dislodged anymore. Sometimes, he even enjoyed the taste, a fact that occasionally made him smile. But that's not why John smiled tonight. He smiled because he knew Henry seethed. He had progressed farther on the humanity road than Henry, since Henry had scarcely tried, and John was eager to put even greater distance between them. They would, unfortunately, remain tied to Simons Mansion and each other until at least one of them returned to life. But soon, very soon, John would be free to roam the world as the celebrated John Simons, and he'd never need encounter Henry until the pre-dawn hour, when he must descend to the gallows. But between dusk and dawn, John could play a house in London or meet the public for drinks in New York before his evening performance with no one guessing his secret.

He was already having fun with teleportation. Every few days, at least one U.S. publication reported a "John Simons sighting," which greatly amused him, and he took amusement where he could, because he always ended the night with a bludgeoning from Henry, a definite drawback to hybridism and not the only one. The farther John climbed out of the grave, the more the torment of Bryony's betrayal returned. For reasons of death, he must return to the cellar. For reasons of pain, he avoided all rooms of his own mansion except the music room – except when he must venture out. As a living-ish man, he still must occasionally make his toilet and change his clothes. But he couldn't reach his room without passing hers – or any place she ever passed. For he sensed her distrusting spirit everywhere he turned.

"Who are you?" He had asked her. "You are not Munsonville."
"Wha...I..."
"Where can we talk?"
"Talk? But we are tal..."
"Privately."

"Sir, this is most improper!"
"Can you slip out? I'm leaving."
"I'm sorry?"
"I'm leaving Munsonville. Now."
"But...you can't leave!"

*"Don't look back," he reassured her. "You are not Mun-
sonville."*

*He reached for her, but she squealed and scooted to the
headboard, pressing her knees to her chin, locking them in place
with arms of steel, whimpering, and watching him with scared
rabbit eyes.*

"Good night, John," she said politely. "Merry Christmas."

"What if we're killed?"
"We won't be killed."
*But she shook anyway and grabbed his arm. "How do you
know?"*

*"We disembark in Detroit," was all he said to her while
they ate. "A second train will take us to Chicago." But that
wasn't good enough for her.*
"How long are we in Detroit?"
"Long enough to board the train to Chicago."
"We aren't staying, like we did in Jenson?"
"No."
*Bryony set down her fork. "I don't understand. Why
would we skip Detroit?"*
"Because I'm impatient to reach Chicago."
"But Detroit is important to you!"
John paused to sip his coffee and study her. "It is?"
*"You mentioned Detroit the night you and Father argued
about marrying me."*
*"So the timing to speak to my father was a convenient
one? It had nothing to do with Detroit?"*
*John slammed down the empty cup and roughly pulled
her close. "Forget Detroit."*

"The owner is French?"
"No."
"I want to go home!"
"Bryony."

He pulled her close, and she drenched his coat with despairing tears.

"Shh, Bryony."

"I can't! I can't! Take me home!"

"John, why is your room locked?"

"Because I'm obviously not using it. Unless you'd rather I did."

"I want you with me."

"Good."

"Then why lock it?"

"But...John...I thought..."

"You didn't think. You assumed I made class distinctions."

"Didn't you?"

"John, I wish you wouldn't fight with my father."

"He's meddling in our lives."

"He's just worried for me."

"Well, he needn't be."

As many times as he'd explained it to her, Bryony still had to gaze up at him with bright eyes and turn the knife. "Welcome home, John Simons."

"Don't do that."

She blinked. "Don't do what?"

"I told you. It's not my home."

"Your Father isn't 'killed.' He had a mild paroxysm of the heart. He's resting quietly in one of the guest rooms."

"But you two argued so!"

"He'll not fly at me and hinder your freedom."

"He's afraid something bad will happen to me! And now it has!"

"His cage of perverted half-truths has harmed you. Not Chicago. Not New York."

"Our trunks are nearly packed. We leave in the morning."

He couldn't wait to show her the White House, to show her off, to feel her support at his side.

Bryony calmly took another sip. "I'm not going."

"Believe, Bryony,"

"Oh, John," she whispered, reaching out to peel the damp strands off his hot forehead and sticky cheeks. "I do believe in us."

"I don't want to go."

"We must." John set the invitation on the sideboard and poured a drink. "I'm the entertainment."

But the tears spilled out and she cried, "No! I can't do it!"

"I'm hosting a reception next week to welcome them to Munsonville."

She laughed aloud. "What will the villagers think of them?"

John shrugged. "The villagers aren't invited. I'm only feting anyone they and Kellen deem useful."

"Perhaps I should remain in my room and not spoil your party."

"With that attitude, perhaps you should."

"Oh, John! Never mind their disagreeable words. Your performance was flawless!"

"Disagreeable words? From whom?"

"Oh, never mind that! Believe in yourself, John. I do!"

"If you believe, why must you convince me?"

"But it's true!"

"Darling, I believe you."

Bryony shoved John's hand away, but he grasped her hair.

"I said I believe you. And when you've recovered from this fright, we shall go down, and you shall show me."

"No baby."

John, I didn't mean now. Obviously, not now. But next year..."

"No baby ever. I won't lose you to a baby."

"But it's fine I lose you to a piano. Have you ever been unfaithful?"

And yet who called out Henry's name in sleep? Bryony.

As a vampire, he was impervious to her loss. But as humanity returned, the agony returned, acutely, as if rewarming a frostbitten limb. With the numb of cold death, John felt nothing. But quicken him with the flame of life, which spread an exuding glow, and the agony returned. This he must address if to survive. He could not live with this degree of pain.

The worst part is that her song became his signature closing song, and audiences would expect it; he couldn't escape it, Kellen would write it into his contracts. But the best part, for him, showed in his original pieces. With Anna's blood, John felt his fingertips as they made contact with the keys, and he felt inklings of other emotions, which edged his pieces beyond mechanically correct, despite the assessment of the others.

"The grieving John Simons," Dr. Gothart remarked to Kellen one night. "Each note perfectly executed and devoid of warmth, like chimes of ice."

Kellen agreed. "They're so brilliantly cold. Oh, how audiences will weep!"

"To my detriment," John argued.

"No, to your advantage." Dr. Gothart looked at Kellen while pointing to the window. "Go and prepare a place for him."

So Kellen sprouted a pair of coriaceous wings as he shrank and passed through the glass.

Now Henry, who wanted no part of hosts or humanity, had monitored the change in John from afar and resented his rival's connection to reality, which Henry thought he didn't want, but lately found himself wavering. Now that he efficiently stalked and fed, he had more time for thinking. And Henry loathed the extra time and thinking. What a waste of a perfectly good hanging. When people kill themselves, they shouldn't end up where they started. The whole point of suicide was to kill pain. And here he was, in pain. He lusted for the life he threw away, he glutted on blood he didn't want, while envy for John's good fortune when John deserved none of it gave him no rest. He burned with wrath because fortune eluded him even though he was too slothful to grasp it, and he was too full of pride to admit his greed and want. Satisfied with anything? Not at all. The crux of being a vampire. The driving force of being a vampire. You are never, ever satisfied.

He strove for oblivion, and it eluded him. He settled for vampirism, and humanity nagged at him. But why? Henry could recall those pursuits that once filled him with pleasure, but he couldn't recall the actual pleasure. Yes, Henry recalled painting, writing, dancing, dining, dressing, fucking, but he recalled them as if detached from himself, as a voyeur might perceive from outside the window.

The way Henry knew he really dwelled in hell was his desire to stay there. Now that he'd dodged oblivion, he didn't want a second shot at it. First of all, hanging himself really fucking hurt, not long, but for that split moment before he lost consciousness. Henry didn't know the affliction level of death by staking, decapitation, drowning, fire, silver, garlic, holy symbols, running water, or starvation by arithmomania – all the methods Kellen listed in his missing notebook. But he didn't want to find out. And with his luck, he had no guarantee he'd wind up nowhere. He could wind up back here – or worse.

No, Henry had no choice. To survive as the undead, he needed some semblance of humanity. And since eternity lasted a long time, he'd need a way to pass it. That semblance of humanity ought to give him just enough "life" as to restore some of his interest in his pastimes.

To get there, Henry needed a host. And he didn't need to look far for it.

Out of state, yes. But now that teleportation came easy for him, the miles between Michigan and Pennsylvania meant nothing to him. And now that he was dead, her cloister couldn't keep him out.

Persuading Agnes King to give up her blood for him would be trickier than coaxing her purity from her, and Henry wasn't taking any chances she'd refuse him. He didn't need an entire order praying against him.

But halfway through the show, they stole to an anteroom where Henry introduced Agnes to an ecstasy not of the religious kind.

"I love you," Henry murmured and then hushed her panting with a kiss before she could reply.

Instead he would infiltrate her dreams. He knew her heart's desire, and he could let her dwell in a chimeric fantasy that would vanish with the morning light and leave her even more despondent than before she retired.

But...

It would make her long for sleep so she could reunite with "her boy." And once she drifted into sleep, he'd pounce.

That's why Henry didn't worry about gaining Agnes' consent, despite the fact he'd postponed the nuptials for years and dumped her when the promised day drew near. He'd used her, and she now knew it. But Henry also knew, she'd let him use her again.

But after the first draughts, Henry pried way her still-full glass, set hers and his on the floor, and kissed her with more passion than he intended.

"So you don't forget me on the way home."

Agnes patted his cheek. "You silly boy."

Nevertheless, he'd been fond of her. And Henry feared that, with some of his humanity restored, he'd be fond of her again. He didn't fear like a man; he couldn't quite remember manhood. He feared like a dog before a cruel master. Instinct told him this and nothing more. Moreover, tapping into Agnes' lifeblood would be tricky. He must be as satiated as possible before visiting her, lest he get carried away and cut short his hosting opportunity with vampiric gluttony. Demise by degrees was out of the question, too. For Agnes, now known as Sister Maria DeLourdes at the convent, mustn't become languid and attract the attention of her community. She must remain healthy and full of robust blood...like now, soft in sleep on her hard bench in her cell under the watch of a stark wooden cross – and him. How she'd aged!

An albino like her mother and sister Emily, Agnes King had none of their cadaver-like features, at least, not when Henry first met her. Agnes' silver hair, crystalline violet eyes, porcelain skin, and pale lips had all seemed, to Henry, quite angelic, as was the voice that spoke from them: fluid melodic tones that hinted of heavenly instrumentations and choirs.

He combed his fingers through her silver strands and held them apart. She watched as he examined them.
"I want to paint you," he murmured.
"Tonight?"
"Not tonight. But soon. Tonight is for..."
She looked up expectantly.

But now as a member of the Cloistered Dominican Nuns of the Perpetual Rosary in Lancaster, Agnes had become a shrunken creature in a shroud. Even in sleep, a skeletal forefinger and thumb, white as bone, gripped an onyx bead from the strand looped to a cincture; her knuckles gleamed like alabaster knots in the dark; a snowy tuft strayed from the ebony band; and blue veins curved over her closed eyelids like tributaries frozen in ice. Had her primitive cloistered life ruined her? Or her extreme sorrow at the loss of him?

Yet whether she looked like an angel or a crone didn't matter to Henry. What mattered is her desire for him and her cooperation at letting him take from her so he could exist another day. The fact she'd welcome the taking is what made her such an easy, attractive host for Henry, and not one he'd have to woo. Agnes never refused him anything, and she would refuse him nothing now.

She was pathetic, really. The thought made Henry smile.

And just like that, he mastered Kellen's first lesson.

r. Parks locked the back door to Dr. Gothart's colonial, glancing up at the mercury in the old Hay & Lyall thermometer as he pocketed the large ring of iron keys: Fifty-nine degrees, and the old clock in the mansion had yet to chime seven.

A sign of a good day. He'd take it.

With his medical bag in his left hand and his right fist in his trouser pocket, Dr. Parks strode across the stone walk to the drive, deliberately forsaking the carriage house in the back, and began his descent down Blue Gill Road, a descent he made at least twice each day. The early morning sunshine brightened the cumulus clouds in a sky of perfect baby blue and sparkled on dewy grass and droplets on the young oak leaves, lingering reminders of last night's storm. The faint scent of timothy grass and wildflowers surrounded him. Such a morning was made for walking or riding, but a walk took longer, and he needed the time to organize his thoughts.

He was a month into his second spring in this fishing village, a village that consistently shunned progress every time it reached for it, a place where he, too, had failed to progress. Eighteen months of paralysis: for Munsonville, for him. Nor had he realized the depths of his yearning until a twelve-year-old angel stirred those waters inside him. Today, he was both doctor and patient, and the latter filled him with dread and unease. He'd rather strip naked and strut across Main Street than bare his soul. Vulnerability did not suit him.

As if sensing his glum mood, the robins encouraged him with their calls: "Cheerily, cheer up, cheer up, cheerily, cheer up."

No more defending himself. Today he would listen and shoulder the burden. Today he would reconcile with the "childless" Orville and Bertha Parks, his parents.

For years he had tried reasoning with them. For years, he advocated for himself, for his profession. But even when he presented the facts in the most elementary of terms, they could not, or would not, perceive the science behind the horror and the humanity behind the seemingly inhumane. They stubbornly clung to their image of "physician" as a benevolent old granddad bearing receipts for chest poultices and rice jelly, even though that image had little to do with reality.

He squinted at the sun's glittering on Lake Munson; he caught the lake's fresh smell on the breeze. Deftly, he turned away from the water onto the unnamed street that led past the Munsonville Congregational Church and toward his destination.

As a boy, he'd gone with his father to Cambridge on weekends for fly fishing at Fresh Pond. He watched father's inexperienced hands struggled to remove the hook from the squirming fish, shredding its mouth in the process. He watched the fish flop to and fro in the pail of water as it struggled for oxygen. He studied the still fish, his dinner.

Well and good.

But cut open a live fish to observe its nervous system, or a dog to learn about its digestive system, or a prisoner to see if men can live without diseased livers, and he's a fiend. How could he safely excise cancer from a young woman's brain if he'd never drilled into a skull or examined and dissected lobes and glands? How else to understand the workings of blood vessels until one studied them in action?

How many hours had he sat at his mother's knee, memorizing Bible verses as she mended his father's shirts? He could still recount the lines; nay, he'd memorized them long ago: Greater love hath no man than this, that a man lay down his life for his friends; Hereby perceive we the love of God, because he laid down his life for us: and we ought to lay down our lives for the brethren; Christ also hath loved us, and hath given himself for us an offering and a sacrifice to God for a sweet-smelling savior.

So why couldn't a thief, a murderer, pay his debt to society by laying down his life to the scalpel to advance mankind?

But his parents had stopped their ears. It wasn't their fault; what did they know of medicine, of science? His father had risen before sunup and labored a full day (and more) at the Boston Sugar Refinery. His mother had cooked and cleaned and led Sunday schools and organized church suppers. Medicine was for men who didn't shrink from reality, however stark and ugly, not to those who blurred reality and hid under bushels in utopian communities when their own son became too real for them.

As if he could not find them. As if he hadn't known where they'd fled.

He paused in front of the weathered sign and read the thick letters chiseled into the wood: Pike Street. He turned right, back up the hill from whence he came, the first of the hill's three streets of homes, in graduated sizes from bottom to top. The sight always made him cringe. The design element was hideous, in his opinion.

His parents were not stupid, and neither were they weak. Look how they'd survived meager wages, inflated rent, the devaluing of silver. Didn't they show immeasurable strength when his paternal grandparents burnt to ash in a house fire? Or when breast cancer gobbled up his maternal grandmother months before she finally expired in their living room? Of course, he'd never known his maternal grandfather, who died when his mother was five, a ruptured appendix on Christmas day.

And now this, a fishing catastrophe so indescribably tragic that only his father had withstood it. Survival did not belong to the feeble and frail. Indeed, his parents' steel fibers ran through his bones; he could not be himself without them. But they were extremely pigheaded.

He smiled.

And a little naïve.

As his parents' small balloon-frame came into view, he saw his father settled in his rocker, wrapped in blankets and not rocking. One dared not touch the chair in any way so as to cause it movement. He did not see the tin of coffee, but he knew it was there. Orville and his mug were inseparable, especially when Orville was outside.

"Good morning, Pops," Dr. Parks said as he squished through the sopping yard. "How are you today?"

Orville in his gray shirt and trousers, clutching his tin mug, slumping slightly, and staring at what Dr. Parks could not see, contrasted with the cheery maize boards, deep blue door and window sashes, and whitewashed trim. A second rocker sat at the south end of the porch; a broom perched in the corner, straws splayed with frequent use. To his knowledge, his mother never occupied the chair. Maybe he could, after today.

The wooden steps thumped under Dr. Park's weight as he climbed them. If his father saw or heard him, nothing in his expression indicated it. A few white hairs marred the brown of Orville's furry mustache, but his father's round face didn't flush with rage at the sight of him, nor did he run him off the property, as he used to do in past years. Orville's mind appeared forever broken, either from the horror of the accident or the horror of surviving it. Dr. Parks lay the back of his hand against his father's thick fingers. Cool but not yet cold. Orville could stay outside awhile longer.

Dr. Parks retraced his steps and steered to the back of the house, noting his mother's cultivated vegetable garden as he passed it. Last year it produced peas, lettuce, parsley, spinach, chard, and onions. Most likely, it would again. In Boston, her potted plants on the windowsills always flourished. The small barn needed painting; he'd hire someone soon for the job. His father's draft horse was living out its days at Fisher Farm, nice of the Fishers to take it. No need for his mother to worry about caring for a horse when she couldn't ride one or drive the cart anyway.

He skipped up the back stairs and easily turned the handle. As much as his mother scorned him, she always left the door unlocked for him and kept three meals a day warm for him, her habit until he'd moved out of his childhood home. Even during the years he practiced in Boston, he always supped well. His most recent cook had graduated from The National Training School Of Cookery in London. Stewed green turtle, mutton with capers sauce, salmis of duck with olives, cream of rabbit in aspic, and ice creams from cucumber and asparagus: none of these tested her skills. But no anchovy biscuit could beat his mother's cornbread, straight from the oven or fried in butter the next day and served with thick slabs of bacon. No celebrated chef could fry a chicken as well as his mother could – or make as tasty a gravy from its drippings.

Bertha stood at the sink, washing the breakfast dishes. She'd developed a slight hunch over the winter, but otherwise stood erect. Her beehive, now completely gray, still towered over her head, every strand in place. A light wind rippled the tied-back yellow curtains; a four-inch stick propped up the window glass. She'd set the table for one. This morning's Times lay near his place, hastily refolded.

Another morning flashed in his mind, this one from nearly forty years ago, of his mother bustling about the large kitchen of their rowhouse. He'd hear her rouse from bed in the middle of the night, and he'd pad after her. While she lit the stove for his father's breakfast and coffee and packed a pail with bread and butter and a cheese for his father's lunch, he'd rest his head on the kitchen table and half-watched, half-dozed. The smells of sizzling bacon mixed with the hiss of the gas and the sounds of Boston at night: a husband yelling at his wife, drunks fighting in the street, dogs barking in the distance, or a vagrant urinating on their stoop.

But three-thirty in the morning was the only time his mother could open the window without grime from horses and buggies blowing into their abode. His mother was forever dusting the tables, chair legs, and picture frames; daily she hung the rugs out the back window and beat them. She liked everything clean, neat, and tidy, and he was grateful for it. In Boston, no germ dared take up residence in his surgical suites. And he'd learned it all from her.

"Good morning, Mother," Dr. Parks said as he carefully wiped his shoes on the mat and set his bag on a chair.

Bertha did not respond, but he did not expect her to respond. She spoke to him only out of the gravest necessity. Hopefully, that, too, would change after today. He crossed the room, gently placed his hand on her shoulder (How thin it had grown these last months!) and kissed her wrinkled cheek.

She ignored him.

"How's Pops this morning?"

"Same as always. You, for one, should know it."

"I also know you taught me to believe in miracles."

She dried her hands on her apron. "I kept your breakfast warm. Sit down."

"What about Pops?"

"Let him be 'til you eat."

He tucked a napkin into his collar and slid The Times closer to him, even though the Simons scandal and the mysterious "virus" had given way to the mundane: the official hiring of a new pianist at church to replace his mother, an upcoming village board meeting, and beginning preparations for Munson Day.

Avoiding his gaze, she served him a boiled egg and fried salt pork and gravy over biscuits on the same blue and white J. Wedgwood Ironstone plate of his boyhood and then she poured coffee into a matching cup. Duty to him fulfilled, Bertha proceeded to the living room with feather duster in hand, no doubt to tidy up the parlor, for she couldn't let old habits and routines go. Traffic dust on Pike Street when even Main Street had little to no traffic, depending on the day. Hilarious to even imagine.

His mother returned as he swallowed the last bite of biscuit; she whisked everything away to the soapy basin before he'd even wiped his mouth. Then she grabbed the kettle from the stove and poured steaming water into the rinse basin. Quickly she scrubbed the dishes clean, dunked them, and them stacked each one in the wooden rack while he pretended to peruse The Times.

Finally she dried her hands on her apron and announced, "I'll call your father."

He pushed back his chair, picked up his bag, and proceeded into the parlor, small and square, not like their spacious parlor of old or even that of his Second Empire home, but cozy, just the same, perfect for two – or three.

Bertha held the screen door open and called out in an overly chirpy voice, "Orville, Martin is ready for you!"

Dr. Parks heard the scrape of the chair as his father stood and the scuff of his shoes as he straggled to the door. Once inside, Orville merely shuffled to the sofa, perched on its edge, and unbuttoned his shirt, while Dr. Parks unpacked his bag under his mother's keen eye. He knew his parents loathed his presence in their home; he knew they'd agreed to it because he forced himself on them after the accident, and his mother wished to avoid the waggle of village tongues should they shun him, even though she ordinally swooped to gossip likes flies to feces.

Just as he did every morning and evening, Dr. Parks sat next to his father, took his father's blood pressure and pulse and then listened carefully to his heart and lungs. His father offered no protest, nor did he assist in any way; he never did. Nor did

Dr. Parks expect a variation in the results, Physically, Orville Parks was as strong as an ox and ought to live longer than a tortoise. But with a feeble mind, who could tell?

He slowly repacked his bag. But after he fastened it, he paused. His mother raised her brows in alarm.

"Martin, hadn't you better..."

"Mother, please refill Pop's coffee. I wish to speak to you both."

Did revulsion pass over his father's face? Or had Dr. Parks imagined it, the workings over an overstimulated conscience?

"Martin, you're wasting your time. You've had your say, and we are full up to our ears with it. So don't waste your breath on us. Just take your bag and go...go...doctor some sick people."

"Mother, this isn't about my past...activities. Please. Refill Pop's coffee and hear me out."

He swore his mother shuddered. Maybe it was the way the sun streamed through the window and lit upon her face. Seeing wasn't always believing as trick photography proved.

To his astonishment, his mother said crisply, "Very well." Then she rose her voice, as if his father was deaf. "Orville, I'm refilling your coffee. Martin wants to speak to us."

Bertha pried the cup from Orville's hand and marched into the kitchen, her heels clicking with supreme authority over the old boards.

Dr. Parks remained beside his father, who still sat as limply as a stuffed dolly with vacant eyes to match. In the next room, Bertha banged the coffee pot to signal her vexation. The curtain to their bedroom was slid to one side. He glimpsed a simple platform bed, the outline of their old bureau.

The parlor curtains billowed. Restless, Dr. Parks cracked his knuckles.

His mother soon returned with a steaming cup., which she placed in his father's hand. Orville's fingers curled around it, and he took a sip. Dr. Parks gestured to the wingback chair in the corner.

"Please, Mother, sit."

She gave a loud harrumph, but she picked up her mending basket and eased into the seat with the dignity of an empress. He immediately slid to the carpet and then slogged on his knees towards her.

Bertha stuck her nose in the air and turned aside. "Martin, get up. You're embarrassing yourself and us."

"Mother." He glanced over his shoulder at Orville and his empty stare. "Pops, please I'm not here to explain my actions or to defend them. I'm here to beg your forgiveness."

His father didn't move or blink. He looked back at his mother. Her eyes, her expression: empty.

"I'm not worthy to be called your son. I'm so sorry for disappointing you, for not being the doctor you wanted. Don't make me go back to Boston. I want to stay here, with you and Pops, and be that compassionate healer you envisioned."

Bertha slowly faced him, still aloof. "Are you done?"

He swallowed hard, but the lump only thickened and grew.

"Mother, I'm pleading for clemency. Let me prove my usefulness to you. Let me care for you in your old age and minister to the sick people of this village. Let Munsonville be my home, too. Mother, I…"

"I don't think folks here want your hack and butcher methods."

"Mother…"

"You're wasting your breath! Now get up and get out!"

In desperation, he grabbed her knees. "Mother, please."

To his surprise, she burst into tears, grabbed his hair with two tight fists, and screamed, "'Please? Mother, please?' Where was your mercy when we said 'please,' when you stole our hard-earned money to fund your vile experiments? Don't you realize upstanding citizens founded the American Anti-Vivisection Society to stop the atrocities of hellions like you! Even my dearest friends in Boston joined. I couldn't hold my head up! The other mothers bragged about their sons, but what could I say? My Martin cuts up a litter of kittens faster than you can fry an egg!"

She dropped his hair and smacked his face hard enough to see stars, and he took the blow.

"And your poor father, what he's suffered! Every day his co-workers taunted him. 'Why can't you control that son of yours?' 'You should have taken him out to the woodshed a little more often!' and 'Didn't you ever hear of spare the rod and spoil the child?'"

She smacked him again.

"Where, Martin, did you get such depraved appetites?" She cracked him two more times, and he didn't even flinch. "Not in this God-fearing home, let me tell you! You've disgraced us! I still have nightmares of your heinous crimes! Martin, child of my womb: oh, how could you do this to us?"

His mother threw her apron over her head and loudly wailed, heedless of the open windows. He was forty-two, yet he felt the familiar wave pass through him. With every ounce of will he held it back, but he was losing. He always lost.

She let the apron go and stared at him. He scarcely recognized her with the swollen face, the blotchy cheeks, the reddened eyes.

"Martin, don't you remember when you were a boy, and you won the certificate for memorizing the most verses? Or that you could recite the Ten Commandments forward and backward when you were still in breeches? 'Thou Shalt Not Kill' Oh, Martin, how could you forget it?"

The pressure in his chest, the squeezing in his throat, the stinging behind his eyes. He hated this feeling, and he knew...

"Mommy!" he gasped, grabbing her knees as his eyes and nose gushed at the same. "Mommy, please don't be mad at me! Please, don't hate me! I love you, Mommy! I didn't mean to hurt you! I love you! I love Pops! Please, please, please forgive me!"

Dr. Parks buried his face in her lap, clutched her waist so she couldn't pry him away, and cried with the terror of an abandoned child in the middle of a mean and bustling city. He'd never in his life done such an act, not even when he was four and a doctor had set his broken leg following a tumble down the stairs. His father, to his knowledge, had never cried, so he adopted that as his standard and did any crying behind locked doors, away from curious eyes. Over the years, he diligently attempted to break the habit of shedding even a single tear as merely thinking about crying disgusted him to the extent of self-loathing. But certain bodily sensations had their personal Rubicon. Once they crossed it; reflex took control, and he drowned in revulsion, powerless to stop it, as he was powerless to stop it now. He moaned like an old seal, certain all of Munsonville heard him.

After a long while, the miracle happened. He felt his mother's rough hand across his scalp and heard her cry over his blubbering: "I forgive you! O, Martin, my own little boy, I forgive you!"

Her touch increased the flow. He sobbed out the many years of anguished separation while his mother hugged and kissed and caressed him, with those motherly murmurings of the mother of his childhood. As the heartache ebbed away, and inklings of joy replaced it, he felt a marveling wonder rise up inside him: the wonder of mercy; the wonder of absolution; the wonder of being ushered into the fold once more.

She was right, he thought. George Clare's little girl was right.

Finally, he broke free. The need to urinate was terrible.

"Mother, I'll be right back. Please, just wait."

He dabbed his dripping nose on his sleeve as he hurried to the back door and then wiped his cheeks dry with his bare hands. Inside the outhouse, he drained the last of his heartache into the earth and decided it was a fitting place for it.

When he returned to the parlor, his mother was patting his father's damp cheeks dry with his father's threadbare handkerchief. That action said more than spoken words. It said his father existed somewhere inside the shell, a father who, of all things, actually cried, a father who, perhaps, pardoned him. As he retrieved his bag, he felt the melting of the last leaden bits. The weight he'd carried, a weight that had grown heavier with each passing decade, was no more.

At the door, he paused and turned around.

"I will make you proud," he said in a low choked voice. "You'll see."

CHAPTER TWENTY-SIX: REDEFINING LIFE

...but for Henry, who must often work by day, needs a reason to shun the sunlight," Dr. Parks said, taking a sip. "And I have found the solution."

"Which is what?" Henry asked.

Although Kellen had decreed that his students had properly graduated his "finishing school," the two mentors still met with their novices from time to time over the midnight hour to refine techniques and finalize their plans to reenter the world while they awaited their full return to life.

Dr. Parks set down the goblet. "A new blood disorder."

"A blood disorder?" Henry asked.

"Yes. People with this disorder must shun sunlight. If they do venture out, they must cover up. This will allow you to move about society and resume your livelihood."

"A vampire with a blood disorder?" John asked doubtfully.

"The blood disorder is real," Dr. Gothart said from his customary place near the fire. "But Henry's acquisition of it is not."

"Correct," Dr. Parks said. "But I can create an outward manifestation of it. Anyone who sees it will believe it. So until you regain more humanity and can thus handle small amounts without crisping, you will have the excuse for only covering evening stories and attending night parties."

Henry considered Dr. Parks' words. With the acquisition of this "blood disorder," Henry could, theoretically, recover part of his old life, the life he lived before he came to Simons Mansion. For all Henry's previous objections to any of it, he felt strangely optimistic. Did Agnes' blood effect this change? Well, this made his suicide rather pointless.

"And even if you don't want to become fully human again," Dr. Parks continued, "hosting will increase your ability to appear human, allowing you to move more freely in daylight without risking severe harm or exposure."

"When you do plan to court again?" John asked abruptly,

"Court?" Dr. Parks repeated, looking perplexed. "I hadn't considered it."

"Why not?"

"For one, it's improper to court anyone this soon after Millicent's 'death.' Furthermore, I'm too old, and too, let's say too 'unconventional' for the average young woman of marrying age."

"But you're staying in Munsonville?"

"Definitely. Like any good son, I hope to care for the needs of my parents." A shadow crossed his face. "If they allow it."

"And you'll continue working with Dr. Gothart?"

"Why all this interest in my romantic rendezvouses?"

"Because when you're ready, I have a suggestion."

Dr. Parks paused and raised an eyebrow. "Oh?"

"She is young but not a maiden, a widow, in fact, so she is experienced. She is also an intellectual, openminded, and not afraid of opposing convention."

"Pray, John, who are you suggesting?"

"Neta Ashmore."

"Neta Ashmore," Dr. Parks repeated, knitting his brows together. Then his face brightened in recognition. "Reverend Marseilles' housekeeper?"

Henry grinned. "Yes, 'housekeeper.' Meaning she cooks, cleans and provides 'horizontal refreshment,' to the reverend at his house."

Dr. Parks smothered his own grin. "Why should I court her? She's apparently already 'taken.'"

"Because by restoring the honor of a 'dear upstanding woman' whose reputation has been sullied by an 'honorable' man, you'll win the trust of the villagers, your parents included." Henry stretched and yawned. "And you'll hurt Reverend Marseilles, which is what John wants and won't say."

Dr. Parks looked at John. "Why don't you just eat him?"

"I'd rather he suffer," John said. "And he'll suffer if you lure Neta Ashmore away."

"Speaking of suffering," Dr. Parks reached into his coat pocket, pulled out a piece of paper, and leaned forward to give it to Henry. "I want you to 'eat dinner' in Evansville tomorrow evening. Here is the name."

Henry read it, and his eyes widened. Dr. Parks reached for the decanter. "I see you know the place. And the victim."

"Any particular reason?"

"Personal reasons," Dr. Parks said as he topped off his glass. "The man is weary of life and doesn't have the tallywags to end it himself. But it will satisfy your bill with me. Tomorrow we shall create your chronic disease. In a week, we'll unveil you, and I know just the person to invite. In fact, I will telegraph him in the morning."

"Anything else?" Henry asked.

"I don't think so," Dr. Parks said. "Why?"

But Henry was already in Pennsylvania holding out his hands; Agnes eased into them with an amazing litheness, as if she still felt young and still belonged there. Not once did he move his gaze from her eyes; not once did he show her anything but the adoration that she needed to see from him toward her. He whirled her around and around and around and around until she grew dizzy from whirling, when he could pull her close and stroke her neck with one hand and then lay her back and fuck her with three fingers, keeping Agnes ecstatic, distracted, and finally, lethargic, while he...

Thus revitalized, he abandoned Agnes to her sleepless sleep, relieved he needn't witness her lonely despair at sunrise when she wakened to the painful reality of her empty cell.

After John cut the bonds, Henry immediately entered the gloaming and teleported to Evansville, much swifter than the four hours it used to take him on horseback. The gravel road had given way to asphalt, and many of the tidy frame buildings now boasted additions, dormers, or completely new and larger tidy frame buildings in the spots where their former structures had met the wrecking ball once they'd outlived their usefulness. Typical Lord Girard behavior. Neighborhoods stretched both north and south now; Henry doubted a single farm survived and briefly wondered the fate of the old Platt property.

But except for briefly noting the growth in the old, rural company town, Henry didn't loiter, and he especially didn't visit The Courier's office. Stopping at The Courier would waste time (as if time pressed Henry, he thought with a snort), but stopping posed a risk, too – of faltering in his task. Now that Henry was regularly slurping Agnes' blood, he was prone to momentary sentimentality. Best to get that "dinner engagement" done – quickly.

Now in all the time Henry had worked for Horace Fuller, The Courier's editor, Henry had never visited Horace's lodgings, but Henry knew his way around Evansville, and he had Horace's address from Dr. Parks. Soon he "appeared" inside Horace's cottage at the edge of town and gazed at Horace's sleeping frame. How old was he now? Sixty-five? Nearly ten years ago, Horace had reached the point of simply putting in his time and collecting his salary. Why was he still in this dead-end place, putting out a dead-end paper?

"The man is weary of life and doesn't have the tallywags to end it himself."

Henry glanced around the empty room. A bed, a bureau, and an old, tired man. Not even a picture or two to counteract the bleakness of the plain board walls. Hell, even Agnes had a crucifix. Hadn't Horace any family? Never mind, scratch that. Henry once had family, and he was altogether poorer for it.

"Henry?"
"Still copyediting."
Horace stretched and reached for his mug. "Warm up?"
"Sure."
Horace set the tin to boil and stretched again. The mismatched buttons on his worn checked waistcoat strained with the effort, especially near the middle age pouch above his belt, but his eyes had a youthful keenness that didn't require reading spectacles for editing copy.
The only sound in the room was the scritch of Henry's pencil. The acrid smell of warmed-over coffee mixed with that of the charred wood from the stove.
"Getting favorable responses on 'Carter Jones and the Sunset Ghost.' Folks here like scandalous and scary."
"Gratifying."
"And profitable, which is especially gratifying."
Steam rose and rattled the lid. Horace removed the pot.
"Hand up your mug, Henry."

Great. Flashbacks. That's what Henry needed right now, a visit from the Ghost of his Evansville past. Henry was dead; Horace wanted to be dead, and Henry was here to get the job done, not stroll down Memory Lane.

Horace blinked. "Babbie's not back?"

"Sheriff and his party hadn't returned when I left." Henry rolled up the sheet and began typing. "It's possible they've found her by now."

The editor grabbed his coffee and leaned back in his chair. "What did Nancy say?"

"That her daughter had been outside watching bluebirds," Henry said over the clack of the keys.

"What's your take?"

Henry sputtered, "She wandered into the woods and took a wrong turn," but he knew the words tumbling from his mouth were lies.

"I don't think so."

The finality in Horace's tone brought Henry's typing to a halt. The room turned colder than it should on an August night.

Henry took a long dry swallow. "Why do you say that?"

"Girl knows the woods like I know the back of my hand."

" You think someone abducted her? In Evansville?"

"No place is above immorality and cruel acts. New folks coming through all the time. I'll wager the sheriff will be questioning a few of those strangers, even if he finds the little miss tonight."

Henry resumed typing.

"But?"

Henry sighed, stopped, and ran a hand through his hair. "I don't know."

"What happened at the farmhouse? A good reporter digs below surface answers."

So Henry told him. Horace listened while pensively scratching the stubble on his chin.

"It's strange tale, Henry."

"I'm aware."

"But you've got good sense. I trust that. It'll be interesting to see how this plays out.

Well, Henry thought as he watched Horace snuffle in his sleep. The disappearance of Babbie Platt played out in ways that even Darwin would have...

Stop it! Do it now! Now!

Henry lowered himself close to the sleeping man's neck, bared his fangs, and hesitated once again. What was wrong with him? This was a killing, nothing more. Henry killed every night, several times a night, and the man lying before him yearned for death, if Dr. Parks had spoken the truth – and who the fuck cared if Dr. Parks spoke the truth about this soon-to-be victim or not? Although Henry, mostly, didn't mind killing, he had just enough of Agnes in his veins to restore a trace of empathy for someone who'd meant something to him in life. Not the type of empathy that would prevent Henry from carrying out the plan, Henry quickly reassured himself, but the type of empathy that spurred Henry to kill and kill quickly, so quickly that Horace could quickly reach eternal rest and never realize Henry had been the one to send him there. For once, Henry was glad of his hypnotic abilities, and he used those abilities now. Soon, Henry was gulping down Horace's blood, and all twinges of regret disappeared.

A short time later, Henry felt a tug, and he crashed to the floor. The room whirred before him with nauseating speeds: gray swirls with color splotches. A hand grasped his shoulder and violently shook it.

"Wake up," Dr. Gothart's voice echoed from faraway. "It's time."

"I can't," Henry slurred, slipping away.

Something pried his eyes open. A leering Dr. Gothart pressed his nose against Henry's.

"It's time," Dr. Gothart repeated, holding out a glass of blood.

"Time?" Henry asked, trying to shake the fuzziness from his brain, which still felt comfortably bloated.

"Yes. Time to create your blood disorder."

"Later." Henry drifted away.

SMACK!

Henry struggled to lift a hand to rub his head as Dr. Gothart hauled him to his feet, saying, "We have to do it now."

But Henry's legs buckled, and he dropped to the ground a short distance from John, who still lay in a somnolent heap on the floor. So Dr. Gothart grabbed Henry under his arms and hauled him up the stairs. When they reached the top, bright light seared through Henry's eyelids and burned his skin — Henry actually smelled the scorching — and still Dr. Gothart kept dragging him across the floors.

"Put him over there," Dr. Parks' voice said.

Henry felt four pairs of hands lead him to a chair. He felt a tightening pressure across his chest. He cracked his eyes open. Dr. Gothart was tightly wrapping a good length of thick rope around him, crushing his chest while binding him to the chair. The drawn curtains barely restrained the sun, which beat against the glass in an effort to cook his flesh, which was already tingling and prickling. He glimpsed white rugs and padded chairs, along with deep blue and bright pink accessories. He knew this room: Bryony's parlor. The glaring warmth swirled Henry into a weird, broiling drowsiness, but he managed to mumble, "Is this a trick?"

"No trick," Dr. Parks said. "But after today, no one will ever suspect your penchant for the night is anything more than a horrible disease. Everyone will completely understand why you shun the sun."

Henry rolled his head back and tried to focus. Dr. Parks standing by a window, his hand holding the cord of the shade. Dr. Gothart stuffed a gag into Henry's mouth, but Henry spat it out with a force that caused Dr. Parks to raise an eyebrow.

"Why the gag?" Henry mumbled again.

"To stifle your screams," Dr. Parks said as Dr. Gothart restuffed the cloth into Henry's mouth and tightly tied and double-knotted it. "Because this is going to hurt. A lot."

"Close your eyes," Dr. Gothart hissed in his ear.

Henry did. And somewhere in the distance, Henry heard the shade release with a loud snap.

240

CHAPTER TWENTY-SEVEN: SCRAP TOSSED TO THE WINDS

ristle and bones, breadcrumbs, chips of pie crust, bruised lettuce leaves, and jelly, custard, and gravy smears, collided with half-eaten chicken slices, bits of buttered biscuits, potato drops, and forsaken wedges of pumpkin pie marked with fork tines.

These filled the inn's white ironstone dishes, which were stacked and scattered all over the table and floor of Room 27 in gluttonous disarray.

For several hours they'd kept the staff hopping with their outrageous requests for more soups, more roasted meats, more roasted vegetables, more rolls and butter, and still more puddings, pies, and jellies, which George called his effigy of the fatted calf, to celebrate his return from death to life. Although he partook of a simpler dish – boiled chicken, boiled potato, thrice-boiled cabbage, boiled custard – and kept the portions modest, he ate with restrained gusto and his face glowed with new-found health and delight.

What the guests lacked in number they made up in noise. They talked over each other and laughed with loud guffaws. Alannah, dressed only in a pink floral day wrapper, reclined on the bed with Eugenia, who nursed and napped through much of the commotion, heedless that a man had struggled for his life on that same bed. But before the child dropped off altogether, she did her part to add to the upbeat noise, giggling her head off whenever Alannah tickled her or spontaneously adding a shriek of her own, a gleeful test of the powers of her voice and elated to be part of the gala. Isabella and Lula, as matriarchs of the madcap, sat tall in two of the chairs at the round table wearing tea gowns of figured silk: violet for Isabella and slate for Lula. George, as the recovering invalid and honoree, occupied the third, shunning formalwear for a red paisley dressing gown with a wide black silk sash over his shirt and trousers. All three cousins, and Milton, sprawled on the floor and ate their meal there. Lillian wore a brown cotton skirt and beige ruffled shirtwaist, and her pompadour had loosened, but that only added to her natural loveliness. Leo had loosened his tie and rolled his cuffs to his elbows – as had Milton, who had also discarded his waistcoat and collar. Luther chimed into their chatter from time to time, and, while he didn't actually laugh, he smiled broadly enough to show he was enjoying the little party.

Marie sat alone on the floor near the table, legs modestly tucked beneath her, and picked at her plate. She wore a proper visiting dress of turquoise silk and puffed sleeves; her grandmother's rose gold diamond necklace clasped around her neck; her oldest charm bracelet silently jingling as she moved her fork.

For whom the bell tolls,
It tolls for thee.

All through the afternoon, George entertained them with one tale after another, stories about the stampedes, fires, shootings, stabbings, and bank robberies he'd covered. He talked about playing calliopes on riverboats and circuses, dancing the polka in saloons, and sleeping in brothels. He shared his experiences about arriving at Haymarket Square the day after the riot, Oklahoma the day after the land rush, and Johnstown the day after the flood, making himself the buffoon of his own inadequacies, but he told those stories in such an endearing and humorous way that they unconsciously leaned forward and closer, enraptured at every word. George, of course, ate up their attention with as much relish as he did the meal. His eyes sparkled, and color crept back into his cheeks – the flush of good cheer, more intoxicating to George, Marie knew, than the finest of wines. George spent his whole life spinning stories. He loved nothing more than an audience, especially an audience that gasped in all the right places, laughed until the tears streamed down their faces, and choked on their own breaths.

"Did I ever tell you about the…" George began again.

Not once did George's stomach rebel. He no longer needed bismuth; Dr. Parks discontinued it a week ago and announced that, in a few days, George might try the stairs. That is why the party came to him, because George's legs needed more strength to make the trek to the inn's dining room, and because he wanted to carouse now. Although they'd eaten to bursting, they continued to drink, and out of respect to George, they drank only tea. But they drank a lot of tea, pots and pots of tea; they got drunk on tea and kept sending for tea until their stomachs and bladders could hold no more. But they still had room for stories, and George continued regaling his little party with one anecdote after the next, except now those heavily exaggerated tales were accompanied with the background sounds of someone filling a pot behind the screen.

Only Marie wasn't brimming with excitement or tea. Only Marie glowered as she pecked at her food and nursed half a cup. To everyone else in the room George was back, and he was back with renewed vigor, elegance, animation, and verve. Neither he nor Isabella cared that the money was gone, the big breaks were gone, and that their wispy future was so far gone Marie could scarcely glimpse its hazy outline.

Mostly, the essence of her papa's vibrancy was gone. Marie saw what the others did not: a semi-forced gaiety. He no longer had hope in his eyes. Just the color blue.

Eventually the hilarity wound down as all hilarities do, and the conversation took a downturn, in Marie's estimation.

"...and we're really hoping with your experience and knowledge, Uncle George, you..."

"...naturally, everyone is curious now that the mansion is abandoned. Will John Simons..."

"Of course, I could make a few phone calls to..."

"I have a source in New York who might..."

"...the rooms are darling and wait until you see the furniture!"

"Yes. My father handcrafted every piece, just for you, and he told me that..."

"...no need to bother about such things. We're planning a housewarming par..."

"...should be ready for occupancy by the end of next week, I should think..."

"Uncle George, any change you'd like to make at The Times..."

"...because Dad really respected your judgment and certainly would want us to..."

"An honest wage for honest work and surrounded by a loving family," George sighed with deep happiness and reached for Isabella's jeweled hand. "Only an ungrateful man would want for more."

At that moment, Alannah strolled across the room with Eugenia and disappeared behind the screen to change the baby's diaper and obtain her own relief, as Alannah had lounged with the baby the whole time. But that act changed the tone. The guests began yawning and stretching, and the help knocked at the door, ready to clear away the remnants and sweep up the crumbs. From her place on the floor, Marie watched the farewells and exchange of hugs, brightened with the knowledge of "next time," but she did not participate in them, nor did anyone make it a point to address her. George, true to his performance form, still had one last yarn to spin, which kept everyone lingering at the door, even the last servant with the last tray, who just had to hear one last story from George.

Before George could turn the locks or slide the bolts, Marie, still on the floor, snatched his ankles and screamed through a sudden monsoon of tears, "Papa! Don't do this!"

He looked down at her in wonder and surprise. "Why, Little Marie…"

"Please! I beg you!"

"Little Marie, it is already done."

"No!"

"It's the right move. You'll see."

"But, Papa! The Dream!"

"Little Marie," her papa began in his kindest, gentlest tone as he crouched beside her. "The Dream is gone. The winds of life have blown it away." He brushed her tears away with the back of his hand, but fresh ones continued to fall. "Please don't be sad."

She jerked away at the hard, quick raps on the door and wiped her cheeks with her dress cuffs like a common girl. Because that's all she was now, a common girl in a common village.

But before George could call out, "Come in!" And before Isabella could react, or Lula reach for the handle, the door burst open, and Dr. Parks strode into the room, where he stopped short, lest he trip over two of its occupants.

Despite his quizzical look at the queer scene, Dr. Parks was smiling, the broadest, most genuine smile Marie had ever seen him smile. The light that once shone in her papa's eyes now shone clear and strong in his.

"Mr. Clare," Dr. Parks said.

He paused, the grin threatening to split his face.

"A man is downstairs looking for you," Dr. Parks said. "Shall I send him up?"

CHAPTER TWENTY-EIGHT: A NEW GASTRONOMY

r. Parks' alibi burned like actual hell.

That was Henry's assessment of the process.

Seared to a crisp like the bread of his old childhood homes, hovels more like it, for his vagrant parents often moved him and his sisters in the middle of the night, forsaking their meager possessions in the quick process.

"Mummy!"

Maggie slammed the pans on the table and kicked the oven door shut. She scowled at the incinerated crust of the salt-risen loaves and watched their centers sink in shame. Her brown eyes blazed with indignation; color crept into her sallow cheeks.

Caroline swiped her apron and grabbed a knife.

"Don't be discouraged, Margaret. Look." Caroline overturned a pan with her knobby hands, and the crisp loaf popped out. "We trim a little here." She sawed through the brick. "And we trim a little there." She brushed the black crumbles into her palm and out the open window for the pigeons.

"See?" Caroline gestured at the naked white lump. "A nice firm loaf that will stand up to gravy."

Well, Henry hoped to stand up to the grave. He'd spent quite a few nights bathing raw, oozing sores beneath the moon now that most of the crumbly skin had flaked off. The radiance penetrated his skin, and he took it like a true coward: he moaned and whined and writhed over the ground. But each night, before submitting to the heat lamp in the sky, he feasted and then he teleported to the convent to fuck with Agnes, which was not the same as fucking Agnes, although either way, she was still fucked. At least, that's how Henry rationalized it, as if anything about vampirism or the attempt at reversing it was rational. After his moon treatment, Henry only had enough energy to catch, kill, and consume creatures within reach as he slogged back to the cellar. When Henry was young and sick and suffering with asthma, he mother and sisters petted him so he could rest most of the day. Well, resting most of the day was impossible when one rested from a noose, none of which soothed the burns on his neck.

Mothers and sisters.

How odd he recalled them now! He'd swept them from memory long before death, much as Lizzie once swept up dead roaches while Pa, ever the cunning gypsy, strummed his guitar and drank quarts of beer. Their recollection stirred little except the recollecting, a collection of names and facts with scant connection to him, better suited to Kellen's memorandum book.

Caroline, his mother: Old, feeble, cheerful.
Etta: Loving, jolly, kind.
Lottie: Somber, brooding, diligent
Maggie: Vain, selfish, diffident
Lizzie: Energetic, ambitious, bold
Kitty: Quiet, dark, hopeful

Fuck it. He didn't need reminiscences; he needed distraction. Since he must play the part of the "old Henry," he ought to pretend the part. And since he spent half his non-existence in an underground room filled with his works, he'd start with painting.

"Portraits?"
"A surprise. For Bryony. For our anniversary."
"Two portraits? Three?"
"I made a list. And prepared a room."

Hoping to punish him for his adulterous sins, the undead John had recently added to that anniversary list by creating an eternal list of paintings, all with Bryony as their subject, he had ordered Henry to complete. Henry scoffed at the order and chuckled inside when John presented it. He was more dead to Bryony than John was, but if John liked to think his injunction tortured Henry, so be it. Actually, Henry only dimly recalled how he met Bryony or why he esteemed her.

MUNSVONVILLLE MINISTER WISHES PORTRAIT FOR YOUNG DAUGHTER - (STOP) - PLEASE SEND HENRY - (STOP) - GREATLY OBLIGED - (STOP) – SIDNEY

"You don't have to accept," his uncle said quietly as he reached for the teapot. "But Sidney is hoping you'll agree...as a personal favor to him."

"Uncle...of course. I'll telegraph Sidney tonight and call on the minister this weekend."

To underscore his decree, John had tacked the list next to the easel, so Henry reviewed the ideas and went with the first one: Bryony in the morning room, teacup at her right, book in front of her. She pillowed her cheek with her left hand as she read; the fingers of her right looped through the cup, as if to bring it to her lips. So Henry set up a fresh canvas, sharpened his pencils, and began to sketch or, rather, tried to sketch. His dead fingers couldn't properly grasp the pencil, and the clumsy and imprecise marks showed it. Plus, Henry's mind repeatedly strayed from the task. He drew a line and then a line and then a line and then a line and then a line. Was it always this dull and tedious? How had he spent hours at this? Had he actually enjoyed it? And yet, the alive Henry doted on art. Some of those packed-up crates in his study held old sketchbooks. His commissioned pieces hung inside the parsonage.

On other nights, Henry abandoned his art and restlessly wandered the vast Simons estate, peering past the seedlings and into the ground to their roots, wracking his mind as to why annuals and perennials once fascinated him, why his uncle built him a greenhouse at Arcadia, and why Henry spent years crossbreeding roses to create a purple variety. What value did it hold? After all, he did sign his paintings with a purple rose in the right-hand corner instead of his name. But from this side of eternity, the entire process of horticulture felt like a futile waste of effort and energy. Every bud withers and drops; in the end, all flowers, no matter how beautiful or fragrant, die. Even bryony wouldn't escape death forever. And in death, only blood was needed. So why bother?

Branches with graceful curves. Corkscrew perennials. Sleek leaves and fuzzy leaves. Flowers: broad and focal, tall and slim, short and bunched, a solitary stem here and there, thoughtfully bedded in triangular and crescent groupings. Pink and white blossoms promising summer fruit.

He paused to study bryony, the noxious weed he crossbred with creeping witch flower at John's pleading, which produced tiny pink, instead of white, flowers — but with the characteristic white glands on the large lobed leaves as the original bryony. He himself had plunged the massive, fleshy, swollen taproots, all of them harboring a toxic milky liquid, deep into the moist soil of John's property. They sprouted hairy vines that grew up the trees and across the vegetation; their tendrils wound around every other living plant with unflinching tenacity and spawned a dizzying maze of curlicues across Simons mansion and the outbuildings.

He gave a short bitter laugh.

Because in the end, "bryony" had outlived them all.

Henry even tried turning his attention back to the typewriter and manuscripts in progress. But, again, his leaden fingers stiffly pecked out the keys. He spent many hours rereading his notes, hoping to spark an interest in the characters or plot lines: dastardly bastards who murdered, plundered, poisoned, butchered, and raped (sometimes in the same scene); gangsters and pirates; women with daggers up their nickers who kidnapped and avenged; and nefarious henchmen and highway men.

"That's the drollest thing I've read in ever so long." She opened her purse and removed a silver dollar. "Will this suffice? When might I expect another installment?"

Henry's heart beat fast at this first sale. "Anytime, ma'am! I've books and books of stories."

He abandoned the typewriter, his notes, his story. All of it: stale and tedious. He swerved his chair to the window and looked out at the dark lake, brooding. He now understood why people engaged themselves in these various pastimes. They passed time. And Henry had plenty of time to pass.

Henry's first instinct was to fall prostate on the floor, so awed was he the magnificence of this dual-story, high-ceilinged palace sheltering the knowledge of the ages. The ivory pillars, the carved balcony that ran the perimeter of the room, the ornate arches, the oversized oils in potent hues, and the everlasting rows of bookcases upstairs and downstairs, all jammed with thoughts waiting for Henry to discover them.

He leaped up, ripped the lid off the first crate, and pawed through one book after another: *The Life and Opinions of Tristram Shandy, Gentleman; The Rime of the Ancient Mariner; Gulliver's Travels; Emma; One Thousand and One Nights; Troilus and Cressida; The Knight of the Road; A String of Pearls.* His mind whirred through the words; not a single syllable stirred him. Disgusted, he slammed The Bible shut and pitched it across the room. Then he pitched *The Poets of Arabia, Song of Roland, Five Little Peppers,* and a few more, whose titles he didn't bother to note. But even the sound of their thuds against the wall failed to stir the least bit of satisfaction.

So Henry headed to the cloister. He needed a return of humanity and not just for his protection against slayers. The frustration and boredom would drive him mad if he didn't relieve it.

Agnes jolted awake, and her face immediately lit up, so Henry knew she saw what he wanted her to see, the dapper Henry that danced with her on New Year's Eve 1888 inside her father's Fifth Avenue greenhouse, away from the party, where the scuffing of their feet on the floor all but drowned out the faint sounds of the orchestra, and where Henry had proposed marriage.

He extended his hand; her hand flew to her mouth to stifle her excited gasp, but Henry caught it anyway. Now she was standing before him, her crystalline violet eyes shining, and he held those eyes as he, smiling deeply into them, brought that wizened hand to his lips and tenderly kissed it. Her smile was wide; her face, radiant; gently, he clasped that hand, slid an arm around her waist, and pulled her close. He stepped to the side, he stepped back, he stepped and stepped with a sway in each step, and she moved with him, gliding like a fairy as he raised her arm and languidly twirled her. She faced him again, and he eased her around the room, her joy at his presence giving him energy; her eagerness for his hunger edging him to ravenous; he spun her around and around and around and around, and then yanked her tightly into him. Back and forth, back and forth, step by step, around and around, and as she arched back, he eased her onto the bed, and her mouth was already opening, and his hand was already under her shift and working her hard. But the effort he expended to teleport to Agnes, penetrate her dreams as the handsome young Henry instead of the disfigured Phlegethon he'd become, and revel in her orgasms as much as she, since they caused the blood to spurt out faster from her neck: all of it felt laborious, tiresome, and pointless.

"I love you, dearest boy," she whispered in sleep.

Temporarily satiated blood-wise and feeling less depleted in his non-spirit, Henry left the languid, pasty Agnes to her revelries and reappeared in the back of Simons Mansion, wondering if he'd absorbed enough of her essence to revive even a token amount of the pleasure he once felt in sweeping pencil strokes across a canvas.

On his way to the gallows, he passed the forsaken kitchen and laundry. Now Henry had vaguely known of these rooms but except for the one day with Anna, the day Bryony labored and died, when Henry had rummaged through the icebox for a make-shift lunch for him and the little servant girl, he had never explored those rooms.

Curious, blasé, and not really finding more stimulating options, Henry wandered into the laundry room and looked at the large stove that once heated water and irons. Wash tubs and wooden frames for drying the clothes also filled the room. His childhood home: one wooden tub, for washing clothes and themselves.

Caroline brushed back a gray lock with a soapy hand and glanced up from the wash tub with a proud smile. "He's gifted, Elizabeth, just like your father."

Recollections as if from a hazy dream: Henry knew these should stir something inside him: tenderness, grief, sadness, affection, yearning, something. But he felt nothing. He could acknowledge the fact of "Caroline was your mother, and you loved her," as Professor Julian Bayard once taught him the basics of the trivium at Arcadia; Henry could accept that truth.

251

But his experience of it – any fervor or melancholy or the lightest tremor of emotion – these remained as foreign and remote to him as Hindustani.

Kitty's eyes met Henry's and then returned to her mush. Silently and slowly, Kitty moved her spoon from bowl to mouth and back again. Henry drained the rest of his coffee and rapidly started on the gray sludge in his bowl.

He recalled other poor and meager meals he'd share with Pa, Mummy, and Lottie, Maggie, Kitty, and Lizzie, that was spoiled or stolen from the storekeeper – what was her name?

Lizzie laid out the treasures while Henry blinked and adjusted to consciousness. Mrs. Variola had sent several cans of beef broth, as well as a string of sausages and two loaves of bread.
"She's stewing a real bone tomorrow!"

As, yes, of course. Mrs. Variola.

His thoughts wandered back to another kitchen, this one in young adulthood. It belonged to his oldest sister Etta, her husband William, and his nieces and nephews: Adelaide, Archer, Emma, Giselle, and Wyatt, and he was thrilled to join them.

To assemble in the kitchen with his bone and blood and prepare a meal they would partake as one, this Henry yearned to experience.

But – why?

Henry drifted into the spacious kitchen and scanned the room. Food-preparation tables with drawers. Several coal stoves. Pumps and wash basins. Shelves for pots, pans, and staples. Utensils hanging from large hooks. An enormous, walk-in pantry. Two cellars: one for vegetables and another for wine. A large oak ice box. A lot of effort for an act Henry could accomplish with a quick teleport and baring of two fangs.

After they'd finished the braised chicken, roasted potatoes, and young asparagus, and then passed the fruit and cheese... and they passed the foie gras, and the chateaubriand, and the braised asparagus...the pork ragout with its emphasis of scallions and cloves, as he preferred it...

Henry understood kill and eat and subsist. Stalk the prey; kill the prey; eat the prey: solitary acts best executed alone. But gathering for a meal had meaning for the living beyond the act of digestion. That's why Kellen assembled them into the dining room. He taught two lessons at once. It's just that...

Wyatt and Archer brought two chairs from the parlor, making a tight fit around the rectangular table, which was covered in green-checked cloth and positioned in the middle of the spacious kitchen, the largest room in the house.

...it's just that gathering for a meal had no meaning for Henry.

Now. Gathering for a meal had no meaning now.

But at one time, it, more than consuming the food. To be recognized in the world as Henry, Henry must recreate elements of his old self.

Dinner was stewed beef with carrots, boiled beans with strips of onion laid across, sliced brown bread, and baked apples for dessert.

Or, as Archer noted after William said grace, "Plain, wholesome food that doesn't arouse the passions."

Wyatt nudged Henry and grinned.

"My brother intended to say that the beef is savory, the beans are flavorful, the bread is yeasty and warm, and the baked apples are spicy and sweet."

Where did the importance lie in a shared meal like? And how could he pretend it mattered?

His uncle tucked the heavy white linen into Henry's collar. "Take what you like and leave the rest. I trust you'll find something to interest you."

It all interested Henry: the tiny thin triangular slices of bread sandwiching even thinner slices of tender meat, exquisite little cakes topped with marmalade, transparent cucumber and radish rounds, and an assortment of berries, all arranged to please the eye and tempt the palate.

He had an idea.

Henry headed to the ice box where he had fished out that lunch he'd shared with Anna and opened the door. The water had long since evaporated but a delicious aroma and interesting colors and textures greeted him. The milk had curdled into a solid yellow lump except for its black-speckled amber layer of cream. The chickens' wrinkled skin hung over their bones like a maize overcoat. The orange cheeses now sported coats of many colors, reminiscent of the Old Testament Joseph. The salted codfish had shrunk to powdery marbles, and the pink leathery ham was topped with gelatinous shine. One mutton roast had melted to jelly; a side of beef had partly dissolved.

Most of that didn't matter since spoilage had no effect on vampires. Still he couldn't use anything in a liquified state, at least not where solids were needed.

He pawed through some drawers, and found not one, but two cookbooks: *A New System of Domestic Cookery* by Mrs. Maria Eliza Ketelby Rundell and *Miss Beecher's Domestic Receipt Book: Designed as a Supplement to Her Treatise on Domestic Economy.*

He also found a stack of hardish squash in the corner, hardish because the skin had collapsed where the flesh evaporated, like the cheeks of an old granny with her teeth out.

Emma handed him a steel butcher knife. "First you cut it in half and scoop out the seeds. Then we'll strip the peel and stew the flesh until it's soft."

He assessed the rest of the stores and discovered a sack of enchanted cornmeal, or so it seemed when Henry peered inside, for the sour, musty grains crawled as if bewitched. Upon closer inspection, Henry noticed an infestation of weevils; the same was true about the beans and the flour. So – all usable, although he ought to supplement the meats in the icebox with fresher catches: rabbit, opossum, giant rats. With the diligence of devoted housewife, Henry ripped several blank pages from the

254

cookbooks (since Kellen's memorandum was full), sliced his wrist for the "ink," and composed a list and four invitations.

> *"Delicious."*
> *With a dusting of the white linen, Agnes brushed the crumbs off his lips. "Your same opinion of the lemon tarts."*
> *"And the chocolate tortes."*
> *"You're impossible."*
> *Henry kissed her cheek, a warm statue. "My dear, whatever pleases you."*

He slid two folded notes underneath front door of the colonial at the top of Blue Gill Road for the doctors, and he left two on the piano bench, one for John and one for Kellen.

> *Mr. Henry Matthews*
> *Requests the pleasure of your company*
> *11 p.m. Saturday, April 25.*
> *Formal Dining, Simons Mansion, Munsonville.*
> *Bring your best appetites.*

Then Henry went "shopping" for additional ingredients, prepared the dining room (tying up the decaying scraps of Kellen's last lesson in the cloth and dumping them onto the growing pile in the corner), and headed to the cellar well before dawn, so as to murder John the moment he stumbled into "their" room. Henry had many preparations for tomorrow evening, so he wanted to get to dead as soon as possible.

The moment John headed to the music room the following night, Henry took possession of the kitchen. He carefully followed Kellen's instructions for the safe lighting of fires, and then sped through the slicing, dicing, chopping, mixing, and stirring, harkening back to memories from his human days of food preparations as best as he could. He kept one eye on the next step in the recipes while nibbling here, tasting there, and licking his fingers, as any cook secretly does when no one is watching.

During an odd moment, a thought that elicited a chuckle as the entire process felt odd to him, he bolted upstairs and set the table.

At the appointed time, Henry appeared in the library where Dr. Parks was drowsing over brandy, Dr. Gothart and Kellen were smoking their respective pipes and cigars, and John was playing a lively waltz.

When John saw Henry, he abruptly left off with a curious stare, which caused the other occupants of the room to turn and stare, too.

For Henry stood before them in a white apron smeared with grease, blood, and gravy, and he had smoothed his hair into a snood. With a queer little bow and a congenial smile, Henry announced, "Dinner is served."

Then he led the little party to the dining room. John and Kellen stopped short in the doorway, speechless. Dr. Parks fled, gagging into his hand, Dr. Gothart actually laughed out loud, literally threw back his head and roared.

For the serving platters held delicacies of all kinds: boiled beans in the stewed chicken broth with strips of slimy ham jerky across the top, rehydrated gray codfish, mutton "jelly," beef "soup," flaky squash, biscuits and cornbread speckled with baked weevils, skewered rats roasted whole, and a variety of opossums, rabbits and moles in their raw dismembered states. He had garnished the whole with dead roaches and live spiders, with the latter desperately trying to scuttle away, which only further buried their tiny legs into the gloop, all to be served up on dusty bryony-pattered china and eaten from green-tinged, coppery silver. He had laid out bottles of John's Bordeaux and goblets of infant blood.

So Henry smiled again and repeated with a flourish, "Dinner is served. Let us celebrate our glorious reentry into society."

Granted it wasn't Arcadia. It wasn't even Simons Mansion at its best.

But it was, to use Dr. Gothart's words, close enough.

CHAPTER TWENTY-NINE: HOPE AND A FUTURE

aving grown up with a keen knowledge of both sacred scripture and sacred art, Marie had also formulated certain images of the term "savior" whenever she heard it.

For instance, she knew the rough, meditative, very human style of Rembrandt's Jesus; the homely, careworn look of Da Vinci's Jesus in *The Last Supper*, and the majestic, nearly ethereal, almost iconic style of Raphael's Jesus.

But none of those concepts even approached the one sitting at the little round table with her father and Dr. Parks. This savior, average in height, stout in width, and wearing a gleaming monocle and an impeccably tailored suit was named Albert Brumfeldt, and he owned many newspapers across the country. And he had pored over her papa's stacks of clippings for three-quarters of an hour by the Arnold and Dent traveling clock.

"These are quite good," Mr. Brumfeldt said. "You have a keen instinct for news, and you report it in clear, concise tones."

George smiled, a little timidly, it seemed to Marie, and sweat beaded on the proud and noble brow. From across the room, Marie saw what Mr. Brumfeldt could not: her papa's hands on his lap, which he absently wrung like a nervous old lady. By contrast, Dr. Parks leaned confidently back in his chair, hands clasped behind his neck, looking as smug as the tabby that had just caught the canary.

Marie glanced away from her sampler and at her mama. Isabella, head bent over her work, slowly moved the needle up and down and through the cloth, again and again and again and again and again. But Marie saw the stiffness in her mama's fingers and the tension in her mama's arms, signs Isabella was on high alert. Lula sat next to Isabella, browsing through Vogue and languidly turning the pages, but every line on Lula's face was taut.

"Here's my proposal," Mr. Brumfeldt said. "My editor-in-chief at the Evansville Courier died quite unexpectedly last week. The paper's small staff is scrambling like cockroaches without leadership, and I need to fill the position immediately."

George's face drooped as he absorbed this final blow to his cherished aspirations, but he feigned a polite smile. Her papa might nobly bury The Dream to help lead a small newspaper, the life's work of his dearest friend and the family of his beloved wife. But he wouldn't forsake his family to scrabble for a stranger.

Yet with his gaze so singularly fixed on Mr. Brumfeldt, George also missed what Marie caught: Dr. Parks, practically wriggling like a puppy with repressed excitement.

"Take the position for a year while I seek a suitable replacement," Mr. Brumfeldt said. "If your editorial skills consistently match what I see here, I'll set you up with any publication in the country, your preference."

Isabella cried out and nearly dropped her needlework; Aunt Lula gasped, clapping her hand to her mouth to stifle her outburst. George's lower lip began to tremble, and he rapidly winked both eyes.

"Mr. Clare, will you accept?"

Marie gripped the chair arms tightly. Her heart practically banged out of her chest.

"Yes," George said in a quavering voice. "Yes, thank you."

"Excellent." Mr. Brumfeldt whisked out his pocket watch, checked it, and then stuffed it away. He removed a thick packet from his briefcase, which slid toward George. "Here is information about my company and my contract. Read it carefully. I'll return later this evening for your signature." He snapped his briefcase shut, rose, and then nodded to Dr. Parks, who also rose. "I have another appointment."

George stood, too, a little shakily, gripping the table for support. When he found his balance, he reached out and clasped Mr. Brumfeldt's hands. "Thank you, sir, for this great favor."

Mr. Brumfeldt slid on his coat and reached for his stovepipe. "I'll ring ahead and arrange suitable housing." He glanced at the flashing of Isabella's diamonds in the lamplight as she obsessively stitched and then at those of Marie, which also caught the light as she stitched, and then back at George "Although it might be less than..."

"Any accommodations will be suitable," George interjected. "I'm...I'm truly humbled at the honor."

"I understand you've been ill." Mr. Brumfeldt glanced at Dr. Parks, who was buttoning his coat "Is a month sufficient time?"

"I think so," Dr. Parks said, but he grinned at George as he said it.

"Dr. Parks, I owe you so much," George said, and Marie could hear tears in his words. "Join us in a light repast?"

Still smiling, Dr. Parks shook his head. "I will indeed share a celebratory meal with you, but, regretfully, it won't be today. I must accompany Mr. Brumfeldt to his next meeting."

"I understand," George said, and he meant it, Marie knew.

Dr. Parks turned to Mr. Brumfeldt. "My other patient is still quite weak, but he definitely wants to meet with you."

Lula murmured to Isabella, "Come walk with me?"

Isabella gravely nodded in return. She set the needle-work aside, stood without a word, and followed her sister to the door, pausing to drop a kiss on George's head and whisper, "Congratulations," on her way out.

After Mr. Brumfeldt and Dr. Parks left, George poured himself another cup of tea and thoughtfully sipped it, but his eyes merrily danced, and a giddy smile kept breaking out as he read through the paperwork and contract.

Marie returned to her sampler, but her mind wandered away from the thread, and she found herself stealing glimpses at her papa. She thought of Dr. Parks and the many months of thrice-day visits, of monitoring her papa's vitals, mixing bismuth, and sharing his own life's blood. He infused George with water, corralled Isabella, prescribed a healing diet, crafted exercises to strengthen the wasted limbs, and, today, hand-delivered the last piece of medicine her papa needed to have life and have it more abundantly. Whereas some men had intelligence and skill, Dr. Parks also had discernment. And where some physicians recovered the bodily health of their patients, Dr. Parks restored the entire man. She knew why people condemned his vivisectionist activities. One can't see into a person without inflicting pain. Stay on the surface, be at ease, as Luther might say. But then never be whole.

Not until after Isabella returned, settled by the window, and, humming in forced cheerfulness, took up her abandoned needlework did George, still sitting at the little table with a cup, address the matter.

"Isabella," he began. "You are not happy."

She stopped humming and gaped at him in astonishment.

"I am very happy," Isabella insisted. "Finally – oh, George! We've worked and waited so long!"

He rested his cheek on his hand and gazed at her, a serious earnestness on his face. "But I am being selfish, uprooting you from your sister – and Little Marie from family she scarcely knows," George paused and added with emphasis, "Would you like to stay in Munsonville?"

"George!" Isabella looked confused. "You'd forsake The Dream?"

"No," George said, quietly, looking straight into her eyes. "I would not forsake the Dream that came for me."

"I don't understand."

He looked down at the stack of papers and fiddled with the pen. The he slapped his hand on it and looked at her. "Let us, for a while, separate."

"Papa!"

Isabella dropped her cloth. "George…separate?"

"You heard Mr. Brumfeldt. One year. A test. A chance to prove my skill. An opportunity for you to reconnect with family."

Isabella began to shake, and her lips quivered. "George, no!"

"After that, we shall begin our lives anew in Chicago or New York, wherever The Dream chooses."

Isabella burst into tears, which quickly turned into hard anguished sobbing. George paid no heed and swerved to Marie.

"Little Marie, would you not like that? To settle down with family, a home?"

"No, Papa. I want to live The Dream."

"Me, too," Isabella sobbed. "You are my husband. One flesh. Where you go, I go also."

"Even though my veins carry the blood of a monster?"

His words startled Isabella into silence, although her eyes continued welling up and spilling salty water down her cheeks. Their eyes met across the chasm. For a long time they remained fixed on each other, the distance between them greater than the length of Room 27. How like pilgrims they were, Marie thought, pilgrims who'd traversed a long arduous journey together on a single-lane road and who now had reached the crossroads, where each pilgrim must decide for himself the path to follow. One signpost said, "proclaim truth," while another said, "family honor," and still a third said, "keep the faith."

In the space of five months and one building, they'd traversed the City of Destruction, where George vomited blood all over the tablecloth in the dining room of Munsonville Inn, destroying, in that very moment, all chances of scooping the story of the tragedy of the Simons family, although no one admitted as such at the time. They went through the Slough of Despond that first night when George became afflicted again, then the Village of Morality when George received a blood transfusion which shook up their religious beliefs, then the Wicket Gate when they returned to and reaffirmed their dietary habits. Through keeping up with the news reports at the Interpreter's House, George began questioning God's plan for his life, and he faced The Cross when his money and health ran out, and he approached Difficulty Hill, where he made the courageous decision to forsake The Dream in favor of his family's needs. He enjoyed some old wine and respite of good health at the Palace Beautiful only to descend into the Valley of Humiliation by vomiting blood once again and losing so much strength as to become delirious. Dr. Parks and Marie kept watch with him in the Valley of the Shadow of Death, and Dr. Gothart literally ran a needle of morphine into Isabella's Vanity Fair. George trudged his way back to recover in the Doubting Castle, only for Isabella and Marie to plunge onto the bed and at his feet in the Giant Despair. But George experienced peace and comfort in the Delectable Mountains of recovery and altered diet and then accepted his new way of life in the County of Beulah, otherwise known as Munsonville. But like true pilgrims, Munsonville was not their true home; The Dream pushed them further still, to the Dark River, where they met the Shining One in the guise of a powerful publisher, who showed the way to The Dream, their Celestial City. Marie clung to Hopeful. Would her mama?

Then Isabella laughed out loud, even as tears streaked her cheeks. "So does the milk of human kindness. And we know what milk does to blood."

Marie did. She recalled how patiently her mama had used milk to rub out every bloodstain from George's shirts, just as George would rub out every incorrect mark he made with the typewriter with a pencil eraser. He wanted a perfect story; she wanted a perfect man. Marie held her breath; her eyes darted from one parent to the other. She watched George's face soften and then crumple as he fought back the tears.

"I can't argue with that," he whispered.

He held out his arms; Isabella and Marie sprang from their chairs and rushed to him, each perching herself on one of his legs. He tightened his arms around them and nuzzled their hair, first Isabella's and then Marie's, and Marie felt the wetness on his cheeks.

"I love you," he gasped, and that's when Marie began to cry, too. "I love you both so much!"

Even Dr. Parks' eyes grew moist as he rode in the hack with Brumfeldt to Simons Mansion, which, of course, the Clares could not see.

Brumfeldt did, though.

Especially when Dr. Parks removed his fine silk handkerchief to dab at the corners of those traitorous eyes.

"Slight cold," Dr. Parks said to Brumfeldt's astonished look.

Brumfeldt snorted, readjusted his monocle, and peered into the woods. "With your history of riff-raff, I'm surprised you've haven't dropped from consumption."

CHAPTER THIRTY: THE WOLF SHALL LIE DOWN WITH THE LAMB

fter the feast, Henry spent most the night scurrying about Simons Mansion in an effort to tidy up for the company. Mostly that meant shutting doors to hide the remnants of Kellen's finishing school (human remains, animals scraps, dried buckets of blood and so forth) and yanking up columbine, forget-me-knots, and everlasting peas from the gardens, which he arranged in as many vases as he could locate to conceal the stench of decay, including his.

After a hurried hunt, Henry dragged a few extras corpses into the cellar before going comatose; these he'd quickly consume later the next afternoon after Dr. Gothart prematurely awakened him. John had also brought a few spoils into the cellar, in case he reanimated before the guests had left. For John was not to exit the cellar until Henry gave leave; that order came directly from Dr. Gothart, who planned to hunker underground with John in case the prideful vampire entertained thoughts of disobeying.

But Dr. Gothart threatened Henry, too.

"Not one bite of one guest," Dr. Gothart had warned Henry. "You'll pay double, if you do."

Henry had no idea what he implied. Nor did he wish to find out. Although he was fairly certain Merlin wouldn't stake him. Soon, all too soon. Henry was crouching on the bottom step of the main staircase, somewhat groomed and somewhat thankful for Dr. Parks' "application" that saved Henry from making a more complete toilet; in this case, changing his clothes sufficed. He absently twisted the gold heirloom ring from his uncle, which Dr. Gothart had insisted he'd wear. Henry still didn't care about his uncle or the ring, but if wearing it fooled Brumfeldt into thinking otherwise, well, why not?

Finally Henry heard the tap-tap-tap of the door knocker. He rose, shuffled to the door, and opened it.

Brumfeldt turned white; his monocle dropped, and he might have collapsed if Dr. Parks hadn't grabbed his forearm to steady him. He quickly replaced the glass and scrutinized at Henry's appearance.

"Good Lord," Brumfeldt whispered. "Henry, I had no idea it was this bad or I..."

"Brumfeldt. Dr. Parks." Henry hoped he correctly articulated the words despite his swollen "hanging" tongue, enough to sound like his former self. He gripped the door jamb to ensure Brumfeldt noticed the gold ring on his right hand. "Do come in."

He led them into the first room on the left, the parlor where once Bryony entertained her guests and where Dr. Parks had roasted Henry, and then gestured for them to sit. Brumfeldt did and sneezed. Without the attention of servants, thick dust had accumulated on the carpet, heavy curtains, upholstery, and the curved, wooden legs of the many chairs and tables. Lacy cobwebs swathed the silver picture frames on every wall, the blue vases resting on the mantle, and the pink bric a brac adorning each table in the room. Dust webs hung in long strands from the oil lamps, like tinsel on a Christmas tree. Even the wavy vine pattern of the peeling wallpaper was barely distinguishable under its grimy haze. So no wonder Brumfeldt sneezed.

"Will you walk into my parlour?" said the Spider to the Fly,

"'Tis the prettiest little parlour that ever you did spy;
The way into my parlour is up a winding stair,
And I have many curious things to shew when you are there."

If only Brumfeldt knew the truth.

"Drink?" Henry asked.

"Sit," Dr. Parks said. "I'll pour. You rest." He looked at Brumfeldt. "Will sherry do?"

"Yes, yes," Brumfeldt waved his hand.

Brumfeldt learned forward, gripping his hands and gaping at Henry while Dr. Parks busied himself at the sideboard, and Henry let him look. Drink it in, Henry silently told Brumfeldt. Does my reddened, swollen, blistered skin cause you discomfort? Henry hoped his appearance tortured Brumfeldt for a very long time.

Dr. Parks returned with three sherry glasses. He passed one to Henry, handed the second to Brumfeldt, and kept one for himself, Brumfeldt quickly gulped a third, stared at Henry, and then gulped another third. Dr. Parks relaxed in a chair, leg crossed at the knee, and casually sipped. Henry allowed the liquid to splash his lips and then quickly set the glass on the little table beside him.

Brumfeldt didn't notice.

"So what happened, Henry? Quickly from the beginning if it won't tax you."

"I can manage it, as I've been resting for many days," Henry said, as if speaking around a mouthful of marbles. "It's best if you ask questions. Forgive my thick speech."

Brumfeldt waved that remark away. "What happened to Bryony Simons? She really died giving birth?"

"Yes."

"A son, wasn't it?"

Just the thought of the tender flesh of a baby caused Henry to salivate. Why hadn't Kellen warned them about drooling in public? He whipped out his handkerchief and dabbed his face, willing back the urge and picturing Dr. Gothart's rage and his injunction about "paying double."

"That's what I've heard," Henry said slowly. "But I cannot confirm it."

Brumfeldt shook his head. "A damn shame."

"Yes. John sent for her physician, but he was too late."

Brumfeldt quickly glanced at Dr. Parks, who said, "Not me. Dr. Gothart, the village's other doctor. He's attended Mrs. Simons since she was a child."

"Yes, Dr. Gothart," Henry said smoothly. "You recall him? He and his daughter Millicent once spent a night at Arcadia when..."

Brumfeldt cut him off with a wave of his hand. "Yes, yes, of course. John is really gone?"

"For now. This place," Henry weakly pointed around the room, "torments him. He had to leave. You understand."

"Indeed I do, Henry. Even now, whenever I think of your uncle..." Brumfeldt's voice cracked, and he took out his own handkerchief and blew his nose. As he stuffed the cloth back into his pocket, he added, "John really sent the servants away? You're here alone?"

Henry nodded again. "It was supposed to be temporary. Overnight. In case her confinement was difficult. Servants can be such gossips."

"But they never returned?"

"They couldn't. Because of the sickness."

"Ah, yes, I'd forgotten. The quarantine. Parasite, correct? Nasty creatures." Brumfeldt shuddered, sincerely, it seemed to Henry. "But that's not the cause of your illness."

"No," Henry said. "It's a blood disease, newly discovered. My tongue can't quite pronounce it."

"It's called 'porphyria,'" Dr. Parks broke in. "Henry's blood contains an abundance of a substance called porphyrin. He must now avoid sun at all cost, or his skin will burn and blister. Even so, Henry is susceptible to attacks, which can weaken his stomach and his heart. Mr. Brumfeldt, another sherry?"

Brumfeldt glanced at his glass, surprised at its emptiness. But he murmured, "Please," and turned his glass over to Dr. Parks. Then he closed his eyes and rubbed his forehead. When he opened his eyes, he asked, "Henry, are you able to work?"

"I have no choice," Henry said. "I have no other means to survive."

Brumfeldt glanced at Dr. Parks and hesitated. Henry held up his hand.

"You may speak freely before him, Brumfeldt," Henry said. "He knows about...Lord Girard."

"Henry!"

"It's not Henry's fault," Dr. Parks quickly interjected, handing Brumfeldt his glass. "Henry blurted out the details one night in a fever-soaked delirium. I spoke with Dr. Gothart, who confirmed everything. Since you know Dr. Gothart, you would also know his discretion. And you would also know he would not tolerate my indiscretion."

"Well," Brumfeldt began, still leery. "Why are we bantering about your survival? If you can work, and wish to work, I'll always have work for you. And if you cannot work, I'll always provide for you, as any caring 'uncle' would do. My

266

homes, your uncle's homes, are still open to you. In fact, if you're recovered enough to travel, we shall leave this very night. The money's yours anyway, Henry. I never dreamed he'd written you out of the will. If he hadn't collapsed after you left for Munsonville, he would have eventually realized your departure was only the loyalty of a friend. But after that, ahem, letter surfaced, you can certainly understand how your uncle mis-understood your true intentions."

"I don't mind, Brumfeldt. He was already upset about Agnes."

"You did your best, Henry. And you succeeded where her father did not. You kept her out of that blasted convent for several years. But for her damn religious fervor – well, I wish your uncle hadn't held you responsible. But it's for good reason he was called 'lord,' Henry. You know that."

"I tried, Brumfeldt. I couldn't compete with God."

Brumfeldt set down his empty glass. "Will you return to Chicago with me?"

"In time. I cannot right now. I'm still too weak."

"Henry..."

"Brumfeldt, you have my word. But I can only cover late afternoon and night events. I tend to rest by day now."

"Anything you want, Henry. Anything you want. However, I'd steer clear of New York for now as Jacob King put a generous price on your head. Although," Brumfeldt gazed around the room and then back at Henry. "I have a plan for your reintroduction, which should go smoothly. But we can discuss that in Chicago. So is John returning to Simons Mansion or is he selling it?"

"He hasn't decided yet," Henry said. "I've tried broaching the subject, but his grief is too raw. He's just recently decided to honor his summer commitments."

"Well, I imagine it's too painful. Old memories. As for Agnes, you can't help she chose God. So don't blame yourself. Still wearing that, I see?"

Henry glanced at the gold heirloom ring on his right hand. "Yes. I'll never take it off."

"Only God knows your uncle's last moments. I'm certain, Henry, he thought well of you before he expired. Your uncle loved you with all his heart."

"I know."

Brumfeldt rose and extended his hand, which Henry gingerly accepted. "Be well Henry. Wire me when you're ready."

"I will."

Dr. Parks stood, too. "I shall accompany you. That is, unless Henry needs…"

Henry shook his head. "I have a little soup and bread from one of the village women. I plan to sup soon and retire early. I'll see you out and lock up."

He led the way to the front door, making deliberate steps lest he hustle them out too quickly. Just a few paces more, and they'd be safe on the other side of the door, where Henry's fangs wouldn't not pierce them. Just a few more minutes…

But as Henry started to shut the door behind them, Brumfeldt impulsively swung around. "Henry, I nearly forgot. I met with George Clare this afternoon. Good recommendation. I think he will work out well."

"George Clare? Who's George Clare?

"The journalist you suggested as a temporary replacement for Horace Fuller."

Henry quickly glanced at Dr. Parks, who quickly glanced away.

Albert Brumfeldt looked away. His uncle looked away.

Two other figures also stood in the foyer, and they were covered in melting snow. The man had auburn mutton chops and thinning auburn hair, gold spectacles, round shoulders, and a slight stoop to his short stature.

The girl…woman…her disheveled red-orange hair tumbling everywhere, gripped him with crystal emerald eyes.

"It's fine," his uncle finally said quietly. "No one is hurt."

"It was the storm, Henry," Brumfeldt babbled. "The storm frightened the horses and overturned the cart before they turned on their occupants, and then, well… it's unfortunate, but it does happen. At any rate they will spend the night here, as it's impossible to travel tonight, and in the morning, we'll wire for transport and send them on their way."

Brumfeldt knew Dr. Gothart. Brumfeldt knew Dr. Parks. And all three knew him.

Well, well, well.

In that moment, Henry wanted. And he wanted with a ferocious hunger that approached his desperate need for blood.

But Henry only said, "Of course. The situation was desperate, and I knew you needed someone qualified right away."

Henry quickly shut the door. The hunger was terrible, not the hunger for blood, which was intense enough, especially with Brumfeldt and Dr. Parks smelling so tasty, but his hunger for *want*.

At sunset, his hunger for blood would drive him deeply into the night to satisfy it. But for now, Henry wished to savor this other hunger, the one that knew better than to kill and devour Dr. Parks and Brumfeldt, in order to satisfy a more delectable and profitable hunger. He returned to Bryony's parlor to celebrate his victory as the rightful heir of Lord Girard. His uncle had sought to shield his fortune from Henry, but Brumfeldt, who bought into Henry's delicate illness, had handed it right back, with apologies. How delicious family blood tasted!

He settled in the chair he had recently forsaken, picked up the even more forsaken sherry, and sniffed it. Then he set the glass down, slid the ring off, and held it up for a better view. Lord Girard, his uncle, had presented this family heirloom to Henry when Henry was just fourteen and a newcomer to his uncle's clandestine paradise, Arcadia.

"Go on," his uncle had said somewhat hoarsely. "Open it."

Henry unfolded the magenta cloth. It held a gold ring embossed with one sharp line, random squiggles, and a wolf. His eyes strayed to the third finger of his uncle's right hand. He wore an identical ring.

"Try it," his uncle said.

The ring easily, too easily, slid over Henry's slender finger. His uncle inspected the fit and slipped it off.

"I'll add a guard until you grow into it. This ring belonged to my father and to his father before him. It is now yours, nephew, as rightful heir to my fortune."

"Uncle?"

"Yes, Henry?"

"Why the wolf?"

"Not an ordinary wolf, Henry. It's the Beast of Gévaudan. Do you know the story?"

"No, Uncle."

" The Beast of Gévaudan is a mythical gray she-wolf. In the mid-eighteenth century, she terrorized the province of Gevaudan in Southern France and tore out the throats of hundreds."

Henry studied the ring. The wolf's eyes were proud; it's teeth were slightly bared.

"Perhaps it seems too vicious a symbol for my lineage. But it symbolizes sharp intelligence, strong instincts, fierce guardianship of family blood, and a legacy so enduring it approaches mythology. That, Nephew, is what it means to be a Girard. Take pride in that ring and your ancestry."

"I shall, Uncle. Thank you."

Dr. Parks provided the alibi. Brumfeldt offered money and position. Dr. Gothart trained him to withstand light, food, drink. Agnes, of course, would deny Henry nothing, not even the blood she needed to live. He thought of Pa, so like the illustration of a reed from an old botany textbook: slender, bendable to winds of misfortune, and, like any invasive species, equipped with a tenacious ability for survival by suppressing competitors, including his own family, wherever he rooted himself. Pa took what he wanted, including Henry's mother. Henry's uncle always willed his wants, and his wants always responded to his will.

And now, Henry had *want* and *will*.

He was his father. He was his uncle. Finally, he'd figured it out.

Henry slipped the ring back onto his finger, marveling at how perfectly it now fit.

EPILOGUE

"...and the glorious return of Mr. John Simons!"

The applause rose to deafening roars as John crossed the stage under the dazzling lights of the newly constructed Smith Opera House in Geneva, New York, and the noise coursed through him better than blood. Their worship was outside him, but it was inside him, reverberations that wove in and out of him like the maggots he didn't have.

Of course, John was still in danger of maggots if he neglected to crawl back to the cellar at Simons Mansion and submit to the slashings every night. Otherwise, John was cruising at a brisk speed toward the highway to life. He felt nearly himself, not nearly as vulnerable.

He'd feasted well; his firm body nicely filled out his white tails, never hinting to the living corruption that lay beneath the white tails. He knew his hair shimmered under the brightness; he saw it earlier when he made his toilet; his hair gleamed with the health of the living. His complexion remained paler than he liked, but no one questioned it. They only saw the grieving John Simons, who'd lost his true love and only child; and this John could use for his excuse as long as it served him. Whether or not he'd wed in the future didn't concern him now. He'd decide in the future, when life returned one hundred percent, and vampirism dimmed to a vague recollection. Tonight, he knew his place, up on the platform in in this Richardsonian Romenesque-style theater with its picturesque massing and rounded arches. He was the fixation of fourteen hundred people who'd tripped over themselves to empty their wallets for the privilege of seeing and hearing the famous musician command the piano, and he deserved every piece of it. He not only owned the space, he ruled it, and as he settled on the bench at the majestic grand, he sat immobile, refusing to move until each and every person ceased their noise. Then, and only then, did he allow his fingers to strike the keys with the precision of a master who knew how to force the sound he wanted out of them, and the patrons exploded into exuberant applause.

John played a prelude, and then an etude and then a waltz, and then a mazurka, and then a nocturne, and then a polonaise, and then a serenade, and then a scherzo, and then a ballade, and then parts of his sonata and his concerto in progress. He trilled the high notes, blithely skipping up and not too far down, a melodic enthusiasm climbing higher and still higher, magical tinkling chords that rose and rose until the waves crashed in a thunderous refrain and merged into dissonant chords and a macabre melody of music that the music swelled, dark and distended, thundering notes and then drowsy waves and plundering shades and downward spirals with hard abrupt chords; a pause and then sad, single notes. Some went up the scale, and some went down; some stayed the same, a monotonous half-melody he repeated again and again.

Deep into the audience, so far back as to escape detection, a man whose sleek hair and goatee were blacker than his coat and tails, gently rubbed his hands and delighted in each perfect note.

"You earn twenty-five percent of his profits forever. And he lets you drink from him again when he's one hundred percent human."

Unconsciously, Kellen's tongue grazed his lips and reveled in the memory of its favorite blood: so delectable, mellow, and full-bodied, with no lingering aftertaste. He mentally counted the spoils from tonight's performance and then mentally squeezed John's neck until the veins popped. He "inched" his fangs to John's neck for the kill, hovered above that swollen vessel, and basked in its throbbing. He nearly sighed aloud as he "ground" himself into John's stiffened and unresisting frame, and he and drank and drank and drank and drank. Finally, finally, finally. The beginning of eternity together...

A hard chord returned Kellen to the theater. Soon, Kellen thought to himself as a lascivious grin overtook his face. Soon, soon.

The luxury coach rumbled past the wrought iron gates and down the long, long drive, the culmination of a tedious jaunt from the train station to his uncle's old mansion in Chicago. However had Henry borne it as a human when teleportation was so efficient? And now he must suffer it again and again and again in order to fool the world. Unbelievable. On and on he rode for nearly a quarter of an hour before he perceived the outline of the carriage house, and the great alabaster mansion with its narrow windows and statues, all hidden among the trees. Less than a decade since Henry had passed this way in the coach for the first time with his uncle, and now...

"Are we staying at the Grand Pacific or the Palmer House, Uncle? Or perhaps the Tremont or the Sherman House?"
"None. I have a home off State Street."

Once the coach stopped, Henry wasted no time strolling to the door or skipping up the tall stone steps. He knew what he must do and was eager to do it quickly.

"Come here, Henry, let me look at you."
Brumfeldt stood in the middle of the west parlor, beaming and motioning for Henry to draw near. So this was it; the reason for, and culmination of, Kellen's "finishing school" had arrived. Henry thought he'd passed the test when Dr. Parks brought Brumfeldt to Simons Mansion, but no; Henry still had one last hurdle to scale. But why should that trouble him? Despite his heckling at those early lessons, Henry had diligently applied the precepts and smoked his flesh in the sun lest anyone cast doubt. So Henry coolly crossed the room, noting that Brumfeldt, although he'd kept his uncle's decorative preferences for white and ornate, had added splashes of blush and pale blue, along with heavy oak furniture and plum upholstery. But it was an observation, nothing more. What Brumfeldt did with the house didn't concern Henry, nor did Henry want the concern. Yes, he was dead, but Henry and his uncle had become dead to each other before either had actually expired. Hosting ten Agnes Kings wouldn't infuse Henry's heart with esteem for Lord Girard.
Henry reached the rug.

Outwardly, Henry modeled unshakable confidence in his ability to wear the mask. Inwardly, fear mixed with the assorted blood in his veins as Brumfeldt, hands clasped behind his back, circled him, looking hm up and down with a curious expression.

Abruptly, he stopped and grabbed Henry's wrist.

"Amazing," he murmured and raised his eyes to Henry. "You're really dead?"

"I…"

Well, this wasn't the way Henry envisioned this evening. But he quickly recovered. The means to the end didn't matter as long as Brumfeldt still met his end.

Brumfeldt peeped into his eyes, his nose nearly touching Henry's. "How much of you is left?"

"This. What you see."

"Well, we've all changed." Brumfeldt moved to the sidebar, poured himself a brandy, and started to pour a second glass but paused in mid-splash. He turned Henry. "Can you drink this? Should I offer another refreshment? I have an uncooked roast in the ice box that…"

"It's not necessary. I've…dined."

Brumfeldt nodded, a little lost, and then settled onto the sofa opposite Henry. "Sit and let us talk, frankly and openly."

"Us?" Henry exclaimed with snorted, but he settled into a wingback chair and regarded Brumfeldt with scorn. "Frankly and openly?"

"Henry, be reasonable! I spoke as frankly and openly as the circumstances allowed. You know your uncle."

"Not as intimately as you."

Brumfeldt actually flushed, and the monocle dropped between his legs, how fitting. Fumbling for it, he said. "I intend to fully protect you, Henry, as long as you mind your p's and q's."

"Meaning?"

Brumfeldt cleared his throat. "You know Lord Girard changed his will shortly before he died."

"How shortly?"

"Within minutes."

Henry gave a bitter laugh. "At the brink of eternity, and money is on his mind?"

"Not money, Henry, but legacy − and a lifetime of investments. Naturally, he'd want to protect them."

"So he cut me from the will?"

"Yes. And added a codicil."

"Which is?"

"That his money never pass to you, not through me, not through anyone."

Henry began to tremble, but he swallowed the simmering rage as best he could as he mind raced for the consolation plan.

"How clever of Lord Girard," Henry said through clenched teeth, squeezing his fists against the impulse to...

"Not clever, Henry, wise. Wise, intelligent, and full of integrity. It's a puissant combination. Even the unscrupulous revere him, if not fear him."

Henry's trembling turned into actual shaking. He gripped the chair arms to control it, and Brumfeldt actually flinched.

"Now before you charge over here to send me to the land of golden harps," Brumfeldt hastily added. "You must heed the rest. Your uncle allocated a sizeable amount for his 'projects.'"

"His projects?"

"Yes."

"Do those projects come with an association with Dr. Gothart?"

Brumfeldt paused and took a deep breath. "Yes."

"And Dr. Parks?"

"Yes."

Henry jumped to his feet, and so did Brumfeldt. "Now, don't get riled. What your uncle did not foresee is that you would become a...a..."

"Project."

"Well, yes. For lack of a better word, Henry, yes. A project."

Henry took a step. Brumfeldt stepped back and held up his hands. "Don't you see? That means, as long as you behave, you may share in the wealth. It's a curve Lord Girard hadn't anticipated, but here we are."

Somewhat resigned, Henry dropped into the chair. Brumfeldt did likewise and took a sip of brandy with quivering lips and a shaking hand. A lot of good Brumfeldt's trepidation would do Henry. He eyed his uncle's former paramour. Had his uncle really cut him out? Or had Brumfeldt forced the hand of a dying man? And did it really matter anymore?

"What's expected of me?"

"You return to work for me," Brumfeldt said, waving away Henry's objections the moment he opened his mouth. "Now don't interrupt; hear me out. The world, remember, knows nothing of this. The world isn't aware Lord Girard was your uncle and that he disowned you."

"He never 'owned' me," Henry said.

"Well, not publicly. But his discretion makes the present circumstances easier for us."

"Easier?"

"The world views you as my nephew. The world recalls how you broke from reporting to manage the household of a good friend and tinker with a novel or two. Now that the friend's had a tragedy, and your novels are completed, you are back to work, same as always, and life, well, life-ish for you, resumes."

"You're assuming I'll cooperate."

"You will cooperate."

Henry raised an eyebrow at the finality in Brumfeldt's voice. "That's rather brazen. What if I just..."

"...persuade me to write you into my will and then feast on my blood?" Brumfeldt shook his head. "Be assured, Henry, your uncle's associates would disintegrate you in milliseconds if you got within a foot of my jugular."

"You mentioned a plan for my reintroduction to Jacob King?"

"I did. And you will sink your teeth into it, well, into him."

"I'm to kill him?"

Brumfeldt smiled. "He's not so much a threat to me as he is a threat to you. And at this stage of the racket, I need you more than I need King. As compensation, you work for me – your caring uncle – live in my homes, receive an unlimited allowance, and keep your night habits discreet and out of this century." He leaned forward and stretched out his hand. "Do we have an agreement? Nephew?"

Dr. Parks stood outside the small, cream-colored, clapboard church and studied its arched windows and ornate steeple. It certainly lacked the majesty of the Gothic architecture of the First Church of Boston, what with its English mosaic glass

276

work, chandeliers of bronze and gold, one hundred and eighty-seven pews, and steam heat and ventilation. But Munsonville's Congregational did have a countrified charm that appealed which helped him will up the courage to step inside, for today was the day.

Inside the narthex, he removed his hat and studied the view, noting the raised platform near the front with only a podium and unadorned wooden cross to embellish it. The windows and whitewashed walls provided sufficient light on sunny days like today; the opened windows allowed for natural "ventilation," certainly not unpleasant. The sounds of the old piano told him his mother was not playing; she missed too many notes, and this execution wasn't bad. But the piano sounds also told him services were beginning. The church's pastor, Algernon Demars, was already motioning people to sit. Gray streaks had appeared in Algernon's thick black hair these past few months, and a few lines marred his youthful face, even though Algernon's eyes still shone deep blue. His wife Gertrude sat at the piano, face aglow, blonde hair frizzing at her forehead; she had not changed. But despite the stresses that caused gray and creases, Pastor Demars' never wavered from his "joy in the Lord" preaching, a bold contrast to the hellfire version Reverend Galien Marseilles used to deliver. "Used to" was key. The reverend had not strayed from the parsonage since the night Bryony Simons died.

Dr. Parks approached the nave but didn't enter it. His parents occupied the last row on the right, near the end, and he did not wish to distress them, especially since they did not cause his sudden turn of piety. On the left, about halfway down, the Clares worshipped with the Hassets, their last spiritual breaking of bread before the Clares' little exodus to Evansville. Today was indeed the day.

Instead, Dr. Parks hung to the rear, bowed his head, gently beat his breast, and pleaded in his soul for God to spare it. Within minutes, he heard the first notes of the recessional and lifted his head. So soon? The faithful began filing out while the "Doxology" filled the air. His parents remained, but they would remain to the end, lest someone jostle his father and cause his heart to flutter and fail. He shyly smiled and nodded as the villagers filed past him. Algernon had passed through the back door and was now greeting his people outside at the front.

The Hassets and the Clares lingered in the nave, exchanging a flurry of last minute "Goodbye for nows," along with huggings and handshakings and promises to write "until next time."

"Dr. Parks," a strong voice said.

It was George Clare, slight frame erect, brunet head and waxed mustache immaculately groomed. Not one fleck rested on his brushed herringbone suit. His blue eyes sparkled as he spoke, and his smile was warm and engaging as he grabbed both of the doctor's hands and said, "Dr. Parks, thank you for all your help."

Dr. Parks returned George's smile with a genuinely warm smile of his own.

"Rise," he said, still smiling. "Take up thy bed and walk."

George dipped his head. "Your servant. Always."

"Mrs. Clare."

Had he ever seen a more beautiful woman than Isabella Clare as she now passed him, in a golden bronze traveling ensemble trimmed in black velvet? Her hat, also black with a large crown and plumes, lay cocked on her golden curls, and her cheeks flushed pink. She had the carriage of a queen, and it suited her.

"Dr. Parks," she said crisply.

Then she marched out the door after her husband.

"Little Marie, er, Miss Clare."

Except for the royal blue and dark hair, she was a miniature replica of her mother, and she stopped and looked up at him from beneath the brim of her regal hat, and the look was blank and devoid of connection. It wasn't trusting. It wasn't knowing. It wasn't a look of anticipation for the future or thankfulness for his role in facilitating that future. It was simply a look.

He hesitated, shaken at her unexpected distance and detachment, and then quoted Paracelsus, "That which the dream shows is the shadow of such wisdom as exists in man, even if during his waking state he may know nothing about it."

Her gaze, impassive still.

He swallowed hard and lightly touched her shoulder. "Don't wake up."

Marie followed her parents out the door, and then, there she was, the reason for his attendance. She looked like the image on his old "carte de visite" of New York actress Kitty Blanchard, although he estimated her age to be around seven and twenty. She had a sweet face, and although she wasn't beautiful like Isabella Clare, she wasn't ugly either. Her features were naturally pleasant and not so plain he'd soon tire of them, and he noted a keen intelligence in her eyes that slightly intimidated him. So he just stood there, hat in hand, feeling like a nervous schoolboy.

"Mrs. Ashmore," Dr. Parks finally said. "May I walk you home?"

The waiting coach was just an ordinary coach, like all the coaches that had taken Marie there and there. The horses, well, she noted nothing special about them, either. They were just ordinary draft horses. But Jesus entered Jerusalem on a colt; why would she expect more?

He held out his hand. "Up you go, Little Marie."

"Thank you, Papa."

She paused on the step and looked out, but not back, at Main Street's deserted buildings and plank walks, for today was the Lord's Day, and the villagers were heading to their homes on the hill for the noon meal and an afternoon of rest and refreshment. A home on the hill had nearly been Marie's home on the hill, but God had delivered her, as he had delivered them from Room 27, and in this she rejoiced and was glad. This place, this Munsonville, had been prison and pain, victory and light, a foaming, spicy wine and their cup of salvation, and now they were blessed, now they were those "which are called unto the marriage supper of the Lamb."

Her papa had come to scoop, but he had blundered, and yet The Dream had found them, not at once as she'd imagined it might, but in pieces, such as one attains dreams through sleep. The premise was so logical and consecutive, how could they ever have doubted it?

The sleeper knows if he readies for bed, puts on the dressing gown, turns down the gas, ties the night cap, opens the window, and draws the curtains; the sleeper knows that if he only places his head on the pillow, the limbs will eventually slacken, and the impressions will eventually form: snippets of fragments – until the would-be sleeper, unbeknownst to himself, finally drops off, and the real dreaming begins.

Her papa had already befriended truth and inscribed the goal onto his heart. He learned and practiced his skills and chased down stories wherever they took him. He did not falter when afflicted but pushed through to the end, even though the finish line appeared to back up when he approached it. But that was merely the mirage of dreams, the pre-dreaming, before the real work of dreams began. The rivalry, the setbacks, the signing of contracts, her mama's adoration and money and sacrifices, and even this coach, hack more like it, were all snippets of the clarity waiting for them as soon as they took the final step.

So she took it.

One step up, and Marie was in the hack.

She settled herself on the hard seat next to her mama; her papa shut the door.

www.ingramcontent.com/pod-product-compliance
Lightning Source LLC
Chambersburg PA
CBHW031945260626
47157CB00017B/2652